MW00737264

JACK ROWE

DOMINION

A GROLIER COMPANY

Franklin Watts/1986/New York/London

Library of Congress Cataloging-in-Publication Data

Rowe, Jack.
Dominion.

1. Du Pont Family—Fiction.   I. Title.
PS3568.0926D66   1986   813'.54   86-11188
ISBN 0-531-15002-X

Copyright © 1986 by Jack Rowe
All rights reserved
Printed in the United States of America
6   5   4   3   2   1

To our children:

Maria, Anne, Joan,
Susan, Michael,
David, Stephen, Mark,
John, and Kevin.

DOMINION

PART I

CHAPTER ONE

1846

The midmorning February sunlight poured a cozy lemon puddle on the Oriental rug, bathing her bare feet. But its warmth was more suggestion than fact, and she decided to wear the slippers after all.

Scuffing briskly to the cherrywood vanity to the right of the window, she studied herself in the oval mirror, adjusted the neckline of her silk nightgown, touched back a vagrant curl at the temple, and smiled. The peach silk was a perfect choice, softening the stern lines of her face and deepening the color of her dark brown hair.

She heard the muffled thump of the front door closing below and moved to the window opposite to watch as her husband and two sons mounted the family barouche. The groom stood holding the door of the carriage as Blanche Feeney climbed in after them. All three males doffed hats in ragged unison as Blanche took her place and then faced upward toward the window and repeated the salute.

Meta du Pont frowned at sharing her husband's deferential gesture with their maid, but she knew it was just another absent-minded reaction by a man whose thoughts always seemed to be elsewhere. She was pleased that the boys were attentive to their gentlemanly behavior even though it was not proper to extend such amenities to the help.

The three arms were still upraised, and she had a sudden image of them riding woodenly in that position all the way to Wilmington if she did not acknowledge them.

She gave a half-wave, and all three hats were replaced at once, triggering the driver's response with his whip, the horse's lunge, the barouche's lurch—heads bobbing back against the strain—and they were finally off, moving smartly down the quarter-mile gravel drive to the main road.

Meta grudgingly accepted the way her boys were attached to Blanche. The old servant had been with the family since the du Ponts built their mansion over forty years earlier. When they died, she and Alfred had moved in, displacing the other heirs to less prestigious homes on the du Pont properties. Although Meta had initiated the move, there was no objection from the others, since her husband was entitled as company president and eldest son. Still, he probably would not have exercised the right if Meta had not insisted. The man needed prodding in anything beyond a love affair with his chemical laboratory. Alfred behaved more like a chemist employed by the firm than the leader of du Pont's substantial gunpowder industry, and she was ever after him to behave as an executive should.

The distant carriage finally disappeared into the turn on the main road and Meta left the window, grateful to have the house to herself. They would be gone for several hours. Blanche would fuss over the boys' shopping, badgering the salesclerks with her oddly imperious haggling.

She crossed the room, paused at the fireplace, and tested the heat, turning her palms toward the bank of glowing coals. The porcelain clock on the mantel chimed softly at the quarter hour, and she returned to her vanity for another look in the mirror.

"You'll be forty within the year, my girl," she whispered to the radiant face in the glass, "But this afternoon you'll pass for twenty-nine!"

She returned to the bed, conscious of the sensuous rustle of silk as she smoothed the turned-down comforter and fluffed the pillows. The tea service resting on a low table in front of the settee caught her eye and she went to it, cupping her hand to the pot to test its warmth. She looked at the clock again. Twenty past ten. Well, it wasn't the first time he had been late.

Alexis du Pont rubbed an itchy crumb of wet gunpowder from the side of his nose and contemplated his brother with good humor. He wished Henry would not get so agitated over minor matters which could easily be smoothed over.

"Murphy and his crew are good men, Henry. They get out their share of cake and more. You can't rush this business too much, you know."

"If they got off their collective asses and got those tubs empty for the bogeymen like they should, we could get another batch started an hour earlier." Henry speared his younger brother with a cold stare. The redhead was inches shorter than Alexis, but his condescending attitude more than made up for his height. "An hour saved between batches means an increase of fifteen percent in production."

Alexis grinned defensively. "The drying house wouldn't be able to handle that much cake, and you know it. Besides, the men need some time to clean up the floor and tubs."

"Let them do the floors while the new batch is mixing. It will keep them on their toes."

Alexis shook his head. "It could blow them across the crick. I don't like rushing them so much that they get behind. That's dangerous."

Henry snorted. "Carelessness is the imp in this business, not hard work. You keep too slack a line on them as it is. Too much tomfoolery. There's no place for larking in a powder yard."

Alexis kept his tongue. It was an old argument. Henry wanted to run the mills like an infantry regiment, all sober business until the shift was done. Alexis saw no harm in occasional socializing, even horseplay within reason. It relieved the tension, and the men went back to their tasks with renewed vigor.

Henry stared at him coldly. "Look to it, young brother. You up the production of powder cake and leave the drying sheds to me. They'll keep up the pace." He pulled out a pocket watch and seemed angered by what the dial told him. Snapping shut the case he added, "You would do well to spend more time supervising these Irish than trying to look and act like one of them."

Alexis started to speak, but Henry spun on his heel and marched over to a knot of powdermen, snapping sharp words as he approached. Their conversation died out to nods, and they scattered to their mills at a trot.

Henry followed them with his frosty eyes. Then, apparently satisfied, he marched out of the yards and up the hill toward the company office and the home of his elder brother, Alfred.

Meta du Pont heard him enter the house through the kitchen door at the basement level two floors below. She could follow his heavy-footed progress up two flights of the servants' stairway at the back of the house, and when he entered the bedroom, his sour mood was no surprise. There was no disappointment in it. Henry's bullish mood swings were rather a challenge. She smiled at him with amusement as he went directly to the settee and began pulling off his boots.

"Would you like tea?" She made no move toward the service, however, and stood near the fireplace watching him. As his second boot fell, she eased out of her own slippers.

"If you had coffee, I might be interested," he said gruffly.

She laughed lightly. "I can imagine the kitchen gossip if I had ordered coffee sent to my room this morning."

He flicked an amused glance in her direction but made no comment. Getting to his feet he took off his greatcoat, folded it carefully on the settee, and continued disrobing methodically, placing each garment in an orderly pile. As he was unbuttoning his shirt, he looked at her again.

"Get into bed."

She gave a sound that was half-gasp, half-laughter.

"Well! You *are* all business this morning, aren't you?"

His eyes were fixed on her now. She could feel him taking her measure, each look an individual thrust. Then those light blue eyes were full on hers.

"All business," he grinned, rubbing his hand across his thickly matted chest. "The kind you like, Meta." He reached out his hand to her.

And again she was mesmerized by this thickset bull of a man. All the dissembling gone, the anticipated dalliance gone, the preliminaries gone. She felt hypnotized by those eyes, at once brutal and appealing. The softly curled copper ringlets covering his chest drew her, and she found her lips on his neck, fingertips searching the hard muscles of his back without knowing she had taken a step toward him.

She felt the gown move under his hands, slipping from her shoulders, sighing into a heap around her ankles. Then his arms were under her, lifting her to the bed. She lay on her back, eyes closed, listening to the gradual deepening of his breath, feeling the thumping of his heart under her palm. His hands were all over her now, gentle caresses made vibrant by the trembling restraint of his powerful arms.

She wanted to hold him off, to extend the caresses, to bring herself slowly to his level of need, but again it was she who gave the signal, opening herself to him, urging his entrance.

Suddenly she seemed to lift within a great vacuum of silence, and Henry crushed her as an ear-splitting crack filled the room. The window sash groaned and exploded inward with flying glass. The whole house shuddered, and plaster chips showered down upon them from the ceiling.

"Goddamn!" Henry's curse was almost a petulant whimper as he crawled off the bed.

"Dear God, what was that?" Meta shrilled. She was dazed, sitting amid a pile of glass and plaster rubble on the comforter.

"One of the mills," he snapped and picked his way over the glass-strewn carpet to his clothes. He was dressed and out the door in less than a minute. Meta continued to sit on the bed amid the devastation of her room, shaken and pale. Then, after she began to hear the shouts of workers from the powder yard below the house, she began to laugh. It was some time before she could stop, and tears had streaked the plaster dust on her cheeks.

The house was probably a wreck, and there was always the possibility of injuries in the yard. But, perverse as it might seem under the circumstances, Meta would not have missed it for the world. It was the first time in her memory that Henry du Pont had not had his own way.

Eleutherian Mills, as the main du Pont residence was called, was literally within shouting distance of the original powder mills. In the years since the founding of the company, the yards had been extended down the Brandywine River for nearly a mile as the stream flows. Pairs of water-powered rolling mills were clustered in sets of a dozen or so wherever a millrace could be placed to provide a regulated supply of water.

Before he burst from the door of Alfred's home, Henry knew from the shock of the blast that one of the nearby older mills had detonated. Once he was clear of the house, that fact was confirmed. A billowing column of greasy black smoke rose from Number Two, barely two hundred yards away. As he rushed headlong down the slope, his eyes took in the entire upper yards. The wind was in their favor. It was weak and pushing any sparks away from the works and into the stream. He scanned over the sloping roofs of the other buildings, the small pressroom, the drying sheds, and the stack of bogey cars waiting on their tracks. These were the volatile places. A single spark there could start a progression of explosions that might kill everyone in the Upper Yard and level his brother's residence instead of breaking a few windows and cracking plaster. Satisfied that there were no wisps of smoke, he scanned the works again, this time concentrating on sources of secondary fire. This inspection included the charcoal ricks, sulfur shed, and saltpeter plant.

Henry clicked them all off in an orderly sweep, missing nothing. He was on a dead run for the middle of the yard and slowed to a walk as he approached the smoking shell of Number Two. It would be quick work dousing that. He could see Alexis forming the bucket line, and one man was already atop the blasted masonry, watering the shattered and smoking roof beams.

Henry strode up to Alexis and pulled him aside.

"Was anyone hurt?"

"No, thank God." Alexis noticed Henry's coat covered with plaster dust. "The house! Dear God, Meta and the boys, Alfred—"

"They're fine. Meta was alone, but I checked. The others are in town. The place is a mess, but it's just plaster and glass." He watched the progress of the bucket brigade for a moment. "Send someone to my place to quiet the alarm and another to Chicken Alley to let them know nobody was injured. We don't need a bunch of wailing wives at the gate."

In thirty minutes every spark in the yard had been doused, but Henry's efforts to avoid a rush of alarmed relatives from the employee quarters did not succeed. Word from the boss was not enough. They had to see their men in the whole flesh.

They were not the only ones alarmed. Alfred du Pont was soon on the scene, white-faced and trembling and flanked by his teenage boys. He was distraught almost to tears. It would not be good for the workers to see that. Henry assumed charge and ordered them all to the privacy of the small office adjacent to Alfred's home.

The three brothers filed into the two-room building with Henry in the lead. He went directly to Alfred's office. As he passed the accountant, Harry Belin, he snapped, "This will be a confidential meeting."

The man rose and reached for his coat, and Alfred, with an impatient look at Henry's back, took the clerk's arm. "Have some coffee in the house, Harry. And tell Mrs. du Pont I'll be over shortly." The accountant nodded and left quickly.

Henry seated himself immediately, and Alfred paused as if to make a comment, then sat behind his desk. He nervously rearranged some loose papers. Alexis looked at the remaining chair, then at his soiled clothing, and remained standing.

Henry spoke quietly. "Who was running Number Two?"

"Murphy." Alexis's mouth was hard, his voice flat.

"He's fired. Give him a week to get his family out of Chicken Alley."

Alfred lowered his head into his palms and massaged his temples. "I think that is rather harsh. Was the man careless?"

"Overworked." Alexis glared at Henry. "He's the best man in the Upper Yard."

Henry spoke with finality. "I will not brook carelessness."

Alfred looked weary and distracted. "Pending an investigation . . ."

"I've investigated, Alfred. The man had not swept up from an early batch. These cold dry days, he should have . . ."

Alexis glared at Henry. "My God," he fumed, "it was your order! Not two hours ago you told me to have the men sweep up *after* reloading the tub to save time!"

Alfred stiffened and turned to Henry. "Save time? You know my orders on unnecessary haste."

Henry sighed and spoke almost with condescension, "I intend to avoid the frivolous *waste* of time. These people take over an hour between batches. You know our quota." ,

"*Your* quota," Alfred corrected. "You know full well my instructions in that regard!" He rose and pointedly turned his back on Henry and spoke to Alexis. "How did it happen?"

"Murphy had just loaded the rolling pan with a heavy batch and started the mill. The floor dust was very dry, and I saw him wet his broom to go back in to sweep. But the bristles froze as he pulled it from the bucket. He had to sweep with a dry broom."

Alexis took a deep breath to still the quaver that had crept into his voice. "He heard the snap of static that set it off. It was just luck that the floor dust burned slowly enough for him to get out before the tubload blew."

"The point both of you miss," Henry injected drily, "is that the man caused the accident by his own poor judgment."

"The point *you* miss, Henry, is that the explosion would not have happened with an empty tub."

"He should have wet down the floor. The salts in the powder prevent freezing."

Alexis choked off further argument. What Henry said was true, of course, but this was hindsight. Murphy had been forced into a deadly compromise. Under the pressure of a dangerous change in procedure, he could not be expected to improvise.

"Do not fire the man," Alfred said quietly. "Make it clear that he made a costly error. And your method of saving time, Henry, will be stopped immediately."

Henry's eyes fairly crackled. As he spun to leave, he muttered, "And the U.S. Army will have to wait for its powder. That will be good news for Mexico, I imagine!"

He went directly to the stables up the hill from the office and gave orders to have his horse saddled immediately. The groom knew better than to smalltalk Mr. Henry, especially when the boss had fire in his eyes. He had urgent business in town and on the way, he detoured briefly to tell his wife. Louisa was grateful that her husband had been spared in the explosion, and delayed him only briefly to clean his coat of the ugly plaster dust. He should look presentable at his meeting.

Henry's "appointment" was a spontaneous decision made necessary by the unfinished business he had begun in the morning. But he was a regular at the brothel, and in this emergency, as always, his needs would be warmly attended.

CHAPTER TWO

Ne give thee thanks, Almighty God, for these gifts which we have received and for all thy bounty, through the love of thy divine son, Jesus Christ, our lord."

"Amen."

The response was a piping shout in Father Francis Reardon's ears, and he winced briefly before hugging the twins seated beside him at the table. Then he laughed and pushed them off either end of the shared bench. "Off with you two, and go play. I want some peace to speak with your aunt and uncle and," he added with a wink down the table, "your old bachelor cousin."

Kevin Gallagher smiled and dropped his eyes at the family jibe. He was thirty-five with no prospects and no apparent inclination toward marriage.

"As usual, Noreen, your table was magnificent," the priest went on, "and again, I was sorely pressed to overindulge." He leaned toward his host and lowered his voice. "I honestly do not see how you keep fit, Brendan. With fare like this I would soon be big as a house. As it is, I make a novena before coming to help me ward off gluttony!"

"Blarney," Noreen said and smiled. She rose and began clearing the table. "If you men will go sit in the front room, I'll find my work easier. And take your cups with you. I'll bring a fresh pot in later."

After they had gone through the curtained doorway separating the two main rooms of the cottage, she checked the single downstairs bedroom leading off the kitchen. It was an afterthought single-story wing with a sloping shed roof. Although it was Brendan's and her room, by day she allowed her niece and nephew to use it for study and quiet play. Their room on the second floor under the eaves was bitter cold, but this room drew some warmth from the kitchen hearth.

As she entered, Denis was reading to Megan from his school writing slate. Both looked up, and Megan jumped off the bed and ran to her.

"Do we have to go to bed now, Aunt Norrie? Please can we stay up?"

Noreen cupped the child's chin in her hand and bent to kiss her on the forehead. "You may stay here until Father Reardon leaves. But only if you behave quietly." Megan hopped back on the bed beside her brother. Noreen went to the lamp and adjusted the wick. "If you get sleepy, just crawl under the quilt. Kevin will carry you to the loft later."

Back in the kitchen she added more coffee to the pot, filled it with fresh water, and hung it over the hearth to reboil. It was blackened with soot and hard to handle without soiling her apron. A little thrill of pleasure lightened the chore when she remembered that the iron stove Brendan had ordered would be coming in another week. What a difference it would make! She was still excited over the pitcher pump he had installed by her sink, making trips with a bucket to the well in the backyard unnecessary. Wonders of the modern world! When she was a girl, only the wealthy had such things.

Beyond the curtain partition the men's voices were heating up.

"Well, I admit Murphy slipped up, but it was young Henry's order. He's pushing the men too hard."

"Dad, you know that the business is risky at best. All Mr. Henry is trying to do is make money in hard times. If he doesn't shave off waste, we could all be out of a job."

"Kevin, sweepin' up dust with a full rolling tub is plain stupidity."

"They won't do that again, of course. Mr. Alexis put the stop to that right away, but we all have to learn to move a little faster."

Brendan snorted. "A fast trip across the Crick is what we'll get."

Kevin got up and paced the room. "The docks from Boston to Wilmington are piling up with Irish. There's already troubles about so many men out of work."

Father Reardon nodded. "I received a letter last week from the Chancery in Philadelphia. There are thousands starving in Ireland because of the blight, God help them."

"He'd better help them, Father," Kevin said grimly. "The times are bad on this side of the ocean, too."

Brendan went to the mantel over the small hearth in the corner of the room and picked up a pipe. He filled it awkwardly and offered it to the priest.

"Wouldja like a smoke, Father?"

Francis Reardon demurred with a light wave of his hand. Watching Brendan struggle with his pipe brought back memories of the massive blast that had claimed so many lives and Brendan's right arm. Brendan caught the look. The priest sighed. "A long time, eh, Brendan? Almost thirty years. That was a terrible day."

Brendan nodded. "Aye, terrible. And many more almost as bad in the years since." He looked at his son, "It's events like those that I'm worried about, Kevin."

Kevin shrugged. "Well, Dad, we could take our chances doing something else, but I for one am glad for the steady work."

"From what I hear, the work will be steady enough what with that business in Texas."

Father Reardon shook his head. "The country is against it, really. There are many who claim it to be a crude attempt to steal land from Mexico. Now that Texas is a state, the question of the legal border can be resolved easily enough." He leaned back in the armchair. "Nobody wants to go to war over a small strip of land."

"I disagree, Father Francis," Brendan said, puffing out a cloud of smoke. "Mr. Belin, the bookkeeper, told me the other day that I must be thinking of moving greater loads of rifle and cannon powder to the docks. It's all consigned to the U.S. Army." He pointed the pipestem at the priest. "You can be sure the government will not buy powder it has no use for in times like these. Something's afoot. Mark me."

The priest thought a moment and then spoke almost as if he were thinking aloud. "It is a delicate moral question. Should I rejoice in the hope of lifesaving employment for starving souls if it is bought at the price of war? For that matter, wishing these men and their families into such a hazardous trade is in itself a moral dilemma. The very church I pray in was bought from the profits of powdermaking."

"Nobody forces us, Father," Kevin said quietly. "We could as well risk life and limb in the mines or on the sea."

Noreen had come in with the steaming coffee. She paused first at the priest's chair.

"A fresh cup, Father?"

"Thank you, yes, Noreen. You come in time to rescue us from an endless discussion." He watched as she refilled his mug and took it from her, cradling its warmth in his hands.

"I have some news for you, Noreen, that I wanted to keep until the children were asleep."

"Tim?"

"Yes. I hear from—let's just say I've heard that your brother will be here soon, to stay a week or so with the children. The exact day I can't be certain of, but no more than a few days."

A brief look of relief crossed Noreen's face. Then her lips tightened, and she tossed her head angrily. "I will not tell the twins their father is coming until he's in the house. They've been disappointed often enough, surely." She nearly splashed Kevin's coffee into his lap as she poured. "Oh, Kevin, here, take this pot back to the fire before I scald you. I am so distracted by all this business!"

The room was silent as Noreen turned her back to them and stared down at the dying fire. "We'll need more on this tonight, Brendan, to get some heat for the children. It must be bitter in the loft."

Then, as if to answer some unspoken argument from the room,

she turned. "I was happy enough to love them as my own when poor Meg died in their bearing, but when Tim went back to that awful trade again—"

Francis Reardon spoke quietly. "You must not be harsh with Tim, Noreen. He feels he must do something for the blacks, and there are those who admire his work. A calling."

"Oh, a 'calling,' is it? I think he owes more to his wee ones. A father close enough to touch day in and day out. He could have had paid help to keep his family together. Instead he runs off like some missionary driven by high ideals."

Brendan rose from adding wood to the fire and put his arm around her waist. "He was terribly upset when Meg died. I'm sure he went back to the Underground to take his mind off that."

"Well, he ought to be cured by now! Dear God, it's been over eight years. I sometimes think Thomas Garrett is the troublemaker the law makes him out to be. It is one thing to break the law by sheltering runaways, but another thing altogether to sneak around plucking them from the plantations, bold as brass." She wrung her hands and went to stare out the window into the cold night. "Truly as I stand here, there is not a day goes by that I don't have some awful vision of him being shot dead by some slaveowner."

The fresh logs began to snap, sending a few sparks beyond the stone hearth. Brendan picked them up idly with calloused fingers and tossed them back. Francis Reardon rose to leave.

"It's getting late, and Mrs. Dougherty will take me to task if I'm not in safely by ten. The poor thing loses her own sleep waiting up to see that I'm in. I'll get sulks and poor meals for two days to pay for her worry."

"Thank you for comin', Father. It's always a pleasure." Brendan went for the priest's coat and hat.

"I'll speak to Tim about the matter," Francis said as he wrapped a woolen scarf up to his ears and buttoned the coat. "Not that it will do much to change his mind. He listens to you more than anyone else—besides himself, that is."

After he left, Noreen was sorry to have made the outburst which ruined an otherwise pleasant evening. She knew that

Father Reardon was somehow indirectly involved in the Underground Railway himself, despite that fact that he was opposed to the practice as being an unlawful means to an end. It was difficult to be a priest and remain completely isolated from these things, though the majority seemed to manage.

She and Brendan had already gone to bed when Francis Reardon showed up at their door again. He had another message.

"Thomas Garrett has been jailed for hiding slaves," he whispered in a voice shaking with the cold. "And there is a warrant out to arrest Tim Feeney."

CHAPTER THREE

The cold rains which had followed the *Quaker City* from the mouth of Delaware Bay north to the port of Wilmington had tapered off to a drizzle by the time Captain David Craith had doubled up his spring lines and had the gangway run out. Free for the moment to concentrate on other affairs, he assessed available open space on the dock for the unloading of his cargo.

Satisfied that the old clipper was properly positioned to make easy use of both booms, he ordered fore and aft hatches unsealed and the winches rigged. There was considerable freight stacked on the wharf waiting for onloading. Most was covered by tarpaulins slick with rain, and he would have to wait for the manifest to see how the lot would be stowed. One pile at the farthest point on the dock, only now being unloaded and hurriedly covered with canvas, was no mystery. He recognized the one-armed man supervising laborers gingerly lifting kegs from his wagon. It could only be Brendan Gallagher, and Captain Craith did not have to use his glass to make out the name on the Conestoga. It would be du Pont, and the shipment was gunpowder.

"Well, Captain, I'll be taking my leave."

Craith turned to the young man who stood near the gangway, holding a bulging valise. He was tall and muscular with strong shoulders, a build which made him seem older than the seventeen years given as his age in the ship's log. His tweed jacket had once been quite grand and not as ill-fitting as it was now, but despite the fact that he had outgrown the garment, it was clean and showed scrupulous care in the neatly sewn repair of its worn places. His rugged facial features reflected more maturity than his years. Although his serious gray eyes seldom smiled, they suggested a deep understanding and quiet humor.

He saluted the captain by gravely doffing his woolen cap and giving an almost imperceptible bow. His hair was the color of coal. A black Irisher if ever there was one. The captain wondered how many generations back the Moorish bloodline reached.

"Good luck to ye, Master Farrell," Craith boomed. He liked the Irish youth to a degree that surprised him. Usually Craith was quiet, almost sullen, in his demeanor. But this boy had captured his attention from the first, and they had had many enjoyable discussions on the voyage from Dublin. The eight other passengers on the clipper never took meals at the captain's table, but the Farrell lad ate there often and was frequently seen pulling his own weight with the crew even though, unlike the others, his was a prepaid passage. Craith had often taken it upon himself to show the boy secrets of the mariner's trade, almost as if he were a midshipman instead of a fare-paid lubber.

Craith gripped his shoulder. A quick grin flashed on Michael's face, suddenly betraying his youth, and then melted so quickly that it might have been a mirage. He replaced his cap soberly.

"If ever ye've a mind to take up the sea trade, lad," Craith rasped, "drop me a line and I'll see what I can do."

Michael nodded. "I'll do that, sir. Though for the moment I believe my fortune lies here on dry land."

Craith laughed. A four-day bout with seasickness had marred the end of their voyage. The mid-Atlantic could be unmerciful with her squalls. "Ah, your belly will settle quick enough. It's a thing we all get over soon or late."

"I tell you, Captain, if this place has any leaning toward earthquake," Michael said with a wry grimace, holdings his stomach, "I may be tempted to cast my luck with the churning seas."

"Fair enough, Michael. Now look here, lad, do ye recall my mention of those gunpowder mills outside town?"

"I do."

"Well, if ye'll cast a glance to the wagon being unloaded, ye'll note a one-armed man in charge. The older man, about my own age. Go and introduce yourself to him, tell him I sent ye, and I'll speak to him about getting you on as a powderman with du Pont."

Michael shook hands with Craith and began descending the rain-slick gangplank with a knot of other Irishmen eager to begin a life filled with the golden promise of the New World. As they laughed at their own clumsy eagerness, stumbling and sliding down the steeply angled ramp, a clot of men, twenty or more, suddenly rushed them and began throwing cobbles. It was a silent attack, and Craith cursed at his failure to notice the toughs hidden behind the stacked barrels and crates on the dock. He rushed aft to his cabin, snatched open the door, and disappeared inside.

The second paving stone hurled at the gaping Irish struck Michael on the shoulder, spinning him off balance, and he toppled off the gangway. The fall caused no damage, but his arm was numb. He sat with a dazed look of surprise, massaging his tingling left shoulder, and felt the shock of cold water seeping into his pants.

"Get back on the boat, y'bloody clod! There's no work for Irish trash hereabouts."

The coarse faces closing in were worked up to a white anger, and the fetid smell of alcoholic breath and sweat came like a warm, sickening wave. They were yanking at his coat, pulling him up and pushing him toward the edge of the dock. He caught a glimpse of the black hull squeezing against the rub rail of the pilings, then yawning out against the straining hawsers to come grinding back again. He had the frightening image of his skull popping like some pulpy red melon with matted hair.

The thought electrified him, prickling his arms alive, and he thrashed out blindly, stabbing with fingers and then fists to break through the encircling ring. He didn't punch but swung his arms like hammers, crashing against necks and jaws. One man ducked his swing and Michael drove a knee into his groin, then fought his way to the gangplank. Somehow he made it to the ramp, clutching at the handlines, and pulled himself toward the ship. Then they were on him again in a shouting rage, clawing him down.

Suddenly his head rang with a tremendous roar, the hands released him, and he saw the four tarnished stripes of Captain Craith's upraised arm. The smoking muzzle of a huge pistol was pointed past him toward the dock. Michael heard a sharp click and looked at Craith's other hand, which held a matching weapon.

"No scum threatens my ship nor her company," he said in the sudden quiet. "It is a capital offense. And I am judge and jury."

There was no movement, no sound except for the slap of the tide against the hull and the creaking lines. Craith sighed with resignation. His thumb pulled the hammer to full cock, and the pistol went up.

"*And* executioner," he cracked.

There was a sudden scuffling, like the clattering of crabs on a shingle beach, and when Michael turned around, not a soul was on the dock but the one-armed man from du Pont. He was grinning up at Michael.

"Now look what y'done, Cap'n Craith. Spoiled the lad's donnybrook just when he got warmed up. A shame, that. It was only twenty to one!"

By late afternoon any hope that Michael Farrell entertained of getting work at the du Pont works had evaporated. Brendan Gallagher had brought him the five miles up the Brandywine to the company office, a distinct advantage over the dozens turned away daily from the yard gates, but Harry Belin, the book-keeper, was firm. Strict orders from the boss. There would be no one hired.

There was one possibility left. Brendan gave Michael directions to the church. Father Reardon might be able to help.

"I'll keep your baggage at the house, and you're to eat supper with us and spend the night. Tomorrow you can make a fresh start."

Michael thanked him and set out. Saint Joseph's Church was

not over a mile from the mills, a pleasant uphill walk along a road winding through lush woods. As soon as he had topped a rise in Barley Mill Road where the woodland abruptly ended in spring-green pasture, he saw a slate-and-copper steeple outlined against the clearing sky.

Father Reardon was impressed by Brendan's recommendation.

"Mr. Farrell, may I call you Michael? You seem to have had a rather abrupt arrival. That is a nasty bruise under your eye. Heavy weather at sea, or did you run into some unpleasant fellows on the docks?" The priest was smiling easily.

Michael's hand went to his cheek. He had forgotten the fight and wondered how bad the swelling looked. "Tell me something of yourself and how I might be of service."

Michael nearly blurted out the simple fact that he needed a job and a place to live, but pride choked it back. He found his words reeling out a casual sketch of his life as it had been, rather than a realistic picture of what it had recently become. The priest absorbed it all, fascinated by his background.

"So you attended Trinity College! I must confess your speech marks your education and upbringing."

"Only two years at Trinity . . ."

"Yes, yes. Well, Michael, you're only seventeen. I must confess I thought you to be much older. You say your home is in Ballingeary. If I'm not mistaken, that is very close to Bantry Bay."

"Fifteen miles."

"Oh, then we might have been neighbors. My father came from Skibbereen."

Michael nodded with a curious glance at the priest. "You do not sound Irish, Father, though I expected you to—with a name like Francis Reardon."

"I suppose I sound more like a Southern farmer. My parents had a tobacco plantation in Virginia." The priest paused, reminiscing. "That was a long time ago, a lovely time. The place had been in my mother's family for generations. When my father emigrated and came to work on the place, Mother fell in love with him on the spot." He chuckled, "Oh, there was much to-do about that! After they married it was years before he was accepted as an equal."

"An equal." Michael's words were a flat echo.

Father Reardon smiled wistfully and fell silent. After a moment he roused himself and looked sharply at his guest.

"Forgive me, Michael, I ramble so. What of your parents. Are they well?"

"Both gone. They died within a year of each other."

"God rest their souls. I'm sorry to hear that. Were they advanced in age?"

Michael shifted uncomfortably. "No, Mother just pined away after he died. I buried her last November."

Francis Reardon felt a door closing on that subject, and decided to skirt the boy's grief.

"Are there others? Brothers or sisters?"

"Only me."

"Then the responsibility for the estate has fallen to you. A heavy burden for one still in university."

Michael looked away, agitated. His answer was sharp to the point of being curt, "I left that to the care of others. And the schooling is done."

An awkward silence filled the room.

"How can I serve you, Michael?" the priest said gently.

The meeting seemed pointless now. All the chatter about social position had gilded his circumstances beyond practical use. He needed a job. Any job. The little money he had left after passage fare would not last a month. But he could not demean himself to ask.

"I think a letter of introduction from you, Father. A general letter would help in my getting settled."

Father Reardon avoided looking at the young man's sorry clothing, but he probed discreetly. "Are you sure that will do, Michael? I *can* make inquiries about work. Nothing very grand, you understand, but . . ."

"No, thank you. No, the letter will be fine. All I need."

Later as he went back down the hill toward the Gallagher cottage, Michael flushed with hurt pride and anger at himself.

He knew the priest had guessed his circumstances and might have been able to help. But he could not tell the old cleric that his father had been killed in a foolish skirmish with the English, losing for his mother and himself the lands and home that had been theirs for generations.

At least he had the letter. How important that would be in this Protestant country he could not tell, but he patted the inside pocket of his jacket to make sure it was still secure. The rich crinkling of the vellum envelope was some assurance. Michael shrugged off the meeting and began to whistle his way toward Chicken Alley. His belly growled, and the thought of a good supper with the Brendan Gallaghers brightened the evening considerably.

Early the next morning, Michael was freshly dressed in his best change of clothes and on his way to Wilmington, buoyed by the optimism of a full stomach and a solid night's rest. The Gallagher family had welcomed him so unreservedly that his self-esteem had gone up several notches, and he was beginning to feel at home in the community. A job would come, he was convinced; it was just a matter of time.

Even the teeth-rattling jolts of the freight wagon were exhilarating, and he listened in good humor to the garbled banter of his driver, whose words were warped by the stem of a black pipe clenched firmly in his teeth.

Michael's thoughts drifted back to his evening with the Gallaghers and the Feeney children. How those two had fussed over him, treating him more like an uncle than a stranger. He wondered if it had anything to do with their father's absence. There was something quite strange about that business. Apparently he had not been seen for some time—the twins chirped that out—but their aunt would not volunteer much beyond the comment that her brother worked as a long-distance wagoneer. He had been impressed with Brendan Gallagher's wife, a striking woman in her manner and appearance. He could easily imagine Noreen to be his older sister or close friend. She had an air of gentle wisdom that did not intimidate and a strangeness, too, almost a mystic quality he could not put his finger on. Twice as he had been speaking with her, the night before and again this morning, he had been amazed to realize she was old enough to be his grandmother. Yet there she possessed a quiet empathy that made her seem like his contemporary.

"Thar she be, young fella." The wagon jarred to a stop, and the driver pointed his wet pipestem at a garish facade. "That's yer Caesar Rodney Inn I been tellin' you about."

"Thank you for the ride," Michael said as he reached for his duffel and climbed down.

The driver leaned over and lowered his voice. "Don't tell them yer lookin' for work. They'll up the price to skeer you off. Tell 'em you're jest passing through. Oh, and another thing. Don't mind the ladies hanging around. They do a busy trade come evening. My advice is leave them be. They'll empty your pockets quicker than a deck of cards!" He slapped the reins over his lead mule's rump and the wagon rattled away.

Michael had arranged for a week's lodging, paid for in advance, and was off looking for work within the hour. His experience of the day before made him cautious in his approach. He tried to appear purposeful in his walk and made certain he had specific locations and directions established before setting out. No one would challenge a reasonably well-dressed young man looking like he had business to attend to.

It was not long before his spirits were considerably dampened, however. Every place he called had signs prominently posted, No Work. And most of them had another, usually scrawled as an afterthought, No Irish. Neither message stopped him from trying. His planned strategy of appearing to be on business carried him past the signs into the places without hesitation. That and the fact that he was well-spoken were enough to guarantee a polite rejection in most cases. But polite or not, the message was always a reiteration of the sign. He returned to the Caesar Rodney in the early evening, hungry and discouraged.

Michael had eschewed communal sleeping quarters, the barrackslike arrangement most inns provided for their cheap trade, because he wanted to avoid an appearance of insolvency. The room he rented was the least expensive available, but even that rate cut deeply into his purse. When he counted out what was left, there was barely enough to eat for a week. Well, there was a way to stretch that. He had had a solid breakfast at Brendan Gallagher's. He decided to skip supper and sleep off his hunger.

It worked for a time, but sometime in the late evening the din from the tavern on the first floor woke him and he dressed. An ale would be cheap enough and might quiet his complaining stomach.

There was a boisterous crowd in the taproom, and many of the patrons were apparently soldiers dressed in a blue uniform that Michael did not recognize. He worked his way to the back of the place, to a bench at the far end of a plank table in the corner, and had hardly taken his seat before a girl settled herself next to him. She flashed an impudent smile.

"Mind?"

Michael thought of the teamster's advice and grinned. She was no more than fifteen.

"It's a free land," he said disinterestedly.

"You're Irish, ain't you," the girl grinned. "You don't sound like one of those micks, but I bet you are!"

Michael recoiled from the loud announcement. It was not exactly the publicity he wanted.

"And why do you say that?"

She twisted her head, an awkward attempt at arch coquetry, "Oh, it's not your accent exactly, but 'free land'—it sounds like the Irish. I'd say, 'It's a free country.'"

"I see."

"Do you want a drink? Let me get us a drink!"

"An ale, yes." He was calculating the financial loss.

"Two ales. I need the company, dearie. To tell the truth, I was lookin' for somebody else, but I don't think he'll show up."

She bolted away from the table, snatched two pewter mugs from behind the bar, and helped herself to the tap. As she slid the foaming mugs along the table, the girl made an exaggerated reach, putting her open bodice inches from his nose.

She clinked her mug against his and took a mighty swig. He laughed, raised his own tankard, and nearly choked on the ale when she slid her hand between his legs and squeezed.

"God—" he spluttered. "Mind your fingers, girl!" he croaked, pushing her roughly aside. Carefully he put his mug on the planks and fixed her with a hard stare. "I might as well tell you now," he whispered, "I've neither the inclination nor the money to buy your time."

She sat unmoving, her hands in her lap, staring over the rim of her mug. She did not even seem to breathe, he thought, for a full minute. Then tears ran down her cheeks and her chin trembled. She dropped her head and quietly wept.

"Look," he said finally, "I didn't mean to hurt your feelings, miss, I just mean, well, I'm not a good prospect for you. That's all."

His words were less than reassuring, and the weeping showed signs of increasing. He would have gotten up and retreated to his room, but the girl blocked his way. Besides, he felt suddenly responsible for the damage to her feelings. He had barely reached out to comfort her when she sagged into his chest sobbing wetly against his neck.

Michael did not see the burly redhead enter the tavern. In fact, he was not aware of the man's presence at all until he spoke and reached across for the girl.

"Let's go," he said and roughly pulled at her arm.

Her head snapped up at the tug, and seeing him, she pried at his grip, twisting free. He reached for her again.

"Leave me be!" She was angry now, eyes flashing, only the tear streaks evidence of her recent collapse.

"I've no time to waste on argument," the redhead growled quietly. He made another grab.

"Leave her alone!"

Michael was as surprised by the sound of his own voice as he was by the sudden stillness in the room. The burly redhead turned slate blue eyes on him. They felt like ice.

"Mind your business, boy, and drink your beer."

The next few minutes were a blur to Michael. He remembered hearing the girl squeal in pain as the man gripped her arm again, and then the table rose, tankards flying, and he was over the upended table, his fists whirling at the redhead. He was floating through it all, a redo of the previous day, arms pounding marvelously of their own will. He was conscious of one solid hit against the bristling heavy jaw, and then he was down, face to the ale-puddled floor, a dozen hands pinning him, someone's knee in his back, and he could not breathe.

When they let him up, he was dizzy with loss of breath. There was good-humored laughter and faces swam out of the gray smiling at him. He looked around for the girl and the bull-like redhead.

"There're gone, lad, and good news that is for all concerned, especially yourself."

The voice was coming from one of the soldiers, the older man with an armful of stripes.

Michael struggled to his feet. The soldier held him back with a bear hug.

"Whoa, me bucko! Yer better rid of any more of that." He held on until Michael sat down.

"That's better, lad. Sit and quiet yourself." He turned and shouted to the bar, "Bring me hero another beer to cool him down!"

The brew was suddenly in his hands, and Michael took a long draught, gripping the tankard tightly to cover his trembling.

"My name is Aloysius Moody, Sergeant of the Army," the soldier went on. "I'm here with these others to recruit lads like yourself for a fine hitch with Uncle Sam, all expenses paid. What's yer name?"

"Michael Farrell."

Sergeant Moody stood with hands on hips, grinning down at this glowering young man who had exploded into such a fierce fighting machine.

"Well, Michael Farrell, if you're interested in a job with travel and excitement, look me up. I'm a lodger in this fleatrap, same as you." He added with a cluck, "Ye've some nerve!"

Michael shrugged and looked ruefully at his torn shirt. "A tavern brawler . . . I was stupid to get involved."

"You don't know who it was y'punched, do ye?" Sergeant Moody observed thoughtfully.

Michael shook his head.

"That was Henry du Pont himself, it was. In the flesh!"

And again the whole room was silent.

The following morning Michael had second thoughts about the whole business of looking for work in the Wilmington area. It was not that he was in the least perturbed by du Pont's reputation, but the prospects were definitely bleak. He had a sudden inclination to seek out David Craith. Perhaps the sea trade would not be as unpleasant as his experience the last few days of the voyage across. It was marvelous how a settled stomach—and the prospect of a permanently empty one—could influence one's thinking.

He made his way to Front Street and the docks, and with each step the idea of shipping on the clipper became more appealing.

But when he rounded the corner of the last block there was no sign of the tall masts, and the entire wharf lay deserted. One merchant seaman standing in the doorway of a pub was able to answer his questions, though.

"She went on the tide last night, bound for New Orleans with a load of gunpowder. Won't be back for at least a month."

Michael was disappointed, but he was determined to run out his string of chances before giving up. He had money enough for six more days.

And after that he would consider Sergeant Moody's offer. Two new sets of clothes, both blue with brass buttons, a rifle to carry, and three meals a day. All that and a dollar a month.

It was not the answer to his dream.

It was good insurance, just the same.

CHAPTER FOUR

Meta du Pont slammed her way into the house, her face a black contradiction of the balmy spring sunshine outside. She snapped at Blanche Gallagher, who was arranging an armload of fresh daffodils in a large vase in the hall.

"Where is Mr. Alfred?"

Blanche dropped the blooms on the table, stooped to pick up one that fell to the floor and, wiping her hands nervously on her apron, approached her scowling mistress.

"Why, I believe the Mister is in his library, madam."

Meta stalked to the end of the entry corridor and briskly climbed the elliptical stairway to the second floor. Blanche heard the library door close firmly.

"Mother Mary!" Blanche whispered and went back to her flowers.

Alfred du Pont looked up from a desk littered with papers and heaped with half a dozen technical books. He gave his wife a preoccupied smile.

"We need to discuss the business."

Alfred's expression changed from a dazed recognition of his wife's presence to mild curiosity. He rarely spoke with her about the operation of the company. It was something the women in his family left to their men. Even his own sisters, who, unlike

Meta, were legal shareholders in the family business, rarely questioned what was going on.

He smiled genially. "I am pleased to see your taking an interest, my dear."

Meta did not return the smile. "It is your *lack* of interest which concerns me, Alfred."

Alfred's expression remained pleasant, but a bemused detachment veiled his somber gray eyes. He rose from the desk, an imposing man physically—six feet three inches tall, with generous shoulders and build proportional to his height. Alfred was ten years older than his wife, and his face looked it. On haggard days he looked older still, the care lines deeply creased in a gentle but apprehensive pattern about his worried eyes. Except for a perceptible stoop in his back, the body seemed to have escaped whatever had so ravaged his face.

"Lack of interest?" he muttered, carelessly waving to the clutter of paperwork on the desktop. "I have been pestered by a nagging guilt all morning that I should spend more time with you and the boys . . ."

Meta had to crane her neck to look up at her husband, but being seven inches shorter had no effect on her manner. He nearly quailed under her hot look.

"I'm not talking about your . . . your . . . hobby, Alfred. What I am referring to is the practical business of running this company."

"You do not understand, my dear," he said mildly. "The need to improve the company product requires constant review of the process by which it is compounded and research as to how it can be improved. In fact, only this morning, I struck upon a chemical alternative . . ."

"In fact," she mimicked, "only this morning I was talking with your brother about how slipshod the operation of the mills has become! Under *your* leadership, Alfred, if you can call hiding away with formulae and books in this dark hole leadership!"

He backed away from her a step and turned slowly toward the light from the window. "What exactly did Henry have to say?"

"That we are losing ground in production to an alarming degree. Henry says that he doubts we are even making a profit!" Her voice was controlled but husky with belligerence. "Henry says that he thinks we may have been losing money for years. Is there any truth to his claim, Alfred? You are certainly not very aggressive in your dealings with our employees. I really wonder if that carries over into the marketplace as well."

"Henry says, eh?" His look was mixed hurt and hostility. "If our Henry had his way, we would long ago have had to replace more than a few panes of shattered glass and cracked plaster as we did recently. He is impetuous and roughshod, his tactics well suited to leading troops against savages, but hardly appropriate to the volatile science of powdermaking."

Meta huffed with exasperation. "You should have had that worker fired on the spot as Henry demanded. It is your attitude, Alfred. You coddle the men and allow the business to drift aimlessly while you hide here dreaming of chemical theory."

"Listen, Meta. You would do well to get your information from a less prejudiced source in the future. For your information, we have just contracted for a substantial quantity of powder for the federal government. That order alone will insure a heavy profit for the year. In fact, we shall have to add men to the payroll to fill it."

She was unprepared for the good news, but it did not sway her argument. One last point had to be made.

"If it is delivered and paid for. I only demand one thing from you, Alfred—that you not allow us to sink into bankruptcy. Your lackadaisical manner might satisfy your own limited ambition, but it must not threaten the boys' inheritance. I will not stand idle and watch my Irénée's rightful future as president be stripped from him."

The accusation of dereliction did not cut into Alfred at all. His own priorities in the leadership of this frightening business were clear. He would take no chances with the black genie manufactured in the mills inherited from his father. There had been too much grief and terror already. The answer lay in safer methods. As to the rest, the profit-and-loss measure, well, he would catch up with that in due course.

But he did not like the implication that he was not looking out for his sons. That cut deeply. "I'll speak to Henry," he said, and abruptly left the room.

Henry du Pont sat comfortably on a stack of new powder kegs in the warm sunshine outside the keg mill and let his brother's anger wash over him. He was not in the least perturbed. Indeed, Henry was enjoying the scene as a deviation from his older brother's usual taciturnity. The anger gave Alfred an animation that his personality needed.

Alfred was not enjoying himself, however. The knot in his stomach twisted more as the interview continued. He had learned long before that nothing he could say, nothing *anybody* could say, would have much effect on Henry. He suddenly wanted the lecture ended.

"In the future I suggest in the strongest terms that you bring your criticism to me personally."

Henry answered with a long, cool stare followed by a curt nod. Then he got up, switched a curled wood shaving from his trouser, and stabbed his walking stick in Alfred's direction.

"Very well. To begin with, I must be given more autonomy to run the yards. To meet production there are the changes I have already outlined."

"Night production is out of the ques—"

"My second requirement is to have access to the office records: sales correspondence, accounting records, payment schedules, profit-and-loss statements."

"Careful, Henry! You are overstepping your bounds."

"The third, and for the moment, the last requirement, is that you support me as second in command or, if you do not have the stomach for it, stay out of my way."

Behind them in the keg mill, a saw whined shrilly through a stubborn grain and settled back to a muted hum. Somewhere nearby in the trees a mockingbird attempted to duplicate the sound, gave up, and improvised its own melody. The song was cut short by a raucous scream, and the bird burst from the leaves above them, diving at a cat which darted under the wood-shop. Something pink and red hung limp in its jaws.

— 33 —

Alfred's face was gray with the effort to control his rage. "I must warn you, Henry, that I will not tolerate such effrontery from anyone, not even a brother. If you do not choose to follow my instructions, you are free to seek employment elsewhere."

"You forget, Alfred," Henry said with exaggerated patience, "I am a partner in this enterprise."

"You are a stockholder and an employee," Alfred countered, an ague of trembling shaking his words. "The president has absolute control over all matters pertaining to company operation. That includes every worker." Then he added a final comment that twisted his lips like a foul taste. "I should remind you that your own home is owned by the firm."

The last threat piqued Henry at last, or so it seemed. He jabbed at a fallen leaf irritably, spearing it with the tip of his cane. When he looked back at his brother, his eyes burned, but his voice was icy calm.

"I see where I stand, Mister President." He turned easily and began walking away. When he had gone several steps, he turned and added pleasantly, "My best to your family, Alfred."

The confrontation ruined Alfred's entire day. He was nearly dismantled emotionally by his implied threat to remove his brother's family from their home. Hours later he was unable to eat and left the table to retire early. The boys wondered what had caused their father to be so upset, but Meta had no explanation.

Henry was ebullient at his own table. Louisa delighted in his rare good humor that evening. He pranced about the house entertaining little Henry Algernon with much of the gusto he had had as a young major with his first command in the Indian Wars.

Henry had reason. Alfred had succeeded in painting himself the villain far better than Henry could have managed on his own. Time now to follow through with the next step. He knew that Meta would be more than cooperative. She might even initiate the move herself.

The career army man congratulated himself on brilliant tactics and promising strategy. Not since he had left the military life at his father's request had a project promised such excitement of challenge and conquest. It had been over a decade since

Eleuthère Irénée du Pont died, twelve years of frustrating subordinate work in the dirty mills with Alexis sharing his inherited burden, a dozen years of watching the inept leadership of his firstborn brother Alfred.

Well, he had sacrificed a brilliant career as a West Point–trained and combat-proved officer to help this foundering company. He had done his homework in every phase of the industry. And now it looked like there would be a promising market in a nice little war with Mexico. Henry's eyes flashed with the prospect of leading a military operation against *that* disorganized mob with their gaudy uniforms and popinjay officers. It galled him to think of Zack Taylor and Winfield Scott positioned to make names for themselves.

So be it! Let them have the excitement of battle. He would content himself with taking over the company which would make most of their gunpowder. Let them get the citations and medals. He would content himself with profit and power of a different denomination.

Meta had not seen Henry for two days, and the suspense was killing her. Ever since her confrontation with Alfred, her husband had moped about the house like an afflicted ghost. He practically went into hiding, eating rarely and always alone in his library. Blanche fussed about the place casting worried looks at Meta and fixing trays of snacks to take up to the man.

"He seems ill to me, madam. I don't wish to butt in where it's not my place, but I think the last accident upset him more than the others."

Blanche's tone suggested reproach, but Meta stifled an impulse to put the servant down. She suspected that it was more than the explosion which had addled her husband, but for the time being it was probably just as well to reinforce that idea in the household. She smiled wistfully and patted Blanche on the arm.

"If he does not improve by tomorrow, I think I will call in the doctor. Here," she said, taking the tray from Blanche, "let me see if I can cheer him up."

Alfred was again sitting at his desk, his elbow buried in the rumpled pile of foolscap, chin resting on the heel of his hand as he stared vacantly across the room. Meta thrust the tray before him on a stack of books where it teetered dangerously. Alfred stirred, raised his head, and leaned back in the chair.

Meta sat in an armchair facing him.

"I want to know what you said to Henry."

Alfred's eyes flickered, but he said nothing.

"And what he said to you."

He shrugged, made an effort to clear some of the papers, and lowered the tray before him. The dishes rattled with the palsied movement of his hands.

"You're very thoughtful, Meta. But I'm not hungry."

"You met with Henry."

He nodded listlessly.

"And?"

"We have an understanding." The pain deepened in his eyes.

She waited, tapping her nails irritably on the arm of the chair. When he said nothing else, she leaned forward angrily. "You are exasperating me, Alfred. Please explain yourself. Will there be changes? Changes in the way this firm is being handled?"

He looked at her steadily for the first time, a sad but firm gaze. "I gave Henry the choice of following my orders or leaving the company. He apparently agreed to the former choice."

Her jaw dropped. "What are you talking about? Alfred, I am half witless with worry over the way *you* are mismanaging things. The question was never over Henry's abilities!"

"You are quite correct, Meta. There is no question as to my brother's abilities. What I cannot countenance are his methods and, with respect to this incident where he sought your sympathies, his arrogant attitude." Alfred's voice shook with agitation, and he paused to compose himself, then continued. "I do not think he will attempt to undermine our relationship again."

Relationship, indeed! Meta wondered what he would do if he knew how much their relationship had been compromised already. She bridled at having been sidetracked.

"I warn you again, Alfred, I will not permit you to mismanage our security into a state of insolvency. Henry may be too aggressive for your nature, but his ideas are better suited for the healthy progress of du Pont!"

"Please, Meta," he said as though exhausted, "I'm afraid you will have to trust my judgment. I do not wish to discuss the matter further."

He could not miss the burning hostility in her stare, but he was relieved when she left without another word.

The next morning Meta intercepted Henry as he was leaving the company office near the house. They stepped behind a huge clump of blossoming lilac blocking the view from the yards below and the main house. She was direct in her proposal, pretty much as Henry had expected.

"He will not bend. Together, you and I will have to bring him down," she said without emotion. "Then you will assume the presidency."

He nodded gravely, icy eyes betraying nothing.

"There are conditions," she added. "Some provision for Irénée and Lammot. Irénée shall not lose his birthright because of his father!" The last comment surprised Henry with its vehemence, but she softened immediately and continued. "As for the rest, Henry, I imagine you have some idea . . ."

He embraced her without a word, the crushing press of his body against her a confirmation of the pact and demonstration of his need. Meta smiled and whispered in his ear.

"Tomorrow at ten the house will be empty."

CHAPTER FIVE

Michael Farrell returned to his room at the Caesar Rodney Inn wet and miserable from a luckless day on the streets. He had been to so many businesses during the past week's search for work that he was beginning to lose track.

He stripped off his sodden clothes and hung them from the bedstead, garment hooks on the door, and the back of his single chair. Shivering in the damp cold of the gloomy room, he pulled a blanket from the bed, wrapped up in it, padded to the window, and stared morosely down at the rainswept street. He had certainly picked a fine time to come to America! The depressed economy was a subject discussed in the newspapers almost daily, with dire forecasts that did not help his spirits at all. Of course, he did not need the papers. The crowds of men out of work were everywhere, and ugly feelings toward them, particularly the Irish, increased daily. He allowed himself the luxury of regret, bemoaning ever leaving home in the first place.

The next morning he was not sure whether it was the brilliant sun stabbing at his eyelids or the din from the floor above which woke him. But the shouted words of an Irishman clumping down the stairs from the dormitory loft spun him out of bed like the touch of a hot iron.

"They're hirin' at the du Pont mills!"

Michael did not waste time packing. In fact, he was not fully dressed when he raced to the innkeeper, pressed a coin into his hand, and shouted over his shoulder as he made for the door.

"Look to my things. I'll be back tonight!"

He began running as soon as he hit the street—a loose, loping stride that had him beyond the town limits in a few minutes. It was a good five miles to the mills, the first four a gentle upslope run and the last almost precipitously downhill into the Brandywine Gorge. He paced himself during the uphill grade, holding the prospect of an easy coast at the end. He dismissed the possibility of hitching a ride on a wagon because it would be too slow, and the chance of being picked up by a carriage was ludicrous.

The morning sun drenched his back and neck, and he was sweating heavily in the humidity even though the air was still cool. Once or twice when he passed walking clumps of men and again on overtaking a freight wagon festooned with hitchhiking laborers, clinging like limpets to its sides, he was cheered on.

"Save a place in line for me, lad!"

"Don't blow up the place before we get there!"

The first three miles were easy, and he was thankful for all the walking he had done during the week, but then his legs began to cramp and he had to slow down, blowing like a winded horse. He gauged his need, forcing the legs to move on the safe edge of their endurance, feeling the deep heaving of his chest subside to easier breathing. As soon as he had control again, he burst into a run and felt the release of reserve energy propel him into second wind, up the last slope, past the blurred cluster of buildings which were the church and rectory he had visited and, at last, the turn down hill into the cool woods toward the distant Brandywine.

He nearly tumbled several times during the headlong, clattering run down the steep gravel road. His legs were rubbery now, numbly following the directions of his brain, and when the road flattened out along the streambed, he slowed again, staggering over the puddled, muddy ruts.

When he finally reached the gates of the du Pont mills, a line of over twenty men was ahead of him.

Michael was too exhausted to be disappointed. He took his place, breathing so noisily that several turned around at the commotion. He was drenched with sweat and too spent at the moment to even wipe his face.

"Look at that one, O'Toole. By the look of him, I'd say he swam upstream to get here."

"Are ye that keen on gettin' work, lad?"

"Work? Whisst! In his condition he'll not last a twelve-hour day."

"Ah, it doesn't matter. He'll have the whole day fer rest. They're hirin' naught but a dozen anyway."

"Twenty, I heard."

There was general laughter.

"You're dreaming again, Flaherty. Is it because there are nineteen men ahead of you?"

"Now don't knock Flaherty; he's just demonstratin' his skill with figures. That lad can count like a wizard!"

"Aye, all his fingers and toes. After that he's stumped."

Flaherty seemed unruffled, he turned and winked at Michael. "A pack o' lies. I can count to twenty and three—all me fingers and toes and the three between me legs."

"That's true," a piping voice agreed. "I've seen him practice regularly."

Flaherty joined in the laughter at his expense. Then he observed soberly, "From what I hear, in this place it is a holy practice to keep tabs on your precious parts. They have a bad tendency to fly apart at odd moments."

Nobody added to that. And after some reflection Flaherty turned back to Michael again. "If I could have me druthers, I think I'd better go all at once, instead of a piece at a time."

The man in front of Flaherty turned around and whispered, "Here comes one who can only count to fifteen."

Michael looked up and saw Brendan Gallagher counting as he walked down the line. When he got to Michael, he grinned with surprise, reached out with an awkward left handshake, and tugged him from the queue. "Every man up to Farrell here, follow me."

"Come on with me, Farrell."

Alexis du Pont paced the Wilmington rail depot with the eager anticipation of a child. He made any excuse to detour to the place if he was in town when the daily trains from Baltimore or Philadelphia passed through. In the ten years since he had seen his first locomotive, the Tom Thumb, the machines had grown in size and power with increases in speed that dazzled him. At thirty, married, with children, he often toyed with the idea of leaving the powder yards and taking a tour as operator of the huge engines. That was dream stuff, unrealistic. He would have to content himself with an occasional ride and frequent looks at the clanking behemoths as they thundered nonstop through town or wheezed clanking to a stop inches from his nose.

More than once the worried stationmaster had tugged him back from the rails, afraid that this youngest of the three du Pont partners would be plucked from life by some thrashing iron lever or another, mashed by his own curiosity, and the finger of blame would rest on the rail agent's carelessness.

Alex, as most of the family called him, hoped that the train now overdue from Philadelphia would be drawn by the new locomotive he had read about. It was a huge affair—horizontal boiler, flaring funnel, external cylinders mounted in line with the horizontal driverods, and spent steam discharged thunderously up the chugging stack. He nearly danced with anticipation.

Leaning out from the platform gave him a clear view for only a quarter mile in the afternoon haze and drizzle. Patches of ground fog drifted in gray veils across the glistening track, and even in the humid dead air, his ear was sharper than his eye. It was coming, and he was a trifle let down when he recognized the huff not of the new machine, but of a recent model of the Clinton.

In spite of the disappointment, he ambled far down the platform to be near the engine when it stopped, and when it rumbled to a halt he was so engrossed in the hot, panting thing that he did not hear someone calling his name.

"Uncle Alex!"

A tap on the shoulder brought him around to face a very tall young man with spectacles.

"I thought you'd be here. Thinking of getting one for the powder yards?"

"Oh, hello there, Motty." Alexis smiled and appraised his nephew. "I think you've grown an inch since last month—taller than me now. Where's your brother?"

"He's staying at school."

"Boning up on his studies?"

Lammot laughed. "Widening his social world, I think. It's nice that you came to meet me."

"I was in town anyway. Some bushings for the new turbines. Where are your bags?"

Lammot cocked his head toward the gleaming locomotive. "I don't want to drag you away, Uncle Alex."

Alexis poked the tall youth in the ribs. "Don't make fun of your elders, boy. Come on, the way I look they're apt to have me stoking the firebox."

The mean, drizzling afternoon lifted under a west breeze, and when they were halfway into the five-mile trip to the mills, the skies opened to scattered balls of cumulus racing eastward over the Brandywine Gorge. At the southern boundary of the du Pont holdings, the river turned into a sharp north-south channel cut deeply into a steep-sided valley strung on both banks with the rumbling millworks and strips of worker housing. The du Pont residences were on the high ground overlooking the streambed and separated generally from the mills and tenants by woodland covering the slopes.

The normal route from town to estate was along the lip of the gorge, out Kennett Pike, north along Montchanin Road to the west entrance to the family compound. Alexis chose instead the lane following the Brandywine. This roadway wound through the working mill yards and employee housing. Each cluster of houses was built into a single row with a common roof, generally with thick walls of whitewashed native granite. All were two-story buildings with four to six dwellings per unit. The communities were generally made up of four or five buildings— the number dictated by the space available under the steep slopes of the gorge—and all had particular names. Chicken Alley, Squirrel Run, and Walkers Banks were originally nicknames that became official in due course. The one cluster near the machine shop below the Belin house was christened Free Park, perhaps to remind the workers of company largess. Within a few weeks of moving in, however, the Irish modified this downward to a more realistic term, and the place was called Flea Park thereafter.

"I want to drop this off at the machine shop before going up to the house," Alexis said jabbing his head toward the box of bronze bushings on the floor of the buggy.

"I can just walk, Uncle Alex. You probably want to get right at it."

Alexis glanced sideways at Lammot and smiled. "You have me sized up, eh, Motty? No, it's almost supper time. I'll get to it after I eat."

"You'll have no one to help after dinner. Can't it wait till morning?"

"No. I want to get the Eagle Mills running first thing tomorrow."

"I could run down and give a hand."

"Thanks, Motty, you stay with the family. Alfred and your mother will want you home. Your father will have a hundred questions about your chemistry studies. Anyway, some of my boys will drift in, Murphy and his gang. They look after me."

Lammot watched his uncle as he lugged the heavy box into the machine shop. He was making small talk with the crew, and as usual he left them laughing over some joke. It was amazing how unlike Uncle Henry he was. Henry was all gruff business and a bit hard on the men. Lammot had heard tales from workers' children over the years. They loved his Uncle Alex; they hated Uncle Henry. As to his own father, who was much older than both Henry and Alexis, it could honestly be said that the workers respected him and considered "Mr. Alfred" to be gentle and fair even if he was a bit distant.

Lammot decided that he was lucky to have a kind and understanding father who happened to be director of the family business, and to have an uncle who was a friend to just about everybody on the Crick.

"Thank you again, Uncle Alex. Are you sure I can't help?"

Alexis shook his head. "Enjoy your vacation, Motty."

Lammot stepped down, dragged his luggage from the buggy, and stood until the rig pulled away. His uncle would be at his own place in minutes, another grand house within the sprawling compound. There were nearly a dozen mansions scattered within a mile of this place, all of them du Pont–owned, all of them a testament to the industry of his family. Lammot was the third generation. His grandfather had started it all forty-six years before, and they had kept it building by sticking together. The sunset afterglow lent a pale blush to the stuccoed walls of his father's home, and he felt a sudden rush of possession-pride. It was a mansion; he lived in a mansion! At that moment, in his sixteenth year, Lammot du Pont knew some day he would lead the company to a greatness no one could yet imagine.

It was a heady sensation, and as he strode to the front door, he could not ever remember feeling quite so good as he did just now.

CHAPTER SIX

The end of Michael Farrell's second week in the United States was cause for celebration. The wolf had been driven from his heels, and he rejoiced in relative good fortune. He was bone-weary when Saturday night arrived. Pick-and-shovel work was one task for which he had not been trained. But the grand fact was that he had been equal to it, blisters and aching back, and now he was richer by four dollars. That was his pay for a week's work after the two he paid to Noreen Gallagher for room and board.

The assignment to bachelor housing at the Gallaghers' had been engineered by Brendan, and work with the masonry crew had been set up by his son, Kevin, who was a construction foreman. Kevin's gang of workers were a happy lot, full of shenanigans that their boss, dour Kevin, did not share but seemed to enjoy tolerating. As long as he was forced to work with his hands instead of his educated brain, Michael decided that he was quite fortunate to be where he was.

That employee housing lagged behind the sudden influx of workers was another bonus. He would have to stay at the Gallagher's, as warm a place as he could imagine, and he seemed to fill a void in the scattered age groups living there. He was the third generation, slipping between their son, Kevin, and the twins, who were children born late to Noreen's brother, Tim.

In point of years, they were young enough to be her grand-children.

It was a lovely time. He literally could not remember being more content. Certainly his early childhood was happy enough, but the strain of his father's political activities had cast a pall. Then, too, he had not really been at ease with the children in his own town. His family was gentry at a time when gentlefolk were suspect—even the families of underground activists like his dad. In time that impression had been rectified, of course, with the sudden notoriety of his name. But it was too late then. He had been disinherited by the grace of the English crown, and anonymity became his very protection. The chance to function as a well-liked member of the Gallagher household was a balm to wounds he had never before had the opportunity to recognize.

On the way to work the following Monday, Kevin mentioned it obliquely.

"You get on well with the twins."

Michael smiled, the fullness of the morning almost over-powering him as they took a shortcut through the woods. Trees were beginning to leaf, the dogwood pink and white, and even maples in loose bud this early in spring. The leaf-mold earth beneath was sprouting violet and yellow blooms.

"They are lovely children. Their playing nearly wore me out yesterday. That Megan is an imp."

The job they had been assigned was to lay a foundation for the proposed addition to a small laboratory not far from the main residence of Alfred and Meta du Pont. The original frame struc-ture contained a single room, and the new wing would triple its size. After laying out the trench lines, Kevin left Michael to begin the pick-and-shovel work.

He had been working steadily throughout the morning and had completed the first shallow circuit of the foundation when someone spoke to him from the stoop of the laboratory building.

"Aren't you stopping for dinner? The noon whistle blew ten minutes ago."

Michael looked up at the speaker, a lanky young man close to six feet, who moved down the steps with the awkward grace of one not yet used to his large-boned frame. He wore spectacles and was dressed in a business suit which was well tailored but looked more appropriate for someone twice his age. He ambled down to where Michael stood in the shallow ditch.

"I suppose I did not notice it."

"I didn't think so." The eyes behind the glasses were gray and sparkled with humor, and under his rather long, beardless face with a somewhat prominent nose, his lips curled happily. Michael knew instantly that he was a du Pont, a junior edition of the company president, probably. "You really concentrate on your work," he chuckled. "I've been watching for some time. I've never seen the turf fly so."

Michael felt rather uncomfortable standing a foot lower in the trench staring at the middle button on the boy's waistcoat. He drove the spade home with a shove of his foot, set the pick beside it, and stepped out of the hole. But even standing level, he noticed, the du Pont youth had an inch or more on him.

"I'm glad to hear that," Michael said easily. "I have been out of practice."

"I *thought* so!" He sounded like he had won a wager. "You appear to have more enthusiasm than skill at this."

"They wanted it done quickly, I was told," Michael countered a bit defensively. He leaned back to sight along the lines strung between corner batter-boards. "It seems true enough to me."

"Oh, I didn't mean that. It's fine, fine. No, what I meant was you didn't seem to have the career pace of a pick-and-shovel man. They do take their time, you know." He seemed flustered, guilty of an unintended faux pas. "Look, I'm Lammot," he blurted, extending his hand. "Lammot du Pont."

Michael exerted more pressure than usual in the handshake, but Lammot's grip was quite strong without apparent effort. "Michael Farrell."

"Two r's and two l's," Lammot observed as if stating a fact. "Glad to know you, Michael. Say, why don't you take your dinner in the shade over there, and I'll go up to the kitchen to see if I can get us something cool to drink."

He was gone quite a long time, and Michael had nearly finished eating by the time he saw the gangly figure striding back from the house with a basket slung over his arm. Lammot's "something cool to drink" had developed into a picnic of delicacies which he set out on the grass next to Michael's dinner pail. He seemed embarrassed by the spread.

"I just asked Blanche for a sandwich and a drink to bring down to the lab, and this is what I got. Please help yourself."

Michael really was not very hungry after having had his own meal, and he limited himself to a glass of lemonade. It was not that he could not have found room for more food, but the finery of it all was rather intimidating in his present circumstances. Even the delicate glass from which he drank seemed at odds with his earth-caked clothing and roughened hands.

Lammot did not press the food on him. After a few moments of silent chewing, he glanced at Michael. "I'd say you are twenty-two or twenty-three."

"Seventeen."

"Really! Well, I was fooled. You seem much older. You have a serious manner, though; that must be it. I'm nearly sixteen."

Michael raised a dark eyebrow and grinned briefly. "I hope you stop growing soon. At your rate you're apt to be twenty-one hands high before you reach as many years." He got to his feet and stretched. "It was nice meeting you, Mr. Lammot du Pont, and I thank you for the pleasant noon break. But," he inclined his head in the direction of the digging, "I have to get back to work."

Lammot jumped up and followed as he left, "Look, Michael, the hour is not up; why not take a minute to look into the laboratory. You'll see how much we need the addition you're building."

Michael was doubtful. It was true that the whistle had not blown ending the noon break, but he did not want to compromise his job either. Still, a look would not hurt. After all, this was the owner's son.

The place was packed with apparatus. There was little room to work, and several unopened crates were stacked against the wall and in the narrow aisle between the benches.

"I love this place," Lammot said quietly. "It is where my father and I spend most of our time together. I think he likes his library better—theoretical study, you know—but I like to fool around with the chemicals."

Michael was amazed at the quality of the equipment. Everything was so advanced, each piece gleamed with a luster that reflected fastidious care, but it was the newness that struck him. He remembered another laboratory, shabby in comparison. A microscope drew him, his fingers delicate on the adjusting knobs as the field came into a sharper, greater magnification than he had ever seen. The lenses must have cost a fortune. Such light!

"Potassium nitrate," he muttered. "But I've never seen the crystals so clearly."

"I knew it!" The voice bubbled excitement. "I just knew it the moment you spoke, Michael Farrell." Michael turned reluctantly from the eyepiece.

"Knew it?"

"Your training. Where did you train?"

"Oh." Michael drew back to reality. "Two years at Trinity."

Lammot smiled as if he had produced a rabbit from his hat. "Trinity. Why that's wonderful news. I'm in my second year at the University of Pennsylvania. Chemistry. It's close by, you know, Philadelphia. I come home often to work right here."

"Benjamin Franklin's university."

"Oh, yes. 'Ben's Business School,' as it's called by the locals sometimes. Not as prestigious as Trinity."

"I did not mean that. Franklin's idea of a school to educate the middle class is well thought of in some circles."

Lammot shrugged with a clumsy sweep of bony arms. "Well, there's not much difference here—the class idea, I mean. Most people here get where they are on their own merits."

It was an unfortunate shift away from his topic, and Michael felt Lammot's distress even before his face reddened. A sound at the door brought them both around, relieved by the welcome interruption.

"Good day, Mister Lammot," Kevin Gallagher said after clearing his throat nervously. "I was lookin' for Farrell here."

As they walked back to the ditch, Kevin mentioned that the noon break was a quarter hour past, and it would be good for Michael to keep better track of his working time. He did not mention the improprieties of hobnobbing with the boss's son.

He did not have to. Michael noticed that Kevin came to the lab door with his cap in hand and did not put it back on until he was out of Lammot du Pont's presence.

Lammot watched them from the doorway. He regretted that the conversation with Farrell had come to such an abrupt end. Perhaps they would have another chance later. He liked the fellow, wondering idly why he had given up his studies.

He pulled a watch from his waistcoat and fumbled open the cover. One-thirty. It was a bit late to try to catch up with his father and brother in Wilmington. Blanche would probably have gone with them for her weekly shopping. He wondered if his mother had left for her twice-postponed visit to his Aunt Louisa. This morning she had hinted again of a persistent headache.

Well, with the place to himself, he might as well go up to his room and change into comfortable clothes. There were several experiments he was itching to begin. He looked around at the crowded laboratory wishing that the new wing were complete. Some of the boxed equipment would have made the work simpler. He closed the door and, after retrieving the lunch basket, again made his way to the house.

Lammot entered through the kitchen, dropped off the basket, and went upstairs by way of the servants' stairway in the rear corner of the house. His own room was closer to this flight than the formal stairway in the central hall. A heavy silence hung in the place and, relishing the quiet, he padded softly through the open door of his room and began disrobing. It was so still the sounds of the working mills below came clear and distinct through the window facing the Brandywine. He was down to his underwear, reaching into the armoire for cotton shirt and trousers, when he heard his mother's voice.

Lammot presumed she was calling for him and was out in the hallway in his stockinged feet about to answer when he heard someone else. His jaws tightened at the sound, and he felt a prickling at the nape of his neck as he carefully withdrew.

There was no mistaking the gruff voice of his uncle. His hand shook as he eased his own door closed without engaging the catch. The words of the two in the other room had been blurred, but their elation was painfully exquisite to his ears. Lammot's tongue went dry in his mouth, and his face burned with images that sickened his mind.

He had been back in the lab for a good half hour before he heard the heavy steps of Henry du Pont pass by and then fade down the pathway to the mills.

At dinner that evening, his mother seemed agitated when she found that he had not gone to town with the others. Her mood relaxed considerably when he claimed to have spent the entire day absorbed in the laboratory.

Alfred du Pont beamed down the table at his son. "All day in the lab, eh? Well, Lammot, you cannot seem to get enough of your science, it appears." He winked at his elder son and added, "What do you think, Irénée, will there be a place for your brother when you assume leadership of the company?"

Irénée humored his father with a smile and looked at Lammot. "Judging from his silence at dinner this evening, I imagine he would be best suited for laboratory work, if not some monastery cloister."

His father rose, went to his wife, and kissed her tenderly on the cheek. It was an unusual demonstration of affection in the household. "Thank you my dear," he said tenderly, "for having given me such clever children."

Meta returned the kiss warmly as Alfred bent to give her a gentle embrace.

Lammot excused himself, pleading the need for study, and went to his room. As he lay staring at the ceiling, he decided that warning his father about Henry would not be worth the damage it would cause. Lammot knew his father's weaknesses—his failing health, his sensitivity, his anxieties over the destructive force of the mills he administered. He also recognized the man's greatest vulnerability, an overwhelming affection for his wife.

Lammot would not risk destroying that. It would destroy his father in the process.

As he fell asleep fully clothed, Lammot almost wished that he had hinted at being upstairs between one and two o'clock. It would have been a way of letting her know—and confirming his own fears. But the confirmation would have cut the slender thread of doubt he clung to for his own love of his mother.

CHAPTER SEVEN

It was inevitable that Michael's and Henry's paths would cross. The meeting took place in the pay line two weeks after he started work.

Michael had hoped that he would not be recognized, that Henry might have been too drunk or that the tavern light had been too dim for him to see well. Beyond that he thought the wealthy boss would prefer not to recall the incident for social reasons or even have the grace to laugh it off. After all, Henry had won the fight—in a manner of speaking.

All of these hopes were wiped out as Henry strode into the pay shed, casually glancing at the new men and suddenly freezing beside Michael. He was close enough for Michael to hear his breathing, and he paused there so long that the men began to squirm awkwardly and give Michael strange looks.

Michael at first pretended not to notice being singled out, but the charade became silly, and he turned to look the man full in the eye.

It was an eye full of searing anger.

"That one!" Henry barked. "What's his name?"

Harry Belin followed the jabbing finger and groped for the information.

Michael stepped out of line, tight as a drawn wire, but he could not unclamp his jaw to speak.

"Fa . . . Farrell's his name . . . ah . . ." The prompting came from one of his mason crew.

"Oh, yes," Belin said, consulting the ledger. He found the name and looked up relieved. "Michael Kevin Farrell, with the masons."

"Not after today. Pay him off and boot him out."

No one whispered in the shed until the crunch of Mister Henry's boots had died in the distance.

There was a deal of buzzing afterwards though. But Michael did not answer any questions. He collected his pay, signed the ledger, and left without a word.

"I would like to have kept him here until he found other work," Noreen said bitterly. "Don't I have any say over who is a guest under my own roof?"

"Mr. Henry was pretty plain about that, Mother. After all, he is within his rights."

Brendan cut in. "The hell he is! It's Mr. Alfred who is runnin' the company, and it's him that says who lives where."

Kevin nodded, but contradicted patiently. "Dad, you know that's how it is officially, but Mr. Alfred hardly makes *any* of the decisions on things like this. The company owns the house, and he's the president, but like as not it's Mr. Alexis or Mr. Henry or Mr. Belin who get things done."

"I've a mind to go up to Mr. Alexis or the old man himself."

"I wouldn't do that, Dad."

"And why not? I've known him since we were kids here on the Crick."

"Well, it wouldn't look good for either of us. I'd like to stay foreman on the mason crew, and you have a few more years running the shipping end of things. After all, he did punch Mr. Henry in public."

Brendan grinned in spite of his anger. "And a lovely sight it must have been," he said reverently. "A pity I missed that."

Kevin shook his head but gave in to a perverse admiration. "More than a few people I know would like to try the same thing."

Noreen rose from her rocker and thrust her knitting angrily aside. "The two of you seem quite satisfied now with having a smile at the poor boy's expense." She sounded like someone betrayed. "It makes me sick to have to bar a pleasant lad like that from my own home because of the likes of Henry du Pont. He always was a bully—and conceited, too, parading in his army uniform. But I'll tell you one thing: I'm glad Michael is leaving. This place would break his spirit, surely."

She left them and began making a clatter in the kitchen. Neither father nor son wanted to continue the discussion. Dreams of independence, ambitious plans, and the breaking of the spirit were things they knew well.

After a few thoughtful puffs on his pipe, Brendan waved it irritably at a droning fly.

"She's worried half to death about Tim. Two weeks now just waiting for the law to pick him up, and not a word as to where he is."

Brendan knew his wife needed privacy to work out her anxieties, that the thing about the Farrell lad was just a convenient issue. He would wait a few minutes and then go to her and have it out—the bottled up worry about her younger brother.

Kevin went out the front door into the damp twilight to look for the twins. It was time for them to be indoors, and he was concerned about Megan. She was quite upset about Michael leaving. Maybe he could have a little fun with them himself to take her mind off the loss.

He was more than a little angry at his Uncle Tim for not being home to support them. Men with grand ideas! He had to admire the man for his work freeing the black people, but what about his own flesh and blood?

"Ah, who am I to talk," he grumbled to the muggy air. "Here I am, thirty-five and a bachelor." A spasm of melancholy tugged at him momentarily, but he brushed it off as he had done countless times before. It was getting easier. In a way his uncle's dereliction helped fill the void. His small cousins gave him a measure of joy, but it was a sham fathering likely to be suddenly withdrawn.

Suddenly. Yes, it was the sudden event which had kept him shy of marriage. He had too many sharp memories of ripping explosions tearing up his own family—both grandfathers, two uncles in their teens, his father's right arm, and friends. Kevin remembered the widows left with little ones, and every time he felt a tenderness for some girl whose looks toward him made no mystery of her heart, there was the inevitable jolt of seeing the pall of widowhood on her fresh face. It was his imagination, of course, and his own job as stonemason was relatively safe.

But his Grandpa Patrick had taught him the trade, and a mill blast had caught up with him even in retirement. No, he couldn't take the chance, even if the girl ended up marrying a powderman anyway. He wouldn't be the one. There would be no joy in it.

He finally saw the twins down by the Crick not thirty yards from the house. They were trying without much success to skip rocks on the glassy deep water above the dam. It was full dusk now, and they were being disobedient to be alone so close to the edge with night coming on, but he would not scold them this day.

"Here, you kids," he grumbled as he selected a smooth, flat pebble. "Let your old cousin show you how it's done."

This time when Michael checked in at the Caesar Rodney, he did not ask for a room. The innkeeper took his coin for a single night in the loft with a smug grin and added salt to the wound.

"A whole boatload of you Irish come in to Philadelphia yesterday. They was a riot, I hear. Not too popular these days. Some of 'em drifted down to Wilmington this morning." He clucked dolefully. "Won't be any better here."

His gloomy prediction was reiterated a dozen times throughout the afternoon by others, and Michael was numbed into inaction. There seemed to be little point in trying another city. The tide of starving Irish had overwhelmed an already weak labor market.

He had not intended to get drunk. The trouble lay partly in not wanting to eat supper, not wanting to crawl onto a louse-infested pallet in the loft, and most particularly, not wanting to face the following morning. The alternative was to spend the evening in the taproom downstairs. He was not even slightly drunk when Aloysius Moody came in. He was only mildly in his cups when the sergeant brought out the enlistment papers and he signed them. He was slightly groggy when Moody ended the rounds of celebratory drinks, told him where to report in the morning, and left. But he was sodden as he climbed to the mattress-covered third floor loft and collapsed on the first straw-filled tick he tripped over.

In the morning Michael Kevin Farrell found that he had acquired a thudding hangover, a colony of lice, and a six-month enlistment in the U.S. Army.

CHAPTER EIGHT

I t was only a little after eight in the morning, but already Alfred du Pont's starched shirt had wilted to limp wrinkles and stuck to his perspiring back. An oppressive humidity had been building for days, covering the valley with rumpled gray clouds that trapped heat along the Brandywine. The stench from the mills' sulfur refinery soiled the air that he breathed, and even the rumble of the rolling powder wheels was a palpable tremble against his clammy skin.

"It's no use, Dad. This stuff is too soggy to work with."

Du Pont started at the sound. He had forgotten that his son was even in the laboratory. What was wrong with him? Was he becoming senile?

"Yes, Lammot. All of the salts have been drawing moisture from the air. I suppose the jars should have better seals."

His son snorted with exasperation from across the expanse of the remodeled lab. "Well, I certainly can't get accurate measurements this way. I think I'll go into town for fresh chemicals."

They made up a list together, the father quietly deferring to his son's preferences, and when Lammot left, Alfred watched his second child hurry along the path leading up to the house. He smiled. There was such determination in the boy—and talent. He would make his mark in the scientific world some day. Alfred knew that as a scientist himself, and if his assessment was colored by a measure of paternal love, it was offset by more than a few comments by university professors who noted the same qualities in his son.

Alfred sighed. Lammot really should be the one to take over the company instead of Irénée, whose right by birth was forever being reinforced by his mother. But Irénée was frail—sickly was a better description—and his infrequent drive was fitful in its aggressive spurts, petulant rather than ambitious. More than once the old generic blight of consumption had seemed to be lying in wait for the boy. It was not pessimism which prompted such a frightful thought; many du Ponts had succumbed to that dreaded ravaging of the lungs.

He turned back to his work, struggling to concentrate on that instead of the grim thoughts that seemed to beset him so much these days. God, but the weight of this industry was heavy on him. He began to tingle with the old apprehension, his breathing became shallow and rapid, his skin clammy, and his vision contracted into a fuzzy tunnel, black around the edges. He gripped the edge of the table and heard the glass retorts, tubes, and fragile apparatus rattle with the violence of his ague.

The worst was coming, visions of the dead, scores of them, terrible images of workmen ripped by the blasts that had shattered their mills. He bowed his head to it again, letting the horror roll over him, holding on, fighting the urge to faint.

When it finally passed, Alfred sat in his chair, drenched with sweat, and quietly waited out the inevitable nausea. Minutes later he got weakly to his feet and shuffled out the door. He cursed again, cursed his own inheritance, this awful industry—child of black alchemy. What a dread legacy to pass on to his own sons.

Henry du Pont was bristling as he left the company office behind his brother's house and swung down the path toward the lower mill yard. He looked like a bull in search of some luckless torero, heavy shoulders and chest pulled tight in controlled anger, eyes snapping, red hair glinting fire.

The information he had extracted from bookkeeper Harry Belin was the capstone of a mounting frustration that had begun with a meeting with Meta. It had been bad enough to find out from her that their meetings would have to be severely curtailed for the duration of the summer because both her sons were now home from the university. In addition, Meta was pretty well distracted by Irénée's perpetual string of illnesses. Even as they spoke together in the downstairs hall, her whispered confidences to Henry were filled with details of the health problems of her pale and skinny child. Henry missed that banter of hers more than he liked to admit. The way she had of intimating things, of turning an apparently innocent phrase into erotic suggestion, could rouse him to more excitement—and more quickly—than any woman he had ever known; and Henry would not deny that he had known many women.

Topping that was this latest information he had just learned about the powder shipments. Alfred had turned down part of an army contract for more munitions. His brother's squeamishness about increased danger from production was going to cost them all a fortune.

A willow branch softly brushed Henry's shoulder, and he swatted it so violently that the green stem snapped and hung limp. "Goddamn!" he cracked aloud to the greenery along his path. The man should step down and let a serious businessman take over. He was better at piddling with his test tubes anyway—should have taken a post with some university and let men run the real world.

He mentally recalculated the profits that might have been realized from the lost contract and swore again. What a fine time for Meta to put her box into cold storage. Well, he didn't give a damn how awkward it might be; the time to move was now. She could be used in other ways, and if the rod between his legs was not reason enough, he could use an appetite over which she had no control. She was no fool even if she happened to be married to one. The health of the company was not only vital to her but to the security of her sons. Henry knew how she felt about Irénée's security particularly. He would use that as a lever. It would be fear he would use, the most reliable tool anyway. "Fear for her precious Irénée," he muttered.

The idea did much to cool his anger, and when he made his midmorning rounds, he did not intimidate the powdermen any more than usual. In fact, he even shared a joke with Billy Dougherty in the keg mill. Billy wore the event like a medal throughout the day.

Noreen Gallagher sat stiffly erect on the seat of the buggy as it rolled easily along the dirt road paralleling the Brandywine. The afternoon was muggy but not unpleasant in the shade along the Crick for someone lucky enough to feel a constant breeze behind a spirited trotter. The horse was well matched to the rubber-tired trap, and Father Reardon held the animal to a steady comfortable pace. Any one of the dozens of women who parted a curtain or looked up from a washtub in the yard would have gladly traded places with Brendan Gallagher's wife as she glided regally along sitting next to the sixty-year-old priest. But Noreen felt numb at Francis Reardon's side. Her regal bearing had nothing to do with pride, and the wind in her face was a mockery to the cold she felt inside. The words of the magistrate still echoed in her ears. "Five years on Pea Patch Island."

That Tim should be sentenced to the prison island in the Delaware River was a horror. A term in the local jail would have been bad enough, but she would have been able to visit her brother, bring him small comforts, perhaps even bring the children. But Pea Patch! It was a grim place for the worst criminals, notorious for cruel treatment, scourged by persistent outbreaks of yellow fever, and barred to visitors. He'd been guilty of threatening murder, assault with a loaded pistol, holding a sheriff at gunpoint, and resisting arrest. They hadn't said anything about the Underground Railway.

Noreen was so deep in melancholy that she was startled when the carriage stopped by her house. The priest alighted and helped her down.

"I'm sorry, Father, I've not said a word to you the whole trip," she apologized. "And you were very kind to go with me."

"I only wish I could have had more influence on the court," he said glumly.

She waved it off. "You did what y'could." She stood there looking up at her house, a solid little cottage built into the wooded slope rising away from the banks of the Brandywine. It was quiet in late afternoon, and she was glad the twins were with the Hallorans. She needed time to compose herself before picking them up and telling them what had happened to their father. The thought made her ill.

"Besides," she added bitterly, "he knew the price he would have to pay for this . . . this business, and the price others would have to pay, too."

"Try not to be harsh with him, Noreen. God knows he was doing what he thought was right."

She uttered a short, mirthless little laugh. "Do you think that will give much comfort to Megan and Denis when they find out he will be in a dungeon until they're nearly grown?"

He could not find an answer for her question nor any words of solace. He remembered other trials she had faced, remembered how he had yearned to give her comfort then.

She put her hand on his arm. "You've done all that you can," she said, almost as if she were reading his mind. "I know what this afternoon has meant to you, too, Father Francis. As for my brother, you know I could never be harsh with him. But," she added emphatically, "I do wish men would think more of their families than their grand schemes."

CHAPTER NINE

Private Michael Farrell marched with renewed energy as the panorama of Monterrey spread before the advancing units of Zachary Taylor's army. The countryside had grown more beautiful with each mile, and as they entered the high plain of the Santa Caterina River, great peaks loomed in the distance. On the broad valley floor which gently sloped toward him, Michael could see the entire city with its flat-topped adobes and magnificent cathedral set like a jewel off to the left in the southwest corner.

A twinge of apprehension spoiled the sight for Michael. The great weight of troops marching on this lovely place suddenly seemed unnecessary, offensive, obscene. He remembered the sullen fear on the faces of the few ragged Mexicans who had been too poor to flee their advance. Each small rancho and its adjacent community had been terrorized by the fierce sweep of mounted rangers. Michael felt a grudging admiration for the Texas fighters, who had a wild disregard for any kind of personal caution, but they were a vengeful lot—barbaric, it seemed to him. There were stories of terrible atrocities that matched the ones told of Mexican brutality, and he had seen signs of wanton destruction visited on undefended towns. More than that, the dark eyes of the peasants left in their wake—scattered figures that peered from behind walls and the darkness of half-open doorways—sent a terrible reproach that chilled him as he passed.

For him personally, it was an unearned hostility. He had not yet seen a single Mexican soldier nor fired his weapon except in drill. He wanted somehow to stop and explain that the war was certainly not of his making, that the uniform he wore was only the badge of a desperation similar to their own. Like their dependence on the largesse of rancho labor, he had traded six months of his life for three meals a day and eight dollars a month. But as he gazed on the bright little city, the virgin musket he balanced so expertly on his shoulder weighed heavily for a moment on his soul, and he wondered what damage it would bring to the people of this untroubled place before day was done.

"Battalion!"

"Company!"

"Platoon!"

The warning commands rippled through each successive formation in an overlapping series of shouts.

"Halt!"

The great column accordioned to a stop.

"Or . . . der, arms!"

Musket and rifle stocks came down in a sequential crash, and at the sound, a few officers gave their sergeants hard looks.

"Rest!"

The men were free to talk at last.

"Well, there it is, Michael. Do y'think there'll be a fight?"

Michael glanced at the dripping face of Liam Kelly, his short and round marching partner for the past three months. Liam's rumpled uniform was stained dark with sweat-muddied dust that clung in damp streaks from the wilted stock around his neck and looping patches under his fat arms. He oozed like a sponge and, as Michael watched, Liam pulled the stopper from his canteen and took a long drink, making a face as he swallowed the warm, metal-tainted water.

"Ugh, 'tis a foul drink, but welcome at that!"

"You'd better save some of that," Michael warned. He had been pressed to share some of his own drinking water with the chubby soldier several times before. "It might be a long, hot time before you get more."

"So y'think we'll fight, then?"

Michael shrugged and looked ahead at the sweeping vista of Monterrey. They were within a mile of the place and he had not seen a thing moving.

The conversation was cut off abruptly as a column of horsemen thundered past them on the left, milled briefly around Zachary Taylor's headquarters group, and then careened wildly down the road ahead of the halted formation. The Texas Rangers looked more like a band of desperadoes than a military cavalry unit. They wore no uniform, yet their grease-blackened buckskins, vaquero boots, and wide-brimmed sombreros were a kind of costume. Each man was armed to the teeth with a carbine, one or two revolvers, and the frightening bowie knife. Their blood-curdling yells carried back to Michael's ears as they galloped in a sweeping arc toward the black walls of the half-built church, and their unsheathed knives flashed like broad sabers in the sun.

The general was a few dozen yards in front of Michael's squad, sitting "Old Whitey" easily, letting the animal amble as he pulled a plug of tobacco from his pocket and worried off a bite of the stiff slab. Then he leaned back against the high cantle, chewed contentedly, and watched the distant horsemen cavorting in the fields.

"Do you think Ampudia has withdrawn, General?"

Michael could hear the conversation easily, but he had no idea who the officer was who spoke. Unlike Taylor, however, the man was wearing a uniform. Michael could pick out the eagle devices denoting the rank of colonel.

"Hard to tell, Jeff. I hope so. I'd rather get him out in the open."

Liam Kelly jabbed Michael in the ribs. "That's Colonel Davis, the general's son-in-law."

Michael was unimpressed. What difference did it make?

"Jeff Davis of the Mississippi Regiment, the lads with scarlet shirts and the new rifles!"

The distant horsemen had nearly reached the unfinished church when Michael saw a white puff of smoke blossom up from behind the walls. A split second later more puffs, much smaller, spit from unseen clefts between the stones. He saw the cavalry unit turn, discharge a volley with their carbines, and begin to gallop back.

At the same instant a hoarse whistling sound like a whip cracked in his ears, and a cannonball crashed to the road directly in front of General Taylor. Old Whitey's ears flattened, and he trembled stiff-legged but held his ground. Colonel Davis's mount was dancing in circles with flared nostrils, fighting the bit.

The general patted his horse's neck, spat a long stream of tobacco juice to the side, and resumed gazing at the returning Texans.

"As soon as you can get your horse aimed properly, Jeff, pass the word to encamp back at that pecan grove I pointed out earlier. I suppose we'll be getting a fight after all."

The following day was Sunday, and Michael's regiment did little more than rest in their camp. Always on their minds was the fortified city two miles up the road and how it would be assaulted. The "Black Fort," as they had come to refer to the half-completed church, was the focal point of any discussion. Its squat domination of the road leading into Monterrey gave it a mysterious as well as awesome power in their minds whenever the rains let up enough for them to see the mountain-ringed stronghold of their enemy.

There was another thing which was unnerving, particularly for the Baltimore Volunteers. They were mostly Irish, mostly Catholic, and mostly leery of shooting at a church, completed or not, even if it held hostile soldiers armed with cannon and musket.

Zachary Taylor certainly had some misgivings himself about the Black Fort, but they were purely tactical. By midday, one of his engineering officers had reported after a reconnaissance that the Mexican left flank was largely undefended against infiltration and attack from the southwest. There were a few ridges occupied behind Monterrey, but the bulk of General Ampudia's army was crowded in strong points within the city itself.

As a result of this report, 2,200 men, nearly half of Taylor's force, began to move out in an encircling maneuver skirting the Black Fort. Michael watched as the column kept well to the right, hiding in the ravines and scrub-covered defilades of the foothills west of the city and finally disappearing beyond the Rio Caterina.

They had been gone several hours when the sound of cannon fire and faint clatter of musket shots brought Michael and clusters of unblooded recruits like himself from the tents to chatter excitedly in the rain and peer toward the distant firefight.

"It's not the proper way to do it!" Liam Kelly shook his head soberly and sucked on his pipe. "Not the proper thing at all!"

Michael looked at his friend without comment.

"Y'see, Michael," he said, pointing with his pipestem, "Old Zack is playin' the fool and splittin' his force. Now, any commander of troops knows that it is asking for trouble to split your forces. Against all military theory. Never split your forces!" He jabbed the pipe back between his lips and puffed furiously. A large drop of rainwater plummeted from the branches above them and splattered into the hot bowl with a steamy sizzle.

Michael forced back a smile and looked down at the older man. Liam was as close a friend as he had in the platoon, excepting Sergeant Moody.

"You seem to have picked up a considerable store of military theory in the last three months, Liam. I wonder if you might not share some of it with Taylor's staff."

Liam laid off sucking on the stubborn pipe and snapped, " 'Tis not theory at all; 'tis a principle of modern warfare I'm speakin' of, and common sense besides. And y'need not be making sport of me words."

"Just a thought is all, Liam," Michael grinned, "Just an idle thought."

"Here comes the Pope's Brigade!"

"Hi, fisheaters, goin' for a taste of powder and ball?"

"Fresh fish!"

The Mississippi Regiment hooted at the lead battalion of the Baltimore Volunteers as it marched out of bivouac toward Monterrey. The catcalls had been sporadic until they drew abreast of the red-shirted Southerners—occasional wisecracks about green troops—but Michael was stung by the deluge laid on them now.

"They ain't fisheaters any more, ain't you heard? They've switched to *piloncillos* and *frijoles!*"

"Are y'all takin' the point and leadin' us into battle?"

"They ain't *leadin'* anywhere. Old Zack just wants to let them desert as a formation!"

Sergeant Moody cracked out sharp commands, and the troop marched sullenly toward the Black Fort, enduring the gauntlet of insults in silence.

It was nothing new. Michael had heard worse things said as individual arguments had broken out during their training. Scores of Irish had slipped away from Taylor's army to join the Mexicans. Some of the Germans and French, too. The most celebrated defector was the infamous John Riley, who had deserted at Matamoros in the spring and was now reported to be in Monterrey with his "San Patricios" artillery.

Michael watched Aloysius Moody's sweating red neck as the sergeant swung along at the head of the battalion. He knew that Moody was burning inside. The man was fiercely proud of both his Irishness and his American citizenship. His noncommissioned rank approached a level of holy orders as far as he was concerned. There was no equivocating. If asked to, Moody would literally die as a matter of military principle. There was no room in his soldier's mind to entertain the morality of the American-Mexican conflict. Moody was a soldier.

Michael admired him for that, his dedication to purpose, and wished he too had a similar line of direction. But he did not.

He had no idea of the disposition of other units in the attack, but he knew that the main force of the army was proceeding in a frontal movement against the city. He was having a difficult time just keeping lined up with Liam Kelly as they crunched through the towering cane. Somewhere off to the right a cannonading began thumping the morning air, and he watched the waving cane for falling shot.

The command to halt and load swept up the line. Michael bit the end off a paper cartridge, shook some powder into the pan of his musket, and poured the rest down the muzzle. He found the point of the lead bullet with his fingertips, and inserted it, paper and ball, after the charge. A quick thrust with the ramrod packed it home.

The whole operation took only a few seconds. A trained infantryman could load and fire three rounds in under a minute. Michael had put his flint on half cock and brought the musket to the order position at his side before most of the platoon had torn off the end of their cartridges. He watched as Liam botched the first attempt, dropping the torn charge from his shaking fingertips. He was the last man to finish.

"Company, as skirmishers, trail arms . . ."

"So it is starting," Michael thought. He lifted his musket slightly and waited for the command of execution. They must be very close.

"By the right flank . . ."

There was a sudden peal of thunder, and he looked up apprehensively at the dark clouds roiling above the waving cane. It was suddenly cool, a wafting breeze on his face, and he could hear a squall of drops slashing into the dry leaves. Huge pellets. Could it be hail? Leaves fluttered away from the stalks with ripping sounds; he saw an inch-thick cane snap in the middle, lopped off as if with a corn knife.

Later he would wonder if he really did not know they were under fire, that he did not pop out of the numb state until the guidon flag wavered and fell. They were suddenly out of the cane, facing a thorny hedge spitting red flashes and soft balloons of white smoke. It was a wall of fire cutting into the company from a range of thirty yards. Men dropped in midstride, tumbling with their unfired weapons still at trail. The Mexicans crouched unseen and protected by a stone wall behind the thornbushes.

He could hear no commands above the deafening clatter of fire, but he needed no direction. Their position was disastrous; in seconds a quarter of the company had been cut down.

"Come on, Liam!" he screamed and yanked the little man sideways in a dead run to the left. The end of the wall was as close as the vulnerable cane field behind them. They had to get out of the frontal fire.

A handful from the first squad followed his lead, but he could see the rest of the company melt back into the cane. A few paused to fire their muskets into the thornbushes. Most of these were dropped by the concentrated fire before they took another step, but it was enough distraction to spare Michael's group. They reached the corner of the wall and tumbled together under the barrier thorns.

For a few minutes they lay huddled listening to the gunfire as it gradually decreased, and the volley fire was replaced by occasional shots along the line. They could hear no return fire from the Americans, and gradually the realization that they had been cut off by withdrawal began to seep in. They were terrified, afraid to speak even in whispers. In their breathless fear they listened to the exultant Mexicans on the other side of the wall chattering and laughing.

Michael raised his head slowly to see how many of them had made it safely to the corner of the wall. He could count eight, five from his own squad and three from the second file in the platoon. As far as he could tell, there were no complete "comrades in arms"—groups of four who worked as a team. Only Liam and he were left from his quartet. He tried not to think of what might have happened to McGuigan and Rooney. The image of Seamus Flaherty lying with his guidon flag had shaken him enough.

Movement and shouts on the other side of the wall made him duck again, fearful that they would be spotted. Liam's face was inches from his own. He was glistening with sweat, white with fear, and stank with a strange, ominous sourness.

"We've no officer!" the face whispered. "Not even the corporal."

Michael wanted to smash him to silence. My God! The idiot would have the Mexicans on them.

"What will we do?" the face bleated.

He had to shut him up, preserve their protection of silence until . . . until what?

The reality of their grim position suddenly crashed in upon Michael, and he realized that even if the Americans attacked, they would be finished, caught in a crossfire or chewed up by friendly artillery before that. If the Mexicans could not see them, the Americans certainly could not. They had to move somewhere.

To run back across that open field was unthinkable. To advance? The idea was ludicrous. Eight muskets against how many of the enemy on the other side of the wall?

He found himself slowly lifting his head, pushing his chest clear of the earth, raising himself into the brambles high enough to peep over the wall. There must have been over fifty infantry crowded against the wall. A musket every three feet. Michael knew even as he sagged down to the welcome earth that they would have to attack. There was simply no alternative. To wait would be worse. Any moment they would be discovered by one of the Mexican infantry and cut down like paralyzed rabbits. Even if they were not, the American assault would be mounted soon, and somehow the idea of being slaughtered by indiscriminate fire was a worse prospect. They would have to use surprise—to feign a strength they did not have.

He felt a surge of decisive determination. It was peculiar to have the cold fear which had frozen him minutes before replaced by a fatalism that was strangely exhilarating. He crawled recklessly to each of the men whispering instructions, positioning them for the attack. Words of reassurance jumped to his lips, and the men, all older than he, drank them in.

Michael squirmed back to Liam, patted him on the rump, and winked as he carefully twisted his bayonet over the muzzle. He waited an agonizing minute, crouched at a gap in the thornbush, then crashed with a yell headlong toward the wall.

CHAPTER TEN

He woke to a spinning nausea, his head throbbing to the slow pounding of his pulse. Someone was speaking too loud, grating on his ears, dragging a wood rasp over his brain. He had to concentrate hard to open his eyes, the lids heavy and sluggish, and when he did, the light splintered new pain into his skull.

"Ah, now there he is at long last." The voice piped louder, piercing. "Are ye finally awake, Corporal Farrell?"

It was Moody. He could tell without opening his eyes again. He lifted his hand to ward off the sound, tried to speak, and managed an unintelligible croak.

"Now listen if you can, me proud banshee. You're all in one piece, the battle's won, mebbe the war too. And you've been out cold for two days."

"Two days . . ." He worked his eyes open again, saw the sergeant's face spin above him, and groaned.

"Aye, lad, two days. And whilst you slept so peaceful, the rest of us took the city."

"What's wrong with me?"

"Ah, nothin' much. Not fer an Irisher, I mean. A Brown Bess ball put a new part in yer hair, is all. But it didn't cave in that thick skull, a blessed heritage of our ancestry."

Michael made a tentative squirm on his hard pallet and winced.

"Ye've various other hurts that are not serious, mostly rips and tears and punctures from that Mexican briar patch you went rippin' through to glory."

"I don't remember anything but poor Seamus Flaherty." His eyes popped open, alarmed, "Liam! What about—"

"Fine, fine. Kelly doesn't have a scratch."

Michael sagged back and shut his eyes again.

"You don't remember routing that whole company with only eight men, do you, lad? Well, it was wonderful to behold. You saved the lot of us terrible damage that day. By the time we got out of the cane and over the wall, all we could see was Mexican asses and heels in a cloud of dust! You lads knocked over at least two dozen before they pulled out. They left a fully charged fieldpiece without ever gettin' a shot off, nor takin' the time to spike it."

The pain was showing on the boy's face, and Aloysius Moody decided to let him rest. A head wound was a risky thing, even when it didn't break the skull.

"I'll be back tomorrow, lad. You rest some more."

"He deserves it well enough," the sergeant thought as he left the grim warehouse crammed with so many of the seriously wounded. He covered his mouth with a neckerchief on reaching the wide doors of the loading dock. Thank God it had turned colder. Rows of litters with those who had died during the night covered every foot of the rickety platform.

He swore under his breath. What a waste! Even now Taylor was giving Ampudia terms that would allow him to withdraw with his surviving troops! Something about President Polk making a deal with Santa Anna to stop the war and give in to American demands. "Christ, when will they learn?" he thought. Nobody could trust Antonio López de Santa Anna; even the Mexicans had learned that.

"We'll have to fight that bunch again," he rumbled as he made his way down the captive streets of Monterrey. "And the next time we'll be farther from home still!"

The street venders were already pushing their wares on the gringo bluecoats.

"I don't like the options any more than you do, Jeff. This whole operation has been lashed up by the politicians since it started." Taylor looked tiredly at the colonel sipping coffee across from him on the sun-splashed patio. "And I'm including the ones in the U.S. Army as well."

"No one will deny that, General, but this action is going to appear wasteful to the nation. To have Ampudia surrounded and then let him go."

Taylor snorted. "Surrounded. Well, yes, but more like holding your knife on a grizzly in his own cave." He tugged at his mustaches and sighed. "We were lucky that Worth did so well in the flanking movement. Brilliant operation—I wouldn't take any credit from those boys—but you know that Ampudia was plain stupid for not defending his left rear. As it was we had twenty percent casualties." He swept his arm toward the fortlike masonry of the city buildings around them. "Can you imagine what we would have left if we had refused the terms of his surrender and tried to blast him out of here?"

"There are those who will say we could have crushed them with artillery, that they were a concentrated target," the colonel went on carefully, "And that is true, of course. We had the advantage."

"The advantage to butcher how many thousands of women and children? They are here, too, you know. That bastard Ampudia would use them as a shield. You know it and I know it. He's done it before."

The reasons for letting the Mexicans escape south to Potosí were now on the table. Jeff Davis mentioned it as gently as possible. He could agree with the general without appearing to patronize.

"And if Polk's intrigue with Santa Anna succeeds, our president will appear the more merciful because of your constraint."

Taylor looked up, surprised at the abrupt tack in the younger man's comments. He shook his head and grinned. "I don't know, Jeff. You're one hell of a fine soldier, but maybe you should have stayed in Washington. The way you can outflank a man with words is downright dangerous!" He jabbed his hand into the side pocket of his ill-fitting coat and pulled out a worn leather case, opened the flap, and extended it over the table. "Here, Colonel Davis," he said. "Have a cigar."

Some time later the colonel took his leave, and Taylor walked him out to the porch of the home he was using as headquarters.

"I'll stop by the hospital to make rounds before going back to Walnut Grove. Is there anything you would like me to do?"

"No, Jeff. I was about to say something about those damned six-month enlistees whose time is up, but I'd better handle it myself."

"The Irish and German volunteers."

"Yes. It's another one of those political mix-ups. None of those men can be held legally because the limit by law was three months. I'd like to give them a few hurrahs and get them to extend for the full year; make them regulars."

"Are you sure you want the Irish—"

"Better with us than to let them drift into Mexico. I don't want more American-trained Irishmen giving us trouble if the war heats up again."

"Like John Riley's gunners."

"Exactly."

"Well, I'd be glad to have my officers and—"

Davis was cut off by Taylor's laugh. The general gripped his son-in-law's shoulder affectionately and growled, "Now Jeff, I know your fellows are a wonder with the rifle and saber, but do you think your Mississippi folk would have the tact to convince a redheaded Catholic from Ireland that he owes allegiance to the United States? From what I hear, they're about as neighborly as coyotes and prairie chickens."

Davis looked uncomfortable. "There's not much love lost between them."

"Correct. Your boys would end up converting those papists at knifepoint; trying to make 'em good Baptists. No, you'd better leave it to me."

The colonel shrugged, dismissed the idea with a wry grin, and saluted as he left the porch. He stopped at the bottom step and turned. "There is one Irishman I'd especially like to keep, General. That fellow who led the rally on the first assault."

"The one who routed the Mexicans at the wall and captured Riley's gun?"

"That's the one. He killed three of the gunners before they could fire and drove the rest off with bayonet. The dead gunners were deserters from Matamoros. All Irish."

"How does he feel about that, killing his own people?"

"He doesn't know yet. He's just coming round from taking a glancing shot to the head."

The general looked bemused. "You seem to know close detail on this man, Jeff."

"Yes, Zack," he said, forgetting his military distance for the moment. "He was the one who drew their fire away from my boys."

Henry waited impatiently in front of the house for Alfred to get back from town.

"Glad I caught you, Alfred," he said. "We have to move quickly on the Mexican deal."

"I thought I had made myself clear on that matter."

"Clear enough. I just think you are wrong."

"I'll entertain your arguments tomorrow, Henry. Frankly, I'm not up to it just now."

"Tomorrow will be too late, brother. A friend in General Scott's headquarters has passed on some startling information."

"Which is?"

"An invasion of central Mexico by sea. A siege of Veracruz and assault on Mexico City. It will take a lot of powder."

Alfred removed his hat and looked wearily at his brother. "We will provide them all we can."

"It's not that simple, Alfred. They need a commitment, a guarantee. There will be a dozen other firms after those contracts. We have to press our interest."

"You'd have me strain the seams of this enterprise, Henry. I want no pell-mell dash after money that will lead to our own destruction."

"Not at all."

"You're rash. We've spoken of this before."

"Brash, Alfred, not rash. We simply must seize this opportunity!"

"I'm tired. I don't want to think of it."

"Let me handle it, then."

"No shortcuts, no hazards?"

"Efficiency will mean higher production and less danger in the long run."

"You want to represent the company in this?"

"I could leave this afternoon."

"All right. See what you can do."

Alfred started for the door, hesitated, and turned back to Henry.

"Mind you, no guarantees we cannot live up to safely. I want no more dead or injured workers in my dreams."

"Leave it to me, Alfred. You'll have no worries. It's a family enterprise."

It was nearly two weeks before Michael lost his mammoth headache. By that time all of the superficial "rips and punctures" Moody had described were healed, and he was able to move about the makeshift hospital helping the staff.

It was a strange experience. The more seriously hurt soldiers from both armies were collected here, and U.S. military surgeons joined with civilian doctors from Monterrey to care for Mexican and American alike. There had been early efforts to keep the two groups separated, but since hostilities were now officially deactivated, the practicality of teaming up to combat their common enemies of suffering and death gradually fused the two groups.

Besides, Michael observed as he moved through the cot-jammed warehouse, few of these survivors would ever fight again anyway. His own wound was exceptional in that it was a temporary disability. The others were either slipping toward death or coming to painful grips with the reality of life imbalanced by amputations.

More would die than survive, he thought. He could spot the doomed ones easily: they had a dark knowledge deep in their eyes. There was little military fervor here.

Michael's return to his platoon was a celebrated affair. Now that his protégé was back with the platoon, Sergeant Aloysius Moody bragged about Michael's exploits. There was even talk of a meritorious promotion to corporal. When he mentioned this to Michael, Moody did not get the enthusiastic response he expected.

"Is your head still ailin' you, lad? On the outside you look as good as new."

"No, that's fine, Sergeant." Michael stretched out on his cot in the deserted squad tent and rested his arm across his eyes. Moody did not take the hint, but pulled a locker box close to the cot, fired up his stubby clay pipe, puffed until it was burning well, sat on the box, and waited.

When the sergeant gave no sign of leaving, Michael lowered his arm and lay there frowning up at the yellow luminescence of the backlighted canvas roof. It was not really canvas at all; most of the tents were muslin, a cheap substitute bought by a stupid quartermaster, and they leaked and ripped when tested by anything stronger than windless sunshine. They would have to be replaced by genuine canvas before winter set in.

Michael sighed. There was much about this war that was shabby, much that was different from what first met the eye. He sat up and swung his legs over the hardwood cot rails. Clearing his throat, he looked at Moody.

"I found out today how many I killed."

Moody grinned at first, about to help him crow about the score, but then he caught the look in Michael's eye and held back.

"There were four, I think." Michael's voice had grown thin. "One with a shot from the musket, and thr . . . three with the bayonet."

"Who told ye this?"

"Oh, *nobody* told me. I mean, who would? Nobody in this troop would want to bring up a thing like that. No, it came to me in fragments over the past couple of days. Just this morning the real bombshell exploded clear."

He waited as if for Moody to say it for him, but the gruff Irishman kept his tongue. He would not be the one either to put it into words. At least he did not drop his eyes as others had done. He kept them fixed on Michael's, hard and unyielding but kindly, too.

"It's a grim irony, Sergeant Moody, too maudlin even as the subject of Irish song. In my first bloodletting, with cold steel at that, two of the men I killed,"—he shuddered briefly—"two of them were my own countrymen."

Moody's face was set like stone. "They were deserters. Traitors to the country we're fighting for. Don't waste yer feelings on that lot of turncoats."

Michael was miserable, but the argument was a lifeline out of his mood. His dark eyes crackled as he spoke. "Aye, Moody, turncoats they were, all right! This army did not turn them away, I notice, when they deserted from the British up in Canada. Were they turncoats when the Americans signed them on? Or was it just that they had a valuable skill as gunners, learned at the expense of the British Crown?"

"It's a different thing. Up there they was just shootin' at the Indians. It's not like changing sides and warring against your own blood."

Michael fought back an image of hands clamped around the slippery blade of his bayonet. He shook his head like a wet dog, and his voice was louder than he intended. "I'll tell you this, Aloysius Moody, I didn't come all this way to run steel through some lad I might have raised a pint with back in Bantry!"

Moody let his shouted plea rest on the silence within the tent. Gradually the afternoon noises of the camp outside filtered through, and then he spoke, softly, easily, and, Michael thought, with the gentle persuasion of a confessor.

"Listen, Michael. We're none of us ever gettin' back to Bantry Bay nor anywhere else in the Emerald Isle. Your countrymen are Americans, not Irish. And that lot of gunners were not Irish neither; they were Mexican by choice, no different because of freckles and fair skin. I admit it's not easy to draw a bead on someone who might look like a cousin on yer mother's side, but it *is* important, I think, for you to realize one thing that might have escaped your notice."

The grizzled veteran paused again to give his words a proper frame.

"That renegade crew you're worried so much about had filled the cannon with grapeshot, and they had it aimed at us."

The sergeant got up then and started to leave the tent. He had just reached the pole and thrown open the flap when Michael called out.

"Sergeant Moody!" The florid face ducked back inside the tent again, and Michael added, "Thanks for helping."

Moody dismissed the thanks with a casual wave, but he came back with an afterthought.

"You'll need to sign a new paper to get the rank, Michael. I guess you heard about the problem with the other enlistment."

"Yes. From what I hear, none of us have been legal soldiers for a couple of months."

Moody snorted. "Politicians and lawyers! I don't see what difference it makes so long as a man swears to serve for a given time."

"Service without pay is what some are complaining of."

"Well, that will all be straightened out in time. I'll have the clerk draw up the enlistment papers on Monday."

Michael grinned. "Good. That will give me time to make up my mind."

Moody raised an eyebrow. "Oh? Do ye have other plans? It's a long trip back to a jobless future. Stay here, lad. At the rate you're rising you'll be a brigadier in eight months."

They both laughed at that, any excuse to slide away from the tension of before. But Michael had had enough of war. Within the week he collected his pay and began a long search for Captain Craith.

CHAPTER ELEVEN

Noreen cupped both hands around the mug of tea and shuddered. The hot brew and warm stove in the huge du Pont kitchen were a sharp contrast to the chill of her bones. The mile walk from Chicken Alley up the hill to Mr. Alfred's home to visit her sister had been more uncomfortable than she had expected.

"You're getting too old for these kinds of tricks, Noreen. What are you now, fifty-five?" Blanche Feeney stood toying with a brooch at her neck, the only ornament relieving her neat but severe domestic uniform.

"Fifty-three," Noreen corrected quietly. "You're forty-nine."

"Anyone that close to sixty should not be taking walks in the woods in twenty-degree weather. And look at you! Only a shawl, for heaven's sake."

Noreen took a sip of the tea, breathing in the fragrant steam. Blanche did make a fine cup of tea. The du Ponts had lemons from somewhere, and that added to the flavor. The heat alone was welcome just now.

"It's only a few weeks till Christmas, Blanche. It's to be a fierce winter, I'm told, and I'm afraid for Tim in that brutal place."

Blanche busied herself adding water to a kettle and putting it on the stove. "Well, it's an awful thing to have our brother in prison. I sometimes wonder that the Mister didn't let me go when it got around." She looked apprehensively toward the doorway leading upstairs into the main part of the house. "I tell you, Noreen, the less said about it, the better."

"I've heard that there's no heat in much of the place. God knows it must be bad in this weather, out in the middle of the Delaware River, with the wind blowin' in from the bay."

"He broke the law, Noreen. You can't expect the authorities to treat him like he was a paying customer at an inn. I do wish you would let the matter rest. It's like we were being punished, too."

"Will you ask anyone here, Blanche? Could anyone help? God knows I've learned to beg."

"The Missus has said we must not interfere in the legal process, though they feel some sympathy for Tim's ideals. From other things she's said, Noreen, I think she feels that all the abolitionists should be locked up for their own good."

"But Mr. Alfred—"

"The Mister is not well at all. He seems so dismayed by the rush of things at the mill. The poor man is terribly afraid of more explosions."

"Well, I wouldn't want to interfere with that. It's about time someone worried about blowin' us all up."

Noreen received an arch look from her sister for the remark even as Blanche was refilling her cup. "I don't think y'can make sport of the poor man's affliction. After all, the mills put food in all our mouths."

Noreen dropped the subject. It was a tired and pointless argument anyway. They had come to accept the threat of explosion as a normal vicissitude of life. It was ironic, here she was trying to do something to save their brother from a slow death in the Pea Patch Island dungeon when the lot of them in Chicken Alley, Squirrel Run, and the rest of the workers' housing could be wiped out in a single blast of the tons of black powder made under their noses every day of the week save Sunday.

Noreen got up and wrapped up in her shawl. "Thanks for the tea, Blanche. I've got to get back to be there when the twins get home from school."

Blanche clucked noisily and her eyes misted over. "Now that's the tragedy," she sighed. "What's to become of those poor waifs with their mother gone and their father in prison?"

Noreen decided not to stay for the show. "I'm raising them is what's happening to them, Blanche. It might be nice if you could stop by to see them once in a while."

Blanche nodded, but she couldn't speak. Her eyes were already red with tears. Noreen knew that some things affected her sister deeply. Homeless children, especially orphaned ones, seemed particularly appealing. Blanche would have a short but fulfilling cry over the twins. It would help her avoid the unpleasantness of thinking about her brother Tim.

It seemed even colder on the way back down the hill through the barren woods. Was it because she had got used to the heat in the kitchen at the big house, or had the weather really turned hard? A deep freeze before January was unusual. She looked downhill at the Brandywine, which was clearly visible now that the leaves were gone, and half expected to see it frozen over. That was silly, of course. It would take a good week of temperatures in the teens to lock up all that water. It was not that cold, surely.

Still, as she shuffled along the path, she noticed that the run which crossed it halfway down was completely sheeted in ice. There had been running water two hours earlier on her way up. It must be terribly cold for a running spring to freeze in late afternoon.

The winter of 1846–1847 settled in like a blight. The severe cold that had ushered in December eased up just enough to dump five successive snowfalls on the Brandywine community. It was picturesque for the season, white snow outside and pine and holly trimmings for Christmas. On the Hill sleigh bells added to the holiday mood, but down along the Crick all the white loveliness added up to more hardship. Firewood had to be dug out of snowdrifts, and trips for food and work were adventures that soon lost their romantic appeal. There were no sleighbells or sleighs in Chicken Alley.

Of course, the children were delighted with it all. And after the snowing was done, a great mass of arctic air settled over the Northeast, pushing temperatures to zero and below. The Crick froze even over the dams, making it easy for cross-stream communities to visit without the need to walk miles around by way of Rising Sun Bridge. Besides becoming a convenient thoroughfare, the ice drew hundreds of folk on Saturday afternoons and all day Sundays to clamp on skates.

Throughout those two months of bitter cold, Noreen was becoming a nervous wreck with worry over her brother Tim. Tim Feeney might survive his sentence, but the toll on Noreen grew more taxing with each week. Besides his wife's fragile mental health, Brendan had Tim's children to consider.

He decided to approach the Mister to see if there might be something he could do to have Tim released or at least moved closer to his family.

The second Monday of February he left the loading platforms and walked up the icy hill to the company office behind the Eleutherian Mills director's residence. When Harry Belin opened the door, Brendan asked if he could speak with the director.

"Sure, Mr. Gallagher. Here, have a seat by the stove. He's having a few words with Mr. Henry, but I'll see if he can speak with you afterward." The bookkeeper was twenty years younger than Brendan, but somehow his position was intimidating. It was certainly not because of his attitude. He always treated Brendan with a certain deference to his age and experience with the company. And it was not exactly their respective job differences, although Brendan reported inventory and shipping data to Belin for record keeping.

Maybe it was the fact that he wore a suit to work, and that his company house was higher on the hill than Brendan's place in Chicken Alley. It might also have something to do with the fact that Belin was not Irish like the rest of them in the yards, and an Episcopalian besides.

All the same, Brendan liked the bespectacled clerk as much as he might under the circumstances. He sat in the only visitor's chair in the three-room building, and when Harry came back from du Pont's office, it was Brendan who started the small talk.

"How is your family, Mr. Belin? Missus and the little girl fine, are they?"

Harry brightened at the question. "Oh yes, both wonderful. Little Mary just had her birthday. She's seven, the same age as your niece and nephew, I believe."

Brendan nodded. Belin was like his father before him, company bookkeeper with a head full of details of every family on the Crick. Well, that was natural. Every man who worked for the company had an account in the "petit ledger" which listed his entire household by name and relationship. It was Harry's job, as it had been his father's, to keep track of wages saved in the company account, expenses charged at the company store, and pension amounts paid out to widows and orphans of men killed by explosions in the yards.

Brendan also doubted that Harry's daughter was as well as he claimed. The Belin house was close by the Sunday school up the road from the machine shop, and Brendan had seen the little girl many times on his way to and from the shipping yards. It was no secret that she was quite delicate and had been ill much of her young life.

Brendan had to wait so long for the conference to end that he became apprehensive. It did not look good to be away from his job this long, even to have a talk with the director himself. He was rolling his cap nervously over his knee when the door to Alfred's office opened and Henry finally strode out. His face was clouded with anger, and part of his mood spilled over on Brendan when Henry stabbed him with a baleful look.

"Last week's shipments were down a few tons, Gallagher. Any bottleneck at the loading platform?"

Brendan started to answer, but Henry immediately turned to the bookkeeper and snapped, "Get me the complete list of government orders for the last three months, Harry. And I mean the ones we declined to fill as well as the contracted amounts."

Then he turned back to Brendan, pulled out a cigar, bit off the end, and spat the tip aside. "What are you waiting for?" he snapped. "He wants you to go right in."

Brendan might just as well have stayed in his dispatcher's shed. There was certainly enough work to keep him busy. The visit with Alfred du Pont was of no value if he expected any help from the director as far as Tim was concerned. He had never seen the man so nervous and preoccupied. Brendan doubted that he really heard much of his plea at all. If he did, there was no evidence that any of it registered.

After standing in front of his desk for what could not have been more than two or three minutes, Brendan excused himself and turned to let himself out. He had the sinking feeling that the director was as upset as Noreen, and he wondered which would collapse first, his own household or the du Pont Powder Company.

The first thaw of that winter did not set in until March, and it was attended by a northeaster that sent sheets of rain into the valley for five days. Stirred by the sudden warmth and lifted by upstream runoff, the frozen Brandywine broke up in a moaning dirge. The stream swelled over its banks in a chocolate torrent that ripped out trees and splintered outbuildings with grinding slabs of blue-green ice. More than a few houses along the banks were flooded, and at its worst a dozen or so people had to be rescued from the roofs of their shed kitchens with boats.

Noreen Gallagher worsened during the rainstorm. Brendan had not seen her quite so bad since she had lost their twins in infancy to the fever. Several times during one afternoon she had asked him if he thought Pea Patch Island had been washed out to sea. As ludicrous as the question might seem, Brendan had to reassure her with patient explanations that the Delaware River in its tidewater section close to the bay was not subject to flooding. The reassurances had little effect on her peace of mind.

She had been to see the priest several times, and Father Reardon had asked Brendan to see him about Noreen's state of anxiety.

"We know that she is more sensitive than most, Brendan. I just wanted to let you know she has been in to see me for help."

"I knew that, Father. It's a great worry, and that's the truth. But unless you can come up with a miracle to get Tim out of that place, I don't see her gettin' any better."

Father Reardon was thoughtful for a time, and when he spoke, his words were measured carefully.

"It may be too early to say, Brendan, but I have spoken to the du Ponts about this matter and they have promised to intercede."

"Mr. Alfred, you mean?"

"Among others, yes. I'm afraid Alfred du Pont is not well himself these days. However, I did mention the problem to others who wish to be unnamed."

Brendan immediately wondered if it might be one of the sisters. All of the du Pont women generally kept in the background, but they were known for some charitable work. Was it Sophie, the eldest child of E. I. du Pont, or Victorine, who had worked with Noreen in the employees' school years before? He stared at the priest expecting more information.

"I'm sorry that I can't say anything else, Brendan. The effort may come to nothing after all. It would be cruel to raise her hopes and then smash them."

"So we just sit and wait?"

"And pray for his release."

"Well," Brendan growled, "we've been doin' enough o' that. I sometimes wonder that Noreen won't have a permanent bend in her knees."

Brendan did not hear anything soon about Tim's release, but there was plenty to keep him busy at the yards. In addition to flood damage to some of the mills, the lower levels of the older powder magazines had been under water, ruining the stored explosive and putting their deliveries farther behind schedule. Word was soon circulated that Henry had ordered night shifts to speed up the manufacture to match the rate at which government orders were pouring in.

Mickey Dougherty, who was Brendan's second in command, announced one morning that night shifts would soon start.

"Aye, Brendan, it's back to the oil lamps again, God help us!"

"I don't think Mr. Alfred will stand for it."

"Well, the night-shift roster is already up on the changehouse wall, and a cart is movin' through the Hagley Yards handin' out the lamps and oil."

Brendan felt his neck crawl with the old fear. The stupid bastard, he thought. There could only be one man behind the madness. "Henry," he muttered.

"Well, o' course! Who else might it be?" Mickey crowed and shook his head sagely. "You wouldn't get Mr. Alexis to go for that! He's up to his black elbows in the cake like the rest of us and knows better. And the Mister is a nervous wreck with a lifetime of seein' heads and arms and legs flying to all points of the compass." Mickey glanced at Brendan's stump tucked in the sewn-up sleeve of his coat and stammered, "Ah, ah, there I go again, Brendan."

Brendan did not even seem to notice. His mouth was set in an angry line, and he slapped the sloping pine boards of his worn dispatcher's desk. A stack of papers jumped and slid, but Mickey caught them before they could cascade to the floor.

"And that's not all," Dougherty went on, recovering as he riffled the bills of lading into an orderly pile. "It's more than just makin' up for losses in the flooding. The papers are full of new fighting down in Mexico."

"I thought that foolishness was done," Brendan snapped at Dougherty as though the renewed war was his foreman's idea.

"I heard a new general landed on a beach, Veracruz, and is going to go all the way to Mexico City!"

"Where is that?"

Dougherty blinked at the question. "I don't know," he said finally, somewhat deflated.

Brendan took the stack of papers from Dougherty's hands, nodded an absentminded thanks, and placed them carefully in the center of the desk. "Wherever it is, it's not just the border of Texas," he said thoughtfully. "It looks like we want to break Mexico's back, not just settle an argument."

"And it looks like Mr. Henry wants to make a quick fortune while he has the chance," Mickey drawled. "Even if it means shavin' the powdermen's chances awful thin."

Brendan had a suggestion of the old feeling again, that flutter in the stomach and quick breathing that sometimes ended up making him a bit dizzy. Goddamn, but why did it always have to be like this? He couldn't let it go. He wasn't going to put up with any close shave this time, nor let his men put up with it either. Before he went under the razor's edge again, he'd have some say about the conditions.

CHAPTER TWELVE

Sometimes you make me feel like a harlot." Meta propped herself over Henry's barrel chest, made an exaggerated pout as she spoke, and ran her fingernail in idle circles through the soft ringlets of coppery fur that ran from the razor line above his collarbone in a continuous mat to where their bellies met and below.

"Why do you say that?"

The question was a flat interrogation, idle curiosity but nothing more. If Meta was hoping for a flicker of concern, she was ripe for disappointment. She knew that in advance but could not stop herself from pouring it out anyway.

"Well, really, my love, sometimes you seem to be miles away even as we are loving."

"Do you need some more?" He made a move, reaching down, and she caught his hand, stopping it. She had a picture of him digging into his pocket for change to make up for a price shortage to some store clerk.

She forced a giggle, trying to rebuild the mood of minutes before, when he had taken her to bed. "Oh, I've no complaints on that score."

He made a movement, and she knew he wanted to get up, to be out of her bed, to be off doing whatever it was that so absorbed him even when they were making love. She slipped to her side and pulled the covers down between them, lying there watching his impassive face. He would stay on his back for one or perhaps two minutes, sit up, leave the bed, and begin to dress briskly without so much as a look in her direction.

"Why are you so preoccupied?" She almost added, "this time," but bit it off before the remark had a chance to come between them. "Something in the yards?"

He sat up, planting his feet beside the bed, his back a block of muscle toward her. "In the yards and in this house." He got up and walked straight to the settee and his pile of clothes.

He really is constructed like a bull, she thought. Strong and deep in the upper torso with thin hips, a flat backside, and stringy hams. Below the knees, though, his calves swelled out like the turned newel posts of a balustrade. There was no flabbiness as he moved.

"Alfred?"

He did not turn to face her until he slipped into his underwear and pulled up his pants. "Not Alfred directly. I'm having some resistance in trying to build up production to meet the government orders. A combination of laziness and womanish handwringing."

"Then you *were* speaking of Alfred."

"It's not just your husband who is flighty about explosions. Now he has dozens of the men as frightened as he is, some of them are old-timers, too."

"I have heard that you plan to work a night shift."

"Word gets around quickly. Did you hear that from my brother?"

Meta got out of bed and wrapped the sheet around her. She crossed the room to an oval rug between the hearth and the settee where he was dressing. She knew that he no longer wanted closeness, but she did and pretended a need for fireplace warmth.

"Yes, but not Alfred. Alexis was here last night, and he dropped the information like some dire prophecy of doom."

"Damn!"

"Is it really that dangerous to use lanterns in the mills?"

"Oh for Christ's sake, we've done it before and there has never been a problem. Every accident has been because of some stupid mistake that could have been avoided by better discipline. I tell you, Meta, that husband of yours—and Alexis, too—will have the workmen dictating policy and sending us to the poorhouse with mismanagement."

"I know that Alfred has been of little use lately, but Alexis—"

"I'll tell you that the two of them have abdicated the family responsibility to such a degree that we might have a workers' revolt on our hands. Brendan Gallagher had the brass to challenge my right to set new quotas for production and shipment."

"Gallagher?"

"Worker for Father since the mills opened; never a complaint from that family before. Now he's beginning to sound like those Irish in the coalfields. I tell you there is a crying need to bring stern leadership and discipline to this company once again."

He was throwing on his clothes now with a vengeance, frustrated in his rush by a stubborn knot in his tie. She stepped close to help him, working at the ribbon with both hands. The sheet slipped from her to a pile around her ankles, and she wanted him again with an intensity that she knew he must feel. She willed his hands to hold her, could almost feel the power of his fingers on her back, his breath on her neck, his lips.

But when she had secured the knot, he finished buttoning his vest and tucked in the loose ends of the tie.

"Thank you."

He turned to pick up his greatcoat and hat, hooked her ungently around the waist with his free arm, and kissed her roughly on the mouth. The warm smell of claret was still on his breath.

"You'd better get dressed or back in bed before you catch a cold," he said without even a final measuring look, and left.

It was still Dorgan's Inn. That is, it was still in the family and run by someone with the family name. But somehow the flavor of the place had changed for Brendan Gallagher. He could remember the early times when the original proprietors and their son ran the place. Old Dorgan—funny that he could not recall the man's first name—his crazy wife, Lizzie, and their son, Joe; all of them were gone now, the parents to natural causes and their son long before that. Brendan cradled the stump of his missing arm in the cup of his hand. The Dorgans had lost Joe and his mother's sanity in the same blast that took Brendan's arm. He tried to remember the exact date but could not. But it had been in March, so this month was the twenty-ninth anniversary of the "Big One."

The "Big One." That was a grim joke. There had been over a dozen bad rips since the one in Eighteen, with a toll of three times the numbers killed and maimed. It was strange how they had all come to accept the losses. It was a grim tribute to their hardy nature, surely. "The Irish fatalism," Noreen's father, Denis Feeney, would say. Brendan looked around the powdermen's taproom; there were certainly ghostly echoes of Denis Feeney in the dark corners of this place.

But it was not quite the same; not with having Dorgan's cousin just pop on a ship and come over to inherit the place when the old fellow wheezed into his grave. Along the Crick it was hard for an outsider to break in. A man was expected to earn his place as a powderman and take a powderman's chances. Of course old Lizzie's husband had not been a powderman either, but they had paid their dues the hard way. An only son vaporized in the flash of a whole wagonload of kegs is costly initiation to any club.

"What do you think we should do, Mr. Gallagher?"

Brendan looked across to one of the other tables and saw Paul Flynn's freckled face topped by a wild red cowlick. The face of a boy, although he was thirty years old. Paul Flynn had the hands and heart of his grandfather and, like old Hugh Flynn, would have been better suited gentling livestock on the farm than tending to the brutal demon he mixed daily in the tub of his rolling mill. Black powder was always eager to devour its shepherd.

"Why dontcha organize?" That was Dorgan's cousin who was so full of ideas that they were forever bubbling out of his big mouth—because it was nearly always open. He pronounced the word like it was some grand solution he was giving away free out of the generous nature of his innkeeper's heart. "Organize!" He liked so much saying it once, he rolled it off his tongue again.

"Oh Christ, shut up, Dorgan," Brendan said mostly to his tin of beer. But at his elbow Sean Taggart heard and chuckled, jabbing Brendan in the ribs.

"There's always one like him ready to start a war."

Brendan took a swallow of the beer he had been nursing till it was nearly flat. "Yes, and always somebody else's war."

"Well, what do y'think of that, Mr. Gallagher? Should we organize?"

That was Flynn again. Brendan tried to ignore the question, and heard Dorgan pump up his own idea. "Aye, lads, that's the trick to make 'em set up and listen. Just organize."

There was a general rumble of agreement with much draining of pails. Dorgan was too busy working the taps to add any more wisdom to the discussion.

But Sean Taggart thought it was a great joke, and jabbed Brendan in the ribs again.

"I see where Dorgan there has reconverted back to bein' Catholic."

Brendan said nothing, sipped at his pail, and made a face at the taste of the beer.

"Some lads from Ulster tell me that he was a pillar of the king's Church of Ireland."

Brendan would not be sucked in. "I don't blame him. If it would keep my family from starvation, I'd genuflect to Robert Peel and bless meself from his chamberpot."

Taggart would not give up easily. "I doubt that, Brendan Gallagher. You're not a man to switch sides."

"Oh God, spare me from where this is leading," Brendan thought miserably.

"But our friend behind the bar there could speak out of both sides of his mouth and kiss somebody's ass at the same time."

"Well, what do y'think, Mr. Gallagher?" It was the pale freckled face of Paul Flynn that had pushed through the excited, bobbing heads of drinking powdermen. Up close you could tell his age from the powder-blackened wrinkles above his eyes.

The eyes were pleading for Brendan to do something. The plea was for a family of four kids he did not want raised by their widowed mother. Somebody, *somebody* had to put a stop to the one they were now calling the Ginger Bastard behind his back. Henry du Pont had to be reasoned with, and the one thing he respected more than anything else was strength. Together the powdermen could be a forceful club for Henry to deal with. All they needed was a leader.

And suddenly Brendan Gallagher wished he were not such a respected elder in this community of proud but frightened men.

Alexis du Pont saw his brother coming down the path toward Eagle Mill Number Four, and he did not have to look closely to see that Henry was in a fuming mood. He was striding with that parade-ground stalk that bunched up his shoulders about his ears and locked his knees like splints.

"Holy Mother," remarked John Moriarity, who was the operator of Eagle Number Four and had seen the yard boss, too. "He looks fit to spill somebody's brains. I wonder who he's after."

"Likely it's me," Alexis observed matter-of-factly and picked up a wad of waste to rub bearing grease off his fingers. He threw the blackened gob into a trash bin and began to walk up the path. "Don't put any load on that pinion gear until I get back, Johnny; I want to start it up myself." He turned his head to grin and wink at the young mill operator. "That is, if I don't get fired in the next ten minutes."

Henry and Alexis met halfway between the millrace and the twin buildings that formed one set in a long string of water-powered blending mills in the newer Eagle section of Hagley Yard. This was the heart of the powdermaking operation, where the critical formula of charcoal, sulfur, and potassium nitrate was first combined in a dangerous mixing process that took up to six hours per batch. These mills produced du Pont's Eagle Brand rifle and artillery powder, and because of its growing reputation for high quality, they were the gem set of the entire du Pont operation.

Alexis stopped at the waist-high stone sluice box, pulled himself onto the smooth masonry, and sat there leaning easily against the cast-iron valve wheel. As Henry closed the last few yards between them, he slipped on the downsloping gravel path and nearly lost his balance. Alexis approved. He needed every advantage he could collect. But his brother's ungainly arrival did little to relieve his anger; in fact, it may have added to it.

"Have you taken leave of your wits, Alexis?"

Alexis tried to carry off a cool and collected attitude, but the truth was that he was mightily intimidated by Henry. As the youngest, it might have been expected of him to defer to his older brother, and he did feel that usual sort of deference toward Alfred. Actually, Alfred was so much older that he might have been an uncle or father figure for Alexis. But Henry was only four years senior, and what cowed Alexis was more than that. He could not put his finger on the reason—or reasons—but he thought of the term "ruthless" as coming close.

"Going to that meeting was an unbelievable error in judgment to begin with, and agreeing with those hotheads was even worse!"

"I did not see a single hot temper in the group, Henry. Certainly no one was as worked up as you appear to be just now."

Henry's head was cocked to look up at his brother sitting on the sluice wall; his eyes were bulging. "You seem to forget that it was the entire family welfare you were compromising by your presence in that group. There are certain responsibilities attached to leadership—and ownership, I might add."

"It was my only reason for attending."

"You agreed with every one of their demands."

Alexis nodded gravely. "I believe they were requests; suggestions, really. Yes, I agreed, and I made a few of my own, if you would really like to know. But I was agreeing as a powderman myself. I was not speaking as a shareholder or spokesman for the family."

"Goddammit, Alexis! Do you think for a minute that those micks think of you as just a powderman? You gave Gallagher and the rest a wedge to drive between yourself and the rest of us."

Alexis was beginning to congratulate himself on his choice of a seat. The perch gave him about half a foot of height over Henry. "The 'rest' did you say? I wonder what Alfred and the girls would say to doubling production by using short cuts and night runs by lantern-light."

"Alfred? Alfred would as soon shut down the mills entirely. His opinion is of little merit these days. Besides, the man is terribly ill."

Alexis allowed his momentum to push harder. "And I would avoid using derogatory slurs when speaking about the Irish. Some of those men are my friends. You're beginning to sound a little like those blue-nosed aristocratic prigs downtown."

Henry swung his head about angrily and glared downstream at the sunlight on the water. When he spoke again, his voice was deadly calm.

"Direct order from the operations director: second shift starts next week on Monday as planned. All worker meetings are prohibited unless called by the director or production supervisor, and we will be using oil lamps throughout the yards."

Henry did not wait to see if Alexis had the guts to reply in contradiction. That would keep until a more propitious time. His brother could be controlled if the workers could. And the workers were now being controlled by their local leader. As he walked away from his brother, Henry began formulating a plan to take care of Brendan Gallagher.

"Henry du Pont called me in today."

Kevin Gallagher looked up from his newspaper in surprise. The house had been silent since the twins had been put to bed and his mother had said good night herself an hour before. His father had been withdrawn all of the preceeding week because of the agitation at work. Kevin had not exchanged more than a dozen sentences with him since their argument over Henry du Pont. That and his mother's deepening depression over his uncle Tim had made for unpleasant hours at home. Only the twins gave relief to the place.

"What did he want?"

"He can get Tim Feeney out of Pea Patch Prison."

Kevin was out of the chair like a shot. "That's grand, Dad! When can he do it?"

"Any time. Any time I choose."

Kevin's look was confused. "Any time *you* choose?"

"Yes. I have to agree not to represent the men nor lead any more meetings."

He waited for that to sink in, watching the disbelief spread across his son's face.

"You mean he wants to buy you off with Uncle Tim's release?"

"That's the arrangement."

"But how can he arrange that?"

"Henry du Pont has a few friends high up in government, and one of them is a soldier friend from West Point who makes the rules at federal prison. Oh, he's an influential man, is our Henry du Pont."

"I know he's always been a cocky one, but I find it hard to believe he'd stoop to that."

Brendan put his hand on his son's shoulder. "Believe it, Kevin. The du Ponts are playing a game of high stakes, and for the most part, they try to do their best by the likes of us. But your grandpa told me once years ago that if it comes down to either or, we're the pawns in their game, expendable sacrifices freely made in troubled times. I didn't want to believe him then, but I've seen it many times over in the years since. I think Henry would not even spare his own family if it came to that. It has something to do with power, and young Henry has a deep craving for it."

"Then you've agreed to go along with his demand to ransom Uncle Tim."

Brendan nodded.

Kevin smiled after a moment, "Oh, Dad, it's not a bad exchange. Everybody will know why you had to step down. It's not as if you had to leave the company or anything like that."

"Oh, it's very much like that. Young Henry wants me at a distance until he has his way. You see, Kevin, I'm to supervise delivery of all that gunpowder to the army in Mexico."

"You mean *take* it there? Yourself?"

"That's the offer. And Tim will go with me, an experienced man with teams himself."

Kevin was thoughtful and then added, "And clever about avoiding losing his cargo to the wrong people."

"Now you see the argument Henry used to get Tim released."

"Clever."

"Oh yes. It looks very good on the face of things. Of course we both know that Henry du Pont would gladly lose a wagon-load of powder to get rid of a labor troublemaker."

"My God, Dad. Do you really think so?"

"Sure," Brendan grinned and clapped his son on the shoulder to make the point. "Once it gets to Mexico the army would have to pay for the loss."

Much later when he broke the news to his wife, Brendan was careful to skip the parts about dangers and the conditions Henry du Pont had imposed. Brendan knew Noreen's pride. He didn't want her to endure the anguish of making *that* kind of choice. He chose instead to underscore their own long separation.

"Two months, Norrie. Maybe three."

She embraced him and the silent tears came again.

"Of course, Tim will be with me right from the start. I'll be looking after him, you see; and after we get back, there'll be a job for him here in the wagon shop."

Noreen wiped her eyes and pressed closer to him. "You're a good man, Brendan Gallagher," she whispered.

"Well, I wouldn't be much of one if I didn't snap at the chance to save Tim, now would I?"

She squeezed his arm and drew back a step to look at his face. "I have a fair idea of the choice you had to make, Brendan, and I thank you for sparing me that."

"G'wan, Norrie," he muttered. "Where's the choice? The Mister offered to get him out, and he gets an expert craftsman for the company in exchange. Simple as that."

"No, dear. I know the kind of bargain Henry du Pont is apt to offer, and I love you the more for pretending otherwise."

A week later Brendan boarded ship at the Wilmington docks as agent responsible for the delivery of eight hundred tons of du Pont powder in her hold. The ship was the *Quaker City*, commanded by her owner, Captain David Craith. On her way downriver, the vessel hove to at Fort Delaware, the prison on Pea Patch Island, and took aboard a single passenger delivered in rags by a shallop rowed by prison guards. The frail man had to be helped up the gangway, and for a time appeared not to recognize his brother-in-law.

Brendan hoped the sea voyage would be good for Tim's health. Of course, all that black stuff in kegs below decks could alter everybody's health quite suddenly. For many nights as the lanterns were lighted on the *Quaker City*, Brendan wondered how the powdermen were faring as they mixed more powder under the sputtering lamplight and Henry du Pont's driving leadership.

When Brendan Gallagher finally got back to Noreen, he felt a bit like the conquering hero, especially being able as he was to deliver Tim to her and the twins safe and sound.

And of course, Mr. Henry du Pont was delighted to have sold all that powder.

PART II

CHAPTER THIRTEEN

1850

Wat do you mean, 'economize'?" Meta du Pont knew that her voice was shrill, unpleasant even to her own ears, but she could do nothing about it. At times like these, when she was so upset with Alfred, her throat closed down upon itself, squeezing the sounds into the quality of a scold. It was infuriating to lose control, especially when she wanted most to retain composure. Well, it was in her nature; she had turned forty and would accept certain things about herself. One of them was an increased propensity toward flaring up when provoked. So be it! Alfred could be most provocative. She glared at him now, glared at the back of his head as he fussed with the ever-present pile of papers on his desk in their library.

"I need an explanation, Alfred," she demanded. "What precisely do you mean?"

Her husband turned his head to answer, but it was a half-hearted effort to meet her glare.

"Some simple economies practiced in the running of the household, my dear," he said faintly. "Nothing drastic, a pruning back to balance reduced income from the company."

"Reduced income? I find that hard to accept. Even the local press has pointed out that du Pont shipped more powder to the government in the last three years than any company in the history of the United States."

Alfred sighed and made a trembling stab with his quill at the inkwell barely visible beneath the scattered papers. He missed, and the nib scratched instead on the bezel inset, breaking the point. He dropped the goose feather and began rummaging in his vest pocket until he extracted a small folding knife. "It is one thing to break records shipping powder, and quite another to pay the high costs of that production." His fingers nearly vibrated as he fought to unfold the blade of his knife.

Meta started to speak but bit off the hot retort building on her tongue. It would not do to get started on the topic of injured workmen and lost lives. Alfred had developed a bleak fascination for that subject lately. Any thump in the house was enough to set him off on a black rambling chatter of self-recrimination. She would keep his head cool in *this* exchange. Her own survival and the well-being of their sons were at stake.

"Are you saying that we *lost* money selling all that explosive to Washington?" Her voice was controlled now, almost gentle, and she skirted his chair coming round to the front of the desk. "Surely there was profit enough in those thousands of tons of powder to make a dozen families wealthy." She was looking squarely into his face now. She wanted answers, not breast-beating. But her tone was soft.

He would not look up. His eyes were fixed on the mess he was making of the quill point, whittling it into a series of uneven cuts until he was deep into the soft feather shaft itself.

"Forget the quill, Alfred. It's ruined anyway." She drew a light side chair up to the desk opposite him and sat down. "As a matter of fact, I think you should forget this study of chemistry, this hobby which so preoccupies you. I think you should set it aside and tend to more practical matters."

Alfred ruffled the sheets together irritably. He thumped the ragged pile with his fingertips as a nervous gesture of emphasis. "This is the very nature of our enterprise, my dear Meta. Without study, without research, the innovative processes which have made du Pont powder—"

"Oh, spare me that sermon, Alfred," she cut in quietly. "I want to know what you have done with the company profits, not how to make better gunpowder. Your customers and dearly loved powdermen may be fascinated with all that, but this family does not wear gunpowder, I do not pay the servants with gunpowder, nor do I serve gunpowder at the table. With the exception of Lammot, nobody else in this house is at all interested in your chemical theories." She took a breath, leveled a finger under his nose, and went on with more ice in her tone. "You are the director of this enterprise, or so says your title. The welfare of everyone in this house depends directly on how well or how recklessly you have managed that responsibility."

Alfred's usual pallor drained so that he looked moribund to her. His eyes glittered with some private fear as he spoke. "My whole life has been spent avoiding recklessness. God knows how I dread the awful responsibility of neglect in this trade. You should take care not to heap such debt on my conscience, dear Meta."

She groaned with exasperation. "I'm not speaking of *that* kind of wildness, Alfred, and you know it!" she snapped. "It is the absence of your financial stewardship that makes me so wretched!"

The man who had once stirred her into passion years ago blunted the reply with a mute stare, and she knew that he had not heard her words. There was another voice speaking to him, the same voice, the same images, that had driven him to moaning in his sleep these past years. The subject was closed again, and knowing that, Meta rose and left her husband to his bleak ruminations.

Later that evening she left the house and walked unseen to the company office a few dozen yards from their home. Harry Belin had left for the day and the small building was deserted. She let herself in with her own key, lighted a candle, and carried it into Alfred's office. She went directly to a small safe behind his desk and, placing the candlestick on the heavy iron cabinet, she reached into her reticule and withdrew a large key.

It was apparent that she was unfamiliar with the lock, and she fumbled with it nervously before managing to clear the tumblers and twist the dead-bolt handle in the right sequence. As the ponderous door swung open with a piercing squeak, she started with alarm and looked toward the office window as if expecting to be caught.

"Ridiculous!" she muttered to reassure herself. But she was on tenuous ground and knew it. No one but the director, not his wife certainly, had ever had access to the company records. There would be hell to pay if the family shareholders knew that Alfred's wife was snooping in du Pont business. Getting the single key from Alfred's desk had been harrowing itself.

It took considerable time for her to make any sense at all of the entries, but ultimately she was able to piece together the calamitous state of Alfred's mismanagement. It was far worse than she had imagined, the company was hugely in debt. All of the profits from government war contracts had simply reduced losses, and although she had difficulty with precise accounting, she found dozens of receivables uncollected for over ten years. The rough total scratched on the bottom line of her list was six figures. Her hand trembled as she rechecked the tabulation.

"My God," she thought, "Alfred has the company a half-million in debt!"

Another woman might have been paralyzed with fear, but the evidence filled Meta with cold fury. As she carefully locked up the books and stepped out into the night, she was already planning. Something had to be done, and quickly. She would not be left destitute, hung on the family dole. She would not pay for the wreckage of Alfred's stewardship, nor would her sons—not if she had anything to do about it.

Henry was the one man who could straighten out the mess if anyone could. He was calculating and ruthless enough. The thought filled her with a tingling rush of desire, and she breathed in a heady draught of the balmy air, humid with the pungent smells of the springtime night surrounding her. Yes, Henry would set the enterprise humming. She knew that with the same assurance she had of his dependability as a lover. There was a ruthless confidence about him that was nearly brutal. She could feel the cruelty thinly veiled, but never bared; at least where she was concerned. No, no. He had been always gentle with her, a perfect love partner but ever an irresistible force. She preferred not to think how he might behave if denied.

After entering the darkened house, she slipped into the parlor and lay on the divan for a long time staring at the dim outline of the west window. Everyone had gone to bed, and she was grateful for the time alone to plan. The safe key rested in her palm, a reminder to replace it in her husband's desk before morning.

The matter of dealing with Henry would require skill. He must not discover the desperate condition of the company until after she had concessions in exchange for her own support of his takeover. He would have to consider the offer a golden opportunity, not a desperation move on her part.

She smiled as she toyed with various options. All of them guaranteed her sons a permanent place with the firm, with significant shares.

Captain David Craith of the United States merchantman *Quaker City* was also swamped with paperwork the following morning. As he doggedly plowed through cargo lading bills at his cramped cabin desk, he had the compensating pleasure of knowing that the drudgery was a direct result of another profitable voyage. Through the open porthole overlooking the Wilmington dock he could hear the squeal of sheaves running in straining blocks as the deckhands off-loaded barrels of rum, cases of fine china, and from deep in the hold, a choice selection of Scot whiskey which had been aging for a full year, gently rocking next to the keel for almost fifty thousand miles of sea-lanes. This last was his personal cargo, an investment in the interest of raising spirits among the well-heeled gentry. Quality liquor brought fine prices from those with discriminating palates and the ability to pay for their tastes.

The stack of new shipping orders was higher than the off-loading cargo, a testament to the high pile of freight on the wharf waiting to be swung aboard and to the reputation of his old clipper ship's speed and security.

On a corner of the table lay another document, and it caught his eye as it had before, distracting him from his chores, and as before, his face cracked into a rare smile. At the same time two sharp raps rattled the hatch behind him and he swiveled to face it.

"In."

The seaman who swung easily into the cabin and stood relaxed but attentive was a far cry from the battered wreck who had been lifted aboard the ship three years earlier. Michael Farrell had filled out his tall frame with the strength that came from the demanding work of a clipper crewman. His arms and shoulders had thickened with muscle, and his deep chest tapered down to a flat belly and narrow waist. His face and bared forearms were deeply tanned as much from the wind as the sun, and his eyes had paled somewhat, giving his serious expression an even more penetrating look. He was every inch a working sailor, but even with spotless shirtsleeves rolled neatly to the elbows he was a cut above the rest.

"So you'll be off to the Gallaghers' place?"

"Aye, sir; if you need me I plan to spend the three days at their home."

"Well, my regards to the family." Craith eyed a bulky sack hanging from Michael's hand. "And presents for the youngsters?"

"Yes. I hope I have not misjudged their tastes. The twins are eleven now." He looked at the sack and grinned awkwardly, his first change of expression since entering the cabin. "Some of the things are a bit childish."

Craith reached for the document on his desk and handed it to Michael. "Here, lad, a belated present to celebrate your coming of age."

"What is it?" Michael turned the sealed paper over in his hands. It was a single sheet folded twice.

"Your citizen's paper. It was in my mail when we made port last night. I had some friends in Boston push it through."

"You have given me a fresh beginning, Captain." His voice quavered almost imperceptibly as he continued. "I am indebted to your trust." He reached out to David Craith, who rose and gripped his hand.

"No debt, no debt!" the old sailor grumbled. "Someday you might be my first mate, and I'll not be having the British plucking you off my ship like they've done before to men at sea, impressing them for lack of papers into His Majesty's service."

Michael Farrell felt more elation at that moment than he had in years, but his face was almost stern as he picked up his sack. Craith gave a parting shot as his crewman stepped through the hatchway. "Oh, before you take leave, Mr. Farrell, tell the bosun to dab grease on his blocks. The sound is bad enough, but if one of those pulleys breaks its shaft while swinging out my whiskey, he'll be doing the squealing and suffer the loss of any future progeny."

"Aye, aye," Michael snapped and left with an honest-to-God smile on his face.

The group assembled in his library was as hushed as a wake as Alfred rose to speak. He looked at his two sisters, Sophie and Victorine, minor shareholders with no direct influence on business affairs; his younger partners, Henry and Alexis; and avoided the eyes of his wife and sons sitting apart from the group at the table. All looked quite sad with the knowledge of what he was about to do. All except brother Henry, whose eye had the look of an eagle about to feast.

"I won't keep you long, dear family. This is probably more painful for you than it is for me, so I will spare us all unnecessary preamble. The blunt truth is that my contribution to our enterprise will hereafter be limited to research. I therefore tender my resignation as your director forthwith."

Alfred blinked several times and cleared his throat before continuing. "May I see a show of hands in support of my request?" His eyes circled the table, head bobbing as he counted each upraised palm. Only Alexis abstained, and Alfred gazed at his brother so long that the others began to squirm uneasily.

"Thank you for that, Alexis, but you see that my own hand is raised. Won't you join us in the interest of family harmony?"

"No, Alfred. I'll adjust to the changes, work for the firm as I've done before. But appearance is not reason enough to add my dagger."

Sophie du Pont gasped, "That's unfair, Alexis. Unfair and cruel, too. We all love our brother."

"Since we're into it," Alexis added, "I'll admit that Alfred needs help in the business end of things. But why not give Henry that responsibility? I could run the yards and Alfred direct all lab and research."

Henry spoke quietly. "I believe we are addressing the problem of directorship."

"May I speak?"

Meta's voice brought every head around. It was an extreme breach of family protocol. She rushed from the back of the room and stood by Alfred.

"I beg you to accede to Alfred's wishes. God knows how much we are indebted to him for his long labors, but I must confess to you my fears for his continued health. No, no, Alfred, I will say it, say it before it is too late and we later regret our narrow selfishness. My husband is ill, worn out with the drain of this awful enterprise. I beg of you a few more years of his loving company. Give du Pont a new director with energy and strength to spare, and give back to this worried family a sound husband and father."

After Meta had withdrawn weeping from the room, the rest of the procedure was mercifully swift. There was no question of who should succeed Alfred. Nor was there any surprise that Henry had prepared a neat agreement outlining redisposition of shares when he took the gavel. Before the carriages drew up to take each family home, Henry had signatures giving him control of the entire du Pont empire.

Lammot was not on hand for the ceremony. He had gone to his room after his mother's speech.

When Henry closed the last ledger on his desk, he made a notation on a figure-covered sheet with his quill, and put the sailcloth-bound book back into the safe with the others. After locking the steel door, he looked idly at the bronze key resting in his palm and then slipped it deliberately into the lower right pocket of his vest. It felt heavy there, a lumpy presence but secure, and he gave it a reassuring pat with his thick fingers. The gesture was in contradiction to the sour expression on his face, and he paced the room, pulling thoughtfully at his cleft, bristly chin.

His desk. His office, too. Now that his brother had finally relieved the family business of his profligate, dreamy direction. The desk was littered with loose sheets on which he had been working since the meeting. Seven hours without a break in concentration. It had been a nonstop assessment of the company begun in the flush of his newly acquired power.

Henry's belly soured as he remembered that first private delight in turning the key of the safe. He had felt like a modern

Aladdin, heady with a sense of power he had so long yearned for. But it had not yielded the promise. Now as he glowered at the squat iron box, it seemed more like Pandora's surprise, and he quietly cursed what it contained.

He had not expected to find an orderly record; his brother's handling of other affairs precluded that kind of hope. But with all of the war business just completed, the sheer volume of their sales, the breakneck production he himself had forced over everybody's objections—all of that should have resulted in a massive profit. He had doubted that the balance sheets would show it, but there should have been at least the *potential* of net wealth once the delinquent accounts had been collected.

There were enough of those. Non-payment on accounts reaching back a dozen years almost to his father's time. Well, he would get cracking on that as his first priority. But even if they were in fact collectible, they would not offset the huge debt Alfred had run up. The interest payable to lenders had gobbled up every cent of profit and more.

Henry reached into the pocket of his coat hung over the chair and pulled out a black cheroot. He bit off the end, wet the end absently with his tongue, and leaned over the flame of one of the three candle stubs in the holder on his desk. As he drew in the pungent smoke his eye dropped again to the paper nearest the candlestick. His own handwriting boldly spelled out the harsh truth; du Pont Powder was a half-million in debt.

Louisa and Henry du Pont's house was a pleasant walk from the main Eleutherian Mills residence, a few hundred yards along the wooded crest of the Brandywine's western bank. When Henry left the office adjacent to his elder brother's home, he decided to make a longer loop, passing Alfred's place and dropping down into the powder yards along the stream, down into the Upper Yard and then south, following the twisting waterway to Hagley Yard, the newer section of the works, which lay at the bottom of the hill below his own house. It was still full dark, sometime after four, but the powdermen would be moving into the yards soon, and he wanted them to see him, note his presence, on this, his first day as director of the company. From this day on laxity would be an unknown word in the du Pont company.

As he passed the main house, he realized with the deepest

satisfaction of his life that the place would be his now—his as the absolute director of all du Pont holdings. This house, the one his father built even before a single mill was raised, and all the homes of his brothers and sisters were company property to be assigned as the director saw fit. It was a practice adopted mainly to humor his grandfather, old Pierre Samuel du Pont, who had peculiar ideas about keeping the family together in the New World. Just now Henry was quite pleased about that little concession to P.S.'s eccentricities, and particularly so since it had the force of law.

Henry slipped past the house, glancing up once at the darkened windows of Meta's bedroom. She had pulled it off for him; he had to give her credit for gall. Convinced Alfred to resign and convinced everybody else in the family that they should vote him in. He owed the woman a lot, at the very least a roll in the bedsheets when she felt desperate.

Of course there was the other thing she had insisted on—making Irénée a partner in exchange for his father's stepping down completely from the board. Now there would be three again, his nephew Irénée, his brother Alexis, and himself. It didn't matter that he had to include Irénée. The boy was showing signs of consumption. It would not surprise Henry if he slipped away before his father, and Alfred was on very shaky footing in that respect. The only sticky part of the deal was having to give Lammot shares in the company. That was unsettling. Even a minority ownership by Lammot could pose problems. He did not like Lammot. The boy was too much like Alfred and did not approve of his father's stepping down. And he had a degree of spunk inherited from Meta that might make him hard to control later on.

Henry took a last drag on his cigar, dropped it to the damp earth of the path, and ground it out under his heel. Lammot was only nineteen, still wet behind the ears. He would be manageable.

So it was a fine conspiracy. Alexis certainly would be a silent partner. He had never wanted more than to muck with his powdermen anyway. He and Meta had put one over on all of them, all right. Henry chuckled, hitched up his pants, and glanced back again at her black window. "Maybe I should reward her with a quick toss right now," he muttered. "Payment joyfully rendered." The prospect had him half-aroused, and he smiled.

The thought suddenly hit him that Meta could have had her own look at the confidential ledgers. If she had, then the entire manipulation could have included himself—a way to feather her own nest with a son on the board and another holding shares. The idea took his breath away and he missed a step on the dark, twisting path. His erotic impulse vanished.

I'll have to watch that woman more closely in the future, he thought, and began composing the letter he would write to Alfred ordering him to vacate the director's house.

Behind him on the hill, Meta followed his progress down the pathway to the mills. She wondered if he had as yet assessed the total damage her husband had permitted to be inflicted on the family empire. Once he did, Henry would suspect her of duplicity, of course.

That did not matter, really. She would never admit to it. That he was in control thrilled her. It was like watching a powerful stallion prance before being tested against the field in his first race. She knew the power he would bring to the enterprise, the wealth he would amass for her and her sons.

CHAPTER FOURTEEN

She gets that from my side, the Feeney red hair." Noreen ran her hand possessively over Megan's head and gave her niece a little squeeze around the waist. Megan squirmed a bit and sniffed impatiently.

"And isn't she lovely? Look at the eyes."

"Aunt Norrie!"

"Now that one—a head black as peat! The Halloran strain settled in him, surely. Black Irish like yourself, Michael. I sometimes marvel that they are brother and sister, much less twins into the bargain." Noreen smiled at Denis who tried to draw his adolescent frame more tightly into the cushioned chair. "Have they changed much, do you think?"

"Almost man and woman," Michael answered soberly and then winked at Denis. The boy grinned suddenly and picked nervously at a loose thread on his shirt.

"And you have changed, Michael. A strapping young man now, aren't you, fine and strong. Brendan will be glad to see you. It's been such a long time. He'll soon be home from work, and Kevin."

Michael nodded, the same faint smile she remembered ghosting over his stern features, but still he said nothing.

"Megan, you and Denis set the table for supper. Michael and I will sit on the porch to watch for the men."

"Will you stay long enough to take us fishing again along the

Crick like before?" It was Megan speaking, but Denis hung back waiting for his reply.

"I wouldn't miss that, now would I?"

A broad grin flashed across her face, and she nearly skipped out, taking Denis by the hand and leading him through the draped entrance to the kitchen. There were only two rather small rooms connected by the doorless opening, a kitchen with table and chairs for meals and the front room, which held the comfortable chairs. In addition to these there were two side bedrooms, one of them a shed wing added to the east wall. The second floor of the cottage was an enclosed loft under the eaves.

Noreen led him out, and they sat together on one of two hickory-slatted settees flanking the front door. The earth below them sloped a few yards to a whitewashed picket fence, the hard-packed surface of Crick Road, and the brush-screened edge of the Brandywine beyond. The Crick, as everyone in Chicken Alley called it, was deep here, but fast moving and broad, forty yards from bank to bank. A series of dams gave it breadth and depth, building its power to feed the races and turn the mills. From where they sat, Michael could hear the muffled roar of the nearest spillway twenty rods downstream. The sound reminded him of his promise to Megan and Denis, and he wondered if the deep, sucking eddies below the cresting dam still attracted the big sunperch they loved to hook.

"There used to be great shad running, but the water is foul from the sewers in town, and few of the poor things can make it up here any more."

Her words shocked him, almost as if she were reading his mind, and he jerked his head around. She was watching him, amused at his slack jaw, then patted his hand as if he were a child.

"You remind me a bit of Brendan. And you needn't think me some psychic fairy, Michael. We're both listening to the dam, and your last words were a promise to the children. The Lord knows I worried enough about your dragging them off to danger when you were here last."

He laughed, partly with relief, partly at his own credulity.

"Well, Noreen, no one can say you are not a good listener."

She looked at him closely, and he had the sensation of balm over raw hurts. His own mother had not ever had that effect on him.

"It takes more than listening," she said.

A clatter from inside the house made her turn, and she started to rise, thought better of it, and eased back. "They are making the *sounds* of industry at least. Oh, Michael, your coming just now is a tonic for them."

He waited for her to explain.

"Their father was in prison. His sentence was commuted. He was here for a while, and now he's gone. He lives across the line up in Pennsylvania. We don't even know where exactly."

"But why? Surely there is no need for secrecy now that his sentence has been commuted."

"All my letters to him go by way of Thomas Garrett in Wilmington."

Michael felt his scalp crawl. He had been reading about the abolition movement. Garrett's name was in the papers often enough. He shook his head. "That seems foolish, Noreen, to get mixed up with a crew like that, even if they do have a moral argument."

"I can't ignore my brother, their father."

"No, I mean Garrett. Find a contact who's not an abolitionist. The last thing Tim Feeney needs is to be connected with escaping slaves. It wouldn't take much more than a breath of rumor to have him clapped in prison again."

She looked miserable, and he wished he had not been so quick to criticize. But when she spoke he realized that was not the reason.

"You don't understand, Michael," she said grimly. "It's not just a wish for privacy and the passing of mail. Tim is back at the old business himself, a 'conductor' again."

"God!" he croaked. "The man's hell-bent to make them orphans. Doesn't he know when to stop?"

His explosive anger was a surprise even to himself. And the sudden protective feeling for the children and Noreen was as intense as it was irrational for him, an outsider with only the ties of friendship.

They both became aware of the silence within the house, and when Noreen turned, the twins were standing at the open door.

"The table's set, Aunt Norrie," Megan said. "Can we sit here with you to wait for them?"

Noreen got to her feet and hurried toward them, "Well, I'll need water from the pump. Denis, there's a good boy." She patted him on the rump in passing, and he followed her into the house. Megan sat on the settee next to Michael.

"Do you really think Daddy will go to prison again, Michael?"

He was jolted by her directness and struggled for a platitude. She seemed too grown-up for that kind of evasion, though, and he ended up silently groping. The child answered for him.

"I think he will, and so does Denis. We talk about it a lot, but never in the house. It's supposed to be a secret, a sad secret that upsets everyone but Denis and me. And of course, Daddy, but he won't speak of it to us."

"The less said the better, Megan." Michael added cautiously. "Especially to outsiders."

"Oh, everybody else seems to know anyway. Some of them think he's crazy to waste his time carting black people up from the South. Some of the kids think he sells them and is getting rich."

"They tell you that, eh?"

"That and other things. Denis got punched in the nose by Jimmy Halloran once in a fight because he said to Denis that Daddy was a nigger lover. It was pretty bad, because he's even our first cousin, but I never liked him."

"Well, there are many people who would call your dad a hero."

"Yes."

Michael wanted to change the subject, to get it on a positive note and be done with it. He didn't need this kind of responsibility. Maybe they were forbidden to discuss the matter at all.

"The thing that makes it hard to swallow, Megan, is that none of us can do any bragging about the thing he does."

"Oh, I wouldn't even try to do that. Personally I agree with Sister Alonza. She's from Maryland, and when she was little her parents had slaves. She says that all the great men of our country had slaves, Thomas Jefferson, George Washington, lots of them."

"Sister Alonza?"

"My teacher at school. She says that God loves the Negroes very much but they have a special place according to his plan, and that is to serve their earthly masters faithfully to enter the Kingdom of Heaven."

"I see."

"Yes, that's why they are colored so, and why they don't need to read or write like us."

"They're quite different?"

"Oh, yes. Like children who never quite grow up. Our children of Africa, she says."

"Umm."

"So I think Daddy is making a serious mistake, though I know he means well, and I love him anyway. I just hope the Holy Ghost comes to his rescue soon."

"I don't quite understand."

"Well, it's like the poor Quakers, you know. Their minds are clouded without the gift of faith, and they have Daddy mixed up in his thinking. He's acting like a crazy Orangeman."

"What do you know of Orangemen?"

"Oh, you know, black Protestants."

That was at last the end of it. Brendan Gallagher and his son were at the gate before either Megan or Michael saw them coming, and the reunion snuffed out any more talk of Tim Feeney's misguided zeal. At supper they spoke mostly about Boss Henry du Pont and how he was worked up like a zealot himself. There was no question that the atmosphere of the powder yards had changed drastically.

CHAPTER FIFTEEN

Lammot du Pont straightened his six-foot frame, gingerly adjusted the crooked angle of his spectacles with grimy fingers, and stretched to relieve the knot in his back. Tending the graining mill machinery was hard work and dirty work. As the damp cakes of mixed gunpowder came in from the pressroom, they were dried, broken, sized by rolling through a drum sieve, and finally—the dirty part of the operation—coated with a slippery coating of graphite. The graphite made the powder more impervious to dampness in storage and more easily poured into cartridges and gun barrels.

He did not like the work—not because it was hard physically but because it was boring. Lammot did not like anything that required repetitive tasks. He missed the excitement of the ever-novel work in his father's laboratory. The thought of that privation made him grimace through the smeared glass of his spectacles.

Well, Henry might force them all into this breakneck race to increase production during the working day, but at least he had the evenings to continue his chemistry. What a waste. With a degree earned primarily through research, he was forced to spend the productive hours of his energy in whatever mind-dulling task his uncle chose to assign him.

"Every man in the family will have to earn his keep."

It wasn't that Lammot disagreed with that. It had been a

family tradition. His aged grandfather had precipitated his own death by insisting on helping to put out a fire in the yards long before Lammot was born. And his Uncle Alexis still slogged through every workday with his men despite the fact that he had been a partner for years. Even Lammot's older brother, now a partner with Alexis and Henry, worked a full day despite his weak lungs.

The galling fact was that his skills were ignored. There were a hundred ways in which the operation and the product itself could be improved. His experiments, his and his father's, had shown that. Safety, quality, and newer, more efficient explosives were within their reach if only . . . it was pointless thinking about it. His uncle had been on a tirade for three years, demanding an end to the search for quality and rubbing his and Irénée's noses in the weak financial conditions of the firm.

"We have Alfred's time in the lab to thank for that," he would taunt, speaking to Alexis, but intending his words for Lammot. "We have to be competitive! Let's get the volume up and forget the improvements. Our black powder is better than anyone else's. Let's make and sell more of it!"

Lammot shrugged off his dismal woolgathering and began jotting down the production figures for his powder run. In an hour or so his uncle would be by on rounds to check the quantity. It would not be pleasant if the paperwork and production were not up to expectations.

"Well, how's our chemist these days?"

Lammot recognized his Uncle Alexis's voice and grinned in spite of his mood.

"I hope you are writing a generous report there, Lammot," Alexis drawled. "The boss likes big numbers."

"They're big."

"Big enough for the French and English?" His uncle's mouth was a red-rimmed white flash as he smiled. His teeth seemed to be the only clean part of a powder-caked body.

Lammot gave him an overall inspection. "Well, you'd better get that cleaned off before he comes. He might have you packed in a barrel to avoid the waste."

"Pot and kettle, my learned nephew, I can't be blacker than you. Don't you love the graphite? Sticky mess, eh?"

They shared the camaraderie with a laugh.

"So we have more business for the Turks?" Lammot asked.

"Not directly. But the news is that the French and English plan to blockade Sebastopol. I think this rush for powder is for them."

"Is that what Uncle Henry said?"

"Said? To me?" Alexis mocked. "His deals are his own secrets, my boy."

Lammot shook his head. It was really silly. He could understand Henry's not letting him or Irénée know what was going on, but to keep it from his brother seemed pointless.

"How's your father?"

"Not very well. He keeps pretty much to his room."

"I'll drop in Sunday. It seems strange not getting to see him often. You know, he was more like an uncle to me, Lammot. You and I are closer in years."

"He'll be pleased."

"I wish he were closer to the office. Now that he . . ."

"Yes. Moving out of the house was hard for him."

Alexis frowned. "I still do not think that was fair of Henry. It was painful for your mother, too."

Lammot made no comment. They stood watching the turning glazing drums for a time, and then Alexis patted Lammot's shoulder and was gone.

Painful for his mother? Oh, yes, he remembered her wailing at that unexpected comedown. Lammot gritted his teeth as he recalled the directors' meeting where she had urged all the others to accept his father's resignation and vote Henry in. It had been the most humiliating moment of his life.

"God!" he whispered and gripped the iron railing of the vibrating glazing platform. It was a scene to close a play on the Philadelphia stage.

He wondered if his mother was still sleeping with Henry, and what the conditions might have been. He tried not to think about it, but the speculation clung like chronic nausea. He was still having black thoughts about his uncle when the man himself strode briskly into the mill, glanced over the paperwork, and snapped at his nephew.

"When you get cleaned up, come up to the house for dinner tonight. There's something we have to discuss." His eyes stabbed at Lammot. "And," he added, "it's confidential."

Without waiting for an answer, he turned on his heel and made an elaborate business of ducking under the door frame, although even with his tall hat, Lammot thought he could have cleared it easily standing erect.

"What are you now, twenty-three?"

"Nearly so."

"Have a cigar, Lammot, and go close that door."

They were alone in the old sitting room which seemed strange now that it was furnished with his aunt and uncle's things. It was the only time Lammot had been in the place since their eviction, excepting of course the two preceding New Year's Day visits that were mandatory for all du Pont males to celebrate the anniversary of the family's arrival in America. Those had been perfunctory, a stopping in the vestibule of each house to present a gift to the mistress of each place. Lammot had made the visit to Eleutherian Mills more perfunctory than the rest.

His uncle seemed to be eager to get on with the agenda. Even during the meal with his Aunt Louisa, whom he liked, and young Henry Algernon, his cousin, a fifteen-year-old brat whom he detested, converation lagged and the eating accelerated. Everyone seemed glad to be done with it. Henry was eager to get on with things, and gobbling up the victuals was a command performance.

After closing the door, Lammot sat down, suppressed a belch rising from bolted food, and waited.

"Yes, well, you're old enough to be getting on with the company. I've been keeping tabs on your work, Lammot, and I think it's time to get you involved in more sensitive matters."

Lammot perked up, but warily.

"You are aware of our powder shipments to the Anglo-French forces in the Crimea?"

"Marginally, yes, sir." Lammot bit his lip. Henry preferred to be so addressed by subordinates, an expected deference to his position and military background, but Lammot seldom gave in to the pressure. This time it was a lapse.

"Now, the information I am about to divulge is confidential in the extreme. It must not be hinted at to anyone. I repeat, not to anyone."

Lammot nodded.

"I have made a separate agreement with the Russians."

Henry watched Lammot's reaction closely. There was barely a flicker in the youngster's eyes as he responded.

"You will continue to ship to the French and English."

"Yes."

"A delicate situation."

Henry permitted himself a chuckle. The boy *was* cool. He had not underestimated him.

"Delicate, yes. An understated truth. There would be hell to pay if they found out."

Lammot weighed the situation before his next question. He had no idea why Henry was giving him all this critical information. It could be very damaging to the company. His next question might seem to be an effrontery.

"And our government? Does Washington approve?"

"I have a letter advising me that trade with the combatants lies outside our national interests."

"That's surprising to me. I would not think they would countenance selling munitions to both sides."

"Well," Henry drawled through a cloud of cigar smoke, "I imagine they assumed sales only to England and France. The sale to Russia was my own idea. Washington does not know about that particular element."

"Is the sale worth risking the loss to secure markets?"

"So far the fight has drained all available powder from European sources. We're the only supplier left. Besides, Lammot, we can't pass international judgment, can we? Don't the Russians deserve a chance to defend themselves?"

Lammot did not feel the need to answer that argument. He marveled at his uncle's pragmatism.

"From a business standpoint," Henry went on, "we stand to make a considerable gain. The people defending Sebastopol are pretty desperate; they offered to pay double the price we charge the English."

"Double?"

"Yes. Two million dollars cash."

The figure was staggering. Lammot's pay was twice the regular powderman's wage of eighty-five cents per day—about five hundred dollars a year. At double the inflated prices paid by the British, a two-million-dollar sale would net clear profits of at least three-quarters of a million. In spite of that, his expression was deadpan.

"Impressive."

Henry's eyes twinkled behind the smoke of his cheroot. The boy was better than he had expected. A wise thing to rope him in before he had too many ideas of his own. Henry had learned long ago to befriend enemies.

"The deal is cash on delivery. And delivery is in Sebastopol." He paused to let that sink in before leaning forward and tapping his nephew on the knee. "And that, Mr. Lammot du Pont, is where you come in."

It was quite late by the time all of the arrangements had been made, including a cover trip for Lammot to "New York on business." There were British and French informers crawling over every dock on the eastern seaboard, checking cargoes and destinations of outgoing vessels. To throw off the snoopers, a ship in Wilmington was loaded with du Pont barrels every night for a week. When she left in a hurry, taking the night tide down the Delaware under steam and full sail, a half-dozen Tricolor and Union Jack pickets gave chase on the open sea. They overhauled and searched her at nightfall the following day. All the barrels were filled with flour bound for Spanish ports. The British were curtly apologetic, and in return the overhauled captain was unusually understanding. He promised not to lodge a protest.

On a dark sea lane many miles south, the *Quaker City* plowed a direct course to Gibraltar and the Mediterranean. She was low in the water, her sealed holds jammed with hundred-pound kegs from keelson to weatherdeck. They too bore the du Pont logo, but were loaded with more volatile stuff. It had taken a whole week for David Craith to stow the powder brought to his ship by longboat as they stood at anchor in mid-channel, twenty miles down the Delaware. When the decoy ship had passed, the *Quaker City* simply waited an hour, then raised the hook and sailed out unchallenged.

On the bridge Captain Craith decided it would be safe to let someone else take over. He had been at the conn since getting under way, a full twenty hours. It was time to rest. He was getting too old for this kind of anxiety.

"She's yours, Mr. Farrell."

"Aye, aye, Captain."

Once below, Craith stripped to his underwear and eased gratefully into his bunk. He could not drop off quickly as in the old days, snatching rest like a cat. A dram of brandy would help, but the thought of all that gunpowder below him queered that notion.

Overhead he could hear the muffled chatter of his Number One and Lammot du Pont. It was a surprise that they had met each other briefly years ago. The du Pont lad seemed honest and bright, and Michael Farrell seemed to enjoy his company. The coincidence of their meeting was the kind of thing most masters clung to as a sign of good luck and a fair voyage.

But David Craith took no stock in omens, good or bad. Planning ahead was his only religion. He liked to have things laid out in orderly fashion.

The thought pulled him out of the bunk and over to his desk. From a packet of papers neatly stowed in a latched pigeonhole he pulled out a folded sheet and carried it back to his bunk. Adjusting the slide of his lantern so that a sliver of light fell upon the page he began memorizing from a long list of flag signals.

David Craith was not shoring up his seamanship because of a softening memory. What he was reading was a list of secret signals used by the French and English warships. It was an ace up his sleeve for later if they were challenged.

Yes, that du Pont fellow showed promising ingenuity. Craith wondered idly how much he had had to bribe the informer to get the secret code.

CHAPTER SIXTEEN

Q*uaker City*'s sharply raked prow plunged and hissed through water so blue that at times it seemed purple. Lammot leaned over the rail and peered down past the jib boom chains into the milky spume thrown up by the racing ship. As Michael had put it in seaman's terms, she was "running with the bone in her teeth." Above him the three jib sails cracked with the rippling strain of the wind, and farther aft the fore, main, and mizzen masts groaned under the booming strain of full sail. They were making spectacular time, three full weeks of running before the westerlies.

Lammot scanned the horizon ahead, but there was nothing but the broad expanse of the whitecapped Mediterranean and a skyline of creamy clouds. Craning his neck, he looked over his shoulder at the humming shrouds of the foremast, following the ladderlike ratlines to the lookout perch high above the rolling deck. He envied the sailor's view but felt a stab of fear at the thought of making the long climb up the rigging to that dizzy height.

"Don't even consider it."

The voice behind him gave him a start, and he spun around to face Michael Farrell.

"The captain has a rule about passengers wanting to be monkeys. He's squeamish about mopping them up from the deck."

Lammot's face cracked with an embarrassed smile. "I have to admit being relieved at that. I'm not sure I would have the stomach for it, really."

"Or the hands and feet. The stomach does a quick turn every time I go up. Personally, I prefer to let them do it." Michael glanced up at the diminutive figure of the lookout. "Privilege of rank, thank God."

"You appear to have done well at sailoring, Michael. Captain Craith must value your work. It is not usual for a man your age to be first mate of a vessel this large."

"He treats me well."

"And the life? Do you want to make the sea a career, have your own command one day?"

Michael took his time answering, and then he slowly shook his head. "I don't think so, Mr. du Pont. It is an interesting line of work with David Craith, an unusual master, believe me. I have seen a good many captains, heard tales from other crews, and the society is not one to uplift the soul. My time on the *Quaker City* has been well spent, but I think it a temporary education, an escape, perhaps. Someday I will have to get on with my life."

Lammot leaned against the rail and studied Michael's face. "Well, that's interesting. Not surprising. Interesting."

"We have company. Did you see?" Michael was pointing over the side at the smoother water just outside the wake from the bows.

Lammot looked and saw six dark shapes in echelon off the ship's prow and just under the surface. They were quite large, seven or eight feet long, and keeping perfect pace with the ship.

"Dolphins," Michael grinned. "They like to play games, racing contests. Watch."

Almost immediately the six animals shot forward with a tremendous burst of speed and disappeared in the distance ahead of the ship.

Lammot gasped, "Marvelous! How did you know they would do that?"

"They do it all the time."

"Surely something on the ship startled them—a vibration from below?"

"No, they do it for sport. See, here they come again."

They watched as the same six lined up as before, paused for several seconds, and again raced forward abreast as though in marked lanes. The game went on for several minutes, and then inexplicably, the porpoises left.

"Just like me," Michael muttered almost too low for Lammot to hear.

"How is that?"

"Oh, this life, I suppose. I know that one day I'll have to stow the experience and go on to other things."

"Just playing the game for now, eh?"

"Something like that."

"Sail ho!" The thin cry filtered down from the lookout.

"Where away?"

Michael Farrell's sharp question stung Lammot's ear.

"Two points, port bow, hull down." The reply was immediate, almost like a rehearsed duet. Then the sailor added his own opinion in a different tone, projected but conversational. "I think she's a schooner, Mr. Farrell. Not sure."

"Course?"

"Southbound, across our bows."

Almost at the words, Lammot felt the deck begin to swing, and the bowsprit began a slow arc to port.

"Damn! He did it again."

"Who?"

"Oh, the skipper. I was just about to give the command and report to him, but the old man aced me out again." He almost pouted. Bested in the game of catching Craith off guard.

"Is it really so important to change course?" Lammot wondered why a small vessel would make any difference in their mission.

"Word travels. We don't want to be seen until it is unavoidable, when we reach the Dardanelles. Even then we'll try to scoot through after dark."

They were closing in. Soon they would pass Athens, then into the Aegean, skirting the ruins of ancient Troy; running the Dardanelles, the Bosporus, and into the Black Sea.

And the waiting armada of British and French warships. Were they even now shelling Sebastopol? How tight was the ring they

— 128 —

would have to slip through? Would they be challenged? Would they be fired upon?

Lammot thought of the tons of powder jammed in the holds below his feet. One shot, one ball crashing hot through splintering hull planks, would be all it would take.

Suddenly he had serious reservations about his Uncle Henry's plan to enrich the firm.

David Craith ached for a smoke. For the past two days he had ordered no lights topside at night, and with their special cargo, no pipes were allowed below decks at any time. All topside smoking was strictly limited to leeward stations. Even the cooking fires in the galley were a constant threat. Thank God for the balmy weather in the Med. The crew had not used heating stoves during the freezing January crossing of the Atlantic.

But the night smoking ban was for other reasons. He was trying to run the Bosporus undetected under cover of darkness. It was a tricky maneuver. He was gambling that all of the French and English vessels would be gathered on the north side of the Black Sea and that night traffic in the Straits would be slim. Even so, the lookouts had been tripled, and his own eyes were burning with the strain of sweeping the cloud-darkened channel ahead.

"There it is, Captain."

He followed Michael Farrell's outstretched arm to a fuzzy outline of the eastern shoreline. He could not be sure. His eyes were not what they used to be, but the boy was probably right. The northern mouth of the Bosporus was dead ahead.

"Thank you, Mr. Farrell," he said. "Lay on all canvas, and quietly, please."

As Michael passed the word, ghostly figures scrambled up the ratlines and spread out along each successive yard, unreefing the shortened sails. As they bellied out, the long hull heeled slightly with the load and slowly accelerated.

Craith slid his binnacle lantern open a crack and brought a fold of chart into the sliver of light. "Steer nor'-nor'east," he said to the helmsman, "to a hair of forty degrees." As the ship eased into a gentle right turn and took up the new course, he watched the canvas above. "Mind the direction of wind, Mr. Farrell. I want to make knots." He handed the chart over and muttered, "Give me four hours in the bunk, no more, and resume normal watch. We'll need our rest for the morrow."

After Craith left the bridge, Lammot walked back to Michael. He could feel some of the tension easing as they raced for the open sea again.

"How long do you think it will be?"

Michael surprised him with an immediate answer. "Twenty hours if the wind holds steady. The Crimean is 300 miles," he pointed directly over the ship's prow. "We've been making a steady fifteen knots, which is considerable for the old lady, trim clipper that she is." He patted the brass hood over the compass.

Lammot put on spectacles and pulled out his watch. "That means we will reach Sebastopol about midnight."

"More or less."

"Hmm. More if we get delayed by shifting winds, eh?"

"Or by a suspicious warship, more likely."

They passed a few minutes in silence, Lammot watching the lightening eastern sky as Michael gave orders for trimming sail and corrections to the helmsman.

"You do this quite well."

"Thank you, Mr. du Pont."

"My first name is Lammot, and I'd really feel more comfortable is we were on a first-name basis."

Michael grinned. "Sorry. Formalities of the trade, I suppose. But then, you *are* the gentleman financing this expedition."

"Like you, Michael, I am only an agent."

"Fair enough. Lammot it will be, at least beyond earshot of Captain Craith."

"I suspect you are quite fond of his vessel, or perhaps proud is the better word."

Michael shrugged. "I suppose. She's not as fast as the others; different keel design. One or two of the newer clippers have marked nineteen knots. The steamers can't make ten, even when they add sail."

He looked to see if Lammot might have lost interest, but he was listening intently.

"She was commissioned from the first as a slaver; that accounts for the strange spacing of the decks."

"I had wondered about that," Lammot commented. "Rather low ceilings down there, but just the right height for barrels."

"Yes. Barrels of molasses, casks of rum, and chained-up blacks. A different cargo for each leg of the voyage. Very efficient."

Lammot mulled that over a bit before adding, "Very profitable, I've heard. But it seems to me like brutal accommodation for living creatures. I must say I do not like the idea of passage on a vessel used for that purpose."

"Oh, you needn't worry on that account. The original owner was bought out by a Philadelphian before the ship was launched. I suppose he wanted to disrupt the slave trade by paying a premium for her."

"That accounts for the name. I presume he was Society of Friends."

"Yes. An abolitionist from the 'city of brotherly love.' And he snaps up a slaver from the Baltimore shipyards." Michael paused to tap the glass cover of the compass in front of the helmsman. The man nodded and took a small correction in his wheel.

"It's ironic when you consider everything."

Lammot looked confused. He removed his spectacles and tucked them away. "You mean naming a Baltimore slave ship after Philadelphia?"

"No. It's how she's being used these days. The Quakers don't exactly approve of war either."

All that day the winds were strong and favorable. Shortly before noon a squall line overtook them, but it was so mild in passing that they barely shortened sail during the blowing rain. Even the expected shift did little more than cause extra work adjusting to a fresh breeze from another quarter. The crew were nearly jubilant with their speed. Making port a week early was a sailor's dream seldom realized.

Then at sunset it collapsed. The power at their backs petered out, and the ship slowed to a wallowing, drunken pace.

"Damn!" Michael grumbled as he watched the square-rigged canvas sag into listless sheets. The weak air barely filled the mainmast skysail, the topgallants alternately tight and slack.

"Run out the logline, please Mr. Farrell."

Michael ran to the reel strung on a stub at the starboard wing of the bridge. He was glad of something to do. This wallowing of the ship gave him an instant dose of dizziness. Years at sea now and he still got sick.

He dropped the line and float overboard, marked the first segment, and began counting seconds when the line drew taut and spooled off the reel. The second marker shot through, the third, the fourth. As he counted twenty-eight seconds, the fifth mark appeared.

"Five knots, sir," he called, and immediately began timing for a second reading.

"Very well, Mr. Farrell. Take readings on the half hour and let me know of any changes. Keep your eyes peeled and mind the rule for darkened ship." With that David Craith went to his bunk and turned in.

When Lammot du Pont came on deck, it was dusk. But even in that light Michael's face looked green. It was a shock.

"Not *mal de mer*, Michael?"

Michael nodded miserably.

Lammot stifled a laugh. "Sorry, old fellow. I did not mean to be insensitive. It's just that I did not expect seasickness in . . ."

"An old salt?"

"Yes."

Michael suddenly hurried to the rail, and Lammot discreetly turned away.

Some time later Michael approached him looking more composed but ghastly in the moonlight.

"Now you know one of the reasons," he grinned crookedly, "why I may not make the sea life my permanent career."

They both laughed at that and Lammot felt some of Farrell's reserve melt away.

During most of that evening they talked of inconsequential things, Lammot sipping cold coffee and Michael nibbling on hardtack to keep his stomach calm. Only once did they discuss the untimely waning breeze.

"Just now a steamer would seem to have the advantage."

"I don't know about that," Michael said. "A boiler room with a hot furnace next to all that powder seems too risky for me."

"Do you think we'll get through before daylight?"

"Not at this rate. We'll just sight the blockade at dawn."

"And every French and English gunner will have a clear shot."

Michael did not comment, but got up again to measure their headway. It had not changed for hours. When he came back, he was excitedly pointing up at the sails.

"We're up to eight! Look at that; it's picking up." He raced down the ladder and rapped on Craith's door.

Some time later the captain assumed the bridge. He eyed the filling canvas, called for another speed measurement, and when it was given, spoke to Michael.

"Shorten sail, Mr. Farrell. Haul back to maintain a steady five knots."

Lammot was just close enough to hear. He could not believe the order. But even as he stammered out the words, he knew that he had overstepped his bounds with David Craith.

"I don't understand, Captain. Do you mean to slow down?"

Craith inclined his head ever so slightly.

"Precisely so, Mr. du Pont."

"But that will position us within range of the armada at daylight. Is that wise? I'm afraid I do not understand!"

"The ignorance you have seen fit to admit twice is duly noted, Mr. du Pont. As to the wisdom of my decisions at sea, there shall be no discussion except at the master's invitation."

Lammot shriveled in the chill of the softly spoken words and fumed at his own impetuousness. Still, there was a rankling at being so put down.

"When we are on dry land, sir. I will invite your opinion of my command over drinks at my table."

Then the Captain turned to Michael and spoke as if the exchange had not ever taken place.

"You're looking well, Number One. Carry on, and keep me posted of anything untoward."

After Craith had vacated the bridge, Lammot followed and went to his own cabin. He was mortified.

Lammot slept soundly through the night. At the ringing of eight bells he awoke thinking it was the midnight end of watch, but a half-hour later when gray light filtered into the cabin, he realized that he had heard the four A.M. signal instead. He bolted from the bunk, dressed, and hurried on deck.

"Ah, there you are, Mr. du Pont."

David Craith was again a fixture on his bridge looking down at Lammot on the weather deck below him.

"A good rest. Wise practice. I suggest a quick breakfast, sir. We will soon be quite busy."

Lammot waved self-consciously and made for the hatchway leading to the galley one deck down. On the way he stole a glance forward into the lifting gloom of the sea ahead. What he saw was enough to kill his appetite. The horizon was a thicket of masts! On the side he could see there must have been twenty vessels, most riding at anchor, a few under sail. They formed a line which bowed to the horizon. Beyond the curving line of ships the smudged skyline of a sprawling seaport rose behind a hooked peninsula of low-lying beach. Sebastopol!

The *Quaker City* cruised easily toward the blockade out of the southeast, making more headway, it seemed to Lammot, although most of her sails were fully reefed. He looked aloft and saw six men strung along each of the three mainsail yards. They were all crouched behind the reefed canvas, out of sight from anything ahead. Something was missing. He could not place it at first, but then Lammot realized that the American flag was not flying.

He heard Craith speak to the helmsman in a moderate voice which carried clearly over the silent ship. "Aye, lad, that's it. Another point to port. I want him to *think* we're sliding by. Another fifteen minutes is all I need!"

The other ships were standing out more clearly as the mists rose from the sea. Behind *Quaker City* the southeastern horizon grew pink with the dawn.

"Broad daylight when they see us, Mr. Farrell. No thief in the night to draw their interest. Better now when they're relaxed, groggy with sleep, thinking only of their morning pee over the side. Ten minutes more!"

"We're gettin' a signal, sir! Starboard quarter, the Englishman, ship o' the line."

Lammot turned with everyone else and saw the distant string of signal flags fluttering from the yard of a squat vessel. Even at three miles, the triple rows of gunports were ominous.

"It's the challenge, Cap'n. Should I run 'em up?"

"Belay that!"

The order was like a pistol shot, and the young signalman ducked beside his flag locker. The halyard trembled in his hand.

"He's too far. We didn't see him. I don't want to be too quick to play our only trump. Send the anchor party forward to make a show of dropping the hook, Mr. Farrell. And be ready for the challenge from the vessels near at hand. That frigate could give us trouble, lying broadside as she is, or one of those sloops with ready sail."

"Challenge from the frigate!"

"Easy, lad. Make it unhurried like the merchantman we are. Now! Two-block the signal flags."

The light pulley of the signal halyard fairly sang as the frightened sailor ran it up.

Lammot watched breathless as they angled closer to the broad frigate. They were a quarter-mile from the double row of gunports, still closed. As they inched past, the firing ports slipped out of sight one by one sternmost behind the curve of the gunship's beamy hull. He saw the challenge flags dip, and suddenly a new set flashed up. They were close enough to make out men on deck.

"It's an order to stop, Mr. Farrell. Well, we can't have that, now can we. Let me see. Time to improvise. Strike the counter-sign, signalman, and run up our standard seventeen."

"*Seventeen*, Cap'n?"

"Aye, lad, signal seventeen. Then follow with number five and twelve."

"Five and twelve, sir."

"Aye, now execute."

The poor signalman was a flurry of arms as he attached the flags and ran the three strings up, one after the other.

There was a sudden burst of activity on the deck of the frigate, and Lammot could see the heavy cannon ports swing open just as they ran under her bows.

"Now Mr. Farrell, give me full canvas please! Helm, hard to port. No more playing buccaneer. Run up the ensign. Maybe the red, white, and blue will worry them a few minutes."

The ship heeled over violently in response to rudder and sail as all three masts blossomed with thundering canvas. In seconds each panel dropped followed by crewmen on handlines sliding to the next yard in sequence unreefing canvas as they nearly plummeted to the weatherdeck.

"Oh, Mr. du Pont! Might I have a word with ye?"

Lammot was dazed with all the activity. Michael sprinted past on his way forward. "I think he means you, Lammot," he panted. Lammot wondered if their lives were being measured in seconds. He found the steps to the bridge and mounted them mechanically.

"Thank you, Mr. du Pont. You might as well view things from up here. It's as safe as any place on the ship. The real problem is below decks, you see."

Lammot nodded, his mouth terribly dry, and he stole a look astern at the retreating shape of the frigate's prow.

"I'm gambling that their bow gun will miss," Craith said as though he were discussing the placing of a wager. "At anchor she can't swing and bring her beam to bear." He pointed to a sloop off to port piling on sail. "That one could be a problem."

As he spoke a geyser erupted behind them twenty yards left of their wake.

"Hmm. Short range and wide of the mark. A four-pounder at that. No worry there." He turned back to Lammot. "Now this is my plan, Mr. du Pont. But before I carry it out, I will need some guarantees from you or, more properly, from the company you represent."

Lammot was amazed. As David Craith kept one eye on the advancing angry sloop o'war and gave occasional corrections to the helmsman, he drew out a tide table, a chart of Sebastopol harbor and, most startling of all, an agreement to be signed by Lammot authorizing payment of loss by du Pont should his ship be damaged or destroyed!

"You can't be serious."

"But indeed I am."

"My God, Captain. If the vessel is struck, none of us will be left, much less that document."

"I don't plan on allowing my vessel to be holed by cannon shot, Mr. du Pont. However, in order to avoid that, it will be necessary to run her on the beach. At full speed we have a good chance of outrunning that fellow," he jerked his head indicating the converging sloop. "But to do it and come under the protection of the Russian guns, I'll be on the beach before the shore batteries can run him off."

Lammot was fumbling for his glasses, nodding dazedly throughout the explanation, trying to read the document he already knew he was going to sign.

"Now, I've studied the tables and chart carefully, and since we've timed it pretty well, we should run aground at extreme low tide. That will make it easier to refloat my vessel at high water, especially when she's free of cargo."

"And rocks?" Lammot croaked. He was beginning to think Craith was mad.

"Aye, there's always a chance. But its a sandy spit, I hear tell. I wouldn't trouble yourself on that score."

"It doesn't matter anyway, does it? We're between their cannon and the Russian rocks."

Craith seemed to study the idea as he fussed with the helmsman over a minute change in heading.

"Y'might put it that way, Mr. du Pont. Yes. A bit fatalistic, you know, but accurately put all the same."

At that moment Lammot heard a rolling, splitting sound like a peal of thunder. He looked up for black clouds, but the sky was clear. Above he heard a loud plop and noticed a rip in the main skysail. Then there was a tremendous splash to starboard and a dull thump to port.

"Hmm. Thirty-two pounder and he has our deflection. Hard to starboard, helm. We'll give him a small target." For the first time that morning, Captain Craith appeared to be genuinely concerned. He gripped Lammot's shoulder. "Better sign that, Mr. du Pont," he urged, "We're heading for the beach."

CHAPTER SEVENTEEN

David Craith squinted toward the port still three miles away. The pursuing sloop was much closer, a thousand yards off his port quarter and closing. There was no question that the light warship would overhaul the *Quaker City* given enough time. It became a game of timing and seamanship. In order for her to bring heavier guns to bear, the sloop had to turn beam-on to give her gunners a shot. Each time she did, she lost headway in the chase. Craith had a similar problem. The long hull of his ship was best protected by presenting the stern as a smaller target. Unfortunately, to steer continuously in that direction would carry them too far south to intercept the sheltered side of a long peninsula hooked under the harbor—and the protecting guns of Sebastopol.

So Craith had to cheat in his hightailed escape, occasionally presenting his port side for long, agonizing minutes as he raced northward toward the harbor. Each time he did this, the sloop immediately swung broadside to loose a volley. Not all of the guns really had a clear shot, but they thundered shot anyway.

Craith snorted with disgust after one of these displays, which he avoided by beginning his turn a few seconds ahead of the cannonade. The volley struck harmlessly in the sea a hundred yards abeam. With his glass he made out the ship's colors.

"I might have expected. A Frenchman."

He had to swallow some of that derision moments later when a single shot hummed directly over their centerline, punched through the topsails, and splintered the foremast yard, showering the bows with litter.

Craith looked astern and saw a second ship after them, a corvette, probably British. As he watched, a puff of smoke belched from her bows.

"Hard over port!"

This was dangerous. Now his steering was a matter of the enemy's choice. The ball crashed into the sea close enough to spray the starboard rail. Craith jerked his head around to the sloop. As he thought, she was angling toward the peninsula, trying to cut them off now that another gunner was on their tail.

He had to gamble. Or give up. It might even be too late for that. A white flag might be ignored by frustrated gun crews or even their masters.

Lammot was standing at his elbow. Craith looked him in the eye but said nothing. It was du Pont's cargo, after all.

Perhaps it was ignorance, perhaps bravado, but the tall youngster preempted the unasked question.

"Here's your guarantee, Captain," he said, soberly handing over the paper. "I had to sign it with pencil."

"Very well, we're in for a race. A little more to port, if you please, helmsman."

They were naked to the sloop's guns now, and as they headed closer to the point, both ships converged beams-on. Craith watched the other vessel, his senses tuned to guessing when the first broadside would erupt. Each minute gave the Frenchman reduced range.

Suddenly Craith called for full left rudder, and the clipper heeled into a course directly toward the sloop. Almost on cue the entire starboard battery blossomed in black smoke that blotted the sloop from sight. Lammot watched fascinated as the line of their original course exploded in a towering cascade of spray.

"Hard to starboard!"

How long to reload? A minute? Less? The seconds rushed by, and the French were so close now they could see the guns being run back into the ports. Lammot was sure he could see a gunner's arm holding his glowing matchcord. This time they could not miss. Somewhere forward he heard a crewman moan. The sloop's commander knew. Perhaps that was why he was holding off till the last second, just when his target would be at close range. Lammot wondered idly if the blast would be great enough to damage the French ship.

When it came, the roar of approaching shells was deafening, and even Craith flinched. Most of the men above decks flattened themselves on the teak planks, so only a few got to see the sloop battered by the Russian shore guns. In one volley she took three direct hits. It was a minor achievement that she had enough sail left to break off the attack and scuttle to safety out of range.

The *Quaker City* roared with cheering for a wild three minutes. It was cut off quickly though, and nearly everybody got a bruising in the tumbling when their clipper shuddered to a halt on the beach of Sebastopol.

David Craith was furious. In the excitement nobody remembered to chop the shrouds, so they hit with full sail. The mizzen took a terrible strain and would have to be restepped. With all the cheering Russians swarming over them, it was hard to be upset, though, even by dark looks from the captain.

It was Lammot who finally forced a smile out of the Old Man, and he didn't have to say a word. All he did was shake his hand.

The Russian commander gave a huge party for the entire crew, proclaiming them all heroes. Lammot was guest of honor with the captain and his first mate at the head table. There was much singing, dancing, and prodigious drinking of potato liquor by the Russian troops and American sailors. The host provided wine and brandy for his special guests, and the conversation was in French, the language of the Russian aristocracy.

During the celebration, Lammot politely asked the Russian when he would like to arrange a meeting to pay for the shipment. When the commandant expressed surprise at the request, Lammot became confused. His grasp of French was limited to the little he had learned as a third-generation descendant, and Michael had to interpret occasionally, an asset acquired at Trinity. The exchange became awkward, and the general surprised them by shifting to English. His accent was strong, but the meaning clear.

"Oh, but that has already been paid. Did you not know of the arrangement? We had to pay your director in cash the day you sailed from America. He has the money, and," he smiled happily, "we have the powder."

Lammot was ready to protest. He was beginning to distrust the ebullient officer, who was loud and a bit the worse for brandy. It was all the more startling, therefore, when he showed Lammot an agreement dated a month before the powder left the Brandywine. There was no question about the signature.

It was signed by Henry du Pont.

Freeing the ship from the sandy grip of the beach turned out to be no problem at all. Once the weight of a quarter-million pounds of powder was lifted from her holds, the long hull rose gracefully with the flood tide.

That event took place the evening of their second day. Lammot and Michael had returned from an escorted tour of the city to change for yet another night of Russian partying. David Craith met them at the gangway as soon as they stepped out of the shore boat.

"We'll be taking the morning tide."

"So quickly?" Lammot was surprised. "I thought there would be repairs."

"We'll do that under way. It's nothing we can't manage in fair weather. The hull is sound."

Michael caught something else in the captain's manner.

"Is there news of anything, Captain?"

"Just a rumor. The French and English plan to start their bombardment in a matter of days."

Getting the crew rounded up took most of the night, but by dawn the ship had her full complement, although a few would probably not recall much of their leavetaking. With the exception of those stunned with vodka, the delicate matter of crossing the blockade was on everybody's mind.

After they had been towed into deep water and were under way, Craith spoke to Lammot.

"From now until we get past the line, Mr. du Pont, your name is Peter Mott, steward and cabin boy. I'd rather have put you with the deckhands to give you a proper workout, but you haven't the hands. You'd be spotted in a minute."

"What earthly reason . . ."

Craith sighed and gave Michael a look of exasperation. "He does not grasp the idea that a du Pont on board might raise a few eyebrows."

"Oh," Lammot gulped.

"Get him some proper gear, Michael. The carpenter is about his size. No cabin slave of mine is to parade in gentleman's duds."

When they came around the point and into sight of the warships, there was no mistaking two things: the bombardment was about to commence and they were the first target of opportunity. The ships with heavier cannons had closed range on Sebastopol, preparing to bombard the city by turn and then sail beyond reach of the Russian guns. Three sloops and a steam gunboat quickly encircled the *Quaker City* as she sailed brazenly into the heart of the formation and hove to.

"Tell 'em I want to talk to their commander on my deck," Craith told his signalman. He ignored the string of flags moving up and down a nearby frigate's mast. All her guns were run out, he noted, every muzzle bearing on him.

It was an interesting conference. David Craith raged at the French contingent which quickly boarded, led—as he had expected—by a junior officer. From their position near the wheel, Michael and Lammot found it hard to keep straight faces. The Old Man did not let up for a minute. He thrust shipping papers, fictitious certainly, under their noses, he pointed to the damaged sails and canted mizzenmast, his eyes bulged, and his words snapped out at a rate the interpreter could barely keep up with.

"Certainly, we used your countersign! I have all the signals"—brandishing the list—"what kind of foolish master do you think I am to pass by a blockade without authority?"

"But you did not pass, monsieur le capitaine, you *penetrated*."

" 'Penetrated'! Why, dammit, sir, your blasted cannon *drove* me through! And ran me aground at the mercy of those thieving, barbaric Russians, who thanks to you robbed me of a whole cargo of provisions meant for this flotilla!"

"We think otherwise."

"Well, bear this back to your skipper, mate," Craith growled. "I'll not stand the loss, not one penny. The British Admiralty will hear from my company. Loss of a shipload of salt pork, hardtack, cordage, and damage to my vessel."

"We think it was munitions, monsieur."

Craith looked astounded. "Munitions? You must be daft, man, in a Quaker ship?"

They did not believe any of it, of course, and in the end a signal from the frigate called the inspection party back. The evidence was gone, and the great bombardment was being held up. The frigate signaled *Quaker City* to proceed.

By midafternoon the last outline of the city had dipped below the horizon astern, and later a greasy smudge lazed up over the spot marking the bombardment. Still later, as the last of the rosy sunset faded off their starboard bow, Michael and Lammot stood on the fantail deck watching an angry red glow spread in the sky above Sebastopol. There was no sound at this distance, but occasionally a brighter mushroom of fire sprouted like an aborted northern sunrise.

"I wonder if any of that is return fire," Lammot said. "I can think of a particular sloop I hope gets it."

"I have no such wish," Michael said quietly.

Lammot glanced sideways, his face suffused with excitement and the faint red glow. Their elbows nearly touched as they leaned against the taffrail.

"That's surprising. Two days ago you risked perdition running from her guns."

"Perdition," Michael repeated thoughtfully. "That's a good word for it, I'm thinking."

Lammot ignored the slanted rebuff. "I feel a measure of satisfaction in pulling it off."

"The whole business is tragic, if you ask me. All that grief over which church controls Jerusalem." He grunted derisively. "Another war for the Holy Lands."

"Oh, come now, Michael. That's hardly the cause, and though I'll grant the outcome might mean a minor switch in church rule, I find it ludicrous to mount a military campaign over the issue."

"Another choice word."

"Really! Both churches are Christian, after all. Eastern Orthodox and Roman, why, they're both *Catholic*, for heaven's sake."

Michael was tempted but bit back the obvious jibe. "What's the grand and compelling reason, then? Do you think the English and French lust so for the lovely Crimea?"

Lammot backed off lamely. "I really do not know the reasons, but I find it incredible that modern statesmen would suffer the immorality of war for the mere protection of a religious shrine."

Michael arched an eyebrow. "You sound like a righteous debater. Does the University of Pennsylvania concentrate on forensics as well as science?"

Lammot's mouth twisted into a grin. "All right. Let's just say I don't know and leave it at that."

"Complete honesty, eh? For what it's worth, neither do I."

They enjoyed a laugh at their own expense. But Lammot probed again. "I think you do not approve of the sale."

"Oh, it's not my business to pass judgment. I just take no pride in it, is all."

"Pride is a bit much to claim, but I'm happy to have given those poor devils powder to defend themselves with."

"Most of the powder on the ships they oppose came from the same mills." Michael almost said, "your mills," but held back from that temptation. Lammot was stung enough as it was.

"Oh, come now, there are a dozen firms eager to have the business. You know that others would fill the need if we declined."

"Certainly. In due course."

"They chose us for quality, price, and prompt delivery."

"And a certain flair for dash," Michael injected wryly.

"The du Pont mills have always delivered as promised."

"I'm not so naive that I believe the bombardment would not have been fed by others. But this particular shipment . . . nobody else could have done it in time."

"Exactly. So we've made the contest fair, at least."

"No, the Russians are going to lose in the long run anyway. If we had missed delivery, they might have surrendered without a fight."

"Hardly in their best interests."

"Perhaps, but think of all the ordinary folk who would have survived."

"Survival and subjugation," Lammot countered, but even he thought it sounded simplistic and a trifle pompous. "Say, what in the world were those other flag signals? Seventeen and five? I can't remember which."

Michael roused the vestige of a smile. "A little joke of the captain's to confuse things and gain time."

"What did they mean?"

"Let's see, 'Master's compliments, please join me for dinner,' and 'Plague aboard.' "

Lammot laughed. "Well, the crusty old fellow has humor."

"He has his moments, but he's a tough old bird. By the way, he gave you a compliment yesterday. 'Very cool for a lubber,' were his words, I believe. He mentioned the guarantee he forced on you."

"I'll stand behind it. I thought it a bit extraordinary at the time, but he's within his rights."

"What was the problem between you and the Russian?"

Lammot's face hardened as he explained the lie his uncle had used to induce him to make the voyage. As he listened, Michael looked puzzled.

"What would he gain by that?"

"That's what I'd like to know."

"He was the one who kicked me out of the mills, you know."

"Uncle Henry?"

"It was comical in a way. I punched him in a brawl."

"Uncle *Henry*?"

"Before I got the job I was nursing my ale in a tavern, and some girl offered her company. Well, I was a bit unpracticed at that sort of thing and not too happy anyway, so I turned her down. She set up a wail, and I bought her a drink to make amends. About the time she was pushing close, a burly redhead came over and started to rough her up. I popped him one, and the next thing I knew, half the tavern had me on the floor holding me down."

"You punched him!" Lammot was awestruck.

"After he left and they let me up, they told me who he was. Apparently the woman nuzzling me was Henry du Pont's favorite slut."

At the word Lammot drew back as if stung. The reaction amused Michael. Did Lammot think his uncle above gamy pursuits?

"Well, he spotted me in the payline after I'd started work in the yards and fired me directly."

It was full dark now, the sea glittering hammered silver under a quarter moon. Lammot leaned heavily on the smooth railing and studied the purling phosphorescence in their wake. The sullen red over Sebastopol had nearly disappeared.

"And from there you went with the army to Mexico?"

Michael nodded and looked away. Then he began telling Lammot of his terrible experience fighting that war. It was a flat, dispirited report, a confession that exacted its own pennance in the telling. But Lammot was awed by his experience and daring. He made a decision then and there. Michael Farrell and Lammot du Pont would be working together very closely from now on.

CHAPTER EIGHTEEN

Thee must realize, Noreen Gallagher, that it is not wise to be seen in my home. This place is watched by day and night."

"I know that, Mr. Garrett, but there is a limit to my patience, truly. All these years keeping silent."

"I would that thee call me Thomas, my good woman. It may seem strange—a bit old-fashioned even among Friends—but we are averse to titles."

Noreen shrugged, anything to humor the man.

"The point is, Thomas Garrett, that you must push Tim out of this slave business. It is unfair to his children to have grown with a shadow for a father. Besides, he's getting on for runnin' pell-mell through black nights with one or another Southern constable at his heels." She paused, wishing she could get it all out without that nervous sound in her voice. "Besides that, I'm his sister and a shaking wretch with the wondering if next time he'll come home in a box."

Her outburst engulfed him, and he sat back with neck arched in surprise. Over the years he had assumed Noreen Gallagher, whom he had never met personally but knew about through her brother, was a willing and silent supporter of the Underground Railway. It appeared as though her cooperation had come in spite of strong negative personal feeling. It was well that her demand was timely.

Her eyes were snapping, an anger there partly to stiffen her sagging composure, partly because she *was* angry at this abolitionist who had helped disrupt their lives.

"Thy trial is at an end, Noreen, just as mine begins again."

"You mean you'll make him stop?"

Garrett nodded.

Her face began to crumple, but he saved her the loss of composure.

"Not out of a sense of thy need, thee must understand that. Thy brother is too well-known these days to be of value to the organization. A message has been sent releasing him from service."

She absorbed that with a tight smile. "Sounds like the dropping of a worn-out shoe to me."

He shrugged off the remark. "Our passengers are precious cargo, Noreen, fragile and vulnerable. There are odds in the gamble that are reasonable, and some that are not."

"Mother Mary, don't get the idea I'm not overjoyed that y're dumpin' him! It just seemed so cut and dried. But I thank God his children will see some of their father before they're man and woman themselves."

Garrett's face tightened into a mask of control. There was understanding there, and kindness, too; she could see that. But he could be hard.

"Small sacrifice, good woman. I celebrate thy pain and theirs for the harvest it has brought. A thousand or more he saved from lives so dismal thee cannot imagine. A thousand! I tell thee, thy brother was their savior."

But Noreen had spent the last decade and a half soul-searching over that argument. She still preferred the father with his children, her brother safe at home. This Garrett fellow might be redeemer of the whole human race for all she cared. Keeping one family was hard enough for her. She had only one more question for the famous Thomas Garrett.

"When can I expect him home?"

The homecoming for Lammot du Pont was low-keyed to the point of anguish. Since the mission Henry had sent him on was secret, he was forced to spend the first few days fabricating a whole series of activities in New York which never took place. The role rankled him more than it might have under other circumstances. Lammot was by nature fascinated with intrigue, and although fabrication did not come easily to him, the humor of fictionalizing adventure might have been an excitement in itself. Of course, the *real* thing made his cover stories pale in comparison, but that was not the source of his gall.

It was the double cross Henry had laid on him that was infuriating, and when his uncle delayed their private tête-à-tête for nearly a week, Lammot was all the more unstrung at being held at arm's length. It was the first point of contention he brought up after Henry greeted him soberly, offered him a cigar, and inquired about his health.

"The trip did you good, Lammot. Good color and a bit thicker of arm, I'd say. Too bad Irénée couldn't go on an excursion like that; he's as frail as Alfred these days."

"I really do not appreciate being put off . . ."

"Yes. Well, it couldn't be helped, the place has been so Goddamned busy. Sit down, sit down. I've been eager to hear your report, of course. A neat bit of work."

The compliment was not showing in Henry's eyes, though, and Lammot lost some of his steam under the frosty stare. He wished vaguely that he could have said what was on his mind while they were still standing. He had an inch or two on his uncle, and the advantage would have helped. Folded as he was into the spindly chair reserved for office visitors, Lammot felt awkward—a gangly target of those hard eyes.

"Why in the world did you send me all the way to Russia on a fool's errand?" A poor choice of words. Henry could make anyone seem the fool without help. Already this was going badly!

His uncle's face darkened. "What gives you that idea?"

"The payment. I was shown the agreement you signed with the Russians."

"Oh, Christ, *that* thing. You don't mean to tell me you think I would have any faith in that?" Henry's face cracked into a grin, but the eyes were not smiling.

"The Russians apparently did. You were paid cash the hour we weighed anchor in the Delaware."

"Certainly. I would have raised particular hell if they hadn't." The smile retracted mechanically.

"Then you did expect payment on sailing." Lammot was becoming confused. He expected denials.

"I would have overhauled your ship and brought her back if they had been short a penny."

He couldn't stand the chair another minute. Lammot got up and towered over the desk. He was beginning to tremble, biting his lip for control.

"Then why send *me*?"

Henry leaned back and luxuriated in a long puff at his cigar. His free hand fell to the head of one of three greyhounds sprawled around his chair, and he scratched the dog behind the ears.

"Insurance."

When Lammot stared dumbly, he added, "I told them that you were aboard as guarantor."

Lammot stammered, "You could have made Captain Craith, anyone, guarantor. For that matter you could even have lied. They would not have known the difference."

At the word "lie" Henry's brows rose ominously. He leaned forward to roll the ash off his cigar into a brass dish. "A weakling lies to protect himself from stronger enemies. I have never felt the need."

Lammot twisted from his uncle's withering stare and retreated a few paces. Turning again to face him, he choked, "Then why didn't you tell me everything?"

"You didn't need to know, Lammot. You knew just enough to behave convincingly. Any more information would have colored your performance." He let that sink in and added, "You see, I know that falsehood does not come easily to you, either."

It sounded plausible. There was something misaligned, but Lammot could not muster the wit to spear it. He finally nodded.

"And as I started to say before all this fluster of yours, your courage and resourceful handling of the blockade are particularly noted. It is too bad that the nature of the transaction makes it confidential." Henry narrowed his eyes slightly, waiting for Lammot's nod. When it came he clipped the discussion closed. "As a prospective director of du Pont you can grasp the delicacy of these kinds of necessary moves."

Before Lammot left he did manage to salvage part of his reason for meeting Henry. He got an endorsement for hiring Tim Feeney back in the wagon shop and Michael Farrell as his assistant in the laboratory. That was significant because policy forbade rehiring any du Pont worker who had left the yards for any reason. It was a touchy industry, and ex-employees were apt to get the bit in their teeth.

Michael Farrell's case was especially satisfying, because Lammot played his cards straight to avoid a later confrontation.

"It's a minor issue, Uncle Henry, probably one you've forgotten. Farrell was in his cups some years ago, and apparently you had to flatten him with a punch in a dining room in town. As I've explained, he is quite well-educated, an extremely loyal sort, and with his university training he could be a decided asset in our research."

Henry mulled it over for some time before he ground out his cheroot and rose with his dogs to leave.

"All right, he's on the payroll, too. But keep him with you, and make sure he behaves. One hint of trouble from him—or because of him—and he's out on his ass. Permanently."

"It's really a foolish idea. The water is so muddy."

Noreen smiled up at Michael, shrugged, and walked to the end of the porch to a weak puddle of April sun. "It doesn't matter that you get a fish. She needs a friend to talk to, is all." She rubbed her arms as though bathing in the lemon light, the pale cotton sleeves of her dress warmed by the sun. "Oh, this feels good! After two months of snow and rain, we all feel gray as potato shoots, and Megan more than the rest, surely."

"I'm sorry Denis can't come."

"Yes, well, he has some business with Father Francis. The two of them are thick as fleas these days." She purred a laugh.

"Now that's a pair. An old man in his sixties and a lad of fourteen."

"He seems withdrawn a bit, not the old Denis at all."

"Well, he is growing up, y'know. Some boys go through the doltish stage in odd ways. I'm glad he spends the time with the priest, a help to him. Most lads would fear ridicule for their kindness."

"Megan is her old self. I don't think she has changed much in the eight years I've known them. Her mood, I mean." He grimaced. "Do you realize how old that makes me feel? I'll soon be twenty-five."

"God in Heaven, old at twenty-five! Y'should bite your tongue, Michael Farrell."

He shrugged, feeling foolish under her glance. He really did feel older, though it had nothing to do with the growing children. There was a part of him that would be forever old, dried-up old, layers of disenchantment locked deep in some cauterized parcel of his brain.

He looked at Noreen and decided in that moment that he loved her much like his own mother. They would have been the same age, though not of the same temperament, and they each had been through trials enough. He probably *liked* Noreen Gallagher more. She was more perceptive, or seemed so. Besides that she had managed to keep something his mother lost—a sense of humor. "I'm a good one to think of that," he thought, "as morose as I am."

"Well, leave then, y'stingy dot, but see you come back to-morrow."

He thought she was talking to him, but she was taking a parting shot at the sun slipping behind the wooded hill behind the house. It was only two in the afternoon, but spring twilights were long in the deep shadows of the Brandywine Gorge. She called into the house, "Megan, is it next week y'plan to go fishing?"

When Megan finally came out lugging a willow pole and wicker basket, she was all business.

"Let's go," she said, marching down the steps and through the gate leading to Crick Road. "I'm catching a big one today."

Michael grinned and winked at Noreen. "A big stump or water-logged branch is what she means, I hope."

"Look at her; she looks like a willow herself," Noreen smiled. "Tall and thin as a stick. She gets that from the Feeney side. Ah, I hope she doesn't shoot up so tall she outgrows her suitors."

"Come *on*, Michael!" Megan piped from the road. Her cotton skirts whipped around long, bony legs as she strode purposefully toward the Crick. Long coppery braids swung rhythmically behind her back, and she seemed unaware of the yellow muck of the roadway rising with each step nearly to the buttons of her ankle-high shoes.

Michael shook his head. "No fear of that, Noreen. No man she sets her sights on will be able to resist. That one will have whom she pleases."

As Michael had predicted, fishing was really out of the question. He made the attempt, but most of the time it was a matter of unsnarling lines from floating debris in the syrupy brown flood that did not whiten even in the crashing turbulence of the dam. Several times he suggested that they give up and try another day after the water cleared.

"They can't see each other, much less our bait," he grumped, pulling in another muddy branch and carefully unwinding the fouled line.

"I'm going to get a shad," Megan said, nodding sharply in self-support. "And he'll be a big one!"

"I tell you, Meggie, he'll never see the meal you're tempting him with. Besides, it may not even be the season for their spawning."

"Oh, it's the season, all right. I asked Uncle Brendan." Her eyes narrowed as she cast again into the swollen floodwater and watched the bobber race downstream with the current. Michael grunted resignedly, wound up his own line, and propped the pole against a tree. He might as well just watch her until she tired.

She didn't miss the action and shot him an impatient look. "You don't have much faith, do you, Michael? I think you give up too easily."

When he did not answer, she went on. "I have a secret that nobody in the family knows but me."

Still no answer.

"Do you know why Denis spends so much time with Father Francis?"

"Your mother thinks it's generous of him to give the old fellow company."

Megan laughed and cast her line again. "That's what everybody thinks. But it's more than that."

She let him dangle long enough to get a response.

"More than that, eh?"

"Oh, yes! Much more."

He watched her line sweep downstream and waited. After some time he pulled a stubby pipe from his pocket and began packing it with tobacco. She cast again, a long sweeping shot that made her grunt.

"He's going to be a priest."

"A priest?"

"Yes."

"Little Denny a priest?"

"He and Father Francis have it all worked out." Her eyes widened with the excitement of telling.

Michael frowned. "He seems a bit young to me."

"Well!" she snapped, "He's the same age as me, for heaven's sake!"

"Aye, an old man of fourteen."

"Closer to fifteen!"

He wanted to laugh at that, but her child's face atop a lanky body was so intent that he stifled the reaction. Noreen was right about her being tall. She and Denis were of equal height and build. It was not flattering to the girl.

"Well, there seems to be plenty of time left to think things over. In a year or two."

"Oh, he's made up his mind. Right after we finish at St. Joe's, he's off to the Baltimore seminary."

Michael wondered what Brendan and Noreen would say to that. Abruptly he realized that it was not their place to make the decision, after all. Tim Feeney was living with them now, working in the wagon shop.

"What does your father have to say?"

"Oh, Daddy doesn't know anything. Besides, Aunt Norrie is the one to convince."

"Hmmm."

She laughed. "I know what you mean. Well, Denny and I are leaving that job up to Father Reardon. He can make it sound like God himself whispered the vocation in Denny's ear, which maybe he did, all right, and who are we to make God cross."

"I wish the man luck." From what he knew of Noreen Gallagher, the logic would have to include firmer facts than that.

"And you, of course. You will convince her, too."

"Me?"

"Oh, yes, Michael. That was my idea. I figured it all out. See, you were Denny's age when you went away to Trinity College, and I'll bet your parents didn't mind." She beamed up at him and gave her line a twitch, jerking the distant bobber underwater. "So you're the perfect one to explain it to Aunt Norrie."

He was so stunned by the predicament she had put him in that he did not notice her struggling with the bending pole. Megan ran far up on the bank tugging barehanded on the twine before he saw the fish break water. He ran to help, but she beached the beautiful silver-and-black buck shad before he reached her.

"My God!" he gasped. "It must be fifteen pounds!"

Megan was quite proud as they gathered it up and started home.

"I always get what I'm really after, Michael," she said.

CHAPTER NINETEEN

$\blacklozenge$

Michael buried himself in the new job. It was a refreshing change from the sea to be back again in a setting that seemed almost like his university days. He and Lammot had the company lab virtually to themselves because Henry was stingier funding research than he was anywhere else, and he was already a legend along the Crick for being tightfisted with his money. The sole exceptions were his own entertainment in town and his insatiable appetite for real estate. He was buying up land at such a rate that already he owned more than anyone else in New Castle County.

Lammot's father occasionally dropped in on the two chemists, but he never stayed long. Alfred du Pont was sliding quickly into depression-fed debility, and although his brain was still sharp in things scientific, he rarely demonstrated an interest. Lammot tried to perk him up, prodding for information on studies the old man had left undone, but Alfred gave only sparse answers and would soon leave.

That was fine with Michael. He and Lammot worked well as a team and better when left alone. They would sometimes spend half the night in the place, so intent on one reaction or another that it would be midnight before they even noticed the passing time. It was work without pay for Michael. Unlike Lammot, whose salary as a family employee was fixed, Michael was paid wages equal to a powderman's. Henry had allowed even that grudgingly, claiming that lab work was easy and safe and did not turn a profit.

For the time being Michael did not care particularly. His room and board at the Widow Carey's with five other bachelor employees cost him two weeks' pay, but he had little need for much else. The balance just rode on the company books. Grog-shop entertainment was not his choice since he had no ties with the other workers and frankly sought none. It was his own difference, the social distinction that had been a barrier when he was a child in the old country. It cut him off from the easy familiarity the other Irish enjoyed, a kind of respectful and admiring ostracism. He was one of their own, and looked up to, but never brought in.

The Gallaghers were a different matter. They were almost family. The children, of course, were as close to him as his own blood, the niece and nephew he had been denied with the dying out of his family line. And so his entertainment was limited to a couple of Sundays a month at their table and some sport or other with the kids.

All through spring and into the humid days of midsummer, Lammot and Michael conducted tests on hundreds of compounds related to powdermaking. Much of the work was repetitive sample testing of production-run blasting and propellant powders, but these boring chores were usually completed in the mornings to make room for more interesting experimental projects. One of these was an imperfect formula for compounding blasting powder which Lammot's father had been toying with for years. The goal was to find a substitute for potassium nitrate in the mixture. The prime source of this ingredient was saltpeter from English-controlled India, and since it had been mined there for over three hundred years, the word supply was dwindling and becoming very expensive.

"All right, Michael," Lammot muttered as he poured a quantity of powder from a small mortar into a folded cone of paper. "What proportion is this?"

Michael checked a grimy ledger. "Seventy-two, twelve, sixteen." He riffled the dog-eared pages. "We'll soon need a fresh book. This is combination number two-eighty-six."

Lammot blotted a sweaty cheek with a shirtsleeve already smudged and damp. "Let's give it a try. Get the éprouvette."

Michael picked up a small iron machine which looked vaguely like a sextant, and they walked outside to a clearing in the woods behind the building. Michael hung the device on a post set in the ground and watched as Lammot sifted a measure of his powder into the firing chamber.

"All right," Lammot said. "Fire it off."

Michael struck a match and raised it to the firing pan. The powder flashed and exploded sharply. The sound surprised both men, and they crowded each other trying to read the pressure scale under the indicator needle.

Lammot pulled out his glasses. "Is that what I think it is?"

"I think you've hit the mark!" Michael grinned. "Almost the same strength as potash powder."

They tried the test again and again, but the results were the same. They had found a combination which was as powerful as saltpeter-based powder using sodium nitrate as a substitute.

Later they celebrated in the lab with a bottle of wine that Lammot filched from Henry du Pont's cellar.

"So it was not just finding the correct proportions after all. Coating the grains with graphite is just as important. It prevents the soda salts from absorbing moisture."

Michael listened as Lammot rattled on, excitedly chattering about their triumph. The details were superfluous to him. After months on the project he knew almost as much as Lammot about the subject.

"Think what this can do for the blasting powder market!" Lammot swirled his wine in the tumbler and took a quick swallow. "Potassium nitrate must cost four times as much as the sodium, and it's seventy percent of the powder compound. We could underprice anybody making blasting powder!"

"For how long? The others will jump in soon enough."

"We'll patent it! Look, Michael, it's a new process—a new ingredient. My gosh, nobody has changed the basic formula for hundreds of years. If the competition wants to make it, they'll have to pay us for the license."

"Suppose the supply of sodium nitrate drops and the price rises, too."

"I haven't told you this yet, Michael, but I've done some research. There's a bed of this salt on the coast of Peru. A huge supply."

"Just how much?"

Lammot's eyes twinkled. "Inexhaustible," he said and drained his glass with a flourish. "The strip is two hundred miles long!"

Henry du Pont was not one to give in to enthusiasm. When Lammot burst in on him with the news, he was skeptical. Even when he observed the tests, the most he would offer was a grudging admission that the new powder did match the strength of their standard blasting explosive. Beyond that, he asked for the data and said he would think about it.

Another month went by before Lammot was called back to the office to speak about his "soda powder," as he and Michael had begun calling it. The frustration of sitting on his discovery was almost too much for him but, with the exception of his father, he mentioned it to nobody else. He was drained of exuberance when Henry's summons came and was well along into a sulk.

"We're going to make the new blasting powder, Lammot."

It was a bit of an anticlimax, especially when put so matter-of-factly, but Lammot perked up at the news.

"I want you to work out production details with Alexis—make any changes in the processing you need to. Alexis will gradually let your brother handle the new compound. Do you think Irénée is strong enough to run the project?"

Lammot was not sure just how his brother's health might slow him down, but he could not hint of that to Henry.

"Certainly. Irénée will be fine."

"Good. You might as well get together with Alexis right away. I want to begin as soon as the sodium nitrate shipment arrives."

Lammot started to speak, but Henry kept talking.

"And I want you to clear up your work as soon as you can. There's another job for you to do."

"Excuse me, Uncle Henry, but do you think it wise to start production before I protect the formula?"

"The patent?"

"Yes, I—"

"It's already filed. Here." Pulling some papers from his desk drawer, he slid them across to Lammot.

Lammot's eyes raced over the sheets, his face paling. "You filed for a patent on *my* formula?" His voice trembled. "It is properly my father's idea. His and mine."

Henry leaned back in his chair, his eyes never wavering. "It is a process patented as property of the family business. You should not forget, Lammot, that any profitable work you do for the company generates company-owned profit."

"But this is a personal creation. My own idea."

"For which you are compensated with a salary and shares in the profits of the du Pont enterprise."

Lammot stared back. He could not speak.

"We are all in this together, Lammot." Henry's voice had taken on a gravelly softness. "Naturally I had the patent drawn in your name. You are certainly entitled to the honor. But as to the ownership? Why, man, if we operated like that, every paddy in the yards could claim a dozen kegs of powder to sell as his own at the end of a shift. After all, they make the stuff."

Lammot knew it was not the same, but to argue was pointless. He was not quite sure how to point up the distinction anyway. Billing the family business for use of the patent never entered his head.

"You have a new project for me," he said dully.

"Yes," Henry rolled on as though the unpleasantness had never happened, "I want you and Farrell to leave for California. Scout the opposition. There's talk of a railroad through the mountains, and the gold and silver mining uses powder by the ton. We need to get our toe in the door."

The proposal shot adrenaline through Lammot, and he forgot the issue of copyright in a wave of excitement. The Barbary Coast. Lammot did not notice the glint of satisfaction in Henry's frosty eyes.

"When shall we leave?"

"Better plan on no more than a couple of weeks."

Lammot's mind was buzzing. It was midsummer. He wondered how far west the railroad reached, what routes the overland stage used.

"Yes. The sooner the better," he mused, only half aware of his uncle. "The snows come early in the western mountains."

"You won't be going that way," Henry said. "At least not on the way out. I want you to book passage on a clipper around the Horn."

The thought of another sea voyage dampened his enthusiasm, and he objected mildly. "Won't that take too long? Why not have us travel light and fast?"

"Two reasons, and the time may not be much different. The faster ships make it in under a hundred days. Besides, you'll be delivering a shipload of powder to San Francisco, something to start business with."

Lammot nodded; he hadn't thought of that. Still, there was no need for him to travel with the powder.

"What's the other reason?"

Henry got to his feet and looked down at his nephew, a signal that the meeting was over. "I want you to stop off in Peru," he rumbled. "We need to tie up leases on all that nitrate."

Lammot grinned and stood up. "Before anybody else can?"

"Exactly."

Lammot studied his mother with a detached objectivity that belied the awkwardness he always felt on being alone with her. Usually he was out of the house or in his room when she was up except for mealtimes. He wondered if she had any idea of the source of his estrangement from her. She looked younger than forty-seven, partly because of her dyed hair and a trim figure maintained by fierce dieting. Compared to his father, she could easily have been taken for the daughter, not the wife.

He wondered if she was still meeting Henry, wondered if his uncle was the inspiration of her battle to preserve an appearance of youth. As much as the thought disgusted him, Lammot was fascinated by the intrigue the two of them had built under the noses of all the family. Perhaps others knew of their affair. With aunts and uncles and a dozen cousins clustered on both sides of the Brandywine, it would have been difficult to maintain a liaison for very long without a slipup. And the servants—surely old Blanche or one of the other household staff must have had suspicions.

"Your father is quite proud of what you have done," she was saying. Was that a nervous lilt in her voice? Did she suspect his knowing? Her hand, resting between them on the velvet cushion of the sofa, fluttered nervously over the fabric, alternately roughing and smoothing the blue nap. "Your 'soda powder' invention, I mean."

"It's Dad's invention," he cut in defensively.

She appeared not to notice the cold edge in his voice, or perhaps it did not come out as harshly as he felt it himself. "Little seems to interest him these days, but when you or Irénée master a problem, it gives him strength."

Her fragrance of lilac water drifted faintly on the air he breathed, and she made a little business of brushing lint from his sleeve before lightly covering his hand with her own. It was warm and soft and not at all moist in the clammy heat of the August afternoon.

"Your uncle Henry is quite taken with you, too. This trip to California is a great responsibility. I think he has plans for your future."

Mention of the man made him want to recoil from her touch, and he had to fight off lurid images of *their* touching, the softness and warmth of her palm detestable now on the back of his hand. He endured the contact a moment longer and then rose to pace the room, feigning an agitation about his trip and not with her.

"It is a bit awkward to leave the lab in the middle of things. But it is an important job, I suppose." He was tossing out the words without plan, a distraction to cover his feelings. "I was surprised that Irénée was not chosen; after all, he is a junior partner and seems better suited to sales organization."

"Your brother is not strong enough, I'm afraid. We look to you, Lammot," Meta said almost in a whisper, "to carry the responsibility for our side of the family."

"Well . . ."

"And Henry, I know, is grooming you for eventual leadership of the firm."

It was at once flattering and humiliating. So she *knew*, did she? And just how, he wondered, had she become so privy to Uncle Henry's plans? Had there been unthinkable concessions on his behalf? He had to get out of the room.

"I have work in the yards with Uncle Alexis," he said, and left.

"Well, it's all decided," Megan announced, climbing up the steep backyard of the Gallagher house toward Michael, who was tossing bits of corn into the chicken pen and watching the hens scramble for it. "He's off to the seminary next month."

"I'm not surprised, Meggie."

"No? Well, I am, and that's a fact." She frowned at him and crossed her arms. "You were no help at all, Michael Farrell. I thought you would do your best to convince Aunt Noreen. In the end it had to be Denis to do it alone."

"And you, I imagine."

"And me, naturally. I wouldn't be the one to let him down."

Michael nearly chuckled at her seriousness and her attack on his disloyalty.

"That is as it should be. I'm glad for your triumph."

She would not be mollified. "And I'm disappointed in you, Michael," she said, and for the first time he saw real distress in her eyes. "We were *counting* on you."

"Oh, now, Meggie, you must understand why I left the house in the middle of things. It was not my place to say one way or the other. It's a family affair and truly none of my business." He threw the handful of cracked corn, and the hens rose to it in a cackling fluster. Taking her hand he went on, "You see, my own opinion might have been against it, too. Noreen and Brendan both had reservations based on good sense."

"You think we do not have good sense?" It was a challenge.

His tone was gentle, but he would not back away. "You know me better than that, I think."

She gulped an acceptance of the reprimand, nodding with tears starting to well up.

"You see, Meg, a thing like that can't be decided on good sense alone, not just like ciphering sums, I mean. It has too much to do with where his heart lies. A bit like falling in love with a grand idea."

She wiped her cheek with a bony wrist and looked away. She seemed suddenly fragile, this tomboy-child fishing friend of his. "Well," she said after a moment. "I certainly know what that is like."

"Oh?"

"Oh, yes." She pronounced it with a tired sigh so like a jaded adult's he had to smile.

"Then you know what I mean. That a man sometimes must do what his heart and soul call for, against the wisdom of others, and sometimes even when it wars against his own common sense."

"And a woman, too?"

"Well, certainly, yes."

The talk appeared to have laid to rest any hurt between them, and soon she was chattering away like her old self, spilling out the details of Denis's great adventure.

"And I'm to apply for a position at the big house. Aunt Blanche has offered to get me on any time I'm ready."

The idea soured Michael's mood. "You mean Boss Henry's home?"

She laughed. "I'd better be calling him the Mister if I plan to keep the job!"

"Your Aunt Noreen has need of you at home, don't you think?"

"Oh, there's more need for the money to pay for Denny's school. Father Reardon offered to help, but Daddy would have none of it. It was the only thing he said, really, and he was *very* serious. Said it was to be paid by the family and that was that."

Michael grimaced. He could imagine why Tim Feeney would have none of the old man's modest wealth. He knew the Virginia priest's money came from his parents' liquidated plantation—including the sale of its slaves.

"Anyway, Michael, you said yourself that we women have to follow our feelings just as men do."

Michael's brows rose. It was certainly no grand calling to be emptying Henry du Pont's chamber pots. He decided not to press the issue. Later he would have a talk with Noreen and Brendan.

"So, we're all of us taking a big step together," she continued, taking his silence as an endorsement. "You to California on a trip, Denis to Maryland, and myself to the big house at the top of the hill. Oh," she chirped, "it will make such a big difference when we see each other again!"

Suddenly she threw her arms around his chest and gave him a noisy kiss on the neck. Then she skipped back down the yard to the kitchen door.

"Thank you, Michael," she called. "I knew you were with us all the time."

Michael scratched his head. He did not quite know how he had fixed things with her, but he was glad for the hug and kiss all the same. It was the first time either of the children had accepted him so openly. He had missed it without realizing it; part of his own reserve, probably. Anyway, it was nice to feel a part of the family. Why, the girl would be calling him Uncle soon.

The thought of her knuckling under to that tyrant on the hill spoiled the feeling, though, and later in the evening he proposed a solution to Noreen and Brendan and Tim. But they turned him down.

"It wouldn't be right for you to spend your pay on Denis," Noreen said as Brendan nodded soberly beside her. "You've your own fresh start to build for," she said. "And besides, Michael, and I don't mean this to hurt your feelings, but you're not family, and it's not your place to pay."

After he left, Brendan questioned her choice of words in turning him down.

"He's got a chance to make something of himself, and I'll not have him weighted down with our load. He's had more than his share with fighting in Mexico." She looked through the curtain divider where Megan and Denis were still jabbering away, oblivious of the talking in the front room. "And God may burn my tongue for the irreverence of saying it, but I just hope our Denny is not walking into a different kind of trap himself."

As it turned out, Michael and Lammot had to delay their trip for some time. Alfred du Pont suddenly became gravely ill and within a month slipped quietly into death. After he was buried in Sand Hole Woods next to his father and grandfather, near the ancestral home from which he had been evicted, Meta gathered her sons about her in the crepe-hung parlor.

"You are my only hope and consolation now," she said to them.

Later she took Lammot aside and limited the statement further. "The whole weight rests on you, dear Lammot. You are the one with the strength to carry on."

"And get control of the company," Lammot thought to himself. That was what she really meant. Well, he had plans to do just that, but they did not include his mother.

Lammot was grimly thankful for one thing. His father would never know how grossly he had been betrayed.

CHAPTER TWENTY

Living at Eleutherian Mills, or the big house, as all the Crickers called the original du Pont residence, was not quite what Megan had expected. The romantic notions of rubbing elbows with Henry du Pont's family and living part of the time in the place were dampened by the harder realities of being a servant.

Megan did not mind the work. If anything, the actual labor was lighter than her chores at home in Chicken Alley. Her room on the third floor was tiny, but compared to the partitioned loft at the Gallaghers', it was almost grand. And the food was good.

The hard thing to swallow was what Aunt Blanche always harped on—proper "decorum." Decorum, Blanche pointed out as she groomed her new assistant, was pretending to be invisible in the presence of employers. Except of course when any one of them chose to recognize her. Then, of course, she had to jump and attend to whatever task was called to her attention.

She realized after a time that most of the rigidity was imposed by Aunt Blanche rather than by the family. Blanche seemed bent on deepening the stiff formalities of her servant staff almost like the nuns at St. Joe's behaved toward Father Reardon and the visiting priests when they came around. Of course, her aunt had worked in the house all her life, first under old E. I. du Pont, then for Mr. Alfred, and now Mr. Henry. She ran the place like some kind of holy shrine and insisted on a quiet reverence even when nobody was home but the staff.

"Honestly, Mary, I half expect her sometimes to dip her hand in the vestibule flower vase and bless herself when she uses the front door." Megan crossed the stone-floored kitchen and brought more cookies from the pantry jar. She dropped a handful on Mary Belin's plate and munched thoughtfully on one herself.

"Meg! You'll have me fat as a toad!" The company bookkeeper's daughter looked apprehensively at the door leading into the main part of the house, then shrugged and took one.

"G'wan wi ye, girl," Megan growled. "We're both skinny as sticks and can use the paddin'."

Mary laughed. The brogue was to mimic Sean Flynn, the stablemaster, whose thick accent became more pronounced the older he got. It was a point of interest mostly because Sean had been born on the Crick and had never seen Ireland at all.

"I don't think you're much of a stick these days, Meg. Have you looked in a glass lately?" Mary bit into her chewy macaroon and teased her friend by running her eyes from bosom to hips. "Has Billy or Young Henry pinched you yet?"

Megan huffed and tried to cover her embarrassment by fussing with the teapot. "You should talk, Mary Belin. My figure will never catch up to yours! I swear I've even thought of tying on a bustle to make up for slighted parts."

"Mother says that is the least of a woman's worry. It will come in due time, she says, and usually a bit more than she wants." Mary looked crossly at her half-eaten cookie and put it back on the plate. "Mother has a bit more than *she* wants."

"Eat the cookie," Meg said jabbing her finger. "It's a sin to waste, especially in this house."

"Did Mr. Henry give you the austerity speech?"

"Not exactly; Aunt Blanche did for him." Megan handed Mary a mug of tea, poured herself one, and sat at the table. "She also gave me a sermon on not 'flaunting' myself in front of the boys."

Mary laughed. "I don't think you need to worry about Little

Billy, though he may start moon eyes in a year or so. And Mister Henry A. is too snooty to give the help that kind of satisfaction."

"Our cadet."

"Isn't he just awful? When he came home from West Point in that uniform at Thanksgiving he just ignored Daddy and me at Christ Church."

"The shiny hat with the chinstrap across his mouth." Megan pulled in her chin and stiffened, holding part of a cookie between pressed lips. They both spluttered into giggles. "I just hope he floats back to earth someday and grows up. I know I'm just a nobody, Mary, but to think that oaf might be director of the company some day! It would be an embarrassment, surely."

"Hmmph! No chance of that! Lammot's the one who'll take over when Henry senior retires."

"Oooh, 'Lammot,' is it? He's Mister Lammot to the likes of us, but I keep forgetting that you're almost family yourself, daughter to Harry Belin!"

Mary shot an exasperated look at Megan, but she could not help smiling. She knew what was coming, and it had nothing to do with class distinctions.

"I should think y'might be calling him Motty like they do, since you're that close."

"He doesn't even know I'm alive."

"Maybe if you should 'flaunt' yerself a bit."

"Oh, Meg, there you go with that thick Irish again. Talk about poor Sean! I honestly think the brogue is deeper in Chicken Alley and Squirrel Run than it is in Dublin."

"Well, what do you think?"

"I certainly won't go *after* him, if that's what you mean."

"But at least let your feelings show, girl. He's after nobody else, from what I hear."

Mary got up and rinsed her cup at the pitcher pump by the sink and set it carefully on the sideboard. Her face was serious now, no more girlish prattle.

"You know how they are, Meg. Half of them end up marrying cousins to keep the family money in one place. Besides, we don't even see one another more than three or four times a year

when there are social events the Belins happen to get invited to."
The disappointment was plain on her face. "And then I'm just
a nobody face in the crowd, the bookkeepers's little girl."

Megan went to her and gave her a little squeeze on the arm.
"Listen, you set your cap for him. I think these men sometimes
need a good push just to have them take notice. He's not getting
any younger and, mind my words, he'll get the notion one day
and snap up the first fluffy head to bob within reach."

Mary absently picked up the cup and began rubbing it with a
tea towel but said nothing.

"You're my best friend, Mary, even if you are a Protestant.
You're the closest to me of all."

Mary's dark eyes widened. "What's that supposed to mean?"

"Oh, I don't mean that to be a criticism, it's just that it makes
us special in a way."

" 'Special'? Honestly, Megan, sometimes you come out with
the strangest compliments."

"What I meant was that I don't care that you're fallen away
from the one true church. It doesn't make any difference. In
fact, it will make the whole thing work out nicely."

Mary was confused.

"You're both the same church, you see? You and Mr. Lammot.
There won't be any friction over different religions."

Megan's earnest smile was impossible to resist, and Mary's
pique died. "You certainly have a strange way of cheering up a
person, Meg Feeney. I suppose if you were Episcopal, you'd be
after Lammot yourself."

"Oh, no," Megan said simply. "I've somebody else picked
out already."

Mary straightened in the chair and laughed. "So. Romance is
blooming on the Brandywine, eh? Who is he?"

"Oh, I wouldn't say. Not for now, anyway. It's too soon, and
I have too much to do before starting up that kind of job."

"Come on, Meg. I told you! What's his name?"

Megan shook her head, a businesslike dismissal. "As I said,
it's too soon for any of it, and that includes the gabbing."

"Well, thank you, Miss Feeney! You make me look pretty
silly with my telling you *my* feelings."

"It's not at all the same, Mary, and I don't think you silly at all. You should be working on Lammot du Pont."

Mary tried to get more out of her, but Megan added nothing. By the time she left the du Pont kitchen, Mary felt slighted at the lack of confidence and wondered if her friend had fibbed about having someone just to keep even.

She was almost to her home on the wooded hill above the Hagley Yards when an awful thought crossed her mind.

"I wonder if it's Henry Algernon she's after. Dear God," she thought, worried about her friend, "I hope not!"

It was a silly idea. That stuffy oaf wouldn't even consider marriage with the Irish serving class. Certainly Meg knew that. If she didn't, she was in for a crushing rejection. Even so, that would be better than his really being interested. Mary would lose a friendship if Meg married him. "Ugh," she muttered to herself. "I couldn't stand anybody who would marry that prig!"

When Michael swung his suitcases onto the porch and clumped the snow off his feet at the front door, Noreen Gallagher beamed on him like a returning son.

"Get in," she insisted, swinging the door wide and plucking him by his greatcoat to pull him indoors. "I can't be heating the whole of Chicken Alley." She jabbed a finger toward the kitchen. "Sit at the table and I'll fix something."

"No, thank you, Noreen. I ate downtown."

"You'll eat." Her look quashed any protest, so he sat obediently as she swept a bowl from the cupboard and ladled it full from the simmering stewpot on the iron range. He was not sure whether it was the steaming chunks of mutton and potatoes or the cold wagon ride from the Wilmington terminal, but his appetite had returned and he wolfed the food like a starving man.

She watched happily, plying him with questions he could answer with a nod or shake of the head, waiting until he was finished before beginning the real talk.

Finally there was just the mug of coffee before him, and he leaned back stuffed and euphoric.

"A year you've been gone. It seems like more. Now tell me

about California. Is there gold as they say, just for the picking up?"

He smiled. "Not for the picking up. But there is gold. The place is wild with hunting for it."

"And people are getting rich overnight, I've heard."

"A few perhaps. But the ones who are getting rich are not the gold miners. All but a few of them go 'bust,' as the saying goes. The moneymakers are the people selling things, supplies for all those eager newcomers with a yellow gleam in their eyes. Most of the ones who come with all their savings are quickly parted from them."

"Then there really isn't much gold at all?"

"No, there are mines making a fortune in a dozen places in the territory. But those stories about kneeling in a stream with a pie pan are mostly exaggeration. All of that surface stuff was gone long ago. Now it takes a lot of digging, crushing the ore, and separating the gold bits from tons of rock and earth."

"A rainbow dream. With backbreaking work and no pot at the end."

Michael smiled. "The real pot of gold is in the selling. Hope dies hard in a dreamer."

Noreen cocked her head. "It's a philosopher you've become Michael Farrell. Or is it opportunity you see for yourself?"

"There is the opportunity for some. I don't seem to be in position for it."

There was a hint of dejection in his tone that she did not like. He was of an age still for a share of dreaming.

"One man is doing a wonderful business in selling breeches made of sail canvas. The miners swear they can't be worn out."

"And how about your selling? Did young Lammot strike any gold for du Pont?"

"Fair enough," Michael grinned. "We sold the whole shipload of his new powder. It's cheap enough and better than what they make in California. They'd wear out a dozen picks and hammers to equal the work of a few kegs."

She noticed how he sparkled briefly as he spoke, his usual seriousness lightened with enthusiasm. "Maybe you should be an agent for the company, Michael. The pay would be better than working here."

"No, I'm not very good at that sort of thing. Lammot is, of course. I don't see how he does it. Just pushes right in anywhere, and people accept him gladly. He's quite a wit in conversation."

"The men like him, I've heard. Kevin says that the powdermen think he will be much like his uncle, Mr. Alexis."

"He treats me well."

"As he should. You're not like the rest of us, Michael, well-born and educated as you are. You have high hopes."

"I just need the purse to match the grand legacy, eh?"

She had wondered if the lack of wealth galled him. Wondered what it must be like to have known the power of position and money and then lose both. She felt a curious mix of compassion and envy.

"The purse will come in time if you carry the other gifts with pride."

He accepted her choice of "gift" with a slight dip of his head —not quite a nod, not exactly a deflection of her implied challenge either.

"In the meantime I will make do as I can. The work is interesting, Lammot du Pont is a fine fellow to work with, and the opportunity is as good here as anywhere else."

Noreen would have bridled at the last statement in past years. She had been bereaved more than once by explosions in the mills, but he was right in this case. Work in a laboratory was a good thing hereabouts, safe from the blasts and a place to demonstrate brains rather than brawn. For that matter, anybody at work in the yards was luckier than the unemployed nearly everywhere else. The slump of '57 following the Mexican War had produced its share of destitution.

Michael left her with the promise to visit again on Sunday when he could see Kevin and Megan and Brendan.

"You won't know Megan, she's that grown up," Noreen said as he hefted his bags for the long walk to his boardinghouse. "Of course Denis is still away at the seminary."

"Has Kevin found a girl yet?" he called back from the road.

"Lost cause," she said. "At forty-six he's too old to change."

Michael gave that some thought as he shuffled through the ankle-deep snow of Crick Road. He was only two years shy of thirty himself.

Christmas fell on a Friday that year, and a week before, Boss Henry had made an announcement that the Saturday after would be a holiday as well. The prospect of three days off was like a bonus. Nobody seemed to care about the loss of an extra day's pay.

Lammot invited Michael to a Christmas Eve party at his home, a surprise because although they always paired as associates in business travel, the social gatherings at home were closed to him. This was hardly a slight, because the social calendar on the hill was more a sluggish eddy than a whirl, and limited to perfunctory observances of the usual holidays by family members only.

The prospect of rubbing shoulders with the local gentry filled Michael with mixed emotions. He had expected to spend some time with the Gallagher-Feeneys and had accepted their invitation to Christmas Day church and dinner. The Christmas Eve celebration was more or less implied, the gift giving a ritual of the night before. But he had not seen either Megan or Denis and had been told by Brendan at the yards that the young seminarian would not get in until quite late. Megan had duties at the big house until Christmas morning herself.

Anyway, he really felt more like hired help himself, despite the easy equality of his relationship with Lammot. Back here along the Crick he was "one of the Irish." He felt the lesser kinship and, in a way that surprised even himself, savored a pride in it.

Lammot was wound up like a child when he announced it. "It's about time we had some fun," he said. "The house has been like a tomb since we moved in. At least when we lived in the old place there were parties. Is there anyone you'd like to bring, Michael?"

"No, I'll be coming alone."

"We'll get a chance to see some new blood, thank God. Irénée is bringing his fiancée from Virginia. She's quite the Southern charmer, according to him."

"Oh? I didn't realize that he—"

Lammot winked. "He's been busy these past months scouring the field. Pretty far afield at that. Doesn't like the slim pickings hereabouts."

Michael tried to shrug off his depression and focus on the conversation. "It must be exciting for your family. How did they meet?"

Lammot laughed. "Not a cousin this time? Yes, that *is* novel for my family. Well, he met her through distant relatives in Hanover."

"Your mother must be delighted. Nothing like a wedding to cheer people up. Christmas can be sad for those who have lost a loved one."

It was nearly prattling, distasteful in his mouth. Michael rarely said anything merely to fill space, and it was a greater intrusion with Lammot. They had been flippant often, but never dishonestly so. He watched his friend's face cloud over with hurt, and Michael felt that he had betrayed their mutual directness. He tried to salvage the moment.

"Your father would have been pleased to see his eldest happily married."

Lammot seemed embarrassed by his own deflation. He patted Michael on the shoulder and mumbled, "Yes, of course. Well, things will begin about seven. An informal party, Michael, just a buffet and season's cheer."

Megan really did not mind working Christmas Eve. Her brother would not be home until the next day anyway, and the excitement of waiting would have been too much sitting at home. Of course, she might have been able to see Michael Farrell, if he happened to drop in, but she was more than a little angry with him anyway. He had been back for almost a week and had not even had the decency to drop in at the big house to see her.

Not that she would have had the time to dawdle yakking away with him about California and such. Getting the du Pont house ready for the holidays under Aunt Blanche's flustering orders was like mounting a major military campaign. If she had not taken some time a month earlier to do shopping, her own gift list would have gone begging. Now that she had spent the money, she almost resented buying Michael anything at all, especially something that had taken nearly two weeks' pay.

Well, maybe he had not had the chance to drop in. There was much he probably had to do himself. But he had squeezed in a short call on Aunt Norrie. Ah, it was silly to make too much of it. Tomorrow she would see him and the slight be forgotten. She concentrated on getting her uniform pressed nicely to serve in at the other house. That would be a change at least. They needed more help at Mrs. Alfred's to tend at their party. It would be exciting to see the house. She had never been past the kitchen in the other place.

As she switched flatirons and spread out her best maid's blouse on the board, she wondered if Mary Belin's family had been invited. Probably so; they had been invited a few times by Mr. Henry to Eleutherian Mills. Certainly the other family would include them. It would be something to observe. Maybe she could manage to bump Mr. Lammot into Mary somehow. Dear God, how men could be so blind. The poor girl might have to set off a keg of blasting powder to get noticed. Lammot's eyes couldn't be *that* bad.

"Hurry, Megan!" The shrill voice of her Aunt Blanche startled her so that she forgot the iron and scorched the white collar. It was hardly noticeable. But tonight she had wanted to look perfect.

CHAPTER TWENTY-ONE

The wet snow covered Michael's new brogans by the time he reached the Nemours estate. He had blown a good deal of cash convincing a Wilmington tailor to complete a suit within a week, but it was worth it. Under his somewhat worn ulster and felt cap he felt rather elegant. If he was breaking into the du Pont circle, he might as well look the part.

He had never been in Lammot's home although he passed the lesser du Pont mansion on his way to work. It was midway between the laboratory behind the big house and the boardinghouse in Squirrel Run where he lived. The distances were measured only in hundreds of yards, but the separation of the two worlds was firm, and it was due to more than the thick woodland covering the highlands of the Brandywine Gorge.

Michael noticed that the slush underfoot was beginning to freeze as he crunched around the circular drive of the house, and a fine sifting of new snow began to fall. It swirled almost weightless through the pale yellow lamplight shafts from the front windows.

At the door he carefully wiped his shoes, brushed the snow from his cap and coat, and pulled the bell cord.

"Ah, Michael! Come in."

He was glad that it was Lammot and not one of the servants.

Strange how intimidation had built up over the years. He felt like a gawking powderman, cap in hand.

Beyond the vestibule he could see figures moving in the parlor to his left. As Lammot deftly helped him out of his coat and took his cap, the conversation in the other room was punctuated by a woman's light laughter.

"Come, Michael, I'll hand you around the group. Not all of them are here yet. It will be less painful in small doses."

Although they did not know him, Michael recognized nearly everyone in the room. Lammot's mother came forward and was introduced first, and Michael was surprised how much her pleasantries contrasted with Lammot's rather stiff presentation. Meta du Pont had apparently chosen this evening to discard her yearlong mourning black and was dressed in elegant holiday satins and lace. She seemed much younger and vibrant than Michael remembered those few times he had caught sight of her on the estate.

A few cousins shook hands, and then a young woman he had never seen before presented herself with Irénée du Pont in tow. She approached with a dancelike step, dark eyes flashing, and swirled to a stop a bare foot and a half from his chest.

"Introduce me to this most attractive man, dear Mottsie," she said, an impudent smile on her full lips. "Irénée, you did not tell me how many beautiful males there were in your family!"

She was speaking to Lammot and Irénée, but her look never left Michael's face, her head tilted back to study him. She underscored her approval with a deep breath, and Michael kept his eyes from slipping down her throat to the artfully exposed tops of pale breasts straining at the lace-trimmed square of her open bodice.

"Charlotte, may I present my associate, Michael Farrell. Michael, my future sister-in-law, Miss Charlotte Henderson of Virginia."

Michael bowed slightly, and Charlotte curtsied. Her décolletage barely survived the test, and this time Michael's eyes drifted briefly. Charlotte raised her head just in time to catch his lapse, and she shot him a quick knowing smile.

"My congratulations, Mr. Iré . . . du Pont," Michael fumbled, and he reached past the girl to shake Irénée's hand. "Best of luck to you both."

"Oh!" Charlotte breathed. "An English gentleman."

Michael was used to the error. "Irish," he corrected mildly, "though not for some years now."

"An American from Ireland," Lammot smiled at his elbow. Then in a voice a trifle louder, "Michael's scientific training was at Trinity College."

"I see," Charlotte lilted. "An Old World aristocrat gracing our shores."

Michael noted that she had deepened her Virginia accent, stressing the melody, broadening the vowels.

"Not very aristocratic," he said. "There is not much of that in the South, where I was born."

"Unless one happens to be English," Irénée injected wryly. "And then there is more aristocracy than the Irish want, I imagine."

"We have much in common then, Mr. Farrell," Charlotte added. "Both Southerners with an irritation from the North."

The whole room stiffened at her comment. Michael could not quite understand why. Strained relations across the Mason-Dixon line were a common topic, as frivolous as the weather. Something else must have triggered the feeling.

"An Irish Yankee?" she went on, oblivious to the chill. "A pity you did not settle in a more genteel part of our country. The weather *and* society would be more in keeping with your refined background."

The barbed words were said so lightly and followed by such a melodic little laugh that she hardly appeared to be serious, but Michael caught a scowl on the face of Meta du Pont that would have split a cobblestone.

"Let me get you something, Michael," Lammot said, wheeling him by the arm toward the dining room. "Would you like wine or spirits? The eggnog is good but not as fortifying."

When they were beyond earshot Lammot poured two brandies without waiting for Michael's choice.

"Merry Christmas, my friend," he said lifting his glass, and took half in the first swallow.

"What was that all about?" Michael said quietly.

"It's been going on all week. Charlotte is a bit blunt about her preference for Virginia society. I imagine . . . God, no, no imagination about it; she considers us to be crude rustics. My relatives are cooling toward the marriage, especially the girls. Charlotte is so beautiful by comparison that they feel rather dumpy around her."

"She is beautiful, surely."

Lammot grinned, "Yes. I noticed that you lost control for a second in there."

Michael sipped his brandy and then countered, "You mentioned the du Pont women. What about the men?"

"Whew! Well, frankly, it's a test. She really doesn't help matters there either. I don't think it will come to dueling matches, though. Irénée is reasonably alert considering his dazzled state. He knows the prize is for his plucking, and that will ease any jealousy for his coquette-bride."

"Things will settle down after they marry. It would be hard not to like someone with her high spirits."

"My God, I hope so!"

The evening moved on more smoothly, and Michael mixed easily with family and guests, mostly relating light anecdotes about Lammot during their trips to Peru and California. He discovered that the family were quite close mouthed about the business, and suspected that it was the result not of secretiveness but ignorance.

When Harry Belin's family arrived, he was disappointed to find out that their daughter could not come because of some illness. That would have been a tidbit he might have shared with Megan over Christmas dinner with the Gallaghers. According to Megan, they had been good friends as children.

Finally a hush fell over the parlor when the bell rang again, and Meta du Pont rushed for the door, her face suddenly alive with excitement.

When Henry du Pont followed his family into the room, Michael was struck by his change in appearance. He seemed much taller, more massively framed than he had the year before. A curly fringe of rusty whiskers framed his mastiff jawline from ear to ear. He had no mustache, his cheeks were clean shaven and glowed with the cold. He looked like a sea captain, hard blue eyes darting to each of his assembled crew, the beard a fiery lion's ruff. Until he belatedly removed a towering stovepipe hat, the illusion of height persisted. But with the topper off, Henry shrank back to his bull-like proportions. The beard made him seem more massive. Henry the Red, Michael thought, or Redbeard the pirate, more likely.

When the blue eyes settled on him briefly, Michael could almost read Boss Henry's mind, almost hear his "What the hell are *you* doing here?"

Lammot did not delay the encounter. He had propelled Michael toward his uncle before either of them had a chance to prepare for the meeting.

"Here he is, Uncle Henry," Lammot said crisply, "the man who helped me pull it off. Our quiet but strongest resource, Michael Farrell."

"Farrell." The greeting was as perfunctory as the brief handshake. "Merry Christmas," he added as he turned away. "Where is Irénée's promised? I imagine she is decked for the occasion."

Charlotte approached the director and leaned forward to permit him a peck on the cheek and a peek.

"Now the party will begin, Henry dear. May I call you Henry? Uncle is so stuffy and presumptuous, really, at least until Irénée and I are properly wed, though I must confess to second thoughts at times with all the strapping men hereabouts." She laughed again, a musical tinkling that cascaded over Henry du Pont, whose lips twisted in a smile as he took yet another downward look into the tantalizing bosom.

She spun away, lifting her silks with the turn and danced toward the pianoforte in the corner of the room.

"Oh, let's sing carols. Mottsie, dear heart, you do play so wonderfully, would you, please?"

The caroling was a dispirited affair carried off by Lammot's playing and Charlotte's singing in a voice so pure that it cowed the others into unhappy mumbling. Henry du Pont smiled contentedly as she exercised her talented lungs. Meta did not appreciate seeing a familiar yearning in Henry's eye directed toward another.

"Ginger bastard," she said under her breath.

Michael was the only one close enough to hear.

"Oh, I do need to rest my voice," Charlotte pleaded to her audience. "Mottsie, do keep playing. We must keep life in the party." She dabbed at her forehead with a kerchief and turned to Michael. "Would you get me something cool, Mr. Farrell? My throat is parched."

Michael withdrew into the dining room across the central hall and studied the elaborate options spread across the table. Most of the buffet foods had been cleared, and the servants had begun replacing the cheeses and meats with petits fours and dessert cups. A spot had been left for something large. They would probably have ice cream. Such finery! It had been a long time since . . .

He wrestled the memory back into a safe corner of his mind and concentrated on selecting a glass from the glittering rows of polished crystal. He had just begun to fill a glass with punch when he sensed someone behind him, a rustling of silk, a hint of perfume.

Michael's hand trembled, spilling a line of red drops onto the crisp white table linen as he dropped the ladle back into the bowl. A yielding softness brushed the back of his arm, barely perceptible.

"You've taken some time in tending to my needs, Mr. Farrell."

"Oh, I'm sorry. Here, but I've made a mess of it, I'm afraid. Let me pour you another."

She laughed, a private little tinkling for his ears alone. "No, thank you, sir. This will be fine. I shouldn't want you to botch another. Oh, dear, you seem to have a bit on your fingers. Let me tend to that. My, how clumsy you men become when about fragile things."

She snatched up a napkin from the table and began to dry his hand.

"Ooh, so sticky. This won't do, we need some water." Holding his hand close, she leaned past him to dip the napkin in a pitcher. The movement brought them closer together.

"Thank you, Miss Charlotte, it's fine." He made to withdraw, but she held firmly to his fingers, hiking them closer as she stroked with the dampened cloth. His arm was pressed deeply between her breasts.

"Let me dry you off," she said, leaning back to pick up a fresh napkin and gripping his hand. They were so close he was over-balanced, afraid of treading on her toes, and aware of a gentle but definite sliding of her hip against his own. As she reached, he lurched awkwardly and pinned her briefly against the table.

"Oh, my, Mr. Farrell," she teased. "I do believe you are taking advantage of my position!"

"Please, Charlotte," he said prying his hand loose and re-covering his balance. As he backed off, Michael saw Henry du Pont glaring at him from the other side of the table. Beside him with a huge bowl of ice cream in her arms and a shocked expression on her face was Megan Feeney.

Later that night, after he had gone to Dorgan's Inn to have a much-needed drink and a chance to think things out in the safety of the powdermen's holiday din, Michael had reason to regret his first and probably last invitation to a du Pont home.

The curt dismissal from the party by that pompous ass was bad enough. But the cruelty of thrusting the event on poor Megan was galling. He had not recognized her at first. How she had grown into womanhood. And then to have the shocked girl witness his humiliation. Perhaps the whole mess would be patched up tomorrow at the Gallaghers'.

He smiled on remembering the one thing that lightened the affair—Lammot's running after him through the snow, trying to coax him back, saying that Henry had no right to dismiss *his* guest. Finally he just slapped Michael on the back and said, "Now that you've met Charlotte, what do you think?"

"Uninhibited?"

"I should have warned you, Michael. Jesus, isn't she a pistol?"

"More like a French seventy-five. Is there anyone she has not flirted with?"

"Uncle Henry."

"Umm. I'm beginning to understand his reaction."

"I wouldn't worry about the randy old bastard. If I know Charlotte, she's probably mending that bridge right now."

Michael tossed his head back and let the snow pelt his face, "I'm really sorry for your brother's sake."

"Poor Irénée."

"Poor Irénée, indeed," Michael chuckled. "While the likes of us go slavering after fragrant wisps of steam, he will have that lovely plum pudding all to himself."

"I hope he saves his strength," Lammot said soberly.

Then they had both laughed uncontrollably, bent over, head to head, and circling each other in the deepening snow.

CHAPTER TWENTY-TWO

After the holidays Henry du Pont gave his nephew Lammot little chance to get much laboratory work done before he called him into the office for another project.

"We've bought a powder mill in Wapwallopen," he said gruffly, after no more of a greeting than a stiff nod when Lammot came in.

"Where is Wapwallopen?" Lammot asked. He also wondered why in the world du Pont wanted another powder company. The depression was deepening nationwide, and most firms were conserving capital, not spending it.

"About twenty miles south of Wilkes Barre on the east side of the Susquehanna."

"Coal country."

"Exactly. I've put Harry Belin's brother in charge of the place, and I want you to go up there to rebuild it."

"Rebuild it?"

"There was an explosion that wrecked the place last month, and they went bankrupt."

"I see." Lammot *was* beginning to see. A powder mill set in the heart of the expanding anthracite mining area would mean favorable advantages over the competition. He wondered how cheaply it had been picked up.

"I want the place to produce only soda powder, so we would have had to reconfigure it anyway."

"Even if it had not blown."

"Yes."

Lammot considered that a moment before pursuing it. "You were thinking about buying it before?"

Henry shifted in his chair. Prying into his reasons for making company decisions was not something he invited from anybody, much less a nonpartner. Still, it would be well to build some enthusiasm in Lammot.

"The coal industry is just starting. Our soda powder is cheaper to make than the potash stuff the others provide, but the shipping is killing profits. Being close to the pits will give us an edge. I know that this damned depression has everybody buttoning up his pants, but I think with soda blasting powder we can sew up the whole anthracite market, small as it is right now."

"And we'll be ready when the market goes up again?"

"Yes."

"Their loss, our gain."

"Whose?"

Lammot laced his fingers and thoughtfully studied his thumbs. "The bankrupt mill owners. I imagine the price was a giveaway compared to what they could have squeezed out of us if they were still producing."

Henry's eyes never moved, never blinked. "Fate sometimes has a timely way of smiling on the industrious," he sighed philosophically.

"I suppose you'll want me to get right at it?"

Henry shrugged and spread his hands. "There isn't anything pressing to keep you here, is there?"

Lammot was about to mention some new projects under way in the lab but decided not to bring them up. "Not really, no."

"Good, I'll wire Belin to expect you."

Lammot perked up. "Is the Morse machine here?"

"A week ago. Within six months we'll have a wire to all of our larger agents. Harry is getting pretty good at the key; not many mistakes, but he's slow."

"I'll have to look at it," Lammot grinned. The telegraph was exciting news. He was surprised that his uncle had installed it, reserved as he was about change. The man still used turkey quills in preference to steel pens.

"By the way," Henry called as Lammot was at the door. "Take that fancy Irishman with you. I don't want him sniffing around the family bloomers while you're away."

Lammot nodded and left. On the way out he skipped looking in on Harry and the new telegraph transmitter. He needed space between himself and Henry du Pont. His uncle's choice of words was irritating.

Henry seldom left his spreading domain on the Brandywine. For one thing he was busy buying up as much of the adjacent real estate he could get his hands on, and these were prime days for the buyer. In the wake of economic woes, tracts of land could be picked up for reasonable prices, and since he was working with company capital swelled by profits from war sales, his coffer was comfortably full. All of these lands were then deeded in his name personally, a process entirely legal for the partnership he controlled though not entirely within the spirit of his relatives' intent. He was thus quite busy putting these new acquisitions into the production of crops and livestock.

The first thing he did after taking possession was to send a team of laborers and masons to the property and have them clear the surface of rock and stones. Using these he would lay out the boundaries of woods or fields and have the masons build mortarless stone walls around the periphery of each tract. His three-foot high stone "fences" soon became local trademarks for "another of Mr. Henry's farms." The labels varied with individual opinion, of course; frequently they were less cordial, "another grab by the Ginger Bastard," for example.

Not many powdermen complained, though. During slack times at the mills, scrabbling for stones and lugging them to the masons was paid labor, and they were thankful for that.

Some felt the mills should be cut back and some of the powdermen let go. Irénée even suggested airily that the whole business close down, the workers be sent off, and the business hibernate until better times. Alexis would not hear of it, to play such a cruel hand against the loyal powdermen and their families. He was backed up by some of the du Pont women whose opinion carried little weight.

Henry would neither shut down completely nor let a single

powderman go. The decision had nothing to do with a charitable nature as some newcomers speculated; it had nothing to do with any belief in democratic rule, as the du Pont women thought; nor did it have to do with the building of his wall-girded empire as the stonecutters chose to believe. It had everything to do with the United States' gradual slide toward civil war. Henry was an avid reader of news. He wrote and received dozens of letters a day, and he knew lots of important people from the North and South. Delaware was precisely on the borderline geographically and politically. Henry knew that his idled powdermen would be invaluable when the conflict erupted, and there would be huge profits for any powder mills ready to swing into action. Getting the laid-off workers back would be made more difficult by speculator mills willing to pay premium wages to talented explosives workers. Better to keep them happy and loyal on realistic pay. As a former army officer, Henry's preference was for the federal government, but he was flexible enough to adjust to the call of his stronger customer.

Another reason for staying on his own turf lately was that he had become pleasantly accustomed to having important people come to him rather than the other way around. It gave just a touch of advantage that he liked. Other business could be handled by mail or through subordinate agents. Some of them were employed directly by the Boss himself, and a handful were known not at all by others in the company.

Loughlin Sneed was one of Henry's personal helpers, but he had never set foot within the Brandywine Mills property although part of their arrangement was that Sneed's apartment was paid for in cash each year by Henry personally. Sneed occupied his rooms in Wilmington only occasionally because he was usually in the field for months at a time tending to Henry's private projects at rival powder mills.

CHAPTER TWENTY-THREE

I'll be gone for some time, and I wanted to say good-bye."

"Come in, Michael," Brendan Gallagher smiled. "Can you stay for supper?"

"Thanks, but no. I have to leave in a few minutes to meet the train."

"Off to Wapwallopen, eh? Well, you're stepping up in the world. I hear you're Mr. Lammot's right-hand man to start the new mills."

Michael laughed. "I'm not sure whether a coal town is moving up or down. The job will be interesting, though."

"Hello, Michael." Noreen came into the front room followed by Kevin. "Can I at least get you some coffee? We wish you could stop for supper."

"Hello, Noreen, Kevin. No, please, I really haven't more than a minute or so. Lammot du Pont is picking me up at the Barley Mill at six."

"It's too bad Megan is not here," Noreen said. "You didn't get to see her at the big house, did you?"

"No. I've been told to give the place a wide berth."

"She'll be upset to have missed you."

"I think she'll be glad to know I'm gone, after that episode at Christmas."

Brendan laughed nervously. "You and the Mister have had your share of run-ins. The wonder is that you've been kept on."

"I've Lammot to thank for that. My real worry was that it might hurt Megan's position."

"It might be a blessing," Noreen said. "I'd like to see her talents put to better use."

"Well, tell her I'll write faithfully of the wonders of Wapwallopen and Wilkes Barre."

When he left, Kevin asked to walk along with him.

"You noticed that Uncle Tim wasn't home?"

"Yes. Is he working late?"

"He's left the company. Gone over a week ago."

"Damn! He's not back into the old business again?"

"Probably. He wouldn't say, but Mother saw a stranger speaking with him before he quit and took off. Just after New Year's."

"Do the kids know?"

"Not yet."

"It will be a blow to Megan, but Denny cut him off some time ago. How about Noreen?"

"Mother and Father are pretty grim about it."

"I would imagine."

"Listen, Michael. I wanted to tell you something else, about Megan."

"She's not in trouble because of that Christmas thing, is she?"

"No, but it does have something to do with it in a way."

"Did Henry—"

"No. I think Megan is upset because she's a little sweet on Michael Farrell."

"What?"

"I know it sounds peculiar. She's like a niece to you. But she's nearly grown, and these things happen."

"My God, Kevin, that really is a daft idea. I'm half again her age."

"Ten years is not really much of a difference, especially to someone like Megan."

"It's more than age."

"Yes, I know. You're like family, but it seems like she finds no obstacle in that. And there isn't, either."

"Did she tell you this?"

"Not in so many words—indirect hints mostly. I guess the fact that she never mentioned things except when Mother and Dad were not around was what made me think it was serious."

"What does Noreen think about all this?"

"Jesus Mary, the girl would have my hide if I breathed a word to her!"

"Hmm. You underestimate your mother's strength and understanding."

"Not her strength. I know that well enough."

"Even if you are right about the poor girl's feelings, she probably has me confused with someone she hasn't even met yet. But I think Noreen should know. Megan will need some understanding and guidance."

"Maybe. But I'll not be the one to tell Mother, and I don't think you should either. Megan would have said something to her—and will—if she wants her to know."

"Then you have to lend her a hand through all this."

"I'm the fine one for that! Not much help."

Kevin's answer was faintly plaintive, and Michael jabbed at him, relieved to change the subject. "Confirmed bachelor, eh?"

Kevin laughed. "Convicted bachelor is more like it."

"Convicted? Well, you're not without your choices. When are you going to pick one and settle down?"

"It doesn't look like I ever will." He was suddenly quite sober. "A time or two I nearly did, even proposed once when I was your age, but backed off."

"Cold feet? You've more than ample chances to correct that."

"I can never quite match up marriage and job prospects at the same time."

"Job? Your job with du Pont is certainly secure. And by now you must have saved enough to get started without worry."

"Secure? Oh, yes. But the marriage wouldn't be, not with the threat of exploding mills hanging over it. I wouldn't put any girl through that, nor our children either."

"What about another job? As a mason?"

"Like I said, Michael, the timing has always been a little off. Besides, my work with the company is pleasant enough and secure, as you said yourself."

Michael knew it was more than that. Part of the reason was

Denny's education, and until she started working, support for Megan as well. Brendan and Noreen were in their sixties, and Tim, well, the least said about *that* the better.

"Married to du Pont then?"

" 'Til death do us part."

They had just reached the crossroad at Barley Mill Road when Lammot du Pont's gig appeared in the distance. Kevin swung the seabag he had been carrying next to Michael's other bags and started back.

"Good luck to you in Wapwallopen, Michael. And take some time to think about marriage yourself. You're not getting any younger either."

The scene at Wapwallopen Mills was not quite what Lammot had expected. For one thing, the damage from the explosion which had driven the small company to sell out seemed trivial compared to some du Pont had survived. A few mills had been disabled, one or two frame buildings flattened, and the saltpeter refinery gutted. Except for the damaged older mills, the rest of the string could be started up immediately. Even as they arrived, an advance team sent by Henry du Pont was busy clearing out antiquated stamping machinery and picking up other debris from the blast.

After they completed a walk through the place, Lammot found a desk in the office shed and started scratching out a list of priorities. Michael looked over his shoulder, making an occasional recommendation of his own.

"It's not as bad as I expected," Lammot muttered when he was finished writing.

"Yes. I was thinking the same. Except for the saltpeter refinery."

"Which we had to redesign anyway for sodium nitrate."

"And those damaged mills?"

"Useless to us anyway."

Michael was confused. Mill machinery was not as familiar to him as was the theoretical laboratory process.

"They're stamping mills, Michael, a half-century out of date. We would have stripped them anyway."

"You mean that the undamaged mills are the only ones we would have used?"

"Exactly."

Michael absorbed the information before speaking. "So the blast destroyed only the sections we will not need or would have had to replace in any event?"

"Yes."

"A selective and fortuitous series of explosions."

"Almost surgically so."

"I would prefer not to think that."

"Neither would I."

In a month they had the converted mills rolling again, and Lammot reported their success in a terse telegraph message to the Brandywine office as soon as the Morse machine was connected. He clicked out the coded words himself.

"Three thousand pounds soda powder shipped this date stop LduP stop Wapwallopen."

When the key responded with an acknowledgment from the other end of the wire, Lammot waited for congratulations. The message was longer than he expected, however, and the text was not pleasant.

"Tragic accident here stop many dead and dying stop Alexis mortally hurt stop urgent your immediate return stop sadly HduP."

It was not until they got off the train in Wilmington that Lammot found out that his favorite uncle had died. And Michael learned of the death of Kevin Gallagher.

CHAPTER TWENTY-FOUR

Because of his popularity with the workers and because he was the first du Pont to die in an explosion, Alexis's funeral overshadowed services for the other four men killed. It was a hero's death, surely, as he doused his burning clothes in the millrace and climbed up on the pressroom roof, yelling for his men to save themselves, and as he reached for the burning timber just as the building exploded under him. He could have spared himself, escaped with only burns from the first blast, but as always he was thinking of his men first.

Of course, the mourners prayed for the perpetual reward of Kevin Gallagher and the others, and they commiserated with the surviving families. Especially Brendan and Noreen, who had lost more than their share to the mills and now were without any sons at all. But it was their common lot, the chance they all took of a sudden trip "across the Crick," in exchange for a sound roof over their heads and a full pot on the table.

The old priest, Father Reardon, seemed to be taking these rites a bit harder than usual. How many boxes he had splashed with holy water was beyond his own counting. It was not the dying, certainly; that was the nature of his business—wrapping up the package safe for delivery out of the hands of Lucifer and his host of fallen angels. But he must have felt a kind of partnership of guilt in the way so many were snuffed out, with more rocks than flesh to weight the box. The church itself was, after all, a gift he gladly took from those du Ponts, the more to keep his Irish flock content with danger. It was a place for them to pray, "From sudden death, O Lord, deliver us," and failing that, a resting place with the church foundations next to their elbows.

There were some who gnashed their teeth. Why hadn't the Ginger Bastard been taken? God knows they would all be better off if he had been blasted instead of Mister Alexis.

"Wouldn't hear of it, Dorgan. The Red Fellow hasn't the right to go up like a powderman."

"I'll sip to that. Mister Alexis was a powderman like us all, God rest his soul, and Henry du Pont ain't worthy of the company. I'd sooner he died of spoiled meat."

"You wish! Ah, he'll outlive us all."

"The good die young, as they say."

"Then Boss Henry'll live out the century."

"Agh, stop that talk, boyo! You're spoilin' me grief with thinking of spending all my days with an eye cocked for red whiskers and a tall hat."

"Here, Dorgan, fill my pint again. And might I point out for the good of your business head, that your uncle never let a man's tin go dry. He'd always swoop it up with an inch still in the scuppers and work the taps to top it off."

"Aye, and charge for a full draught all the same! Old Dorgan, and I'm not about to dishonor the dead, mind you, but he was a close man with his pennies."

"It's Brendan Gallagher and his missus I feel sorry for."

"Aye, in their old age to lose another one. Her brother Tim that worked here, he didn't show up at all."

"Tim ain't too smart, if you ask me. He's up to his old tricks again. I don't know what gets into a man to get mixed up with that nigger business."

"More grief for his sister, and letting his own kids grow up like orphans. He's a queer duck."

"I wouldn't put him down, lads. He has good reason."

"What do you mean?"

"It's a long story. You're too young to remember it."

"Well, I'm listening."

"I said it was a long story—too long. Let it rest."

"Young Denis looked fine in his cassock on the altar today. He'll be a fine priest."

"That he did. What is he now? A deacon or what?"

"A growed-up altarboy is all he is. It'll be years yet before he gets ordained."

Noreen Gallagher sat next to Brendan and closed her eyes. She gripped her husband's arm tightly with both hands.

"I really do not want to talk about it."

Father Reardon balanced his cup and saucer easily in one hand and gazed at them with compassion.

"I know it is painful."

"Painful?" She opened her eyes and glanced sideways at Brendan's ashen face.

"Sometimes we find it hard to accept God's will, Noreen, especially when he takes one so close. It is not much consolation, I know, but at least Kevin did not leave a widow and little ones."

"Yes."

"A greater sadness avoided."

"No, I meant it was not much consolation."

The priest had already opened his mouth but closed it without speaking. His glance flickered from the dark anger of her emerald eyes to the sunken grief of Brendan's face and back again. He was compelled to reach out to her.

"Do not harden your heart, dear Noreen."

It was a plea, and she knew it came from feelings deeper than from his priesthood and friendship. Did she have to salve his conscience, too?

" 'Harden'? It's more like finding the broken pieces. Are we to rejoice that Kevin was canny enough not to share his chances with a woman and the children she would bear? Small reason for celebration! What's left? What is there to show for all the work and love of this man?" She stroked Brendan's arm and searched his face when he turned briefly to give her a wooden smile.

"I wish we had brought along the fishing poles. It would have seemed like old times." Denis stooped to pick up a stone and skip it over the oily sheen of backwater below the dam. "Do you ever try your luck any more, Meg?"

"Mother of God, Denny! The things you pop up with. Everybody sick with grief and you think of that."

"Well, I meant no disrespect to Kevin's memory, and why not, anyway? Surely he's with God, and that's reason for happiness. What do you think, Michael? Father Francis said himself we should not distract ourselves with too much grief. It's a rebellion against faith."

"Not everybody can look at death quite so dispassionately."

"It's coldly, you mean, Michael. Humph! Sometimes he makes me sick with all that theology."

Denis skipped another pebble and rubbed a fleck of mud from his fingers. "Girls are more emotional, I suppose. Do you know that I can't remember ever feeling sad about Dad's being away, except when he was on Pea Patch Island, of course. But you gushed like a fountain sometimes. It doesn't do any good. That's why priests don't marry. They need clear heads to lead more objectively."

"Your head is so clear it's empty."

"See? You have to get emotional. And it doesn't affect me in the least because I *know* you are getting back at me because of your emotions. If you were stating a logical fact based on reason, why then I'd give it serious thought."

"I think you're a bit weird, Denis Feeney, and I pity the poor people who'll have you for pastor, *if* you ever make it to Holy Orders." Megan's eyes flashed, but as she spoke the last words trembled.

"Hey, you two. Fishing would be bad enough on a day like this, but fighting like nasty children is certainly worse."

"You're right, Michael. I'm sorry to have upset you, Meg. Let's drop it."

She did not answer and turned her back on them to stare across the Crick. In the silence a bass slurped almost at her feet, snapping short a dragonfly's last flight.

"Look at that!" Denis gasped. When there was no response he pulled a watch from his vest and glanced at it before adding,

"I think I'd better go. I'm driving Father Francis back to the rectory. You're staying on a few days, aren't you, Michael?"

"Yes. We'll get together again before I leave."

"I'll see you at the house tonight, Megan." When she did not respond he shrugged and left. Michael watched until he disappeared on the path bending through the undergrowth along the banks of the Brandywine.

"You were a bit hard on him, don't you think?"

"He's as cold as that fish."

"You don't know that, Megan. He may have been covering up some tenderness himself. He always liked Kevin."

"Oh, I know that. But he never really gets close to anybody. Kevin was like a comfortable uncle to have around. To tell the truth, I'm more upset about what it's done to Uncle Brendan and Aunt Noreen. Did you look at him? Did you see how he's shattered? And the only thing holding her together is holding *him* together."

"It was a cruel hurt, terrible."

"I don't wonder that Denis is so . . . so isolated. God knows both of us have learned to keep our love bottled up."

"Have you heard from your father?"

She shook her head. "Indirectly, we have. That's another cross for Aunt Noreen. The day after the blast, she went in to see that Thomas Garrett, to see if he could reach Daddy."

"What did he say?"

"He had no idea where my father is. He isn't with the slave underground, at least. The man he is working for is somebody from Connecticut, I think. They're raising money to help with a different organization."

"Who is that? What organization?"

"I don't know exactly, but the man's name is Brown. John Brown is what she said."

"Christ, not *John* Brown?"

"What's wrong?"

He wanted to bite his tongue for the outburst. She did not need more worry.

"If it's the one I'm thinking of, well, he is a bit eccentric. But that was Kansas, now that I remember."

It was not a lie exactly, a little distraction. But he knew it was the same man, John Brown of Connecticut, leading raids against Kansas pro-slavers. God. Feeney was hooked up with a firebrand, and the money raising was to arm Negroes for rebellion in the South.

Megan apparently was sidetracked. She ambled down to where a fallen tree sprawled across the path and sat looking at him. The dusky light of waning afternoon filtered softly in the shadowed gorge of the Brandywine, and the onset of twilight rose in humid layers from the stream. He was struck again with how she had matured. A death in the family would have that effect, sobering even children into adultlike behavior. In Megan there was a deeper sobriety he had noticed as soon as he returned this time. It had much to do with the sudden responsibility she faced now that Kevin was gone and Brendan aging so. She was close to being sole support of the household. The contrast with her brother was striking. Denis seemed almost blasé by comparison.

"Have you seen her since coming back?"

He went to the log and sat beside her. The light cologne she wore was no more than a hint of scent mixed with other smells of the woods and stream and the warm pleasantness of Megan herself. He recognized the perfume as one of his own gifts to her from a year or two before, and felt strangely elated that she was wearing it.

"Whom do you mean?"

"Charlotte Henderson."

"Charlotte Henderson?"

"Yes."

He smiled. "I don't think it would be wise for me to see that young lady."

"Wisdom has little to do with it."

"Oh, I think it does, Megan. You saw how Henry du Pont reacted to that little scene at Christmas."

"And if Mr. Henry did not disapprove?"

She was watching him closely, her chin slightly elevated. He was aware suddenly of the graceful line her throat presented when she turned to face him. The sunset afterglow softly highlighted her smooth skin, and he could visualize a pendant resting in the gentle cleft of her bosom. A green stone would be lovely, he thought, emerald and gold to accent her natural coloring.

"In that case, I would have to rely on gentlemanly behavior. She is Irénée's fiancée, you know."

"Gentlemanly behavior? Was that what you were up to when I caught you two in the dining room?"

"*Caught* us? Well now, Miss Feeney, just what do you think I was 'up to' in the dining room?"

"You weren't after the goodies on the table. That was clear enough."

Her eyes were snapping, and he rankled at being challenged so by this snippy inquisitor. Besides that, there was a little knot of hurt at being unfairly judged. It had been Charlotte, after all, who had made the advance, not himself.

"You sound a bit like Henry du Pont, Megan," he said sourly.

"Oh, rubbish! That old goat leers at her himself, not that she minds. It's disgusting how every man swarms after her like bees after a warm honey pot."

"She's warm indeed."

"She's a trollop."

"Well, it doesn't concern me. She and Irénée du Pont have set a date. He considers her to be quite a catch."

"She caught him, is more like it. Or caught his money."

"Can't blame her for that."

"Would you?"

"Marry for wealth?"

When he did not answer, Megan looked away toward the sheen of the river, purplish with a reflection of the twilight sky. "I still have those letters you sent, the long ones to Aunt Noreen and the little notes to us. They mean much more to me now, now that I can understand."

"Pretty idealistic, I imagine." His laugh grated harshly on his own ears.

"I don't like that."

"Oh?"

"You shouldn't look down your nose at those wonderful feelings. I think it's mean of you to ridicule the things you did when you were young now that you're—"

"Old?" he grinned.

"I was going to say 'disappointed' or something like that, but it's not the word exactly."

"Disenchanted."

"Oh, yes. Disenchanted. That's it exactly. You're disenchanted. Not at all like being old. All you need is to become enchanted again."

"There's hope for the old boy still. Do you know of any honest leprechauns about?"

Megan laughed at that, a trilling little-girl laugh that pleased him to see her lifted mood, that she was still resilient enough to rise above the gloom of the past few days. And he was glad he had been the one to trigger it. But she turned quickly serious again.

"When you criticize the way you felt, it hurts me, Michael, because I am the way you were; the same age exactly. Do you think that I am foolish for my feelings?"

"You are perfect, young lady."

"Ah, there you go, putting me down as a child again."

"Truly, Meggie. I'm not patronizing you; I think you are as nice as can be."

" 'Young lady' is what I mean. Why not 'young woman'?"

"Why not, indeed. The same thing, isn't it? My God, but you can be contentious when you set your mind to it."

"Yes, I can, as a matter of fact. I'll come right out with what I think to set wrong matters right, Michael Farrell. You can count on it."

"I'll remember that." He swatted a mosquito sucking at his neck and got up. "Come on, it's nearly dark. I don't want you to crash into nettles on the way back, or get a dose of poison ivy on your legs. Noreen wanted to skin me the last time."

"I haven't worn short dresses for some time, Michael, or hadn't you noticed?"

"I've noticed."

He caught the little satisfied glance she gave as he helped her to her feet. They walked in silence for some time, threading the darkening path abreast. She clung to his hand, a familiar little grip made strange by her head at his shoulder instead of at his hip. There would be no more fishing poles, he thought. The suitors would be coming soon, and her twilight walks would be filled with breathless expectation. And, he hoped, with few if any shattered dreams.

"One more thing, Michael," she said as they gained the higher level of Crick Road and saw the dimly lighted windows of Chicken Alley ahead, "It's nice that you wanted to spare me the worry, but I want you to know that I read the newspapers too."

"What do you mean by that, Megan?"

"I know more about John Brown the abolitionist than you gave me credit for. Just say a prayer for Daddy now and then when you think of it."

CHAPTER TWENTY-FIVE

W hat have you decided about replacing Alexis?"

"Nothing. His boys are too young, too inexperienced."

"And your Henry Algernon will pursue an army career?"

"Yes."

"So much like his father. Do you wish that you had not resigned from active service?"

"I had no choice in the matter. With father so ill and Alfred mismanaging. It was a long time ago."

"You must have been disappointed. Such a dashing young officer! I still remember how you looked that first time you came home on leave when Alfred had you over for dinner."

"You have a good memory, Meta. That was thirty years ago."

"It doesn't take a strong memory to remember the first time one falls in love."

"I remember the first time I gave you a roll in the hay well enough. I wondered if Alfred would find out and come after me with a gun."

"He never did suspect."

"Just as well. Poor bastard, he probably would have wept like an old woman."

"Oh, you're harsh!"

"Truth is truth, Meta. I won't gloss over what he was just because he's gone. It's the same with Alexis. He never could remember that he was an owner and not a powderman. I'm afraid his boys are just like him."

"Then you will not hold a partnership open for them?"

"No. I've bought up their shares for a fair price."

"But you will need somebody. Irénée can handle his share of the burden, even distracted as he is with his fiancée."

"Hmm. Charlotte is well equipped to do that."

"I was referring to the discord the girl is capable of generating."

"So was I."

"I know quite well what *you* were referring to, Henry dear, and I would prefer not to go into that. I meant her pompous social pretentions, bizarre political statements, and general snobbery."

"You're beginning to sound like a mother-in-law, Meta."

"Heaven knows I want my Irénée to be happy, and I have gone out of my way to help her feel welcome, but I certainly think she is ill suited to his pleasant temperament." Meta felt a constriction in her throat, heard the shrill creeping into her voice, and paused to let the tension ebb. She rested her cheek on his chest and idly traced the contours of his thigh and abdomen with her fingertips. Even in repose there was nothing soft about him. Henry may have thickened with age, but it was with hard muscle, not fat.

"You have something else on your mind," he growled contentedly. "What is it this time?"

"I'm concerned about Lammot."

"He is well enough, it seems to me. Doing his job. I've no complaints."

"I'm sure of that. Do you know that he is seeing Mary Belin?"

"Harry's daughter?"

"Yes."

"A bit of a mouse, isn't she? I didn't know she was old enough to keep company."

"Oh, she's old enough, and not so much of a mouse as you might think. She was brazen enough to flaunt herself for Lammot at the funeral."

"I didn't notice."

"Men do not notice, usually."

"One of your womanly tactics, eh?"

"I do not appreciate being included with her type, Henry."

He reached down and cupped her firmly between the legs. "And what type is that, Meta?"

She twisted away from him and left the bed, stabbing her arms into a robe and tying the sash with flying fingers. Her eyes were black with anger when she turned to look at him.

"You can be crude. Do you know that?"

"Very well. What type is Mary Belin?"

"She is a manipulative little Jewess."

"A Jew?"

"I know you respect Harry Belin and the service his family has done for the firm, but I do not relish the idea of Lammot being involved with his daughter. I shudder to think of compounding the problems I already have with that vixen from Virginia. It is bad enough that he is keeping company with an employee's child. Can you imagine what it would be like having a pack of Jewish in-laws?"

"Harry is no Jew. They are all dues-paying Episcopalians like the rest of us."

"Harry is not, but his wife is."

"Isabella?"

"Really, Henry. It is common knowledge. You certainly remember the raised eyebrows when Harry courted her. Isabella's mother was the daughter of Moses Homberg of Philadelphia."

"Hmm. So Mary Belin is one-quarter Jewish, eh? It must have slipped my mind. Even so, don't you think that's reaching a bit for troubles?"

"If she were a quadroon would you think me as unreasonable?"

Henry laughed suddenly, rose from the bed, and began pulling on his drawers. "You'd better not let Harry hear that argument! A quadroon! His grandfather was tossed out of Haiti by his own slaves, you know."

"Frankly, I could not care less as to how they got here."

"Well, it's not as though Lammot's kids would be black or brown. And I don't think he would allow some rabbi to snip an inch or so from their private parts."

"I wish you would not be so coarse. And it is no laughing

matter. Unless you consider mixing du Pont and Jewish blood comical."

Henry finished dressing without further comment. For the rest of the day he gave considerable thought to Lammot, but it barely touched on Meta's immediate worry. The loss of Alexis and his easy leadership of the rank and file was a costly gap he had to fill. There was no question that his nephew was well liked by the powdermen. Beside that, he was a near genius in the laboratory, much like his father but with an aggressive side that could be put to use. A valuable asset to the company, too valuable to lose to a competitor. He would need a strong tether to keep him in line, but that would be simple enough to arrange.

When he got the message to meet his uncle after work at the company office, Lammot expected a litany of orders to take back to the Wapwallopen mills. He never expected the statement Henry greeted him with.

"I want to make you a partner in the firm."

"A partner?" Lammot's mouth went dry. "In the firm?"

"Your hearing is not impaired, I see. Yes, a junior partner like your brother."

"I . . . I don't know what to say."

"I'll presume a refusal is not forthcoming."

"Why, no. Certainly not. Naturally I'm delighted."

"Good." Henry extended his hand, and in a daze Lammot gripped it. "I suppose I should have had Irénée here, but I wanted to speak to you privately first. Have a cigar and look over this contract."

The offer was simple enough. Lammot read the single page through twice before looking up. "You're offering me equal status with Irénée. I would like his approval first."

Henry shrugged. "As you wish. Not that it matters. The other shareholders will have to agree to your buying in anyway. That, too, is a formality. They really have to go along with the director."

Lammot smiled faintly at Henry's use of the third person in referring to himself.

"As to your payment for shares, I can advance a loan against your allowance as a family employee. I imagine cash payment might be awkward."

"An understatement of my close means, Uncle Henry. I'll have to negotiate a loan, certainly."

"Very well. It's done. Now there is something else to discuss, something which will bear directly on your plans for life." Henry puffed easily at his cigar and fixed his eyes on his nephew as the smoke billowed softly between them.

Lammot endured the long silence and stare placidly, but his heart was racing. His own hand was steady as he drew a single puff and waited.

"In not too many years I would like to step down with the assurance that I'll be leaving this company in capable hands. The man to run du Pont will have to be aggressive, resourceful, knowledgeable, and firm. I think you have the potential to acquire those qualities."

Lammot was steady as a rock.

"You need to get a feel for our competition, find out what they're up to, dig out new processes for manufacture. I want you to meet the important people in our business, get to know them on a friendly basis."

"New England and the South?"

"No. We've nothing to learn from anyone on this side of the Atlantic. I want you to scout Britain and the Continent. Woolwich Arsenal, Maresfield, Waltham Abbey. Visit Spandau in Berlin, the Paris arsenal, go to the Wetteren mills in Belgium. Use your eyes and ears, and take notes. Get samples when you can." Henry paused and then added, "Do you have any questions?"

"I'm overwhelmed. You're offering me the Grand Tour."

"Don't get the wrong idea. I want you to *look* like a tourist, but you'd better bring back the right souvenirs."

"Sounds more like a spy mission."

Henry flashed a rare smile. "More than that, Lammot. It's to be a one-man invasion of Europe."

"It seems you want to compete for a piece of their market, Uncle Henry."

"By the time I hand over this office to the next director," Henry said, tapping his finger on the desk, "du Pont will be the *only* major producer of explosives on the globe."

There was no question in Lammot's mind that Henry was quite serious. It was heady stuff indeed for the new junior partner to absorb.

"By the way," Henry said as Lammot left, "be sure to tell your mother. I imagine she will be quite proud."

Lammot did tell her that evening. Meta was nearly ecstatic with the news.

"You deserve it, Motty. A proper recognition of your work. And a wonderful gesture from Henry, that thoughtful, magnificent man."

For Lammot, that was the only sour note of his day.

When Mary Belin popped into Eleutherian Mills practically at dawn, Megan suspected news. From the look on her friend's face, it had to have been good news. Megan risked a rebuke from her Aunt Blanche and took a break from laying out the table for breakfast. A few minutes wouldn't hurt.

"All right, girl," she said, handing Mary coffee. "Out with it quick."

"I did what you said."

"And?"

"And it worked!"

"Lammot du Pont."

Mary nodded, sipped at her cup, and winked.

"Oh, girl! See what I told you? Has he taken you out? What did he say?"

"Slowly please! My heavens, Megan, we've just *talked*."

"He's come calling then?"

"No, not precisely. We had a nice conversation after his uncle's funeral. We'd all gone to pay our respects and thank God for my uncle Charles rattling on with Henry about Wapwallopen. We all had to wait, and it gave me time to spend with Lammot."

"Motty."

"Oh, Megan, you're an awful tease. I'll not say another word!"

"Yes, you will, unless you want me to chatter about the whole thing to every ear on the Crick!"

"Well, there isn't much more to it than that, really."

"Mary!"

"Of course, he *did* stop by the house twice since to speak to Papa about the new mills and such."

"Were you able to get him alone?"

"Merciful heavens, Meg Feeney! You make me seem like a clawing wench."

"You know what I mean."

"We had lemonade in the garden once. Alone, if you must know. For about an hour, I think."

"Umm."

"Oh, it was all very ordinary. We just reminisced about when we were children, or rather when I was a child. He teased a bit about some things I prefer he'd not known. It's a disadvantage having him eight years older."

"That's no disadvantage."

"I mean he can remember my growing up through those awful awkward years safe himself because he had outgrown his before I could notice. It can be embarrassing."

"An older man is better. He's established, for one thing, and besides that, he's outgrown all that foolishness and strutting about they all go through."

"Well, Lammot managed to strut just a bit, thank God. That was about the only sign he gave of being interested."

"What do your parents think about his calling?"

A small wrinkle briefly creased the smooth skin between Mary's brows and then faded into a puzzled expression in her eyes. "Only Papa has said anything, and he was no help at all."

"What do you mean?"

"Oh, he just told me not to get any silly ideas. Can you imagine? As though I was throwing myself at the man. It was so unlike Papa. He's so sensitive and kind usually. And really, I did not ever mention the way I feel about Lammot to anyone except you. My stars, I hope my feelings are not that transparent to Lammot."

"Well, it's a grand idea, if you ask me. Why in heaven's name would he want to discourage you?"

Mary shrugged. "It doesn't matter much at the moment, anyway. I found out that Lammot is leaving on a trip to Britain and the Continent to do some work for the company."

"For how long?" Megan asked sharply.

"That's the unhappy part. He doesn't know, really. In fact, I only found out about the trip indirectly from Papa last night. He said that Henry du Pont appears to be grooming Lammot for a larger responsibility in the company."

"Will he be going alone?"

"I imagine. Oh, you're wondering if the mysterious and aristocratic Michael Farrell will be going this time. Well, I doubt it. He's created quite a stir among certain ladies on the Hill, I'm told. And he's not exactly a friend of Mr. Henry."

At that moment Blanche Feeney bustled into the kitchen. She leveled a withering stare at Megan and snapped, "The Mister is already at table, and the Madam is on her way down!"

"I'd better leave," Mary mumbled and carried her cup to the sink.

Blanche said nothing to her as she ducked quickly out the door, and Megan was already a blur frantically loading up her serving trays. As she retreated from the humiliation of having ruined her friend's day, Mary felt a hot resentment toward the old servant. Blanche Feeney was a dried-up old witch, a perfect type to work in Henry du Pont's household.

CHAPTER TWENTY-SIX

During the week of the funerals, Michael had reported for work in the laboratory, which was only sporadically manned by a single chemist hired to replace Lammot while he was at Wapwallopen. There was not enough work to keep the man occupied with powder batch analysis, so he had been assigned elsewhere on alternate days. In the empty lab, Michael filled his days puttering with experiments unfinished when they had left months before. It was fine with him. Everyone else was crawling over the wreckage of the blast, clearing debris for the rebuilding. Although he was not afraid of heavy work—he had certainly had his share of it—the challenge of swinging a pick or loading a barrow with stone could not match wrestling with laboratory experimentation. Probably no one knew he was even at work. That suited him as well. He needed the isolation.

He needed time to think. There were disturbing things twisted like fouled mooring lines inside his head, snarled knotty lengths that defied a neat coiling, strands that led nowhere when he tried to sort them out. It was no good in the boardinghouse. Even his room this time was shared with two other men, young bachelors who tried to be friendly by filling every minute with conversation. Solitary walks did not seem to be productive, and in desperation once he had even sought out the flickering gloom of the church.

The workbench and equipment were what he needed. Somehow the brain could sort things out more clearly when occupied with a mechanical distraction.

Kevin Gallagher's prophetic end had sobered him more than anything he could remember. The old troubles at home had been constant, but he had been stunned rather than quickened by the events. Kevin's life now seemed in retrospect to epitomize emptiness. He had held back from every chance to fill that vacuum for forty years, a mason-monk cloistered in the walls he built, a martyr dedicated to the capricious demon that took him.

God, he was getting carried away. It was hardly martyrdom, although some of the powdermen accorded it that kind of reverence. Black Irish fatalism. But looked straight in the eye, it was more like apathy. The whole community seemed to accept the threat of an awful payoff in exchange for the security of a steady job at average pay. There was no hope of greater reward, and they all accepted those conditions with a cheerfulness that outsiders considered stupidity.

Michael knew it was not quite that simple. There was a pride in confronting the danger, too, a spirit that the grimy workers wore like a badge. And if their trade was terrifying at times to themselves, they knew it seemed all the more so to outsiders. They were living closer to the edge than most, they were proud of the fact, and du Pont cultivated their peculiar esprit.

Now the du Ponts had their own martyr. Michael wondered how much Henry's driving had brought about that calamity, and whether any of his family thought to lay the responsibility on Henry's leadership. He doubted it. The feeling generally prevailed that Alex was too directly involved with the workers anyway, an opinion reinforced by the manner of his death. If he had kept his distance, run his crews like a gentleman overseer should, he would have spared himself a lifetime of grime and a painful death.

Well, he had bequeathed his sons a large share in a prosperous business. As bad as times were now, profits from the recent past must have piled up, and future opportunities would swell his children's legacy when they came of age. Some contrast to Kevin Gallagher's meager savings on the company books.

He wondered if his own end would be as inconsequential. Would he drift along in the limbo of the company shadow, dependent on the friendship of one du Pont to shield him from abuse by another? Would he ever achieve a level of success, of pride? And what about marriage, a family of his own?

"It's time you meshed gears and got your own machinery moving, Michael Farrell," he muttered to himself.

"Took the words right out of my mouth!"

The voice came from the doorway behind him, and he started, dropping a pestle to the floor as Lammot du Pont sauntered in.

"Sorry to have startled you, old boy." He stooped to retrieve the tool and set it back in its mortar. "Hmm, what kind of porridge is this you're making?"

"Double-F rifle. I had an idea to go along with your hydraulic pressing theory."

"Oh? I'm all ears."

"It's fairly simple, too simple perhaps. We know that compressing the grains slows combustion, and that is one way to build pressure gradually as the ball moves along the tube. But as you pointed out some time ago, even dense grains of powder lose surface area as they burn."

"Ergo, fat breeched cannon with short, inaccurate barrels."

"Or long, accurate barrels with an occasional blown breech because of the tremendous first pressure."

"Your idea?"

"To even the pressure throughout the bore. A smaller sustained charge would give greater accuracy, longer range, allow for lighter cannon, and save powder."

Lammot looked bored. "Really, Michael, isn't this rather elementary? We've tried compressed grains of all sizes with only modest success. An even burn behind the shot from breech to muzzle is excellent theory, but achieving it is another thing entirely."

"Let me show you something." Michael began sketching over-size shapes of powder grains: sphere, lozenge, cube, and last, a hexagon. Lammot watched with growing impatience.

"Look, Michael, we've tried all those before, and I have something more important to announce."

"We haven't done this." Inside the last sketch, Michael drew a smaller hexagon, shading the lines to indicate a six-sided opening in the exact center of the shape. "Now, watch what happens as it burns. As the periphery of the hexagon erodes into a smaller burning surface, the inner walls are burning outward, spreading into a progressively larger area."

"My God!"

"I haven't tested it on the linear éprouvette. In fact, I was just about to stamp the shape on your hydraulic graining press."

Lammot picked up the sheet and paced the room. "Incredible! Burning from the inside out, so simple. We could experiment for the ideal size and machine a plate to stamp them out. This is some porridge indeed!"

"It's still untested."

Lammot took off his spectacles and began polishing the lenses vigorously with his handkerchief. His gray eyes twinkled, and he grinned. "Well, let's not waste any more time theorizing, Dr. Farrell." With that he slipped on his glasses, shucked off his coat, and began working the mortar and pestle.

It was well after dark by the time they had pressed several of the experimental grains and set them in the autoclave to dry. They would have to wait until morning for test firing.

"What was the news you were about to share before getting sidetracked?" Michael asked as they were leaving.

"Great Scott! I'd completely forgotten. But you must be starving. What's say to a dinner on me in town, eh? We need to celebrate."

"Maybe we should not tempt fate by being premature."

"I didn't mean your powder idea, Michael. We'll wait on that. I want to celebrate what happened to me today, and indirectly what it may mean for you."

"I'm intrigued," Michael said looking down at his rough work clothing," but I should clean up at Mrs. Walsh's first."

"All right, I'll get something in harness and meet you there in a quarter hour. On the way to town I'll fill you in."

When the buggy stopped at the widow's bachelor house in Squirrel Run, Lammot had difficulty keeping his horse in check. Michael missed the step twice as the rig jerked and, as he swung aboard, they were off instantly.

"You picked a lively animal tonight."

"The horse is just reacting to my news. I whispered it in her ear when I slipped on the harness."

"Well, I'm all ears."

Lammot took a breath and began, the excitement a rising pitch as he spoke.

"Uncle Henry and I had a meeting today. You know that he and Alexis held controlling shares in the company. Of course, my aunts have shares, but they have always been silent partners, and my brother was made a junior partner when Father died."

"Three active partners?"

"Yes. Uncle Henry, Uncle Alex, and Irénée. With Alex's death, something had to be done about the partnership. His boys are still in school, and a third male was needed."

"Henry Algernon."

"No, my cousin plans to continue at West Point and stay in the military indefinitely. Thank God for that, he knows nothing of the business. Of course, Willie is a child. For that matter, I don't believe my uncle likes him very much. He dotes on Henry A. like the crown prince."

"So he picked you as the new partner."

"We signed the agreement today."

"That's marvelous, Lammot. You deserve it."

"I *wanted* it enough, that's certain."

"What changes will it make in your work? Does he want you to continue at Wapwallopen?"

"That's the other news. I'm to go abroad for several months. Uncle wants me to probe about the powder industry in Britain and Europe, ferret out new processes, assess the competition."

"Sounds exciting. When do you leave?"

"In a few days. I asked if you could come along as my partner, Michael, but he wouldn't go for it. He's very tight with 'non-essential expenses,' as he put it. But I did wangle a promise that you could work in the lab meanwhile."

"I appreciate that."

"No increase in pay, I'm afraid. As it was he was upset that you were drawing powderman's wages. When I get back we'll work on that problem."

"I understand."

— 215 —

"Look, my friend, I value your ability and loyalty more than you can imagine. It will take some time before I have the power to do much about it, but you and I can become rich in this company. Do you trust me?"

"Certainly. But it is not quite that simple. I'm not at all sure that a permanent job under Henry du Pont is likely as far as I am concerned. I might turn out to be your particular Jonah."

"Let me take care of that."

"Also I think it time that I took more responsibility for my own direction. I had dreams of my own once."

"Please, Michael, give me six months, a year. We are a team; I can feel it. I need your talents, and you need the opportunity that this company can provide."

They fell silent then. The heavy mist of evening settled over the Brandywine, stretching gauze layers that muted the frog and cricket calls as they rolled along. Even the trotting hooves were deadened by the soft earth of the roadway. At Rising Sun Lane they turned sharply away from the Crick, and Lammot laid the whip to urge the mare up the steep climb out of the gorge. When they reached the top of the hill, the layers of moisture thinned to reveal sharp pinpoints of stars in the moonless sky.

"I'm not particularly delighted at the prospect of working under Henry du Pont's nose," Michael said finally, "but I'll stay on until you get back."

"You won't regret it, Michael."

"Well, *somebody* has to keep an eye on your lab."

"*Our* lab," Lammot corrected.

Michael smiled. It was a mutual indulgence they allowed each other. The laboratory was Henry's and both knew it.

"Someday the situation will be quite different," Lammot said quietly. "My uncle alluded to the day when he would step down from the directorship. He made it clear that I would be the choice as his successor."

Michael turned. "He wants you to take over the company?"

"Oh, not in the near future. He will certainly stay on for another ten years, but he wants me to take over all the research and development operations in addition to setting up new plants."

"Hmm. Well, he knows how much he needs you. I give him credit for that, recognizing your contribution at last."

"The European trip is a step toward taking over. I hope they will give me what we're after. None of my contacts know me. I'll have to make friends quickly."

"You'll do that well. I've never seen a man who can stumble into people's good graces so easily. How do you do it? Is is an acquired skill or an inherited trait?"

Lammot looked at Michael curiously. "I've never given it much thought. Frankly, my family are considered a bit drab and stuffy by outsiders, or haven't you noticed?"

"That's what makes your own situation the more remarkable. I honestly think you could walk away with nearly anything you asked for. Europe had better lock up her secrets."

"Perhaps it's my flawless French."

Michael raised an eyebrow. "You'd better stick to English. Unless of course you want to cultivate the impression of a helpless bumpkin."

"That may be my secret charm, old fellow, that and my obvious lack of means."

"Well, that has changed."

Lammot grimaced. "Not much, I'm afraid. My allowance has gone up five hundred a year, but the contract to buy shares has put me deeper than that in debt."

"That's none of my business. I did not intend—"

"To pry? Really, my friend, there are few people I can share my secrets with other than you. Besides, three shares of the business is rather small potatoes when I could buy only one with my own cash. Thank goodness I have well-heeled aunts I could tap for the loans. Irénée is the lucky one; his three were part of the deal for father's estate."

"I imagine Henry has a larger piece of the company."

"Considerably. More than the rest of the family combined, as a matter of fact. He directly controls twenty shares."

"So you had to *buy* into the business. As an heir of the family, that seems rather strange."

"Yes. It is rather an unusual situation. You see, my grandfather felt the director of the company should have complete say over the administration of all assets. That included the real estate, the actual homes we live in, in addition to the powder works themselves. Even decisions on when to paint, pay for household servants, food budgets, are subject to the director's approval."

"Just like the tenant workers."

"On a somewhat grander scale, yes. Everything belongs to the du Pont Company, subject to disposition by the director."

"That kind of control is absolute."

"Absolutely." Lammot chuckled lamely at his word play. "It is terribly autocratic, but it seems to work for us. The family business does not suffer from internal bickering, nor is there any weakening from dilution of ownership as evolving generations spread."

"A benevolent dictatorship."

"You might put it that way."

"The family puts enormous trust in the ability and ethics of their director. He has a free hand."

"I have to give credit to Uncle Henry, somewhat grudgingly, I'll admit. He has a sharp mind for business even if he does run the place like a martinet."

"And ethics?"

Lammot thought for a moment and then appeared to choose his words carefully. "Ethics of opportunity. He is rigidly honest in business affairs, a stickler for exact accounting, but the advancement of the company is his measuring stick as far as ethics are concerned. I think he'd do anything necessary to keep the business strong."

Or to keep a valuable person like Lammot du Pont under his control, Michael thought, but he did not say it to the new junior partner.

Their meal was excellent, and the wine flowed generously. It was a proper celebration worth the hangovers they suffered through the following morning. Their heads had cleared by afternoon, but the test firing did not go well. More work would have to be done on the density or shape of the grains. It was just as well as far as Michael was concerned. He had a challenge to keep him busy. He did not think it was procrastination at all. There was ample time, really, for him to make up his mind about his own goals.

As Lammot was leaving, he stopped by the lab to give Michael some advice.

"Keep the powder ideas under your hat until I get back. No sense creating a stir or unwelcome curiosity."

"From everyone but Henry?"

"Especially Henry," Lammot said. "He's the last person I'd want to know."

Michael left work early one evening. The powder graining research was taking so much of his time that he never left until dark, and gave up then only because he could not work with much accuracy by lamplight. But another problem nagged him more than the lab project, and he had to get it off his mind to think clearly.

When he got to the Gallaghers', they were at supper. He chided himself at the lapse of good manners, but accepted Noreen's invitation to share the meal.

"I'm really sorry to barge in like this," he said and immediately felt foolish for saying it. "The truth is that I seldom know the time. I've been working on a stubborn project."

"We haven't seen much of you the past few weeks." Brendan was making conversation.

"We haven't seen much of anybody," Noreen said with a little smile. "Everyone is so busy."

The table seemed shrunken—they seemed shrunken. Without Kevin's presence the meal seemed perfunctory, the very house had a closed-in quality Michael had never felt before. So many bright and noisy meals he had had with them. It was nearly stifling now.

"I haven't done justice to your cooking, Noreen," Michael said, putting down his spoon and pushing the half-eaten food away. "Indian summer, I guess. The heat takes my appetite."

"We understand." Noreen gave him a compassionate look and cleared his plate. Brendan excused himself to a pipe in the back yard, and over their coffee they watched him pacing slowly through his smoke, driving two laggard chickens toward their coop at the edge of the woods.

"He's better than he was, poor thing," Noreen said smoothing

— 219 —

out a wrinkle in the tablecloth. As soon as her palm lifted, the fabric sprang back the way it had been before.

But he'll never be quite the same again, Michael thought. There was nothing he could say to comfort her. She seemed to understand his silence and appreciate the honesty.

"Noreen, I don't know how to begin with this so I'll just plunge in and get it out."

She smiled and patted his hand. "Best way to do it."

"You have made this place the only home I know, this family the only one I know. You have made me feel a part of this home. I truly feel a kinship with all of you. You would not deny that, would you?"

"No."

"Once before I tried to claim the right of responsibility toward this family . . . my family . . . and it was denied me."

"Michael, you need not—"

"I don't want to bring agitation upon you, Noreen. Please hear me out without taking offense."

She looked away, and he ignored her swimming eyes to press on.

"Megan makes two dollars a week, and Brendan needs to set aside all he can for your own security. I have no idea what Denny's schooling costs, but it certainly took all that Kevin saved on the company books and his pay besides. Now all of that is gone."

"We can manage, Michael. Truly we can."

"You should not have to. That is the point. Megan should not be cleaning slop jars for Henry du Pont, and Brendan deserves the hope of a secure old age with you."

Noreen bit her lip, and he knew he had hit a nerve with the comment about Megan.

"I did not mean to be crude, Noreen, but the little she makes is hardly justification for that kind of work."

"You need not tell me that!" It was an outburst, the only time he had ever seen her crumble, but still he pressed on scarring her pride, appealing to her pride.

"She should be in school, too. There are places for girls with her talents, with *half* her talent. The only difference is the money.

Denny is making a break for a better life. We can't let Meg buy his position with her servitude."

"Oh, you do know where to thrust the knife."

"It's myself that I'm accusing. Can't you see that? I've the same means that Kevin had. It's my turn now. It's my right by adoption, if you will. I demand it."

"You love her dearly, don't you? I did not realize until now how deep the feeling was."

"Like my own, Noreen. The two of them, but Megan always had me in her grip the stronger."

She looked at him directly, and he had the feeling that somehow she was challenging his sincerity.

"You are a good man, Michael, and I respect your feelings."

"Then grant me the right to help."

"I respect your feelings, yes, but I also think that they are clouding your better judgment."

"I do not see how giving the girl a chance to better herself can be an error of judgment."

"She's a woman. Certainly you have seen that. It would not be right for you to tamper with what she is to become."

"Tamper!"

"Ah, let's drop that. It was a poor choice of word surely. All I meant was that she must be free to reach for whatever she wants without any burden on her affection for you."

"We wouldn't have to tell her."

"Blarney. She'd know in a minute. And even if she didn't, *you'd* know."

"I'd know." His expression was blank.

"You'll need time to let that explain itself. You are still quite young, you know."

"Your logic escapes me."

"Then trust me."

He was about to plead his support from a different angle, but Noreen interrupted.

"It was meant to be a surprise from her. But your mind must be put at rest, I can see that. You see, Megan is already taking her steps upward. She is being tutored in French and, I imagine, in the proper ways to carry on among the rich. Louisa du Pont herself is the teacher; can you feature that? Megan is to accompany her to France. And in another month she'll be off to Europe on a ship."

"France?"

"Oh, she's dizzy with the wonder of it. Like a child on Christmas."

Michael felt a cold disappointment knot in his stomach. It was a reaction that surprised him with its meanness. He could not understand the sour resentment that gripped him.

"And who's paying for that?" he asked evenly.

"Henry du Pont," she answered.

CHAPTER TWENTY-SEVEN

It was her letters that made him face up to it at last. The bright, cheerful, newsy letters she sent faithfully each week and which he now waited for so impatiently at the company post office. He admitted to himself that there was nothing in any of them to suggest any change in her feelings, nothing that even hinted at anything more than friendship. Her closing was always the same as it had been through the childhood notes, "Affectionately, Megan."

Perhaps it was the emerging friendship itself that brought him around. Suddenly it claimed an equality that demanded his sharing of everything she saw and heard, her sharp reactions and opinions, her delights. She was no longer the child-mind doting on what he could bring to her. Now the roles were reversed, and he was caught hanging on her every word.

"You will not think me vain to have sat for the enclosed photographic portrait, I hope. The new science is terribly popular over here, and Mrs. du P. insisted that I give it a try. This one is yours to keep—so that you will not have forgotten what I look like when we get home next month. I have sent another, one less flattering, to Aunt Noreen and Uncle Brendan who will think me pretty regardless."

It was a simple pose, a three-quarter shot of her sitting with hands folded in her lap, her head turned full face toward the

camera. She was not smiling, but there was mischief in her eyes
—and pride, too. She was beautiful, and she knew it.

He had stopped to read the letter on his way back to the lab
during noon break. The route he took wound through the woods
uphill from the company store to the small "chapel," as Lammot
called their lab. He loved this time of year, especially after the
first frost had driven insects into hibernation and the trees were
still in full leaf, beginning to turn color before dropping in
November. Today the midday air was balmy like a misplaced
spring, the earth underfoot soft with last year's humus. He
ambled as though on a Sunday stroll, choosing a different pattern
in his return to work, avoiding as always a regular path.

Lammot would want to know if he had got his weekly "Con-
tinental news" when he got back. Asking again if Megan was
still holding her own with all those hot-blooded French boys.

He drew a great breath of the clear woodland air, fresh and
clean of the rank smells of the sulphur and saltpeter down lower
by the mills.

He stole another look at her face in the glass plate, folded it
carefully in its wrapping, and slipped it inside his jacket next to
his chest. He was conscious of its pressure there, its presence
building a warm, pleasant, breathless feeling in his throat.

He could not resist the feeling, did not want to stifle it, and
felt suddenly conspiratorial. What was happening to him? Dear
God, she was almost young enough to have been his own child.
Had he always harbored this dark affection? He tried to recall
her from those days but the lovely face now resting against his
heart blocked all remembering. A shaft of sunlight flashed across
his eyes, and he could see the edge of the woods, the clear lawns
of the estate, and beyond, in its own clump of trees, the white
outline of the lab.

One last time. He opened the parcel again, stared at the picture like one baffled by a puzzle, then tucked it away. He would
not mention it to Lammot.

When Michael came into the building, Lammot said nothing
about the mail, but he was excited about something else.

"I think we've solved the grain density problem."

"That's good news."

"It is the design of the hydraulic plate. There is uneven pressure on the outside edges of the mold. See the weight differential?" He pointed to a glass-covered balance scale holding two identical pellets of black powder. The beam was tilted. "The heavier sample came from the center of the press."

"How can we correct it in production?"

"I saw a design in Brussels, a press with multiple cylinders arranged so that the plate receives equal pressure to minimize flexing at the edges. I've jury-rigged our press to do the same. Now look."

He replaced the two samples with others which appeared to be duplicates, but this time the balance settled perfectly level.

"What would you wager that the charge will work this time?"

"I'd rather not take the wager. I've lost betting against myself too many times while you were away."

They ran the charge in the small éprouvette behind the lab a dozen times that afternoon, pressing out test samples of varied drying times. Each firing showed a common result: the pressures were nearly constant along the tube.

"Now we'll have to spend a week pressing out the larger grains. That will be the real proof," Lammot said eagerly at the end of the day.

"But we have no way of testing full-size cannon powder. To do that we'd have to go to a federal arsenal."

"Exactly."

"The nearest is Philadelphia, but perhaps you'd like to demonstrate it in Washington," Michael observed. "Might impress the right people."

"Not yet. I want privacy until it's proven. The process is unprotected by patent. I don't want to risk losing it to the competition. Also, Henry might get wind of it."

"Where then?"

"I've a friend, an artillery officer stationed at a less conspicuous arsenal eighty miles west of here. I want you to go with our samples, Michael. You won't be missed as I would."

"Where is this place?"

"The northeast corner of West Virginia on the Potomac and Shenandoah Rivers," Lammot said as he locked the door of the lab. "Harper's Ferry."

"I'm impressed." The young lieutenant scratched out his computations, neatly tabulated the results, and handed the paper to Michael. "Has Lammot been in touch with Captain Rodman?"

"I really cannot say."

"I see. The less said the better, eh? Well, you might mention Rodman to your boss when you get back. His gun is likely to be commissioned, *and* since he is an ordnance chief, this powder should be brought to his attention."

"I'll certainly mention that."

The officer smiled. "After you apply for patent."

"Thank you for your understanding, and for your discretion."

"No thanks needed. Lammot du Pont helped me through hard times when we were in school. He has a pair of sympathetic ears and buttoned lips. He can count on my silence about your remarkable powder. I owe him that much, at least."

Michael spent the afternoon killing time before his train connection left for Baltimore. Harper's Ferry had been only a cluster of buildings before the arsenal was built and had little to recommend it otherwise. The place was active enough by day with freight traffic to the army installation and transient shipping over the ferry itself, and at night all of those transients converged on a scattering of public houses flanking the waterfront. Two nights in a loud inn had been enough. He looked forward to getting home.

The connection in Baltimore was in time to catch a train to Wilmington arriving well after midnight. He slept through most of the next day and did not see a newspaper until Thursday when Lammot brought it into the lab.

"My God, Michael, my friend at the arsenal was killed in the raid!"

"What raid?"

"That maniac, John Brown. You had a close shave yourself!"

Michael took the paper, his eyes racing over the story. The dead included the artillery officer he had worked with, and there was a separate list of men captured by R. E. Lee's marines. The only name he recognized was John Brown.

"A rotten shame," Lammot muttered. "He was a good friend in college."

"Was he married?"

"I don't know. Lord, I hope not! Well, how did the tests go? Did the powder measure up?"

"I have the data in my grip. It's very good."

"Excellent! Let's get at it, shall we?"

When Michael laid out the sheets, Lammot became instantly absorbed in the figures. Michael found it hard to concentrate on the neat penmanship, knowing that the hand that had written it was stilled forever. But Lammot seemed to have forgotten that sad coincidence in the excitement of their invention. He marveled at Lammot's detachment. These du Ponts were a strange, cold clan.

CHAPTER TWENTY-EIGHT

Irénée du Pont moved with his bride into their new home in time for the start of the winter holidays. The house had been built over a mile from the du Pont residence compound, a decision partly justified by Irénée's distressed lungs but mainly to build a comfortable distance from Charlotte's mother-in-law.

"To be truthful about it," Irénée confided to Lammot, "I have become more tolerant of the sulfur and saltpeter from the mills than the vitriol our mother discharges so innocently."

"Tsk! Rather strong words from her elder son."

"Rubbish. She has made it so unpleasant for Charlotte lately that I sometimes detest the woman."

"She's our mother."

"Oh, yes. That is a bond, isn't it? But I could tell you stories that would curl your hair, Motty. The trouble is, I would think them laughable, well, ludicrous, if it were not that she is our mother."

"Stories?"

"Forget that. I have held my tongue for years. Forget it."

"She has been cruel to Charlotte, but face it, Irénée, your wife sometimes rubs the ladies against the grain."

Irénée laughed, "I love her for it. My own little Secessionist. But it's not only political, I think our family—Mother included —resent her beauty."

"And the competition for affection from the men?"

"Oh, bosh, Motty, that's just her Southern manner. They were reared that way. I find it appealing. Frankly it's less hypocritical than the behavior of others I could mention."

"Another secret? What were you going to say about Mother?"

"I wasn't," he answered quickly, but Lammot noticed he had paled slightly.

"Uncle Henry likes her very much."

"What? What do you mean?"

"Charlotte has an ally in Henry."

"Oh, Charlotte, yes. Yes, well, when it comes to women, the man makes no secret of his universal and sometimes indiscriminate taste. If he is Charlotte's ally, she has no need of enemies."

"He knows about Henry and Mother," Lammot thought sadly, but covered the realization with a smile. "I wouldn't worry about Charlotte, brother. She is a breath of fresh air, and clowns like our uncle are no match for her."

Irénée flashed a rare smile. "I appreciate that particular analogy, Motty. I need all the air I can get."

"How is that coming along?"

"Oh, you know. I have bad days, but I think better."

"You should get out of the yards. All those fumes—they can't help. Have you thought of trying something else? Just because Uncle Alexis—"

"It's not what I want to do, you know that, but I don't have your brain for invention, and the job has to be done."

"Someone else can."

"Oh, *anybody* else could. But don't you see, Lammot? I have to protect my interest for Charlotte's sake and our children when they come."

Lammot gripped his brother's arm in a rare show of affection. Irénée was startled by the contact.

"That's a practical loyalty, Bish, and noble, too, if you don't mind my saying so."

Irénée did not mind. It had been years since Lammot had used his childhood nickname. "Grim as a bishop." Some had thought it a cruel label reflecting his bleak years with the cough.

But Irénée had secretly delighted in it. And now Lammot's brief sign of affection soaked into him like a balm.

"Try not to forget the party, will you, Motty?"

"A week from next Saturday."

"Yes. And will that Michael fellow be coming?"

"Hmm. I'm not sure he thinks it a good idea."

"Oh, I know what he's worried about. Tell him Henry won't be there."

Lammot raised an eyebrow, and Irénée explained, "It's just for the younger set. Tell him to bring someone, and you plan to bring someone, I hope."

"Will Mother be there?"

"No."

"This will be rather like an employees' party, I take it. Are you picking up Uncle Alexis's role?"

"Hardly. Charlotte especially wanted your man to be there, to make amends for his embarrassment, I think. Besides, she thinks Farrell a misplaced aristocrat rather than just one of the rank and file."

Lammot smiled, "I have someone in mind, then."

For Megan Feeney the exciting days leading up to Irénée du Pont's party were breathless.

"Try to stand still."

"Here I am almost twenty with more thrills behind me than any girl I know on the Crick, and this has me close to passing out from dawn to bedtime."

"Please give me a rest from it, Megan. I'm gettin' cross-eyed on this hem with all your twitching."

"Oh, Aunt Norrie, do you think Michael will think me pretty in it?"

"He'll be proud to show you off."

"That's not what I mean."

"I know what you meant." Noreen groaned as she stood up and glanced critically at the gown. "Turn around slowly and mind y' don't fall off the stool." The stern look left her face as Megan made a tentative pirouette, gently flaring the skirt, and she smiled up at her niece.

"You'll be the loveliest one there."

Michael thought so. From the time he picked her up at the Gallagher's in a rented trap until he brought her back late that night, she dazzled him. If there had been fears that she might yet seem a girl, that she might bear some adolescent trace to mock his own age and tinge his new longing with guilt, they were gone now. Gone with the first look at her in that elegant gown cut so simply yet daringly, softly draped but stating her figure with unadorned frankness. He had never seen her so radiant. He could not keep his eyes off her.

"Well, what do you think, Michael Farrell?" she asked after he had clumsily bundled her in the sleigh robe and touched the horse's flank with his whip.

"I'm honored to be in such regal company."

"Not blarney, please."

"It's not overstatement, Megan. I think you'll turn every head in the place."

"It's what *you* think. That's what I'm interested in."

"You're lovely. Perhaps the loveliest young woman I've ever laid eyes on."

"Hmm. That sounds a bit distant. Or maybe like something Uncle Brendan might say." She was looking at him keenly. He could feel her eyes as he minded the lines, guiding them through the fresh unmarked snow of Crick Road. The runners hissed, the harness slapped, but there was no sound of hoofbeats.

This was sticky business. How could he say what he was truly thinking? It was a wild hope anyway. Had she agreed to go with him only because it was a chance to rub elbows with the du Ponts, her escort a vehicle only like some doting relative?

"I can't wait to see Mary Belin!"

She had changed the subject, thank God.

"Harry's daughter. Will she be there?"

"Oh, yes," a laugh rippled like music from deep inside her throat. "She's coming with Lammot du Pont."

"With Lammot? How do you know that?"

"She told me. It was quite a telling."

"What do you mean?"

"I mean she'll be stunned to see me there."

"You didn't tell her?"

"No. She tends to lord things over me a bit."

"Oh, I see. Sweet vengeance, eh?" Part of his elation ebbed.

"You might say that. I don't think she thinks me good enough to attend one of their parties without a serving tray. And there's not much difference between us. Her father wears a frock coat to work is all the difference."

He was suddenly thankful that he had not made a fool of himself a few minutes earlier. All the enthusiasm she had shown when he had asked her to the party had been for quite another reason than what he had hoped. When would he learn! He lashed the horse into the steep grade up Breck's Lane, and the sleigh lurched so that Megan was thrown back with a gasp.

"Let's be on with your social entrance then, little lady," he said almost grimly. "Make way for the up-and-coming Irish!"

"Really, Michael," she said with a confused look. "I'm not out to show anybody up, and I wish you'd not call me 'little lady' anymore. I'll soon be twenty."

"And I'll soon be thirty-one," he thought dismally, "with a bad habit of making premature assumptions."

Megan was introduced as the "niece of Brendan Gallagher," the relative with highest standing in the company. A few ladies mentioned her own service as traveling companion to Louisa du Pont, a tactful observation which gave her more status. It was a young crowd limited to contemporaries of the host and hostess. None of the ogres of the family were there to intimidate. A room had been cleared for dancing to the strains of a local quartet, and their music filled the house. It was a small party, no more than thirty, and she suspected that many guests were from Wilmington society. It was certainly not the usual clannish gathering of cousins.

By the time Mary Belin arrived with Lammot du Pont, Megan was beginning to feel quite at home and prepared to enjoy her friend's reaction. Mary, however, was not surprised at all.

"You," Mary whispered when she had filtered through the reception line. "Some friend you are, letting me prattle on about my invitation and saying nothing yourself." She poked Megan in the ribs with a gloved finger, and they both laughed. "Lammot told me that Michael was coming, and dunce that I am, I was still able to put two and two together. Hmm."

Megan winced at another jab and felt small because of the deception. Her friend seemed so genuinely pleased to see her, relieved to find an ally perhaps, that her own lack of confidence turned suddenly into childish spite.

"You look beautiful, Mary."

"Now let's not make it worse. Compared to you, my dear, I probably rank with a wilted dandelion. Where did you get that *gown*? It must have come from Paris. You bought it in France, didn't you? Oh, I hate you for being so lovely. I do hope Charlotte isn't jealous. Hmm. No worries about that as far as I am concerned."

Lammot du Pont angled toward them, intercepting Michael as he returned with a glass of punch in each hand. He made no attempt to cover a rather direct and admiring look at Megan. Mary could not miss it.

"Look at him! Oh, Megan, I swear if you turn his head, I'll put a powder keg under your bed."

Megan was too preoccupied to respond. Her eyes were on Michael, shorter by an inch than Lammot, who towered over everyone else in the room, but broader in the shoulders, handsome. He was in his element in this room, she thought, a quiet, commanding presence that could not be ignored. No wonder Henry du Pont disliked him so. A thrill vibrated through her as he drew closer, she was enveloped by his look, a strong possessive grip of eyes locked on hers as he negotiated his way through the guests, a look that went beyond affection. She was convinced as surely as she knew her own desire. He wanted her.

"Well, Miss Feeney! Do you remember me?" Lammot du Pont was suddenly towering over them, stooping slightly to bring his face in range. "I'm the one your uncle scolded so for wearing out one of his draft animals on a wild ride. You were there when he dressed me down."

"He mentions it often, Mr. du Pont. But he admitted later that the stallion was less fractious after your training."

Lammot chuckled. "I nearly got both of us killed, crashing through Hagley Woods over rocks at a gallop. Is he well? And your Aunt? She tried desperately to correct my spelling, you know, worked with my Aunt Vic at the old school. I failed them both, I'm afraid. Bad grammar and bad spelling. But they tried valiantly."

"They're both well, thank you."

"Look here, have you danced yet? Michael, let me show off this young lady for the crowd, do you mind? Mary? Say, you two sip on that punch while we make a few circuits, that's about all it will take. My feet have a way of finding ladies toes, eh, Mary?" He slipped his arm under Megan's hand and propelled her to the center of the floor. "Two circuits, Michael, and then you can rescue her!"

Michael smiled wryly and offered a glass to Mary. "It looks like you are stuck with me for the moment, Miss Belin. Would you rather dance or drink?"

"He's such a clod, isn't he! My word, if he were not so clumsy in these matters, I would be angry. But the beast is so transparently innocent I find it hard to fault him."

"You are perceptive and magnanimous, under the circumstances."

"Neither, Mr. Farrell. I think 'smitten' better describes my circumstances." She took the goblet, but immediately set it on a table behind them. "I really don't want any of that awful punch. It sours so after the drinking. As for dancing, well, I'd rather have my first dance with the tall fellow with spectacles. You don't mind?"

"I understand perfectly," Michael said, and they both watched the couple gliding around the room.

"Oh, don't be such a sour fellow, Irénée. You *are* the host, and should make an effort to see that everyone has a good time! It's not going to hurt for you to ask a few of the ladies to dance."

"My cousins will do well enough on their own, Charlotte. God knows I've danced with them enough before this. Let me rest on my laurels. You're my prize, dear. There's no more threat of getting snared by some dowdy kinswoman."

"It's the others I mean," his wife pleaded. "It was *your* idea to have some of the help attend. Poor things, they seem so *over-*

whelmed by it all. It's our duty really. Just look at that Mary Belin, practically ignored."

"Oh, if it will make you feel better, I'll ask Mary to dance, but really, dearest, I want to save my energy for you."

"Irénée! I swear you do scandalize me at times, but, yes, dance with Mary and I'll start with that fellow standing with her, the one who works for Lammot."

"Michael Farrell."

"Yes, his face is familiar. The Englishman?"

"The Irishman. I didn't think you could forget easily."

"Oh, my, yes. He had a row with Uncle Henry. Well, I'll try to make him feel more comfortable, poor thing."

"Not too comfortable, my dear."

By anyone else's measure, Megan Feeney's first entree into society was a resounding triumph, but Megan herself had reservations.

She was not sure how many partners had claimed her for a dance, and that was certainly pleasant. But Michael had been with her only twice, both times interrupted by a double cut-in that left him waltzing off with Charlotte du Pont. Those brief interludes when she was in his arms were not satisfactory either. He held her as awkwardly as he might a child, elder indulging minor in a mimic of grown-up games. She knew that her own response had been stiff, but how could she penetrate his reserve? She felt anything but childlike tonight; her thoughts almost wanton when he was close.

So he was wooden and she aloof. Of course he was anything but stiff when dancing with Irénée du Pont's wife. At least he seemed to be making a hit with the hostess. Her laughter rose above the music, and once their execution of an involved step drew a ripple of spontaneous applause.

It was almost time to make an exit without appearing rude, and at a break in the music, she was about to suggest leaving when Henry Algernon du Pont made his entrance, stag, and resplendent in tailored West Point dress uniform. He approached the dance floor, waiting until he was in full sight of everyone in the room, removed his cape and visor with a flourish, and handed both to a servant who had to scurry briefly to keep the hallowed garments from striking the floor. He struck a pose of indifferent examination of the crowd, appearing to glance slightly above the heads of everyone present, and waited.

"Do you think he's lost?" Lammot said drily.

Mary Belin choked on her drink and began to giggle. The buzz around them subsided as those who had not seen the entrance were prodded into taking notice. There was a flutter of gloved applause, which Henry Algernon accepted with a faint smile, and as if cued by the response formed his procession of one toward the host and hostess.

The orchestra struck up a martial tune, and the partying resumed, but not before Charlotte's voice rang clear in greeting.

"The South is secure, thank God," she said, "with gallants such as this to lead the way."

He let himself be led by Charlotte on a round of renewed acquaintance with his kin and scions of the Wilmington gentry.

Megan wanted more than ever to leave. She dreaded being seen by the stuffy cadet. Up to now there had been a sense of mutual celebration of the holiday, a near equality that was certainly feigned, but was nice all the same. It could never be so with her employer's son. If anything, he was more aloof than his father. And he would make a point of their separate stations. She had not seen him for over a year, thanks to his schooling in New York and her own trip abroad. To extend that pleasant separation was most desirable.

"Others are beginning to leave, Michael. Perhaps we should too."

"Of course."

She was glad for the look of relief as he spoke and took a step toward the foyer when Charlotte and Henry Algernon blocked their way.

"Once more into the breach, my dear," she said tossing her head toward the uniform. "Please? As a favor to me and for God and country." She was gone then into the swirling dancers, her head tilted up with a pouting smile for Michael.

"May I?"

Anger was iced water in her veins, but she allowed Henry to take her into his arms, and they flowed with the dancers. It was deliberate, she felt it, a private joke between this prig and the Southern belle. She wondered when the charade would end, how he would manage to humiliate her. Well, she could play the game and give this bore a run for his gall.

They danced halfway through the set without speaking. It was a waltz, and Megan began subtle changes in her step, gradually easing herself into the lead, forcing him to follow. And then a flirting smile, a look into his eye, shifting into hauteur. She would play the game. He had unwisely chosen the ballroom floor to exact her humiliation. Already his clumsy effort was squeezing beads of sweat on his brow. She pressed for more advantage, always smiling, looking him right in the eye.

"I say, miss, I must apologize for my sluggish feet."

"Too much marching on parade, Mr. du Pont?"

"Well," he laughed, missing a step again, "I am not very clever at that either, I'm afraid. My preference is the saddle."

"Oh, a cavalry officer. How exciting."

"My dream," he puffed, "To lead a horse troop. At home I have my choice of several mounts. I am quite good in fact. My father, whose name is also Henry, was a soldier. You undoubtedly have heard of him, director of the Powder Company."

Megan nearly stumbled when she realized with a shock that Henry A. did not even realize he was dancing with his father's downstairs maid.

She withdrew from the attack and they chatted like new acquaintances, maneuvering through the maze of dancers.

"What may I call you?"

"Anything you choose, I suppose."

"Well, your name? I did not get it." He was at ease again, comfortable with the simpler step she had resumed, and smiling with the familiar arrogance. "You just forgot, Henry dear," she said so low that he had to tilt his head to catch the words. She could feel his breath on her neck, but the effect was worth that temporary annoyance. "Perhaps if I put on a dust bonnet you might recall."

He reared back suddenly and stumbled to a halt. She could see his face redden as the recognition dawned in his close-set, bulging eyes.

"Megan!"

A few couples stared curiously at them. Megan smiled genially and gripped his elbow.

"Yes, Henry. Now, would you be gentleman enough to escort me off the floor before we're trampled?"

PART III

CHAPTER TWENTY-NINE

APRIL
1861

"Well, Dorgan m'boy, it looks like yer business will be pickin' up."

"How's that, Dougherty?"

"That fracas down South, Fort Sumter."

"More trouble in bad times."

"Agh, look beyond yer nose, man! In six months you'll have to expand."

"Close down is what you mean. The country's goin' to hell in a basket."

"That's what I mean, the mills are hiring on again."

"What's the point?"

"Boss Henry is no dunce. He sees a war comin'."

"Who will he sell to? He tried to get you powdermen to vote for John Bell, didn't he?"

"Aye, that's my meaning. He's a cagey one, that Henry. He wanted to be right in the middle—just in case."

"In case of what?"

"In case Delaware went for the South. If you're on the fence, you can fall to either side."

"And now he's for Lincoln, I suppose."

"*For* him? Jesus Mary, he had all of us line up under the flag and swear allegiance to the new man. Made a special trip to Washington to pledge the mills behind the Union."

"That wasn't too smart. The politicians in Dover would rather side with Maryland and Virginia. Henry might end up losing the whole shebang."

"Aha, boyo, that's where you're wrong. The governor made him a major general."

"Boss Henry?"

"Himself. Now he commands the whole state militia."

"Just a title."

"Oh? Well he had all the rifles removed from the two south counties and shipped up here. Took out their teeth before they got the idea to bite. No, he's in charge, all right, and it's 'the General' we'll be callin' Boss Henry from now on!"

"Nice touch. He makes the gunpowder and decides how fast it should be used up."

"Now you get the picture."

"What about his own family? I hear some of them are not sweet on Lincoln."

"All of them were there, all the du Pont clan, swearin' to uphold the Union. All but Mr. Irénée's new bride. She wouldn't show up for the ceremony. Her folks are from Virginia, I hear. Hates Lincoln with a passion, and the du Ponts too."

"I can understand that. Her own husband making powder to blow the kinfolks to kingdom come."

Michael and Lammot had been in the mining country north of San Francisco for nearly a year when Lincoln was inaugurated. That was a month before the fall of Fort Sumter. As removed as they were from the turbulent East, the tensions were building with speculation of war.

Michael took little note of the rumors. He was nursing his own turmoil. Not even a note from her. He tested Lammot once to see if he knew anything. "Have you heard from Mary Belin?"

"Frequently."

"I was wondering how things were with the Gallaghers and Megan Feeney."

"Only that you seem to be remiss in your correspondence. Haven't you written?"

"There is little to report."

"I suppose they might feel the same."

Michael shrugged. Lammot gave him a curious look.

"Look, I make it a practice to stay out of others' affairs, but Miss Belin suggested that I prod you a bit to write."

"Megan's suggestion?"

"I presume. Women can be terribly oblique. But since you've brought the matter up, I wonder that you have not pursued the matter of Megan Feeney."

"There's little point."

"Ah, I thought so. You *are* interested. That being the case, why all the hanging back?"

"I'm sure she has someone else in mind."

"What makes you think that?"

"It seems reasonable. She's at the age to attract men."

"According to Mary that's not the case—unless you count Henry Algernon. Apparently my cousin has made advances."

"What do you mean?"

"Oh, nothing beyond his usual, I imagine. Young Henry's eyes are bigger than his heart, if I may bend the saying, but Miss Feeney is in no danger of succumbing. Mary thinks she has better taste than to be interested in someone like him."

So it was true! The pain registered on his face, and Lammot caught the look.

"See here, Michael, I was kidding. Young Henry has a reputation like his father when it comes to women, but Megan is certainly more than his match. She can put him in his place."

"I was thinking of something more permanent."

"As a suitor? Don't be silly, man. Henry A. wouldn't think of courting a . . . Megan is an employee of the household. Above all things my pompous soldier-cousin values his station."

"She's stations *above* them!"

It was a belligerent outburst, and Lammot realized how deep the hurt was. His friend's face was black with fury.

"I only meant to reassure you, Michael. You have no competition from that dunce." He waited a moment, unsure of Michael's control, then slapped him gently on the shoulder. "You can't expect her to make the first move, old fellow. Write to her."

Michael was still angry and later wished that he had held his tongue, but the words lashed out as they formed in his head.

"Is that why you have not said anything to Mary Belin?"

Lammot paled at the suggestion. His open smile disintegrated into a formless waxen line, and his gray eyes hardened. His voice was curiously gentle when he answered.

"My love for Mary is genuine enough, though I have doubts as to my own worth in courting her. It is not the love I distrust, my friend, but the marriage. My family has not been blessed with reassuring examples."

It was to be their last conversation for months. The following day, when he had returned from a test blast using a mixture of sawdust and the frightening oil called nitroglycerine, the newspapers were headlining war, and there was a note from Lammot. He had left for the Brandywine.

The research, or espionage, went on. Their competitor was not only producing blasting powder more cheaply than du Pont could ship soda powder around the Horn, but they were making inroads with Sobrero's dangerous but powerful liquid explosive. It was so unstable that most miners were afraid to use it, but a cup of nitroglycerine would shatter bedrock a keg of black powder could not budge. A thimbleful could blow a man apart with whimsical impartiality. Everyone was looking for a way to make it safe. Whoever tamed the genie would reap a fortune.

Michael buried himself in the project.

In the months following Lammot's return, there was such a concern for the safety of the powder yards that the workers were organized into local militia for their defense. The first thing he did after being appointed captain of the Home Guard was to send for Michael Farrell.

"I hate to pull you away from our work with blasting glycerine," the letter read, "But the current fracas takes priority. I need your skill in drilling men under arms. The mills have been threatened already and the goldfield market will have to wait until the Rebellion is put down. Please take the most expeditious route."

That meant overland by stagecoach as far as the Missouri River, a bone-jarring four weeks to reach the nearest railhead, followed by six days on the train. Michael would have preferred returning under sail. He needed some exposure to the sea again and the time to compose himself before seeing Megan. But that would have taken months. In a few days he had collected his notes, stored the lab equipment with du Pont's local agent in San Francisco, and was on his way through the September flurries of the Donner Pass. He had a crawling apprehension as he passed the site of death and cannibalism and remembered Lammot's words, "drilling men under arms."

A uniform again? More carnage. It made less sense than what those emigrants had done twenty years before. Which was worse, to survive by eating the flesh of your dead brother or to kill him for a political belief?

His six-day ride from St. Joseph on the Missouri River had spanned half a continent, a dizzying prospect compared to the eternity it took to cover the same distance from California. Such a huge country! The railroad west would open it up, but it would take more than blasting powder to carve a gentle grade for track through the granite wall of the western mountains. As the landscape of Maryland and Delaware flickered past his coach window, he thought more and more about harnessing Ascanio Sobrero's terrifying compound. The solution had to come. Tame the demon without losing its blinding power. Again he opened his satchel and studied the thick accumulation of notes.

He could not keep his mind on them. The Brandywine was a few hours down the line, and Megan was there. A forbidden love awaited him, taunting him out of his concentration, building the sour homecoming he would somehow have to endure. By the time his train shuddered to a stop at the Wilmington station in the autumn twilight, he was exhausted physically and mentally. As he swung off the coach and began to walk wearily down the platform someone called from the dark doorway of the waiting room.

"Well, look what the cat dragged in."

"Hello, Lammot."

"Hmm. Not much of a greeting for someone who has met the train for three days." He took one of Michael's bags.

"Haven't had much sleep. I'll be in a better mood after a bath and shave."

Lammot wrinkled his nose. "Your closest associates will appreciate that."

"Anyway, thanks for picking me up."

"Hmm, how you gush! But don't waste your extravagant gratitude on me, old fellow. It was not my idea. Better save some of that enthusiasm for the one who forced me into it."

Michael stared at him, puzzled by his huge grin.

"We've had a long talk, and I covered *everything*."

Then Lammot took the other bag and nudged him forward. Megan was at the edge of the depot, smiling.

CHAPTER THIRTY

Henry's second trip to Washington turned out to be more than just a pledge of Union support. There was a crisis meeting between himself and the ordnance chiefs about reserves of gunpowder and the raw materials for making more. It was a shock to him that except for a million pounds of saltpeter stockpiled by du Pont, there was virtually none on hand in the loyal states. Indian saltpeter was controlled by Great Britain, with the world supply funneled through England. It was no secret that Anglo sympathies were with the newly formed Confederacy.

"A simple problem, Mr. du Pont, we need enough potassium nitrate to see us through the war and to keep it away from gunpowder factories in the South."

Henry nodded and waited for the lawyer from Springfield to proceed. The new president was more impressive than he would have imagined. He wore the office as though born to it—casual but commanding, unintimidated by the responsibility. This was certainly not a backwoods politico.

"The complication lies in acquiring the saltpeter indirectly." He inclined his head toward Secretary of War Cameron. "I cannot send Simon here to the English with hat in hand. They wouldn't sell to us."

"My company is at your service, Mr. President."

"Thank you. Mr. Seward will arrange for funding. How *were*

you doing that, Seward? Not State Department money, certainly?"

The secretary of state shifted uneasily before answering. "We thought to disburse through the Secret Service, Mr. President."

Lincoln smiled at Henry. "Well, that seems appropriate, doesn't it?" The face went quickly serious and he added. "I would suggest that your nephew act in this matter. If I am not mistaken, he has engaged in clandestine affairs for you before."

Henry was stunned. How had he heard about Sebastopol?

"Lammot."

"Yes. A bit young, but I am given to understand that he has recently established contact with several munitions brokers in Europe. Quite a persuasive fellow, they say."

"Most capable young man."

"Good. I'm pleased with the choice. Could you have him come down to go over the matter with me personally? We are most eager to get under way."

"I'll wire him today, Mr. President."

"Thank you, General du Pont. I will sleep more easily tonight knowing you have assumed this desperate enterprise."

On the train back to Wilmington, Henry mulled over the proposition. It would be most lucrative for the company to corner the world saltpeter supply, even if it had to be parceled out to some competitors. And no du Pont money would be involved. But the best part of the entire meeting was the surprise at the end. He was not aware that Lincoln had known of his appointment.

General du Pont. It had a nice ring.

"We'll let them think we had work at Wapwallopen. It should not take more than a month."

"I really see no need for secrecy. What is so strange about your going to England to buy potassium nitrate? Du Pont has bought it from English brokers for generations."

Lammot frowned. "It's not that we are buying saltpeter that is important. It is the quantity. I want to get every sack they have, and if I can, any more that's en route from India."

"Afraid of rising prices?"

"Not primarily, but that is a consideration certainly. I can't let Confederate agents buy it out from under us. The South is in worse shape than we are."

Michael thought for a moment. "All right, the secrecy is important."

"Crucial."

"But dragging me along increases the risk of notice."

"Not at all. If we do run into any questions, your presence as a lab researcher strengthens my tale of assessing new manufacturing processes. Besides, your skill in lining up reliable vessels is essential. I'll be quietly buying up the saltpeter while you are contracting for sound bottoms with dependable crews."

Michael absorbed the arguments with a frown. Finally he shrugged. "All right. But you and Mr. Lincoln have a bad sense of timing."

Lammot laughed. "In a rush now, eh? Don't worry, she'll be here when you get back. A little waiting is good for the soul."

"I've done more than my share of that. And she can't be told?"

"Not a word, Michael. You're going to Wapwallopen for a few weeks. That's all."

"I'm beginning to feel like a spy."

"Oh, another thing," Lammot remembered. "The General wants to see you this afternoon."

" 'The General'?"

"Everyone calls him that now. I think he rather likes it."

"I imagine. Nothing like skipping rank."

"Yes. I wanted to mention that you may dispense with the ceremony in private, as far as I am concerned. Of course, in front of the men . . ."

"Captain du Pont."

"Excellent, Mr. Farrell."

"Small potatoes, if you don't mind my saying so. If Henry rates Major General, you should be at least a colonel or brigadier."

"Not in this command, Mr. Farrell. I own only three shares of the company!"

"Privilege hath its rank?"

They laughed at that. "Nice turn of the phrase, Michael. You know that I could get you a lieutenancy. Won't you reconsider?"

"I'll never wear another uniform, Lammot. That's final."

"But you will help me with the drill and maneuvers?"

"I'll do that."

"Then you may find this familiar reading," Lammot tossed Michael a small book bound in cloth. *Hardee's Rifle & Light Infantry Tactics* was printed on the spine. Michael opened the volume and looked for the printing date. It was a recent edition, Lippincott, 1861. When he turned the page, he saw a brief directive inscribed by the U.S. Secretary of War, April 1855. He read the paragraph, glanced at Lammot, and shook his head.

"It's ironic. I met this man in Mexico, General Taylor's son-in-law, and now every loyal Union officer will be directing troops using the Army text issued under his direction."

"Who's that?" Lammot asked.

"Jefferson Davis," Michael said quietly. "You know, he once wanted to give me a medal."

Megan's announcement to Henry du Pont of her betrothal was made by way of his wife, Louisa. They discussed the need to make arrangements for her replacement. But that could wait until later, and Henry had to be told, of course.

He had not been surprised when Louisa mentioned it to him some time later in the day, commenting, "News like that travels faster than a powder fuse." He added that he saw no reason for Megan leaving her post—as long as she was childless.

Michael had strong reservations when Megan said she might be able to keep her job.

"I never liked your working for the man," he scowled. "As my wife it would be even less appealing."

"My new station?" she teased. "As the wife of *the* Michael Farrell?"

"That's not what I meant, and I think you know it. I simply do not trust the man. Somehow he would use the relationship to his advantage."

She turned serious, suddenly caressing his cheek with her palm. "Really, my love, I'll be quite safe. The Mister is turning fifty."

He smiled at her touch, suddenly consumed with yearning to hold her and wishing they were out-of-doors. The Gallagher sitting room was such a public place. He struggled back to their conversation.

"I was not thinking along those lines at all. I meant his overbearing manner, the subservience he exacts. I've seen it among his own family." He took her hand. "No one shall treat you like that."

Later as he walked through the frosty night to his boarding-house, he wished he could have said more. She would be his wife in a few months but was still not deeply in his confidence. Why was he privy to things he dare not share with her? He felt himself a cheat, withholding from her with whom he was to share all things.

And now this escapade with Lammot. Had she noticed his discomfort, he wondered, when he spoke of the Wapwallopen excuse? Noreen had caught something, of that he was sure. It had been so plain to her, his discomfort when questioned about the trip.

"Are you sure of your heart, Michael Farrell?" she had asked when once they were alone in the kitchen.

His look convinced her of that. But then she said, "It is something else that troubles you. Don't let it sit long enough to sour your mind. Trust her," she said. "She's not the little girl you felt affection for. She has strength to share."

"Tell that to Abraham Lincoln," he thought, and viciously kicked a stone in his path.

The next day, on the morning of their departure, Lammot met him at the lab.

"We have to swing by the office, Michael, to see Uncle."

"More secrets from Washington?"

"No, he wants to see you. Alone."

"Ah, Farrell! Come in, come in, and congratulations. A fine young woman." He extended his hand, which Michael took automatically. "Have you set a date?"

It was a barrage. Fire for effect, Michael thought, the old artillery command given to batteries when deflection and range of the target were precisely known.

"We do not have the date yet."

"Just as well, at least until the business at hand is disposed of. Damned nuisance of the war. I really thought it would be over in a trice, get back to normal business, but it looks like I was off the mark there, too."

"It does not seem to be going well."

"No, and this little trip of yours will give us a safety margin. Anything we can do for the Union, eh? Well, I'd better not say more about it. Security, as you know."

Michael nodded, waiting for him to come to the point. This rattling on was so uncharacteristic of Henry that his defenses seemed pointless. Maybe he had misjudged the man.

"When you return, Farrell, I want to make some changes to reflect your marriage needs as well as your changed status with the company. You'll need a place of your own, one close enough to the laboratory and my home as well. Miss Feeney will continue in her role as director of domestic services at Eleutherian Mills until such time as nature may contrive otherwise, and your duty will be to oversee the research activity under Lammot du Pont. I have ordered the stableman's home vacated and refurbished for you and your wife."

"Sir, I do not wish to push him out."

Henry waved away the objection, "They need more space anyway. I'm building a gatehouse at the other end of our drive."

"Well, it may be premature. As I said, we have not yet set the date."

"You'll move in anyway. After the wedding your bride will have but a hundred yards to move her trappings."

"Look, Mr. du Pont, I have strong reservations about Megan's continued work in your household after our marriage."

"I know, I know. Commendable feeling. But her brother's expense at the seminary is a considerable burden to the family, and the additional income will relieve that. I wouldn't want an up-and-coming employee to be distracted by financial woes."

Michael smiled in spite of his reserve. "You have me bracketed."

Henry's eyebrow twitched. "I haven't heard that for some time. A trace of army experience?"

"You leave me small room for maneuvering."

"And, Mr. Farrell," Henry added with a faint smile, "I have very large cannon."

They faced off for a moment, appraising each other, then Henry snapped his fingers, crossed the room to a file basket, and returned with a packet of envelopes bound with twine. He handed it to Michael.

"Those were forwarded from the California office. Arrived after you left, I imagine."

The parcel was smudged and tattered, and some of the envelopes were smeared with company stampings, "No Addressee," "Delayed Enroute," and "Reroute to Home Office." Michael knew who had sent them.

"The mail has been terrible," Henry said flatly.

"I understand, Mr. du Pont."

"I'd prefer you not use 'Mr. du Pont' in the future. It seems stiff discourse between two who have seen military service, wouldn't you say, Farrell?"

"I don't mind . . ."

"Let's try something more in keeping with the times, especially now that it's official. Yes. Why not just just call me 'General' from now on?"

Their steamer crossing had Michael and Lammot on the London docks in twelve days, and using that city as a base, they split the operation into two activities. Lammot made discreet calls on chemical brokerage houses to line up multiple orders for saltpeter, and Michael roved the waterfront to contract vessels. Within a few days Michael had to travel northwest to Liverpool and then farther north into Scotland to locate shipping near the scattered stockpiles of nitrate. By week's end four ships were contracted for, and 33,440 bags of saltpeter were being loaded at three different ports. After making payments to several brokers totalling three million dollars, Lammot met Michael for a quiet celebration of their success.

"Three and a half million pounds of saltpeter!" he said raising his glass. "We bought every pound of the stuff in England at bargain prices."

"And the inbound shipload from India besides. Nicely done, Lammot. You have a winning way with merchants. I can imagine what the price would have been if they had an inkling before of what they know now."

"Couldn't have done it without your managing the ships, old man. Smooth as oil." Lammot dipped the end of a fresh cigar in his brandy, fired it up, and blew a huge cloud of smoke.

"I'll rest easier when the lot has put to sea. The *Times* has been printing angry headlines about our seizing those two Confederates from the *Trent*."

"Hmm. Ill-timed, perhaps, as far as our little venture is concerned. But turnabout is fair play. These people have certainly stopped their share of our shipping in the past—and kidnapped our citizens."

Michael scowled, "I have no love for the British, but it was a breach of maritime law. Taking Slidell and Mason from a Southern ship is one thing. Overhauling a neutral ship and abducting passengers is quite another."

"It'll blow over."

"I'm not sure. I understand Lincoln has commended the *San Jacinto* and her skipper."

"You worry too much about ethical standards, Michael. When it comes to money, governments are easily greased."

Michael's attention was drawn suddenly to a man hurrying toward their table. "Maybe you'd better get that grease ready, Lammot. Here comes the skipper of one of our ships. He looks a bit upset."

The embargo imposed by Parliament on their shipment sent Lammot back to Washington for new strategy, and Michael was left in charge of three and a half million pounds of saltpeter that the English press was screaming to confiscate for a new war with the United States. It would be two more months before

Mason and Slidell were released with an American apology, and the ships were loaded and under way.

By then the sale to du Pont was a transparent subterfuge, an obvious plan for the Union to stockpile all the available gunpowder chemical worldwide. The Confederacy would have to await new production from India at hugely inflated prices.

Michael was amazed that Lammot was able to convince the British to lift the embargo even after he returned, ironically on the same ship with the Southern agents.

"I did not even talk to Palmerston this time," he said. "It wasn't necessary."

"But how did you convince them?"

"Grease."

"Grease?"

"You've forgotten? I simply told a number of London brokers that I would have to unload the stuff at half the market price. Can you imagine what that would have done to their current sales?"

"I'm beginning to."

"Good old-fashioned greed, Michael, the best lubricant for meshing international gears."

CHAPTER THIRTY-ONE

O h, I'm so jealous I could spit!" Mary Belin circled Megan as she stood on a footstool in the Gallagher front room. Noreen was pinning the hem of the wedding gown as Blanche Feeney gave advice from her rocker.

"A bit lower, Noreen. It should just sweep the floor."

"Get tattered from those splintery planks in the center aisle is more like it."

"Green, I'm absolutely green. It's not fair, really." Mary sighed. "And here I am no closer than a year ago."

"Just a suggestion," Blanche sniffed delicately. "I wanted to help."

"If you got on your knees with a mouthful of pins it would go faster. I must have been daft to make it so full."

"I'd never get up . . . my joints."

"Agh, in church I notice you're limber as a spider, all that genuflecting and kneeling through the Stations of the Cross."

"Maybe it's the war, Mary. Everything is in such turmoil."

"It would help if we could stay in the same place for more than a week's time. When Lammot's off somewhere, I'm at home. The minute he gets back, I'm sent off on some errand or another. I honestly think it is a conspiracy."

"You're not really jealous."

"I'm getting anxious. That's certain."

"Really, ladies. I hardly think it proper to speak so directly about your feelings."

"Let them be, Blanche. Here, Mary, give me a hand up and help her out of that, will you? I'm off to Hackendorn's for more thread."

"I'll come with you," Blanche said and bustled off to get her hat.

"That was the idea." Noreen winked at Megan, "Then you two can visit without getting a sermon."

After the two older women left, Mary watched them through the window. "I think your aunt still thinks we're possessed."

Megan laughed. "Probably. The poor thing means well, but between being saintly in church and putting on airs she has a hard time walking the common earth here on Chicken Alley."

"I'm beginning to commiserate with her—being a fish out of water."

"What does that mean?"

"I have the distinct impression that there *is* a conspiracy to keep Lammot and me apart."

"Don't be silly! Everyone in his family likes you. They like the whole Belin clan, it seems to me."

"They may like me well enough, but not as someone for Lammot to court. Something's out of joint."

"What does he say about it?"

"Heavens, I'd never breathe a word to him. He hasn't spoken of love."

"What about other things?"

"He rattles on about everything under the sun."

"I mean what does he do along that line?"

"He doesn't *do* anything. We have a maddeningly chaste relationship. Oh, he's kissed me on a few occasions, but even that was not quite satisfactory, if you know what I mean."

"He doesn't strike me as a man who would be reserved. In fact, I would have thought him a bit aggressive."

"He seems always to be holding back—afraid of going too far."

Megan laughed. "Maybe he's waiting to get Henry du Pont's permission."

"Megan! That's not at all kind."

"Oh, I was joking. Lammot is not one to bow and scrape."

"I notice that Henry is having his way with you and Michael."

"What is that supposed to mean?"

"You know, locked up in the stableman's house where he can keep his eye on you."

"I'm not sure I like the way this conversation is going."

"The joke is not amusing any longer?"

"There's a difference, Mary. You're not joking."

"Neither were you, Megan. But as you say, there is a difference." When Megan did not counter, Mary made the point anyway. "With you and Michael, the General *is* having his way. You just don't like to admit it."

It was a childish spat blown into irreconcilable proportions before either could stop it. Megan knew that. She also knew that Mary had been right; the barb about Lammot and Henry had been only half jest. She swam in a red shame over that, her own stupid, cutting remark. But there was the deeper shame, the acceptance of so many gifts from Henry du Pont, the clothes, the small bonuses at holiday times, gifts that were in addition to the regular gratuities from the mistress of Eleutherian Mills. And now the very house in which she was about to start her marriage had been picked by Henry.

"I can manage getting out of the dress myself, Mary," she said, reaching back for the tiny buttons. "Thank you for stopping by." She had not yet made it to her Aunt Blanche's room off the kitchen before hearing the front door gently close behind Mary Belin. She knew it would be a long time before they spoke as friends again, and the tears began.

It was not just for lost friendship. Megan knew quite well what drove Henry du Pont to make his favors. Up to now she had not let herself think of it.

One of the pearl buttons ripped loose under her frantic fingers, but she tugged at the remaining loops, careless of further damage, eyes swimming, desperate to be out of the gown.

It was an early June wedding, celebrated at mass said by Father Reardon with young Denis Feeney filling in as subdeacon and witness for the groom. Blanche Feeney stood up for the bride. They had a party afterward in the church hall, a room tacked on to the school across the cemetery from the church itself, and a few of the powdermen made music for dancing. Dorgan dropped off a few kegs, and there was punch for the children and ladies. In the stable behind the rectory the sexton found a couple of empty jugs the next day, but no harm was done, no fights broke out, and everybody was in his own bed by dark.

It wasn't your normal Crick wedding, even if it was done at St. Joe's. The couple seemed aimed for loftier things, and there were little touches nobody could remember happening before. It wasn't just young Denny almost a priest helping to tie the knot at his sister's marriage. There was the fancy brougham with four horses that whisked them off afterwards, the fact that they went to a hotel in town to be alone, and the biggest thing was the Mister himself sitting on the bride's side of church during the ceremony. Of course, General du Pont didn't stay long, but it was the first time he had ever come to an employee's wedding.

After a three-day honeymoon, Michael and Megan moved into the comfortable little house near Henry's great barn and stables.

For Michael the summer of 1862 seemed a turning point in his life. His marriage to Megan gave a quiet focus to life, and for the first time he felt a sense of direction and solid foundation of purpose. Somehow Megan had magically removed his concern about being older. It amazed him, from that first morning when he awoke to her studying him, eyes full of love but deeper still with an understanding that humbled him.

"You have aged ten years since yesterday," he had said, meaning it as a compliment.

She had laughed at his clumsiness, knowing what he meant and accepting it. "Not so, my love," she whispered, snuggling up to him again. "I'm just reviving your wasted youth."

It was true. He measured every day against the time they would be together again, knots of the past uncoiling in his eagerness to be with her. Being with her in long summer twilights consumed his thinking, erased the harsh memories.

He attacked the laboratory work with a new enthusiasm. The usual testing went on, and he gave it perfunctory attention, rifle powder, cannon grains the size of lawn-tennis balls, an occasional batch of blasting samples. But the promise of glycerine was his excitement. Each experimental compound renewed hope of success. Harnessing the giant explosive was close. When that happened, black powder as a blasting agent would be eclipsed.

Lammot was rarely in the lab these days. The crush of war orders had the mills working by lamplight. His brother was weakening under the strain of his lung disease and Henry's pressure for more production. And there was a third reason for Lammot's relief of Irénée—Charlotte now raged at him for his part in supplying powder for the North. Between his burdens of overseeing a string of mills and the organization of the Brandywine Volunteers, Lammot sometimes went days without even stopping in to see Michael. When he did it was usually on military missions.

"Can you spend some time with us next Saturday?"

"Megan and I were to visit her family."

"An hour or two in the afternoon? This drilling is out of my reach, Michael. I think you could set my bungling right with a few corrections."

He would always agree. There were subtle pressures that he should take a Home Guard uniform himself. All the powdermen had been exempted from the new draft laws. Henry had seen to that, saving his trained workers for more strategic service to the Union and more profitable production for du Pont. The others were excused in exchange for signing up to protect the mills and block any rebel attack on Wilmington shipyards and war factories.

"I can't take that uniform," he had said when Lammot offered him a commission.

It had caused some talk among the recruits.

"Is he too good for the likes of us?"

"D'you think he's a Secesh, Dougherty?"

"Don't be daft. Why would he be helpin' Mr. Lammot with drillin'?"

"Maybe he's doing it all wrong—to make us easy meat."

"A spy?"

"Stranger things have happened."

"Ah, g'wan. He's been workin' with the Mister for years. In the old country, I hear, his daddy give considerable pain to the English."

"That's no guarantee. There's as many fisheaters carryin' muskets for Johnny Reb as there are for the Union."

"Pangs of a new bridegroom is what it is. That little girl he married has got him tied to the bedpost."

"I can't fault the man for that, surely. Have you seen Megan Feeney lately?"

"Y've made a point there, Dougherty. If we was all fixed as well, the Volunteers would go begging."

"Ain't that the truth!"

In late August Megan began spending several evenings a week away from home. As part of a local soldiers' relief organization, many women along the Brandywine, including several of the du Ponts, began organizing foodstuffs and medical supplies for evacuation trains beginning to stream northward through Wilmington. The first trainload of wounded was met by the group as it was switched to a siding in the shimmering heat of a brutally humid Saturday afternoon.

As she and the other women labored over the rails and ballast stone with heavy baskets, Megan caught her first impression of war floating on the stagnant air. They were still several yards from the string of cars, but the sweet stench of gangrene was already in her nose and quiet moans drifted from the open windows.

It would be worse inside, she knew, and as a burly soldier boosted her to the coach steps, she gritted her teeth behind a fixed smile. It was not enough. The moans were suddenly cut off as she entered the car, replaced by an embarrassed silence peopled by a hundred gaunt eyes all fixed on her, and the death smell brushed her face with a palpable, suffocating push. Her stomach wrenched and she had to swallow hard against the gagging bile. For an awful moment she was not sure that she could endure it. Panic clawed at her shoulder to turn from the ghastly smell, the nightmare oozing stumps, the rusty bandages, the gross tears in belly, chest, and face.

But she clung to the spot, both hands gripping the wicker handle of her basket, hanging on as if it were bolted like a stanchion for her support. She counted the seconds and fought each bobbing thrust of nausea, stripped herself of the silly ineffectual smile. Finally she was able to breathe without heaving, look without reeling, and speak without shrieking.

"Dear men," she said as sternly as she could, "I have a little food and drink . . . and some fresh linens to make you more comfortable. I . . . I'm quite new at this . . . and . . ."

Halfway down the car a young man whose left arm ended in a bandage at the wrist struggled to his feet and came toward her reaching for the basket with his remaining hand.

"So are we, ma'am," he said with a painful grin. "New at this, I mean. Let me give you a hand with that. You're doing fine," the young man whispered as he helped unload the food and pass it on. "Just fine."

Megan wanted to cry at his compassion, but there simply wasn't time. There were so many to serve, so many to tend. As she worked her way from one end of the car to the other and back again, she noticed that one soldier had spilled his drink, and his uneaten sandwich had fallen to the filthy floor.

"Here," she said, lifting the tin handle from his hooked finger. "Let me get you another."

The one-handed soldier stopped her at the jug and took the cup.

"Never mind, ma'am. He doesn't need it now."

Megan turned around and saw the soldier leaning against a friend, eyes closed, a faint smile on his face.

"That's the first time he's rested since we got on," the friend said. "Moaned all the way from Baltimore."

It wasn't until she saw them carry him across the rails to a wagon as the train lurched off that Megan realized the man was dead.

The troop of women made the five-mile trip back to the Brandywine in silence. Their shared horrors had drained them of commentary. The company omnibus made the circuit of homes, and as the passengers were dropped with quiet good-byes, there was an equality they shared for the moment that would not likely be experienced again. Even the desperate calamities of blown powdermills had not prepared them for this day.

It was full dusk by the time the last stop was made at Eleutherian Mills. When the heavy rig ground to a stop at her front door, Louisa du Pont gripped Megan's hand once as they dismounted and made their separate ways home.

"I'll drop ye at your door if y'like, Miz Farrell," the coachman said.

"Thank you, Mr. Flynn, but I need to walk a bit, and you can use what little light is left."

She ambled along the wooded path from the main house, behind the barn, then into the damp hollow below the little rise where their cottage perched. She could see a dim light flicker from their kitchen window as she looped along the tree-lined track.

Michael was there waiting for her and the thought made her so tender that tears began to sting her eyes. Now she had some idea of the trials he had endured so long ago. How clear now was the reason he abhorred the very thought of war. Small wonder that he would have nothing of Lammot du Pont's uniforms. But the overriding fact was that he was there—whole and strong, waiting for her return. She would have run the last thirty yards if she had not been so exhausted.

If she had run she would have crashed into Charlotte du Pont as she slipped from the door with a hooded cloak on this hot night and disappeared up the path in the opposite direction.

Megan was not really certain why she delayed going into her own house for several minutes. She could see Michael through the window as he paced the floor and ran his hands through his hair. After a time she went up to the porch and let herself in. Michael met her with a concerned smile and swept her into his arms.

But he didn't mention the visit by Charlotte Henderson du Pont, and for that reason, neither did she.

The first week of September ended with near panic in the city of Wilmington. Harper's Ferry had fallen to Lee, and he was reported marching in strength through Maryland. A chilling report mentioned a large cavalry unit poised for a sweep through Northern Delaware to destroy the ironclad shipyards in Wilmington and blow up the du Pont powder works.

"I know your feelings," Lammot pleaded. "But our situation is desperate. I have a section of cannon with no trained gunners."

"My help would be insignificant." Michael got up from his chair and peered out the doorway down the path leading to Eleutherian Mills.

"You know that Lee's cavalry could cross over in a matter of hours. With cannon—"

"You have two hundred green volunteers. Even with the best gunners in the world you couldn't slow them ten minutes. Two six-pounders and some foot soldiers are no match for a cavalry battalion. There are a dozen approaches to this place. Where would you make a stand?"

"We don't *know* that it's a battalion."

Michael shook his head. "For that matter we don't know that they're coming at all."

"We've got to do something."

Michael looked down the path again. "Do what your family is doing, Lammot. Bury your silver in the woods, cart away the finished powder. Better still, dump it in the Brandywine, and let them have the mills."

"I can't believe my ears!"

"Look, with no powder in storage, how long would it take to completely wreck the yards? Without explosives the Rebs would have to take it apart piece by piece. They won't have the time. This has to be a hit-and-run attack. They won't have the equipment to do much except start a few fires."

"Suppose it is a full-scale maneuver with Lee's whole army pushing east to the Delaware?"

"He wouldn't do that—too likely to be cut off from his support. No, he wants to sweep north to Harrisburg and then east to Philadelphia."

Lammot was over his depth and knew it, but he would not give in. "That's even riskier. He'd be twenty miles farther north."

Michael nodded. "And surrounded by all that open Amish farmland with plenty of room to move. Not at all like being funneled south with the Delaware River on one side, the Chesapeake Bay on the other, and his back to the open sea."

The argument was over. Lammot rolled up his chart and handed it to Michael. "At least look over the defensive positions I have proposed. You owe me that much for giving in. I want to give them some kind of show for their trouble."

Michael took the map with a grimace. Some kind of show, indeed. It would be more than the fireworks display at Sebastopol. He wondered if Lammot had ever thought of what a well-aimed shot of canister could do to a neat formation of infantry, or what a saber could do in concrete terms.

"All right."

"Thank you, my friend. I'll be back later tonight after I've alerted the men."

Michael did not study the chart. He did not have to. He had mentally placed batteries and infantry in these hills for years, even before the war broke out. On recreational walks, from the jouncing seats of wagons, even when he was with Megan. It was the lifetime curse of a combat leader. Once learned, the tactical use of topography spoiled every wooded glade, every gentle slope, every meandering meadow gully. Instead of sights to give pleasure, they became tools for defense or attack.

The only reasonable place for defense was one overlooked by Lammot. The prime location was the high ground of St. Joseph's Church—best for observation and especially for its excellent fields of killing fire. He went to the door again to look for Megan. Surely Henry's collection of family silver and jewelry was boxed by this time. Michael wanted to go over his own plans with Megan to ensure her safety in case the attack did come. He would have no part in the senseless defense of a losing battle.

He had another problem, too. What to do about Charlotte du Pont.

"There's no more time," he muttered. "I'll drop it in *his* lap."

Then he was off the porch and up the pathway to Henry du Pont's office.

CHAPTER THIRTY-TWO

Man yer pumps, Dorgan. The gang will soon be here."

"Now what, Dougherty? Is there a bunch of thirsty Rebels on the Crick?"

"Not likely. Ain't y'heard?"

"I've heard so much in the last week my ears are ringing with rumors."

"Well, McClellan whipped Lee at Sharpsburg. Druv him right back across the Potomac to lick his wounds."

"That's a surprise."

"I suppose so. But it was a draw, anyways, right from the start. Two Irishmen sluggin' it out."

"Have the volunteers left the Kennett Pike for home?"

"Aye, I hear Captain Motty du Pont is marching them direct."

"Direct to where, might I ask?"

"Direct to Dorgan's Inn, y'ninny. Where else?"

"I thought maybe to Campbell's up the hill. There's a few Protestants in the Volunteers, y'know."

"Now that's lunacy, Dorgan. There's not a Protestant can drink worth a damn, and you know it."

"I just didn't want to build me hopes unnecessarily. Here, Doc, help me lay out these mugs. There's an extra tub of suds in it for you and a dram besides. Y'know, for an Episcopalian, Mr. Motty is a Christian man, and that's a fact."

When Megan had withdrawn from him the day she tended the wounded, Michael was not surprised. It was obvious that she had been through a shock, and he did his best to be comforting. But their estrangement continued, to Michael's utter confusion. Finally, Megan admitted that she'd seen Charlotte leave the house.

His face betrayed him, first the shock of surprise and then a subtle covert shading just before he looked away.

"It is not what you think."

"Tell me what I am thinking, Michael."

"It was no tryst."

"Oh? Was she making a duty call on her new neighbors? How thoughtful. I must drop her a line. And when were you going to let me know about this casual and innocent meeting?"

"I had hoped to spare you that."

"Spare me!"

"Yes, dammit! I didn't want to spoil our beginnings with anything unpleasant. She . . . she came here with some wild plan—it was really crazy—and I turned her down. She's afraid the South will lose the war."

"You couldn't tell me that?"

"You had some idea about Charlotte and me before, you know."

"Some idea, yes."

He did not respond. It was too complicated. He feared for their love, for the safety of the people in the mills. A rumor like that could be disastrous.

"What your silence says, Michael, is that you could not trust me with her little conspiracy."

"Trust has nothing to do with it."

"Oh, I think so. Just keep my silly little head free of concern? Don't take the chance that I might not be mature enough to handle it?"

"That's not it at all."

"That I might blurt out her plan to the wrong person? That I might take steps to protect people I love from being hurt?"

"I'll see that it does not come to that."

Megan studied him sadly. Her face was drained of passion. "I'll speak to no one of her deranged idea. That means I'm placing the lives of family and friends in your hands—a token of *my* trust in you, Michael."

"I'll not let you down."

But he had already let her down, and they both realized it. She would not let herself think of the greater betrayal, that he might have been tempted by whatever offer Charlotte made in exchange. She would not stir those embers though they smoked enough to choke her.

The laboratory became Michael's escape into isolation from the war and a channel to direct himself toward greater recognition within the company. As always, the routine gunpowder testing took most of his time, but he managed to squeeze in extra hours on the nitroglycerine project. By late fall he had the lab pretty much to himself. Lammot's added chores of supervising the additional production were unexpectedly complicated by military orders from Washington.

"I have to take a company of volunteers to Fort Delaware," he said one day in late November. Lammot was in full uniform when he tramped in, looking rather grand but a little self-conscious. Michael grinned as he inspected the new winter blues. The tailored cut was obvious.

"Lovely," he murmured. "The quartermaster has improved his skills. What Army business is it this time?"

"They're worried about a prisoner breakout from the island. We have nearly three thousand Rebels locked up with more on the way."

"What about protection for the mills?"

"A battalion of regulars from Pennsylvania is setting up permanent camp at Greenville. Washington apparently had enough of a scare last spring. I'd rather be a part of that group, but being sent to Pea Patch is a bit of a pat on the back for our little group."

"I think you are beginning to like soldiering. Have you been reading too many pamphlets?"

"To be truthful, Michael, I confess to a certain feeling of patriotism. To have others my age trooping off while I stay here protected from the draft grates on my pride. It seems unfair to spend my war days making more money for Uncle Henry and myself, I'll admit that."

"Well, at least you're honest enough about it. I am surprised that Henry is letting you go. It will leave him shorthanded for supervisors."

"It was his idea. Made some little speech to me about the du Pont men doing their bit."

Michael smiled faintly. "Why is it that I feel you think he had other reasons?"

"His other reason, as you put it, is that I have been objecting to some of his techniques to speed up production."

"That again?"

"We had a row last week about crowding so many men into the packing houses. They are getting in each other's way, moving too fast, encouraged to be slipshod."

"I've noticed the quality of powder is slipping."

"And if there is a mistake, it will mean more than one or two killed. Yesterday I counted twenty-six laborers in the Hagley pressroom."

"My God."

"When I complained, he just waved me off. 'Men in the field are taking chances too,' he said. It makes me ill."

"What about your family? Are they pleased about your move?"

"Mother is quite upset. Thinks I'm wasting my mind on a romantic adventure."

"That's partly true, isn't it?"

"Well, yes. I'll admit to a little stirring, but don't be too hard on me. The rest of what she said was not very democratic."

"Not democratic?"

" 'Any Irishman can be taught to drill and shoot a gun,' she said, 'but someone in your class should not be sacrificed.' "

"Apparently your uncle thinks an Irish powderman is too valuable."

"Precisely. I'm not fooled, Michael. Both of them are consumed completely with their own interests. Mother wants me to keep watch on her stake in the business, and the General doesn't want a snooping conscience. I'll play their game. The long range payoff is worth it."

Michael was not so sure. "All your eggs are in his basket, Lammot."

"Someday he'll have to let me carry it," Lammot grinned. "It's just a matter of time."

After Lammot had left for the Delaware River fortress on Pea Patch Island, Michael divided his time almost equally between home and work. The waking hours with Megan were still shaded by the Charlotte du Pont bitterness, but life moved smoothly enough until the day he was called to meet Henry at the lab. Seeing the boss at the lab was unusual, and the look on his face was not encouraging.

"I want you to explain this," he said. All of Michael's notes and samples had been stacked on a table in the middle of the room. A man Michael did not recognize was systematically searching the place.

He would not bluff innocence. To have been discovered researching new explosives without periodic reports to the boss was cause for chagrin, but he would not pretend ignorance of Lammot's methods of keeping secrets from his uncle. He was flaring into anger as he watched Henry's lackey work across the room and had a great temptation to say it was not Henry's business to pry into his personal research, but that would be foolish and untrue besides. The man had every right legally. It was his company to run.

"I'm waiting."

"Apparently what you have found does not meet with your approval. I assume my notes are clear enough."

"Your job with this company is to test production samples. If that doesn't fully occupy your time, I'll find a profitable way to use your excess energy and curiosity."

"The work was largely done on my own time. You're getting a day's work for a day's pay."

"I'm the one to decide that."

"If my work has not been satisfactory—"

"You're on dangerous ground, Farrell. Don't press my indulgence."

Michael bridled. "I am not accustomed to indulgence from anyone, Mr. du Pont."

Henry chose to ignore the challenge. "When your supervisor gets back from his war duty, I'll speak to him about keeping you better posted as to the limits of your duty to the company. In the meantime, stick to production testing."

Michael nearly smiled at that. Keeping the nitro experiments from Henry's knowledge had been Lammot's idea.

"Is that clear?" Henry was wrestling with his own composure. Michael met the frosty glare placidly. The man didn't want to lose him.

"Perfectly. I would like my notes returned after you have had time to examine them."

Henry stiffened. Turning to the lackey he barked, "Get this out back and wait for me in the trap." The man scurried to gather up the journals and sample boxes, and hurried from the building. When the door closed, Henry turned a baleful glare on Michael and spoke with a voice graveled with emotion.

"Listen, you cocky bastard, you'll never see that stuff again. Anything, *anything*, that grows on my property *is* my property. I pay for it, I take the responsibility for it, and I decide whether or not to keep it. I pay you for your brain and hands. What you produce belongs to the company. If you want to tinker with that Goddamned oil, you'll have to do it somewhere else. Let some other fool like yourself waste time and money on it."

Michael conceded the point, wondering if he might not have reacted the same way if the roles had been reversed. He was amazed at his own sudden calm.

"I think you are missing a great opportunity."

The comment took Henry by surprise and he relaxed, but the piercing eyes never wavered.

"It's a doomsday chemical. I'll have nothing to do with it. Just last month a whole factory blew in Austria. Not a scrap of metal or flesh bigger than your fist. Wiped out the firm in one second."

"It can be tamed, and when it is, black powder will all but disappear from the market."

"It will never be safe. Nobody will allow it to be shipped now. Not ships, railroads, not even wagon lines. Its production is banned in countries all over the world."

"That will change."

Henry sighed, clamped his mouth shut, and studied Michael for a long time. When he spoke again he was in full control, almost paternal. "That's where you're wrong, Farrell. You are the one who will change. Black powder has been around for five hundred years. It will be king for a millenium."

"You're entitled to your opinion, of course."

"Around here," Henry warned as he left, "it's the only opinion allowed. Make certain you remember that."

It took Michael two hours to straighten out his equipment and the remaining ledgers in the lab. There were rough drafts of some of the later work on nitroglycerine which Henry had overlooked. At some point, he'd have to tell Megan about the run-in with Henry. There would have to be a change now. He was sure of it. Besides, he was sick of war and his contribution to prolonging it.

"It's a cowardly role," he told Megan. "Suppose there was no gunpowder. Suppose we had not been able to get all that saltpeter in '61. Would the whole mess have ground to a merciful stop for lack of fuel?"

"Someone else would have done it."

"The great rationale for evildoing."

She took his hand in both of hers and caressed it. "I can't think of this hand ever raised for an evil purpose."

Henry's orders notwithstanding, Michael spent every spare moment reconstructing his notes on the new explosive. This time he kept all the papers at home. The actual experiments themselves would have to wait because he knew the General would not be satisfied with one inspection.

He was also compiling a list of rival mills where he might find better opportunities for advancement. Megan did not know this. He wanted to have something definite before laying his plans before her. The matter of Denny's education would trouble her, and until he could demonstrate with better pay that they could move and still support her brother, the least said the better. He did not even go into detail about Henry's ultimatum for the same reason.

One Wednesday in late February, Charlotte du Pont convinced her husband to stay home to help her with some legal documents involving her personal assets. It was not a pressing matter as far as Irénée could tell, but she seemed so upset when he asked her to wait until evening that he agreed to spend the morning with her. The work seemed beyond her grasp, and he had to reexplain so many of the passages that the noon whistle blew before they were half-finished. Following lunch they attacked the problem again, plodding through the interminable hours of early afternoon. He was becoming worried that work in the yards might slow because of his absence.

Megan was enjoying a half-day off. She decided at the last minute to put off doing her wash until a warmer day. It was so bitterly cold at noon that the clothes would freeze stiff before she hung them on the line. A walk to the Gallaghers' to visit her aunt was long overdue. She bundled up warmly and started for Chicken Alley a little after one-thirty. The barren trees clacked frozen branches in the gentle wind, her boots clunked on the rock-hard path, her breath stung deliciously, and the sky was cobalt clear. She felt wonderful.

Megan was rounding the hill above the pack house at two. The yards below were like a diorama she had once seen in a Paris museum except that the small figures were moving. She smiled at the scene, an animated show for her pleasure. When the blinding, deafening flash drove her sitting against a tree, her only sensation was a vague disappointment that someone had ripped the canvas, torn up a make-believe world. As her vision cleared she saw a peculiar ball floating toward her, a little black thing no bigger than her foot. She raised her hands to catch it, a looping plaything raining down with hundreds of others that bounced like rubber off the frozen ground. But when her stone struck, it didn't bounce at all, and she had a terrible pain in her stomach before drifting off.

Michael was out of the lab, running before the last shard of glass had fallen. Off to his right he saw the great plume of greasy black boil above the yards, but his mind was on the small house behind Henry du Pont's. Figures were tumbling from doorways as he sped past—contorted faces, shock, wailing—but he did not stop. Distance was the great enemy. He flung headlong into the hateful space that separated him from her, sprawling twice before he reached the house. When he did not find her there, he roared through the kitchen of the big house, to be told by a dazed cook that Megan had been seen on her way to Crick Road.

Through the smoking, flesh-strewn yards he ran, searching faces of the wailing stream of women drifting as close as they were allowed. Then, finally remembering her shortcut through the woods, wild nearly, he thrashed up the path until he found her, like a bundled, broken doll on a hillside strewn with shattered rock.

"Thank God it was so cold. Without all the thick clothing she would have been killed, surely." Noreen watched Michael's face closely as she spoke. Some of the wild look was gone. She wondered how far she should go.

"Is she still awake?"

"She drifts in and out. But you know, Michael. You know she will be well. Nothing broken as far as the doctor can tell. A bad bruise."

"I want to see her."

"Of course, when he has finished tending her."

"You're not telling me something, Noreen. I can see it in your face."

She had seen it before on the faces of men, the gray pallor of quiet wrath. Could she trust his control with more reason to grieve, more reason to rage?

"There is bleeding."

He stiffened—and waited.

"Had she mentioned she might be with child?"

His lips were a white line.

"It was very early, dear Michael, but she's losing it, I'm afraid."

For nearly an hour he sat unmoving by the bedroom door. The whiskey Brendan had set beside him and the fresh cups of tea all untouched until the surgeon came out at last.

"A few weeks and she'll be fine," he said. "As to her bearing other children, I can't be sure."

Michael nodded curtly and went into the room. He stayed there for the next twenty-four hours, holding her hand as she slept, eating nothing, drinking nothing, watching always for her fleeting moments of consciousness.

"How many?" Henry asked Irénée.

"Thirteen dead and a dozen badly hurt."

Henry looked around the darkening ruin of Hagley Yard. Every building within a hundred yards of the blackened crater of the pack house had been flattened. "How many with families?"

"I don't know yet. So many were new."

"They were your men, Irénée. I want the list by morning—and no mistakes."

"Such a shock."

"Yes, well, save your shock for later. We have to get this place cleaned up and rebuilt. Let the others indulge themselves in shock. It's a luxury we can't afford."

"I'm worried about Charlotte."

"You should be. If you had been here this might not have happened. I understand she coaxed you away from work again."

"There were some family papers."

"You'd better keep her in tow, boy. She's leading you by the nose."

"I don't think that's quite your—"

"Business? Whose business is all this?" He swept an arm toward the wreckage around them. "I'm the one who has to answer for it all—award the pensions, visit the widows, keep the men from running scared. And rebuild a third of our powderworks."

"That's not what I meant, Uncle."

"What you meant was for me to keep my nose out of your marriage. Well try this for fit. There is talk of sabotage already. Your addled wife is mentioned as a possible agent."

"That's preposterous!"

"Do you think it strange that she kept you safe at home today? Nice timing."

"Coincidence. Nothing more."

"Here's another coincidence. She blabs Johnny Reb talk to anyone who'll listen, and months ago she approached Michael Farrell with a hare-brained scheme to cripple the mills."

Irénée's jaw dropped. His silence was ample reason for Henry to suspect that Charlotte might even have tried persuading him.

"Now hear me closely, Irénée. Before the week is out you pack her off to a nice sanatorium up North. I want her there for the duration of the war. Nervous breakdown or threat of invasion or any damned reason you come up with is fine with me. Just get her the hell out of here."

"I'll go with her."

"You'll stay here and earn your keep like everybody else. When things slow down after the war you can do what you like."

Charlotte was on her way to New York that weekend, and after he returned from putting his wife on the train, Irénée had the first severe hemorrhage of his losing battle with consumption.

Henry did not miss the chance to go after Michael. A map with military symbols detailing a rebel attack was found among his papers.

Dougherty drained off his pail, wiped his mustaches, and banged it on the bar for a refill.

"I know a few parties who'd part with a rope gladly."

"And be willing to give it a pull."

"It's hard to believe he'd do a thing like that. And Meg Feeney hurt in the blast. His own wife!"

"Well, he was caught dead to rights. They found that map."

"And stuff for making blasting oil."

"Devilish stuff. One bump and off she goes. The Gen'r'l won't have it on the Crick."

"Small wonder. And where did they lock him up?"

"Pea Patch Island. With all the other Rebs. I'll be surprised if Mr. Motty don't use the Volunteers to have him shot."

"Why waste a trial?"

"Mulrooney might shoot him. His brother was at Hagley."

"No. I saw him today. He's back for the funeral."

"I never liked the man, to speak the gospel truth."

"Come off it, Doc. You didn't like his education, is what it was, nor his bein' upper class."

"Well, his daddy is rollin' in his grave this day, mark my words. That grand liberator—to have his only son blowin' up half the Irish on the Crick."

"We don't know he done it. If y'ask me, it's the Ginger Bastard covering up his own sins. They was so many in that pack house they could start a fire with all the shufflin' feet."

"Who's askin' you, Murphy? None of your family was hurt."

"They was *all* me family, Doc. Ain't that the way of it?"

CHAPTER THIRTY-THREE

Perhaps others may think you magnanimous, but what you are up to is clear to me. I'm not fooled. I know exactly why you pointed the finger of accusation at him."

"I did not point, my dear. Others did that. The man's a traitor."

"Spare me the patriotic posturing, *General*. The pack house should be laid to you more than anyone else."

"Careful, Meta."

"Oh, I'm pleased to get Charlotte out of our hair, I'll admit to it. She is a monumental embarrassment to us all. But you know the conditions were unsafe—at your insistence."

"I'm busy. Too busy to elaborate on your son's dereliction that day."

"But not too busy to install your current mistress in the stable house. How convenient. Her husband in prison and her bedroom down the path from this office."

"Your petulance is getting uglier by the day, Meta."

"I don't see how Louisa can stand it. She must be blind."

"At one time you were happy enough with her ignorance."

Meta stared at him across the desk. Her face began to work and then collapsed into a spasm of weeping.

"I would be as happy again, dear heart," she managed through trembling lips, "if only you'd come to me."

He cleared his throat and rose to offer his handkerchief. It was getting awkward. Belin would be back from lunch soon.

"We're all a bit older now, Meta. The fires are banked."

She threw his handkerchief on the floor. "Go slaver after a child if you will!"

Later that evening Henry had more explaining to do. His wife wondered how Megan would fit in now that she was so badly compromised. They could hardly have a felon's wife running the downstairs staff.

"I'm keeping her at the stable house for the time being."

"And her duties?"

"I'll use the space for bachelor workers. She can run the place —cook and wash. I can't turn her away into hard times."

"I like the girl, Henry. She deserves gentle consideration."

"Yes, I think she can handle the job. She'll need time to let the hard feelings among the Irish die down."

"Then you do not plan to install any men in the place for some time?"

"Not just yet."

"I see," Louisa murmured. "You need not be concerned for my feelings any more, husband, but please spare that child any further humiliation at your hands."

Henry stared at her as if she were mad. Louisa did not flinch and withdrew after a long, thoughtful look.

Henry did some serious thinking over a cigar later that night. And as usual, he was writing letters in the company office until after eleven. He looked out his window through the leafless trees toward the stable house. A single light glowed. Megan was up, too.

Mary Belin's visit in March was the first time Megan had seen her since the wedding.

"I don't feel the need for apologies, do you?"

"We're past that kind of insincerity, Mary. Some friendships have long spaces; the lasting ones, I mean. When you walked in today my feelings were the same as always."

"Exactly! All these months . . . but I knew you were there for the asking. Does that sound selfish, Megan? It's not coming out like I mean."

"The words don't matter. And it's not selfish. I know why you came."

"I think I can help."

"Your being here is a great lift. The Farrell name is not proudly worn along the Crick these days."

"I didn't come until there was more for me to do than hold your hand. I had a letter from Lammot."

"He hasn't answered mine."

"I know, Megan. He told me. You have to be patient for a bit longer. Until the trial Michael is better off at the fort. You know that."

"Why hasn't Lammot answered my letters? Dear God, I've been nearly at wit's end."

"He doesn't want to write anything that might hurt Michael before the proper time. He told me that you should keep faith."

"I'm finding that very hard to do. I have not had a word from Michael, and because of the unrest on the island no one is allowed to visit."

"They're afraid of a break by the Confederate prisoners or an attack by Rebel ships."

Megan abruptly broke down, and Mary went to her, holding her close until the weeping passed. Megan got up and bathed her face at the sink. When she returned, she was frowning and spoke through gritted teeth.

"I hate doing that," she said hoarsely. "I feel so damned weak since all this happened."

"You have reason enough. I know that you lost the child."

Megan's jaw trembled as if she were seized by a chill. "That's not the half of it, Mary. God help me for saying so, but I'm not sure Michael didn't set off that blast."

"You can't mean that."

"Oh, I know he would never plan to hurt anyone. But suppose it was like they said, that it went off at the wrong time. That he had planned to destroy the cannon powder when the men had gone, after midnight, but the timing was wrong."

Mary looked at her closely. "Like who said?"

"Henry du Pont. He showed me the evidence they had taken from Michael's things. A new explosive he was working on, that military map. It shook him terribly at the time. He said it saddened him because Michael showed such promise."

"I can imagine."

"And under the circumstances he has been more than kind to me."

"Watch your step, Megan."

"What do you mean?"

"Don't start thinking you should be overly kind to *him*."

CHAPTER THIRTY-FOUR

Brigadier General A. F. Schoepf regarded his prisoner thoughtfully for a full minute before speaking. The tall, well-built Irishman stood at casual ease, dark hair neatly combed, face ruggedly handsome and clean shaven. His gray eyes never wavered, showed neither hostility nor fear.

"You have no complaints about treatment?"

"None." The voice was strong, vibrant, commanding. It was easy to see how others could be taken in by such a man.

"You have asked several times for this audience, Mr. Farrell. What is your request?"

"I have three: mail delivery, visitor rights, and I would like to speak with Lammot du Pont if he is still posted here."

"I assume you know from your past misadventures in the military service that to inform anyone, much less a convicted traitor, of the wartime assignment of Captain du Pont would be a dereliction of my duty. With respect to the other two, the particular complaint lodged against you now demands close arrest without privileges."

"Any prisoner of war—"

"Don't sully the term, sir! You are a traitor, stripped of citizenship fraudulently obtained, who, in case you have forgotten, is currently suspected of mass murder and espionage."

"Common decency would allow me to get a message to my wife."

"Whom you nearly murdered as well. Since you appeal to my decency, I must say that she is in restored health and has been given regular reports of your own condition."

"Thank you for that. Is there any news of a trial?"

"None. You will be informed, of course, and counsel assigned."

That he was held separate from the other prisoners on the island fort was a mixed blessing. His quarters were primitive, a cramped, cold cell, but he was dry. The tent quarters of the captured enemy were festering corrals of mud and slit trenches. But they could at least communicate with each other, a need that grew within him each day of solitary confinement.

A week after his meeting with the commandant, Lammot walked into his cell. He was not smiling. When past the sentry's view, he pressed a finger to his lips and winked.

"I want to speak to you about a lawyer, Farrell," he said gruffly. Your trial date has been set." Then he turned and gestured toward the door, and a man in civilian clothes entered. "Take a break, Corporal," he said to the sentry. "I'll relieve you for a while. Wait for my call at the guard desk."

After the soldier drifted away, Lammot sat with Michael on his cot and gripped his arm hard.

"Sorry, old friend, I can imagine what you must be going through. We have to speak quickly. This is your 'lawyer,' E.J. Allan, Esquire. His real name is Allan Pinkerton, of Mr. Lincoln's Secret Service."

Michael looked first at the grim detective and then at Lammot. His friend's face was suffused with excitement.

"What are you up to, Lammot?"

"Not me, old fellow. This time it's a solo performance, and you're heading the program!"

The news of the prisoner break from Pea Patch was in all the papers two weeks later. Thirty rebels had slipped away on boats supplied by Confederate sympathizers from Kent County. The accused saboteur of the du Pont powder works was listed among them.

It was an incredibly smooth deception. From the time of the first whispered instructions from a prisoner in the compound, to the landing weeks later at Dragon Swamp Delta on the western shore of the Chesapeake, Michael could not tell where the operation shifted from Union to Confederate control. It was a tense two weeks of silent drifting in small boats by night and painful, cramped bouncing over side roads by day buried under everything from cabbages to feed sacks. The escape party had been broken up into small groups as soon as they came ashore, and there were three in his, a Confederate captain of cavalry, one of his sergeants, and himself. They barely conversed. He had little idea of the route taken except that it traversed the peninsula south from Delaware into Maryland and across the Chesapeake. Once in the bay itself, he was able during the night crossing to remember landmarks from his many trips on the *Quaker City*.

After being dropped by their boat, Michael followed the two soldiers inland for nearly a mile over wild marshland until they came to a road crossing. In the predawn light he could make out a wagon stopped on the shoulder. The team was sleeping in their traces.

"You're in Virginia, Mr. Farrell," the captain said quietly. "From now on you are in my charge."

It was the longest speech the man had made since they had begun, and it was not altogether friendly.

"I suppose we can relax now. Where are we bound?"

"I'm not at liberty to say."

There was a movement in the wagon, and they watched the dim figure of a man climbing down. Michael's mouth felt dry; it was about to begin. He'd better sharpen his wits.

A voice floated over from the rig. "Bring any oysters, gentlemen?"

It was apparently a password. The captain replied instantly. "I prefer Chincoteague."

A low laugh from the wagon and they approached.

"You're a bit bedraggled. Any complaints?"

Any complaints! The hair crawled on Michael's neck as he heard his own voice with the countersign.

"I may have a stone in my shoe."

"Better than a Minié ball, friend."

The cluster of buildings on the outskirts of Richmond was the headquarters of a military unit whose identity and purpose were deliberately vague. There were as many people in civilian dress as there were uniforms, and when they arrived at noon, Michael's escort delivered him to the parlor of a rambling gingerbread structure that appeared to be a combination boardinghouse and bachelor officers' quarters.

"The sutler's store is down the street. Get whatever supplies you need—within reason, of course."

"I'm not sure of my status here."

It was a stupid comment, and Michael felt a sickening fear grip his belly. What a start as an undercover agent. The captain looked at him with a curious mixture of surprise and loathing.

"You're no longer a prisoner, if that's what you mean. In fact, you're considered a guest of the Confederacy with some esteem. And since our own association is at an end, Mr. Farrell, I should mention that I do not share that feeling. I am not comfortable with those who wear sheep's clothing—on either side. I prefer to fight my wars against uniformed enemies with comrades who do likewise."

It took some faking to appear insulted at the remark. "I am not interested in your military philosophy, Captain," he said. "Only curious as to my instructions."

"You'll be contacted," the captain answered curtly as he left.

No salute? Michael thought dismally. He wondered what the man would think if he knew the whole truth about his fellow escapee's current mission. Or that he shared the cavalryman's sentiments exactly.

Later that night Michael decided he had had quite enough of safe deliverances. The choices offered him by Pinkerton were pure extortion and he told him so. All the years of work on projects of which the Union was now enjoying the benefit were sour in his mouth. Large grain powder, the saltpeter deal, the painstaking lab work to provide quality powder to its armies were as much to further his own interests as those of the United States, but the record certainly bespoke his loyalty and service. And he had warned Lammot of Charlotte du Pont's wild attempt at conspiracy, as unlikely as it seemed she might ever have carried it out.

Thoughts of Lammot galled the most. Was he a willing party to this plan? Was it possible he might have engineered it? The thought burned at his brain. Lammot was as opportunistic as his uncle. He could almost understand Henry's position against him. The evidence must have seemed a windfall chance to avoid the blame of thirteen deaths himself. But Lammot?

"A dirty business, old fellow," he had said. "A dirty business. But what a chance to clear your name forever!"

Perhaps. Out of his window the lights of Richmond illuminated low clouds scudding across the higher overcast. It would rain tomorrow, soft April rains in the south. He loosened his collar and ran a finger around the sweat-dampened fabric. Tomorrow he might be called to begin his charade. It was humid in the room, suffocating with the heat of the building and the sodden air of the oncoming rain. Could he carry it off? His status as accomplished saboteur would help, but he was not very good at hiding his feelings. Later as he lay exhausted on his bed, he forced Megan's face into his mind, blotting out all other thoughts. She was with him until sleep blotted her out, too.

CHAPTER THIRTY-FIVE

JUNE
1863

Allan Pinkerton quickly scanned the report his aide had given him, grunted with satisfaction, and picked up a handful of smaller notes.

"What are these?"

"Letters from Farrell to his wife. They're clean. Just reassurances that he is well, with the usual personal yearnings."

"Don't forward them. I don't want to take any chances."

"The report is optimistic?"

"Keep your fingers crossed. Get this to the President and General Meade. No one else."

"Yes sir."

"No one else, not even Hooker. Understood?"

After he was alone, Pinkerton permitted himself a smile. J. E. B. Stuart was probably exulting about his little victory near Culpeper. The place was called Brandy Station and that was a coincidence. Even now he was reported making a dashing sweep north of Washington to pester Hooker. Would he take the bait and try to hang another scalp from his victory belt? It would be a temptation, particularly for such a young and dashing general. The feat would have a nice ring, too. "Brandy Station to the Brandywine!"—a chance to capture the powder mills and Wilmington at the same time.

Pinkerton spanned the distance on his wall map with thumb

and forefinger. Two days to cover the distance and overwhelm the weak defenses around Wilmington. Three or four days away from Lee's army, and a chance to capture half the powdermaking source of the Union!

He'd go for it.

Pinkerton felt it in his bones. And Robert E. Lee, on his way to Harrisburg, would founder without the eyes of his cavalry as Meade drove North to cut him off.

He scribed a circle around the towns on the map. Where would they meet, he wondered. Chambersburg, Carlisle, York? His thumb was the pivot for the arc, and it covered a little town not worth considering. Gettysburg.

"A most bizarre twist of fate, Mr. Farrell."

The man was familiar, but Michael would not have recognized him on the street. He was struck with how similar the face was to pictures of Lincoln. Perhaps it was the haggard look, about the eyes especially. Michael found it difficult to look at the eyes.

"A small world, Capt . . . Mr. President."

"It's been some time since anyone made that mistake. I'll consider it a compliment." The face was not smiling, however, and his hand had not been offered. "Sit down, please."

Jefferson Davis studied his visitor. It was a severe test of Michael's composure, but he held on as he had for weeks now, fueled by a small knot of anger at all of his manipulators.

"I've been told that you have struck a blow for our cause."

Michael shrugged.

"You can imagine why your future service might be of value to the South?"

"I have been briefed, sir."

"You have been given to understand that this service is voluntary and that you will be compensated?"

"I am not interested in rewards for this kind of work, sir."

"I have been told of your feelings in that respect. Just what *is* your reason for playing the role of informant, Mr. Farrell?"

He had been expecting the question for some time, and he could answer it truthfully enough.

"It's a way to bring this madness to an end."

Davis smiled grimly. "You would do well not to speak those sentiments too loudly hereabouts. Our rebellion is not considered madness in Richmond."

"War is madness, Mr. President. Without the means to wage it, perhaps thinking men will devise a better way to resolve their differences."

"You speak like a visionary, Mr. Farrell. Did your conversion come like some bolt from heaven? As a powdermaker yourself, I find your rebirth somewhat in question."

"Explosives have a proper peaceful role."

"Is that why you destroyed a dozen men in the du Pont mills last February?"

Michael could not speak. He was back in the woods above Hagley, seeing the rumpled doll among the shattered stones.

Davis held onto Michael's bleak stare and then sighed heavily. "Forget that. It is a question I should not have asked of one who has further distasteful chores."

"Distasteful!" The word was wrenched from Michael's mouth like a vile epithet.

"Come now, Mr. Farrell. You are no stranger to disloyalty to your fellows. If I recall correctly, you saw fit to abandon your soldier comrades within weeks of my recommending you for citation."

Michael's face was black with rage, his voice growled with emotion. The charade was done, and he spoke from years of suppressed fury. "You question my loyalties, sir? What about your own?"

The President of the Confederate States of America was silent as he looked upon Michael Farrell, Irish immigrant, twice dispossessed of promise. He remembered the youthful soldier who had stormed the Mexican batteries that day long ago, and single-handedly saved them all from grape and canister.

"Touché, Mr. Farrell," he said soberly, "I've overstepped my bounds."

When an aide came in later with a questioning look, Jefferson Davis slowly nodded. "But watch him," he added. "Watch him carefully."

It was Sunday, June 28, when Lee learned of Meade's advance to his rear. By then the Army of Northern Virginia was scattered over the southeastern Pennsylvania countryside. It would be days before they could consolidate at Cashtown. He put out a desperate search for his cavalry. On Tuesday one of A. P. Hill's Confederate brigades blundered into a Union force at Gettysburg. The following day the battle was joined. Because of his late arrival, Stuart's cavalry could not break through to Lee. By July 1, Meade's entire Army of the Potomac was massed before Lee's uncoordinated divisions.

To the Brandywiners this was not just "another of Jeff Davis's annual visits North." This time there was a report of cavalry in force at the Susquehanna, and they were heading east into Delaware. Newspapers pleaded for volunteers on June 30 and in every edition for the rest of the week. Militia companies on Pea Patch were released to protect the mills, and finished powder was carted north as fast as wagons could be rounded up to haul it away. People were leaving, too, all but the local Copperheads. It was not considered healthy to be Unionist. Everybody was making plans either to pick up and run or stay and face fighting against the Rebel hordes, and Independence Day dawned as a day of fear. That Saturday morning nobody was planning to set off fireworks. They were worried about hearing the real thing.

When Lammot du Pont had his companies in position, he called for his horse and galloped all the way to Mary Belin's home above Hagley Yard.

"You and your mother should leave, Mary. I've made arrangements in Philadelphia."

"Cancel them, please."

"The news from Gettysburg is bad. I had thought this time our army might have won, but the reports are not encouraging."

"I'm staying."

"But why take chances?"

"Because you'll be here, Lammot, not in Philadelphia."

"That's hardly reasonable."

"Who's speaking of reason? I've been subjected to 'reasonable' decisions far too long. This time I'll follow my heart, thank you."

"In this case, dear Mary, that may be unwise. The General thinks evacuation is prudent, and Mother especially suggested that you be removed to a safe place."

"Yes. I can imagine that Meta wants me removed."

"Somehow that sounds ominous."

"It does to me. For the past two years our paths have been allowed to cross so briefly that I really suspect manipulation."

Lammot looked at her incredulously. He laughed gently. "Such intrigue. I think it unfortunate coincidence."

"Think about it sometime."

"But you have been away as often as I."

"Always at my father's insistence."

"There you have it. Would you call that Mother's manipulation?"

"I only know that Father once said rather angrily that he didn't want to make trouble. It may seem harsh to say this, Lammot, but I think Meta has come to dislike me."

"Since when, Mary?"

"Since the first time we went together socially."

"That's going to be awkward."

"Awkward?"

"After we're married, I mean. I was hoping you might agree to marry me. What do you think, Mary? If I asked, how good are my chances?"

"Dear God, Lammot, you are the most unromantic creature I know!"

"It will mean long separations from my mother. Can you handle that? We'd have to survive without her winning smile and enthusiasm."

"Is this a proposal?"

"Not yet. A preliminary survey to establish feasibility. The actual tender should be made only when a contract seems likely."

"Ugh. It sounds like you're buying some company."

"Oh, it's a mutual decision. A merger for the good of both parties. Joint strength, shared exploration, multiplication of assets—"

She pushed away his hands. "It's a bit early to examine *this* company ledger!"

"Fair enough. Anyway, my preliminary survey is most promising. We're prepared to make an offer. What are my chances?"

"Unfair tactic, sir!" She stepped into his arms and rested her head on his chest. "However, I will say that I've been interested in your company for some time."

"You drive a hard bargain, my dear. Very well, here's my proposal: a merger of our assets. May I say at this juncture that *your* assets are terribly attractive. A merger—delightful word— of our assets in common, share and share alike, toward the mutual prosperity and success of both parties."

"Agreed."

"Shall we shake on it?"

"I've a better idea."

After a rather long kiss, Lammot mumbled in her ear, "I feel an urgency to consummate the contract, my dear."

"I think we'd better get our signatures on the paper first."

"Distressing formality."

"I'll make one concession, sir, if that will help. We'll use your name on the new organization."

"Whatever you say. I must confess to being more interested in getting on with the internal operations of the venture."

"Some externals first. When should we announce plans for our 'merger,' as you so romantically call it?"

"The sooner the better. You tell your principals and I'll tell mine."

She pushed him back to arm's length and looked him over. "You are terribly handsome in that uniform. Go back now and protect me from those awful Rebel invaders!"

He snapped an exaggerated salute and clicked his heels. She felt a terrible fear then and clutched him close, holding him until she could trust her lips not to tremble when they kissed again. Then she broke away and walked up the path to the house.

Lammot had two other calls to make before returning to his troops. He decided to tell his mother immediately about his engagement to Mary Belin, but first he had important information for Megan Farrell.

When he called at Eleutherian Mills, Louisa greeted him.

"I had heard you were back, Motty," she smiled warmly. "It is good to see you looking so fit and dashing."

"How are you, Aunt Louisa? I'm afraid I haven't paid my respects as I should."

"As if you had the time. You are taking care of yourself, I hope. I'm sorry, but I am so concerned about all of you boys. Young Henry tried to get himself assigned here to defend us."

"We'll be fine, Aunt Lou. I don't think they'll try for us this time. The Gettysburg thing will keep them too busy for us. Don't fret." He grinned with more reassurance than he felt. "I came to speak to Megan Farrell. Is she downstairs?"

Louisa looked away. "She is no longer with us."

"I don't understand. You mean she is alone in the stableman's place?"

"No. Discharged a month ago. I understand she is staying with her aunt again."

"Brendan Gallagher's? But discharged? Why, for heaven's sake?"

"I really can not discuss it, Motty. And if you don't mind, I am not at all well today."

After his aunt excused herself and he let himself out, Lammot considered seeing Henry to clear up the matter. But he did not really have the time and decided to go directly to the Gallagher home instead. Megan was in the yard and saw him as he rode up. As he dismounted and tied his horse to the fence, she approached apprehensively drying her hands on her apron.

"It's good news, Megan."

"Thank God for that! Where is he?"

"We're not sure. Probably he's on his way to Washington. The information is sketchy."

"What do you mean then, 'good news'?"

"The charges have been dropped. Michael has become a hero of sorts. The General will probably make an announcement clearing his name next week—after it is safe to do so."

"After it is safe? What is all this? Is he in some danger?"

"I don't think so. All that is past now. There was terrible danger that he might be discovered as a federal agent, but that's in the past. Now all he has to do is find his way home to a grateful community. I tell you, Megan, what he did could well have been instrumental in our winning the war."

"Find his way home, you said. Where in heaven's name was he? What was he doing?"

"Pretending to be a Confederate agent. It was part of a rather elaborate plan to split the Rebel forces. A trick to draw off their cavalry while our army moved in to intercept the invaders. Our powder mills were the bait."

"Do you mean he might still be leading them here?"

"Oh, no. The Rebels have already galloped off to rejoin Lee. We just hope all of them broke off the attack."

"Then Michael might still be with them."

"That was not the plan."

"And if he's discovered in this wild scheme, he'll be shot!"

"He'll certainly not be discovered. Besides, the cat's out of the bag by now. The operation worked just fine."

"Do you mean others know his identity and his real reason for being in the South?"

"Well, yes. That's why I have been authorized to tell you."

"Dear God, why not wait until he was safe at home before telling anyone?"

"According to plan he should have slipped away by now."

Megan nodded incredulously. "According to plan. God spare him such planners." Suddenly her eyes widened and she gripped Lammot's arm. "You mentioned General du Pont making an announcement. How long has he known about Michael's work, about his innocence?"

"Why almost from the beginning, I imagine. He has direct access to the President's office, you know."

Megan made a little keening cry and began to weep. She smeared the tears away angrily and nearly choked on her words. They sounded murderous to Lammot.

"That bastard!" she growled.

"I don't understand."

She glared at him. "You wouldn't. You're a du Pont. Why do you think I'm living here instead of on the hill? Why do you think I was 'let go for reasons of health' as they say?"

"I just learned of it."

"Because your uncle tried to make my bedroom his personal brothel."

Lammot let his breath out slowly and swore.

"Don't be so quick to condemn, Mr. du Pont. Didn't you offer Michael as a government harlot? Didn't you know he might be paid with a Confederate noose?"

Lammot tried to explain, but the reasons sounded hollow even to himself.

It was late in the day before news of the twin victories by Meade and Grant reached the Brandywine. Not only had the Union won at Gettysburg, but Vicksburg had also fallen to the federal armies on the same day. Harry Belin at first disbelieved the message and keyed back a request for confirmation. In minutes the story had spread up and down the Crick, shouted from house to house, drawing knots of jubilant families into belated celebration of the Fourth. The war would not last more than a week or two. Dorgan's had the biggest sale in the pub's history, and more Irish powdermen spent the following morning sleeping it off than made it to Sunday Mass.

Later on, Father Reardon would have some stern words for their behavior in the confessional, but on the morning of July 5th, it was difficult to keep from smiling. This was particularly true when, right in the middle of the last gospel, Denis Feeney came galloping up the altar steps, tripping on his cassock, and whispered excitedly into the old priest's good ear. It was very unclerical for a deacon, but under the circumstances, understandable.

After the interruption, Francis Reardon picked up where he had left off, reeling off the Latin smoothly, and Denny backed off to stand red-faced but piously attentive in the sanctuary. When the priest finished, he moved to the center of the altar and gave the final blessing.

"In nomine Patris, et Filii, at Speritus sancti."

"Amen."

"Ite missa est."

"Deo gratias."

When he picked up the veil-draped chalice and marched down the steps, the altar boys were startled because he went directly to the communion rail. Some thought he might be having words for Joe Haley, who always skipped out during the three Hail Marys at the end.

He raised his hand and motioned for someone in the vestibule to come forward. "Some of you know Colonel Aloysius Moody, whose soldiers were sent to protect us," Father Reardon said with a smile. "He has something important to say. I think we should all sit." Moody looked uncomfortable, standing up to speak in church.

"Last February a terrible thing happened here. A good many men were killed and as many badly hurt. A few of us pointed the finger of guilt toward one man. I speak of Michael Farrell, who was my friend. Well, the short of it is that he had nothing at all to do with that awful explosion. I have a letter here from Captain Lammot du Pont stating why it could not be so."

Moody cleared his throat and held up the sheet. Then he pulled out another, holding it up and turning so everyone could see.

"This other one is a telegraph message received only this morning at General du Pont's company office. I'll read it. 'Please accept our thanks for temporary services of your employee Michael Farrell whose intrepidity contributed to the great Federal victory at Gettysburg.' And it's signed by the secretary for President Lincoln."

There was some buzzing in the congregation, and everyone kept swinging their heads toward Brendan Gallagher's pew and back to Colonel Moody again. Then young Denis Feeney stepped down from the sanctuary, went over to his family, and led them down the aisle.

Most everybody in church could tell from the sounds drifting in that there had been a happy reunion.

Lammot du Pont did not have a chance to see Michael until the following day when he called again at the Gallagher home. After being greeted deferentially by the family he was left alone with Michael on the front porch.

"Well, old fellow," he said warmly. "You're the talk of the Crick these days, eh? How does it feel to be savior of the Union?"

"In a few days when the casualty figures come home, I may be known as the butcher of the Brandywine."

Some of Lammot's ebullience faded. "Always the pessimist. Think of the numbers saved by a quick end to this awful affair."

"I prefer not to think of it at all, if you don't mind."

"Just a temporary letdown. After a few days rest you'll be right as rain; mark my words."

"Why did you do it, Lammot?"

"The mission? Well, old fellow, that should be obvious. Pinkerton's idea seemed the best way to clear your name."

"It could have been done with a single letter from you to Washington."

Lammot laughed. "But not with such dash." He reacted to the dark look Michael gave him and added more seriously, "Really, your part in the strategy was pivotal."

"That's hogwash. Any number of alternatives could have been used. This war is no stranger to spies and false reports."

"But your notoriety because of the blast was too much of an opportunity to pass up."

"You realize that the genuine saboteur reported to Richmond that I was an imposter. It nearly meant a rope for me."

"But no one expected that. I really assumed the explosion had been a regrettable accident. Who knows, the man may have been just a glory seeker. At any rate, the important thing is that it came off handsomely with no damage to you."

"No thanks to you and Henry du Pont."

"Well, Uncle wants to make amends. You're to take a few days off and report back as supervisor of the lab until I'm released. Then we'll work as a team again, finish this distressing war, and get rich together in the high explosives business!"

"No one is getting rich but Henry. I don't like the way he

plays his game. But I might even manage to cope with him, bad as he is. He has a clever, avaricious mind, but narrow. He could be controlled with the right amount of pressure."

"Well, then, stay with me and we'll nail him up in one of his own kegs. Honestly, Michael, we could do great things together. When I'm director, you can state your own terms."

"Come off it, Lammot, how can you be so naive? You will never be director of du Pont, not while Henry is alive. And even if you were, I wouldn't stay."

"For God's sake, why not?"

"Because too much of Henry du Pont has rubbed off on you, my friend. You're getting more like him every day."

"That's one hell of a thing to say."

"Just a minute ago you said you were quite willing to put my life on the line because of an opportunity too good to pass up."

When Lammot did not answer, Michael slowly nodded. "I think you know where I stand."

"If you won't reconsider, at least think of it as a temporary move. Can I ask where you will go?"

"Out West. I've had an offer from California Powder."

Lammot sighed. "May I offer a letter of recommendation?"

"Thanks, no. Considering Henry's competitive tactics, I might be welcomed better as the bomber of Hagley Yards than as a valued du Pont employee."

Lammot smiled uneasily. "Is there *anything* I can do? Please don't let me stand by useless while you go off in a tiff."

"You can do one thing. Draw out all my money from the company books. We're leaving within the week."

"Glad to. The General probably will want to hand it over personally. He has a ceremony planned to honor your service to President Lincoln. He's quite worked up about it."

"He can forget any ceremony. I don't want to risk hanging again."

"Well, there's no risk of that any longer."

"I understand you spoke with Megan, Lammot, so you know why. If I ever see your uncle again, I'll kill the bastard with my bare hands."

CHAPTER THIRTY-SIX

See that last bit of land jutting out?"

She sighted along his arm, cheek against the billowing sleeve, against the hardness of the muscle underneath.

"Yes."

"That's Henlopen. We're at the mouth of the Delaware. The open sea's beyond."

She breathed deeply. "I can almost smell it."

Michael smiled and pulled her close. It was so good being with her that he felt waves of giddiness sweep through him. The prow of the square-rigger plunged gently under their feet and then rose with a sinuous rhythm.

"It's our honeymoon," she whispered.

"Reading my thoughts."

"Oh, Michael, I'm so in love at this moment I think I may be ill."

"Lovesick?"

"Oh, dear. I don't think I've ever had the sensation before, even years ago when I thought I would go out of my mind with wanting you."

"I know. It's contagious, I think. Perhaps we should lie down in our cabin and nurse ourselves back to health."

She jabbed him with her finger and laughed. "Not when we're the only passengers on this ship. I can feel the eyes of the crew as it is."

"Any regrets? Think you will miss the family?"

The glance she swept up at him was more than a denial. He had an almost uncontrollable desire to carry her back to the cabin like a buccaneer. She slipped out of his arms and stepped closer to the rail.

"Off to port you can see Cape May. It's behind us now. We'll soon feel the ground swell."

"I will miss Aunt Noreen and Uncle Brendan," she said soberly. "At least they have Denny to look in on them from time to time."

"You'll see, Meggie. Just wait till I get the right combination for blasting oil. We'll be rich as the du Ponts, with the biggest house on the Barbary Coast!"

"A decent living is what I want, husband, for me and my wee ones when they come. You can forget the grand dreams."

"You'll have that in the meantime, Mrs. Farrell. I've a decent job waiting at the end of this voyage, and I'll give you as many babies as you want."

"Oh," she pouted. "I have to wait on both until we get to California? What a waste of the fine cabin Lammot du Pont booked for us. Are you that upset with the man? Not to make use of his gift?"

"All right, I'm only flesh and blood, woman. To hell with the ogling crew. Do you want to walk to the cabin or must I carry you like a savage?"

"I'll walk," she said, but according to the foretopman, who told the story at mess that evening, it looked more like running.

CHAPTER THIRTY-SEVEN

Like everyone else in the country, Lammot thought the twin defeats at Vicksburg and Gettysburg would mean a quick end to the war. But the South clung on desperately for nearly two more years. His service at Pea Patch became a more horrifying experience as the captive Confederates were packed in by the thousands, with wild outbreaks of dysentery and typhoid. When he could manage leave, the burden of relieving Irénée at the mills was a constant homecoming duty. Irénée was a shell, sucked bitter by his recurring illness and worry for his wife. As the months dragged by, the fictitious rationale for Charlotte's confinement became a diagnosis in fact. She was certifiably disturbed.

Mary Belin withdrew from his embrace and touched his face. "You look terrible. When did you last eat?"

"Hmm. After two months' separation I banked on warmer words."

"I'm serious, Motty. You've lost *pounds*."

"It's all the exercise, Mary. This constant rushing up from the fort to see you has worn me to a frazzle."

That was a sore subject. He seldom called on her. There were reasons certainly, she knew that, but letters could only do so much.

"I think that I'm playing third fiddle to the war and powder mills."

She was not being petulant. It was matter-of-fact.

"I know it seems like inattention, Mary. It's not. You're in my thoughts constantly. I wish we had more time together."

"It *is* inattention, dear Lammot, whatever the reason. I hope it is not oversight, pure and simple."

"Ah, Mary. You know my feelings."

"I had thought so."

"Well then?"

"Actions speak louder than words."

He shook his head as if to clear his thinking. The damned headache was back again. "You know the action I want to take, my dear. And I will when the time is right. This frantic time will soon pass, and we can get on with our lives."

"Soon? I've come to suspect the word."

"You certainly would not want to marry with things as they are."

She smiled up at his worried face. How haggard he appeared! "I would want to marry you with things any way at all."

He slipped his arm around her waist and held her close again. "I want this marriage to be right from the start and forever."

She went up on her toes and kissed his cheek. "It will be right."

His head was pounding. A sudden splitting pain cracked between the temples, and he sagged backward toward a chair. The room spun at a tilted angle.

"Lammot!" He was aware of her terrified expression floating out of focus and felt her cool hands on his face. "Lie back, lie back, oh dear God. I'll get a cool towel."

When she hurried in from the kitchen and pressed the damp cloth to his forehead, he was already coming around. The ache was still thumping sullenly behind his eyes, but his vision had cleared and the giddy sensation was gone. He started to rise, but she pushed him down.

"I'm fine now. Just a headache."

"You're not fine at all. Just sit there and I'll send for a doctor."

"Silly. Just a sudden headache. I have to go, Mary. The Hagley pressroom, meet with the General, and some tests at the lab before heading back."

"To Pea Patch? Certainly not! And you should stay here until

Father gets home. I will not have you riding a horse in your condition."

He struggled to his feet. "Really, you have enough to do caring for your mother, and I'm not unwell at all. Besides, it would not be proper for me to spend the afternoon with a young lady alone in her house."

"I'm not just any young lady."

The pain was increasing, and he needed air, needed to be out of the house. "You know what I mean, Mary. I hardly wish to compromise your position."

She tried to tease him out of his pique. He mustn't go, not as ill as he seemed. "Very well, I'll announce our betrothal to any raised eyebrows."

"That would be unwise."

"Mother knows."

"Yes. I imagined you would have confided in her."

She was fighting for time. She had to get him to stay for a cup of strong tea, something. "I have not told Father."

"I should think not." His voice was thick, almost sullen.

"You have mentioned it to Meta, naturally."

"No."

She was incredulous. "You have not told anyone, have you?"

"She will learn in due course."

Mary stared at him. There was no mistaking the pain in his eyes. How could she have been so dense. No wonder he was so upset.

"I must go now. I'll write."

She nodded, unable to look up when he squeezed her hand and then left her alone in the Belin parlor.

He managed to mount the horse and let the animal find its own way up the hill and through the woods to the stable. There would be no working the rest of this day. He was barely able to dismount, stagger into Nemours, and climb the steps to his room.

The typhoid had gripped him so fiercely that he collapsed in the upstairs hall, dizzy and barely conscious. He was dimly aware, however, that it was his uncle who caught him as he fell, and half-carried him to bed. Henry was in his stocking feet, and the woman making clucking sounds as she stroked his brow was his mother. She was still in her nightgown.

"Now do you understand my fear, Mary?" he muttered to himself, gibberish from his lips but starkly clear in his tortured mind. "It's in my blood. Can I even trust my own fidelity?" The question reeled in his brain and spun him into nausea as he blacked out completely.

That evening Harry Belin got home later than usual and was surprised to find Bridget Flaherty cooking his supper. He was doubly confused. The girl usually came in for cleaning once a week, but this was the wrong day, and she never stayed to help for the evening meal. His first thought was that his wife had suddenly worsened in her illness.

"Y'mustn't be alarmed, mister," the girl said quickly. "The missus is just fine, but I'm to tell you that Mary left suddenly to visit the family in Pennsylvania. I'm to stay and look after Mrs. Belin."

"Wapwallopen?"

"Aye, that's the place, 'tis a hard name to recall. With your brother's folks, I believe."

He wondered what had prompted his daughter's sudden trip North. It was unlike Mary to be precipitous about anything.

Isabella Belin gave her husband the answer as soon as he leaned over the bed and kissed her. "She needs time to get over a broken heart."

"Broken heart? My word, who's the scoundrel?"

"Lammot du Pont."

"Not that again. Poor thing, I warned her not to entertain foolish dreams."

"It has not been one-sided, Harry. Mary is not so dense as to allow false hopes to build without reason."

"Don't get me wrong, Isabella. I love the family, Lammot especially, but you know their record of close ties."

"Incest would be less delicate but more accurate."

Belin's raised eyebrows did not intimidate her. Angry red splotches colored her pale cheeks.

"Well, the matter is finally at rest. I am saddened by her hurt, but it is best for her in the long run. How long will she stay with Charles?"

"She has no plans. A few weeks."

"How was she told? A letter? I hope the boy was gentle."

"He was here this afternoon. Mary said he was so distraught in telling her—hinting really—that he became ill."

"Poor Mary," Harry Belin murmured, "And poor Lammot."

"It's his loss, not hers. She would have made that family jump." Isabella Belin allowed herself several tears, wiped them away angrily, and lay back against the pillows. "Now leave me in peace to collect my strength. Go eat your supper."

It was not until the following morning that he found out about Lammot du Pont's grave bout with typhoid fever. Four others from the Brandywine Volunteers had contracted it as well. In the week following two of them died. Lammot clung on, hovering for weeks between delirium and consciousness. The Belins decided not to add to Mary's problems with additional worry. They never mentioned Lammot until she returned six weeks later.

Meta smiled at her visitor and led her into a small reception room off the entry hall. They sat facing each other across a small mahogany table inset with alternating squares of teak and ivory. It was chilly in the room, but she did not call for tea.

"It was thoughtful of you to call on us, Mary."

"I did not hear about his illness until I got back, Mrs. du Pont. Otherwise I would have written weeks ago."

"It is the thought that counts, my dear. I would have welcomed your support, of course, but then there is not much you could have done."

"Just to let him know."

"Your father has already extended his support as head of your family. I appreciate that. He is more than a loyal employee, much more."

"Do you think I could visit with Lammot? I feel quite badly about this."

"Oh, dear me, no. I'm afraid that is out of the question. His doctor has given strict orders. Mr. Lammot is not to be disturbed any more than absolutely necessary. Just members of the family."

"I see."

"I knew you would understand. I'll tell him you were asking after his health. He will be pleased."

Mary felt a flush creeping up her neck, but she kept her eyes on Meta and pulled open the drawstring of her reticule, withdrawing a small envelope. She handed it over the table. "This is for him."

Meta rose as she took the note. "How sweet, my dear. I did not realize until his illness how many of you young people feel kindly toward Mr. Lammot." She took a step toward the vestibule, paused until Mary rose to follow, and smiled pleasantly as she led her to the door.

Afterward Meta toyed with the idea of opening the letter, but thought better of it. She would not deliver it for a few days, however. Motty's eyes should not be strained. The doctor had said so himself. In fact, keeping the note for a few weeks might not be a bad idea.

"It was as if we were playing chess across that table. What has the woman got against me?"

"Perhaps you imagined it, Mary. After all, your feelings have been under a strain lately."

"Mother, it was like petting a dog with flattened ears. I could *feel* it."

"But she was civil?"

"Butter wouldn't melt in her mouth. I felt like a costumed child come begging on Hallowe'en."

"Mary dear, you said that Lammot had not mentioned his feelings for you to his mother. I don't see how you can fault the woman for being solicitous as to his health. Typhoid is no light illness."

Mary gritted her teeth. "It's so frustrating! Look, Mother, I just *know* she was holding me off for a different reason. I could *feel* her dislike for me."

Isabella reached out for her daughter's hand and pulled her down to sit beside her on the bed. "Let it go, child. Lammot has apparently had a change of heart. You'll destroy yourself with bitterness if you do not accept that."

Mary patted her mother's hand. "You're right about one thing, Mother. I'll not let bitterness sour me, and I'll not let it distract you anymore. But," she added as she got up to leave, "I'll not give him up without a fight."

Isabella Belin followed her footfalls on the stairs, listened as they sounded firm little dots across the parlor, through the hall, and into the kitchen.

"Brave little girl but foolish woman," she thought. "God help you."

Two days after Mary Belin's visit, a second envelope for Lammot was delivered to Nemours. Meta recognized the hand. It matched the first exactly. The girl was persistent. She considered destroying both letters, but steamed them open instead. The first envelope contained only a hand lettered prayer for the sick, but there was a note in the second.

> *Dear Lammot,*
> *How distressed I was to return from Uncle Charles' and hear of your illness. Please God you will recover quickly with no lingering weakness. Know that you are in my prayers till this awful trial is over, and we can again share your good spirits, rejoicing in your renewed health.*
>
>

Affectionately,
Mary Belin

>
> *P.S. I so look forward to further discussion of our joint community project. Let me know when you are well enough to reopen negotiations for future planning.*

Meta resealed the envelopes with a feeling of relief. The postscript itched at her curiosity, and she wondered what charitable organization was using the Belins as a way to inveigle du Pont money for its support. She resented the imposition, knowing how gullible Lammot was in such philanthropies, but it at least explained his occasional visits to Mary Belin.

Well, no danger there apparently, but Lammot was still a vulnerable bachelor. She promised herself to renew social connections with a few families endowed with reasonable wealth and tractable, marriageable daughters. In the meantime she buried the messages under a pile of cards Lammot had already opened.

Six weeks after the onset of the fever, his doctor was willing to concede that complete recovery was probable. Lammot did not need the advice, his appetite had returned. The headache persisted, but it was not the blinding pain of before, and he had some difficulty with his eyes when reading for more than a few minutes at a time. But these lingering ailments were a bother more than a debility. He felt a surge of urgency to be up and about, picking up his life where the typhoid had stalled it.

Picking up his life meant a fresh beginning with Mary. The long delirium had fuzzed over their last meeting, patches of some disagreement he could not focus on clouded his memory. And she had not been in to see him, which had been strange, but he was glad for it. His first glance in the dressing mirror that first day he had struggled weakly out of bed was terrifying. The naked image in the glass stared back at him like a parchment-wrapped skeleton with dark, hollow eyes. He certainly did not want her to catch him in this state!

Still, there was hurt at her disinterest, and judging from the stack of get-well wishes, his ailment was widely known. Was she giving him a sample of his own medicine? On more than one occasion his preoccupations certainly had left her in the dark. He tried to justify it that way but could not visualize Mary being that vindictive. It just was not in her nature. Nor was she, he thought with remorse, as insensitive as he had been himself.

The loss of forty pounds had left him spindly as a scarecrow, but after those first shaky steps to the mirror, he began to eat ravenously. His strength was slow building, however, and a few more days passed before he was able to make the trip downstairs.

"You mustn't rush your recovery, Lammot dear."

"I feel like a penned animal." He paced stiffly through the rooms, paused at a window to savor the swirling color of the blustery, leaf-blown autumn and returned to the library desk. "I suppose I must tend to these before they crinkle with age," he muttered, shuffling a scattered pile of cards and envelopes.

"Don't be silly." His mother tugged at his arm. "You'll see most of those people before long, and a response is not called for anyway."

"I want to clear away the clutter. They prey on my mind, a block to my getting back to work."

"Why don't I just get rid of them? Toss the lot."

It was tempting. He was not up to writing anything, much less a bunch of plodding thank-you notes. He nodded.

"Good, I'll have one of the girls clear it away later. Would you like something? Soup or—"

Something had caught his eye on the desk. She watched as he pulled out first one, then another envelope from the pile.

"I seem to have overlooked a few." He held the two and riffled through the rest.

"Or a nice cup of broth?"

"Only these two. No, nothing, thanks. Oh!"

"Is anything wrong?"

"Why, they're both from Mary."

"Mary?"

"Mary Belin. Strange. This one was not posted. Did she come here, Mother?"

"Mary Belin. How nice of her."

"Did she deliver this one?"

"Oh, my, yes. I recall now. What with so many callers when you were delirious, yes. I remember promising to put it in with the rest of your mail, for when you were up to reading."

She watched for a moment as he opened the card, read it quickly, and went on to the letter. As he scanned the last few lines, a broad smile lit up his face.

"A happy message? She is such a dear child. No employee's family is nicer."

Lammot did not answer. He was studying the postmark with a puzzled expression. Meta drifted toward the doorway.

"I'll have cook prepare you broth and toast."

She did not know if he heard.

Not long afterward the anxious cook came to her room. "I

thought you should know, madam," she whispered. "Mr. Lammot is dressed to go out-of-doors!"

Meta dropped her embroidery hoop and rushed for the vestibule where Lammot was buttoning on his greatcoat.

"Just where do you think you're going? Get out of that coat this instant!"

"I have a need for air, Mother."

"I'll open a window. You get back to bed, Lammot."

"No. This is quite important. I'll be back soon."

"Where in heaven's name are you going? What is so important that you risk a serious breakdown?"

"I'm going to the Belins'. A quarter-mile, and Flynn is driving me in the trap. No risk."

"Madness! You'll follow in your brother's footsteps. Oh, I can't bear another trial."

"It'll do me good. There are some questions that need answering."

Meta flared suddenly. "I *imagine*! Miss Belin and one of her ambitious plans? What community project is she negotiating that can not wait for our funding?"

Lammot's face turned white. "What did you say?"

Meta was fighting between tears and anger. When she did not answer, he tugged a folded paper from his pocket, opened it, and read aloud.

"Community project—reopen negotiations. Is that what you said? Mother, you unsealed and read this note when it was delivered four days ago. Tell me, did you commit the prayer card to memory also?"

In the long silence between them in the hall, in the hushed household behind them, the autumn wind soughed gentle background under sounds of the approaching horse and gig beyond the door. Lammot released the latch and backed out. His black eyes never left Meta's face until he slammed the door between them.

Mary knew it was Lammot coming to her even before the buggy stopped and he emerged unsteadily. She watched from the parlor window as he clung momentarily to the dashboard, fumbled to the whiffletree, followed the harness trace along the belly of the horse, and patting the curious animal's inquisitive muzzle, turning finally on his own to cross the open ground between the rig and steps to the Belin front door. He staggered so she wondered that he did not fall.

She was at his side before he reached the steps, unaware of the cold, the wind tearing at her hair. Only his ravaged face filled her mind. She rushed him up the steps, little spasms clutching at her throat as she felt the wasted bony frame move beneath his coat. When they were inside he gripped her to his chest and looked down at her upturned face. His gray eyes were never more sober, more filled with love.

"I've been a fool, Mary. Let's set the date and tell the world."

CHAPTER THIRTY-EIGHT

I have never been treated so shabbily in my life."

Lammot regarded his mother with cool detachment. Her puffy red eyes and hoarse voice were the result of heavy weeping, but he felt no compassion. It was strange. He was suffused with a feeling of freedom unlike anything he had ever before experienced.

"To find out about my own son's betrothal in the newspaper. Oh, Motty, how can you have been so harsh?"

"Your access to my mails makes you privy to my private plans. An announcement to you, Mother, would seem redundant."

"You thought enough of your brother and the entire Belin household to let them know."

"And no one let you in on the news? Apparently there are some people who respect my requests for confidentiality."

"Cruel. Cruel."

"Prudent, Mother. Nothing vindictive at all. I had to make sure your feelings about my choice would not infect our close little community until the announcement was a fait accompli."

Meta rose from the settee and paced the room, chiffon robe twitching with her agitation. "Well, my impetuous child, there are festering feelings enough without my help, I can assure you of that!"

"Meaning?"

She shot him a hot look and then stared at a a placid portrait of Alfred above the mantel. "To marry an employee's child is effrontery enough, but mixing race is quite another. There are furious reactions to *that*, I assure you."

Lammot frowned and spoke slowly. "I'm afraid you lost me there."

"Oh, don't play the fool, Lammot. You are aware of her genealogy."

His face was blank. She paused, her tone softened. "Dear heaven, you *don't* know, do you?"

He snorted a nervous laugh. "Well, perhaps if you simply told me I could answer. Race?"

"It pains me terribly to be the one. You mean she did not have the courage herself? Oh, my poor Motty. So unfair!"

"If you don't mind."

Meta took his hands, fresh tears welling in her eyes, he was rattled, she could tell. She whispered the words. "The Belin girl is Jewish."

The words stung him. She felt it in his hands, saw it in the gray chill of his eyes, the hardening of his jaw.

"Remarkable," he said at last. "How did you come by this revelation, Mother?"

"It was not difficult, my dear. Her maternal grandfather was a Jew. I am sorry to shock you so."

"How did you find out? I mean, digging back . . ."

"I have a letter from a Philadelphia firm which does research into such things. She's one-quarter."

"As much as that."

"Yes, dear. But the matter can be resolved. It would have been easier had you come to me first. The General will be piqued, but I'll speak to him."

"Uncle Henry."

"You *should* have sought him out first, you know. As director and head of the family his approval would have been crucial. Now that you understand the problem, it will just be a matter of smoothing his ego. Thank God you did not elope and face the awful notoriety of an annulment."

"What about the rest?"

"The rest of what, dear?"

"The other seventy-five percent. What else is Mary made of?"

A flicker of confusion crossed her face. "Is that important?"

Lammot felt her fingers relax, and he gripped her hands firmly enough to prevent her pulling away. "Oh, yes, I think so. Any Indian blood? Irish, even? A trace of Slav to dilute the French?"

"I don't think that's amusing."

"Neither do I."

She extricated herself from his grasp, made a business of patting at her hair, and crossed to the window. "I'll speak to your uncle this afternoon to get his advice on correcting this unfortunate affair."

"I'll speak to him."

She spun around with a smile, "Oh, that would be so much nicer, Motty. Man to man."

"Yes, I'll tell him the date so that he can clear his calendar. Arrange for my replacement during the honeymoon. Perhaps Aunt Louisa will want to host a bridal shower for Mary."

Her smile sagged, and she took a few faltering steps toward him, then froze.

"You are welcome to attend the wedding if you choose, Mother, although I really do not give a damn one way or the other."

"Lammot! Consider before you see him. All that you have worked for. Do you think he will ever step aside for a director with a Jewess for a bride?"

"I see. First Irénée with consumption, now me with an unacceptable marriage. All your well-laid plans, eh Mother?"

"Dear God, what can I do?"

"Nothing. I am moving in with Irénée until the wedding. After that, Mary and I will live here. My business with Uncle Henry will include setting aside a company house for your use. If you have any preferences, make them known to Uncle. I'll expect you to vacate before our return from the wedding trip."

She was ashen. "This is my home."

"Was. The house belongs to the company."

"I'll not move."

"I think it would be wise. Consider how awkward, how demeaning it would be to subordinate yourself to a mistress who is Jewish." Without another word he left the room.

The ordeal had drained him, but he still had two things to accomplish. The move to Irénée's was simple enough. He would just throw a few things into a valise and drive over. The other would take more energy, and he was woefully short of that just now. He had to beard the lion in his den.

"It's good to see you up and around."

As his uncle coolly appraised him from his desk chair, Lammot could easily imagine the naked vulnerability of a slave on the auction block. He's wondering how long till I'm fit for work, he thought. It was some consolation. The snub about his wedding announcement was not uppermost in Henry's mind.

"Feeling fit?"

Ah, yes. He was thinking about the work.

"You have lost weight, boy. You'd better sit down. Eating properly again?"

"I'll be fine in a few more days."

"We'll be glad to have you back in harness. It hasn't been easy."

Demoted from slave to draught animal. Oh well.

"Are you up to some serious conversation, Lammot?"

"Ready or not, I've been having much of that lately." Here it comes.

"Good. I've been waiting for you to recover enough to do some long-range planning. Rather ambitious planning, at that."

"I'm all ears."

Henry flashed one of his typical smiles, a quick baring of teeth that left the face impassive, the frosty blue eyes penetrating and cold.

"The war is winding down. Afterward there'll be a dozen or more powder companies clawing at each other's throats to get whatever business they can find."

Lammot struggled to frame the discussion. His mind was on other things and muddled besides with fatigue. He tossed in a comment while the gears meshed.

"And surplus powder."

"I've taken care of that. A promise from the War Department to keep government powder off the market. The thing I want to get started is a cooperative among the larger firms to hold fast on prices. Someone has to convince them to keep firm so that we all profit."

"That will be hard to do, General. There must be a score of small companies willing to sell at rates we can't afford."

"We'll make sure they hold the line."

"How can we? Those bare-bones operations always undercut us in small production runs."

"There are ways. Persuasion."

Lammot smiled at the simplistic solution. "When a man is hungry it takes great persuasion to make him wait. How do you plan to do it?"

"You'll do it."

"I don't wish to be impertinent, but why don't you try yourself? You head the largest powdermaking company in the country. Surely your leadership would be respected."

"I don't want it to be du Pont. It has to be an independent organization."

"But directed by du Pont."

"Exactly. You have a way with people, young man. Put it to use again, for the family business."

"What would be my role?"

"Call on the big companies, get them to endorse the plan, and then go after the small fry."

"Seems rather ambitious."

"I have a name picked, a nice fraternal name. We'll call it the Gunpowder Trade Association. You'll be president."

Lammot tried not to be flattered. It was a rubber-stamp title, but he smiled. "Suppose I'm not elected?"

"Leave that to me."

They studied each other for several seconds before Henry spoke again. His hardened expression suggested that the niceties were over. "You have been going off half-cocked lately. Has the fever destroyed part of your brain?"

"What do you mean?"

"You know Goddamned well what I mean. I want you to make an announcement that the whole idea of this betrothal was an unfortunate misunderstanding. If you can't stomach that, then I'll do it for you and try to make amends to the Belin family."

Lammot seethed. It was not that it was unexpected, but the voicing of this ham-fisted demand was the difference between anticipating the blow and actually feeling the lash bite. He gripped the spindly arms of his chair so fiercely that the wood groaned. "I'll do nothing of the kind," he glared. "And neither will you."

"Don't try to cross me in this, boy. You're not in a position to dictate family policy."

"Don't you mean company policy?"

"It's one and the same, and you know it."

"Very well. Explain to me very carefully how you dare to interpose yourself in my personal life."

The flare of anger that had suffused his uncle's face was ebbing into controlled conciliation. Lammot saw it and in the heat of his own controlled fury was ready for it. Uncle Henry was not as clever as he imagined himself to be.

"We du Ponts, especially the ones on whose shoulders great responsibility lies and will lie in the future"—he pointed his finger at Lammot's chest—"we have more circumscribed lives. Personal choice is sometimes a luxury we can not afford."

Lammot waited.

"In the matter of marriage particularly," Henry's voice took on a patriarchal rumble, "it is important to choose a mate suited to the social and economic realities of our lives. An inept selection, even one dictated by the highest level of affection, can be disastrous. It is wonderful if affectionate love and prudent choice go together, but"—here he leaned forward with a smile obviously intended to be warm—"honestly, my boy, they seldom do."

When the words stopped flowing, Lammot waited for precisely ten clicks of the pendulum clock on the wall behind his head. A flicker of annoyance crossed the General's face.

"What precisely are Mary's disqualifications?"

Henry twisted perceptibly but kept a pleasant tone. "It would be unseemly to lay these things out like parcels in a trade. Really, Lammot, a gentleman doesn't—"

"Is it her father's employee status? I, too, am an employee of the firm."

"Not in the same sense. You are—"

"Or is it her family heritage? Does the company have a policy regarding miscegenation?"

"Now look, boy, I'll not have you carry this to extremes. The girl is not suitable as your marriage partner, and that's that!"

"Suitable or not, she will be my wife."

"Have you considered the consequences?"

"Apparently I have already endured them."

"Not nearly!"

"Is that a prediction or simple threat?"

"Take it any way you damned please. There's another thing; what about Harry's child? You should think of her feelings as well as your own, her future as well as your own."

"Is there reason to fear for Mary's feelings? Is there *anyone* who would dare suggest that she be received coldly?"

"Tongues will wag."

"Then hear me, Uncle. I charge you with passing the word. I will not tolerate the slightest bruise to her feelings. Not one whisper about class distinction, not a breath about the other thing."

The General stared at his nephew's intense face for some time before speaking. "Who is making threats now, Lammot? I think you're gambling with a poor draw."

"All right, General. I'll call. Do you want my resignation?"

"Don't be absurd. I would not be that vindictive to my own flesh and blood."

Lammot smiled grimly. "Nor will I. You'll be getting an invitation."

If he had not been so exhausted after leaving, Lammot would have whooped with triumph. Flesh and blood, indeed! He was not fooled by the excuse. Henry du Pont was afraid of losing the company's best asset, Lammot du Pont. That was the reason he backed down. It was the only reason.

Later in the month he learned of plans for a bridal shower being hosted by Aunt Louisa at Eleutherian Mills. Mary was ecstatic. About the same time he was called in by Henry to begin serious planning on the Gunpowder Trust.

It was a full year. That spring the mills went wild with celebration at the news of Lee's surrender to Grant. As suddenly the crushing news of Lincoln's assassination subdued everybody. Lammot and Mary were married the following October in Christ Episcopal Church with all the family attending.

During their honeymoon at Niagara Falls the mother of the groom moved to her new house. It was as substantial as the old place, but somewhat removed from the inner circle of Eleutherian Mills.

PART IV

CHAPTER THIRTY-NINE

SAN FRANCISCO
1866

"Wmat in the world is kieselguhr?" Megan handed back the paper she had been reading to Michael, unfastened the top of her blouse, and made a face as their baby began to nurse.

"Easy there, sweetheart, we've plenty of time."

She pursed her lips and let out a slow breath, began to rock in the chair, and smiled down at the child. A two-year-old boy with carrot hair and pale blue eyes slid off Michael's knee and came over to watch soberly.

"What do you think of her, Sailor?"

"Sailor wants a drink."

Michael laughed. "All sailors want a drink. Come on, I'll get you a drink."

Megan looked up. "Give him a tart, Michael. Supper's a long way off."

"Just the thing for a sailor," she heard as they disappeared into the kitchen. "A drink and a tart, eh? You've a very liberal mother, lad. Do you realize that?"

"You didn't answer my question," she said after he came back.

"Sorry, I was distracted with all that shore leave business." He leaned over her watching the baby. "Lusty devil, isn't she?"

"Kieselguhr."

"Ah, yes. A kind of clay dust, tripoli, diatomaceous earth. Made up of microscopic marine fossils."

"You have given it more than casual study?"

"As soon as I heard of Nobel's patent. What do you think of the name? 'Dynamite.'" He paced the room.

"Is it everything he claims?"

"Everything. It will revolutionize the explosives industry."

"Oh, Michael, you've worked so hard on this. To have that Swede just take it away. It isn't fair."

He smiled at her and shrugged.

"Well, I must say you are taking the loss with a good deal of self-restraint."

"Why not? We've a roof, a good table, fair pay, and they think I do my job well."

She shifted the infant to her shoulder. "It's the other thing, Michael. What about independence? Wealth?"

"Ah, you're talkin' about my great dream. Is that it, girl? Y'wouldn't want a dreamer for a husband, now would you?"

"Come off the blather. You're no dreamer, and you know I know it. You've worked too hard for any dreamer and too hard not to be disappointed. Unless . . ."

"Unless I have an ace up my sleeve?"

"Do you?"

"Is Ireland green? Look at this."

He scribbled a single line of characters on a scrap of paper and handed it to her. She twisted her head around the sleeping child to read the scrawl.

"You know I can not decipher chemical symbols. What is it?"

"Saltpeter, a bit of magnesium carbonate, a cup of sugar stirred gently into three parts nitroglycerine. My secret recipe for blasting rock. As safe as dynamite, and about twenty-five percent stronger."

"Your estimate."

"No, my darlin', my measurement."

"You've tested it?"

"I have."

"And Nobel's dynamite? How did you get that?"

"He's been letting contracts for months. Ever since he applied for a patent. I got a sample last week."

"I don't understand. What is the difference?"

"It's really very simple. Nobel was able to stabilize nitro-glycerine by absorbing it in kieselguhr, an inert material. The ratio is three to one, the same proportions as my formula. The difference lies in the stabilizing base. Mine is an explosive combination so that the entire charge produces energy."

"Is it as safe to handle? You said the mixture of black powder and blasting oil was terribly unpredictable."

Michael was pleased at her questions. "Black powder mixed with nitroglycerine is a nightmare. The miners don't trust it for good reason. But this formula really works, Meggie. Nothing will set it off but a Nobel blasting cap. I've tried everything. It's as safe as a candle."

"But if Nobel already has his patent . . ."

"Mine is a new process. Absorption of nitroglycerine in a non-inert base."

"Oh, I hope they agree with your thinking."

He smiled broadly. "They do. At least in theory. It will be some months before the paperwork is completed."

"What do you mean? Oh, you're a devil, Michael Farrell. How do you know what they think?"

Slowly he extracted a yellow sheet from his pocket and handed it to her.

"It came over the wire this afternoon," he said, grinning as her eyes raced over the brief message. "It's my surprise for you, Megan. They're issuing me a patent."

Noreen Gallagher acknowledged each new face with a mechanical nod. She was too much in a daze to recognize any of them, not even Lammot du Pont, whom she was told later had come on his own and not as an official company mourner. That General du Pont had not shown up bothered her not at all. It didn't matter. What mattered was that Brendan was gone, and no show of mourners could bring him back.

That night after the funeral when all the others had left, the house seemed crowded with Blanche; young Denny, who still seemed like a boy pretending instead of a real priest now; and

Father Francis, who was eighty but looked seventy. They age like expensive furniture, she thought idly, with no family terrors to wear them out.

Father Francis was speaking around her to Blanche, the both of them talking as if she were deaf and dumb—or senseless.

"A blessing that he was not ill. Like a thief in the night, when we least expect it."

Blarney! What did they know. The man was torn bit by bit over the years. They didn't have the chance to look deep into his eyes as she had. All that grief shouldered. The miracle was that he survived as long as he did.

"He would have been seventy-seven next month." That was Denny talking. How much he sounded like Francis Reardon. She wondered if they were all taught voice lessons at the seminary, groaning like wind through a hollow log.

"Megan is coming on. A month or so, the wire said. She'll be a tonic for her. They were so close." She felt Blanche staring at her like a robin eyeing a worm. Abruptly Blanche spoke directly, her voice a register higher. "Can I get you something, Noreen? You have to keep up your strength."

"I'm not deaf, Blanche," she said quietly and then looked her sister straight on. "Why?" she asked.

They all looked at each other. Father Francis cleared his throat.

"Why what, dear?" Blanche asked. Her voice was still loud.

"Why do I have to keep up my strength?" Noreen asked.

Nobody seemed to have an answer.

Megan was not able to return at all in '67 or '68. By the time the arrangements were made, she was into another pregnancy. Confinement and subsequent nursing eliminated any thought of either the rough overland trip or the long sea passage.

It was not because they could not afford it. Income from Michael's job and license royalties paid to him by California Powder for the new explosive gave them comfort and security with a bit in the bank. They were a long way from riches, but the future looked very promising.

"We'll wait for the railroad," Michael said. "By the time it punches through we can all go."

"Another year," Megan grumbled. "By then I could have a baby on the way."

"I'll try to cooperate," Michael drawled. "There's saltpeter in the lab."

She ignored his comment. "If I wait too long Aunt Noreen will be in her grave, too."

It was midsummer of 1869 when she boarded the new transcontinental train, but she was traveling alone. Michael's work load was too pressing to leave, so they hired a full-time woman to look after the children. The rail trip was so fast, seven days from coast to coast, that Megan regretted not bringing them with her. Noreen would have been delighted. She was in Chicken Alley only a few days when it seemed they had exhausted all topics of conversation.

"Why don't you go see Mary Belin?"

"Mrs. Lammot du Pont now. Is she living in their house?"

Noreen nodded. "Just up the hill."

"I wonder how she is?"

"Quite happy, I hear. She stopped off to see me a few times after Brendan died. Very nice of her. Not many of her station would take the time."

"She wrote me about that; said you looked well. I was relieved."

"You shouldn't be looking for relief at my well-being, Megan. Don't waste your care on me. My life's complete."

"If I didn't know you better, Aunt Norrie, I'd say you sounded maudlin."

"Just an honest statement of the fact. You've your own to worry over now."

Megan was going to send a note and then decided instead to walk up to Nemours uninvited. But as she approached the imposing place, she had second thoughts and was about to slip back down the hill when someone called.

"Megan!"

The voice came from a roundish figure under a sunbonnet rising from a thick rosebed at the west end of the colonnaded entry. "Oh, Megan!" With a great crashing of watering can and dropped shears, Mary Belin du Pont thrashed wildly free of the thorny bushes and rushed heavily down the path to her friend.

"At first I thought you were one of the staff." Megan smiled as they sat over tea in the parlor.

"Or something out of a circus? I've put on so much weight this time."

"I thought I was doing pretty well with three in five years. You've outshone me there, Mary; four babies in less time. Maybe you're Irish under the skin." In a minute they were rattling on like old times.

The warm feeling stayed with Megan until she began to wonder why Mary had not invited her to dinner some evening during her stay. Maybe it was an oversight. Maybe their calendar was full. Maybe it would have been awkward not to include Aunt Noreen, or Blanche.

If Mary had been visiting in San Francisco, there would have been no oversight. Nor any awkwardness. Mary Belin from up the Crick? As she prepared for bed in the house of her childhood, the wet musk smell of the Brandywine drifted in—familiar but no longer comforting.

CHAPTER FORTY

What do you think of it?"

They stood on a stack of fresh lumber on the cleared lot. The late afternoon sea breeze riffled her skirt, and out beyond the bay entrance she could see the wall of fog moving in. Below them the Presidio gleamed in the sun, and the bay itself stretched like a huge crescent of hammered silver.

"It's breathtaking!"

"It'll be our home in six months."

Michael helped her down, and they called for the children who were busy exploring the construction on their own. They ambled back to the spring wagon and piled in, squealing for choice of corners in the cargo box. Michael took the reins, checked that they were settled, and released the brake. "Hold on, everybody," he called and snapped the lines on the horse.

"I'm concerned about the cost, Michael. It'll be a grand house, not as big but every bit as lovely as Eleutherian Mills."

"I took a loan from the company. They think I'm good for it, I imagine, otherwise they would have refused."

"But we can never afford it on your pay."

"It's not just my pay, Meggie, though a thousand a year is nothing to sniff at. It's the license fees for Hercules."

"But that's not sure. You haven't got a penny yet."

"Just a matter of time, love. Just a matter of time."

The house was finished in a year, and they moved in a month

before Megan gave birth to their fourth child. By then the payments on the explosive patent were trickling in. Only California Powder was exercising the license, and the production was low, but reports from the field were enthusiastic. Plans for increased manufacture were under way. By midsummer of 1871, black powder had been rejected in favor of high explosives for blasting rock. There were only two safe choices available, Nobel's Dynamite and California Powder's Hercules. The mortgage payments seemed assured. "In fact," Michael reported happily one afternoon after a huge railroad order had been placed, "We're going to be rich!"

"You are certainly doing quite well, old fellow."

Lammot du Pont smoothed the loop of clipped beard that followed his jawline from ear to ear and gazed out at the velvet black hills.

"Now that we're both forty, 'old fellow' is getting too close to the mark." Michael handed Lammot a brandy. "Would you like a cigar?"

"Ah, you know my great weakness. Delighted."

They settled in facing chairs on the terra-cotta-paved patio, whose far edge appeared to float suspended over the distant lights of San Francisco Bay, sipped at their glasses, and puffed on the cigars.

"It is about time that we came to the meat of the conversation. What really brings you West?"

Lammot sighed. "Never attempt diplomacy, Michael. You'd be an utter failure."

Michael smiled faintly and waited.

"Very well, I'll come directly to the point. We need you to exercise your influence. As you know, although your interest is in high explosives, there is a huge market for black powder and California Powder controls the entire western territories of the United States. As a matter of information, they are moving eastward at, well, an alarming rate. There are plans to erect more plants on our side of the Mississippi. Naturally we are concerned."

"Go on."

"We are concerned that their pricing may be unrealistic in the current powder market. Quality black powder, as you remember, is costly to produce. Any influx of cheap, inferior explosives could ruin the industry."

"Ruin the company that makes it."

"In the long run, yes, of course. But in the interim, a price war would be disastrous for all."

"What happened to 'we'?"

"I don't follow."

"You used 'we' until the last, then switched to 'all.'"

"Well, I'm glad you mention that, Michael. We are trying to put together a cooperative effort to benefit us all."

"The Trust?"

"Again I do not follow."

"I'm not sure of the name, Lammot; I've heard it called the Gunpowder Trade Association, among other less flattering terms. I mean the trust that Henry and you cooked up to control the black powder market."

Lammot leaned back with a strange veiled look that Michael had never seen on his face before. He glanced at the cold tip of his cigar, struck a match, and puffed it alight again.

"I see that you have not entirely abandoned the espionage track I set you on years ago."

"Common knowledge," Michael commented drily, "old fellow."

"Hah! You have me there. Mary says that I'm getting slow-witted with all these shenanigans."

"You still have not made your point with me, Lammot. I confess to some apprehension about two words, however; 'we' and 'influence.'"

"It's very simple. Try to show your owner the wisdom of co-operating with us for the common good. Naturally a commission of substance would be yours in recognition of our gratitude."

"Tell me, Lammot, what is Henry dangling in front of *your* nose? Is it still the hope of running du Pont some day?"

"There's no one else. I needn't mention what your role in the firm could be when that happens."

"I'm in high explosives now. Henry is trying to outlaw all of it. He's pressuring the railroads daily not to carry nitro, Dynamite, or Hercules. If he had his way, the government would outlaw everything but black powder."

"Exactly, old boy! That's why I'll need you in the organization to turn it 'round. Together we—"

"Ah. A different 'we' this time. You and I, Lammot; not you and Henry du Pont."

"At last you have the picture! A rather tempting prospect, eh? We could control the entire explosives industry in this country."

"Shades of the Ginger Bastard," Michael muttered as he stared at his old friend.

Lammot waved off the hard look and grinned. "Don't you see, Michael? I want to bring California Powder into the association *because* of your patent. Once your employer is a member, I can use their influence to force the General into high explosives."

"We're doing quite well on our own."

"Don't count on it lasting. I know my uncle's strength in gaining control of other companies."

"Yes, I know. Sycamore Mills, Brainerd, Austin Powder, and a few small operations are in the Trust."

"Common knowledge?"

"It's no secret when a firm knuckles under and joins the Association, as you call it."

"That's only part of the picture, Michael. They are not just part of the association."

"What do you mean?"

"Du Pont has bought them out."

"You *own* them?"

"You might say that Uncle owns them. Bought with the help of du Pont cash."

Michael whistled. "I knew they were in difficult straits, but I hadn't heard that . . ."

"You never will hear, my friend. Not in public, anyway."

"There were some explosions."

"Never proven to be anything more than unfortunate accidents."

Michael's eyes narrowed. "I have memories of Wapwallopen."

"I haven't forgotten either. It was certainly sabotage."

"You believe that now, believe that he's up to the same thing again, and allow yourself to to be used as a paper front for his operation?"

"I can't prove anything, Michael. Even if I could, the end result would be punishment of a few of his shadowy agents. We could never catch him red-handed."

"Then why persist in this crooked charade?"

"It's the only way to wrest control away from him. Can't you see that, old fellow? With giants like Laflin and Rand, California Powder, and a few others, this Trust, as you call it, could strip my uncle of his dictatorship."

"It sickens me, Lammot. I won't get within reach of that tyrant. He can't vault the Rocky Mountains. You apparently have made your bed with Henry. Sleep with him if you will. I won't stoop to that level of prostitution."

Lammot's gray eyes smoldered. "Your metaphor cuts deeper than you could ever imagine, Michael. Well, I'm not here to mince words either, I suppose. You are wrong about your own safety, however."

"California Powder is a large enough giant for me, thank you. I respect the man I work for, he respects me, and for us the West is market enough."

Lammot hunkered forward, his eyes fierce. "If I told you that Lake Superior and Hamilton are in the General's bag, would you be surprised?"

Michael's shocked look was answer enough.

"Something else, and I'm laying myself naked telling you this, Michael. Not a word or my goose is cooked back home."

Michael nodded.

"California Powder will be next."

Michael tossed off his brandy and gazed down at the bay. In the darkness pinpoints of light abruptly faded and winked as the unseen fogbank bellied in from the sea.

"Spectacular!" Lammot took off his glasses and walked to the edge of the patio for a better view. "Like an invisible moving wall. I imagine you and Megan never tire of this view."

But neither the vista nor Lammot's comment had registered. "If Henry hates dynamite so intensely, why would he be interested in California Powder?"

"He doesn't want the high explosives business, obviously. But your plant in Santa Rosa produces most of the black powder sold in the West."

"And as you agreed, Lammot, black powder's life for mining, and construction is coming to an end."

Michael paced the terrace with deliberate steps, moving in and out of the yellow light spilling from the house behind them. He stopped beside Lammot, drained the last swallow of brandy, and reached for his guest's glass.

"Let me get you another."

"Thank you, no. I really must be leaving."

"Before you go, Lammot, let me say that I appreciate the information. I won't mention it, of course. As to encouraging my people to join the Trust, well, I imagine you know how I feel about that. If ever I did—and I won't—it would have to be above the table, with no favors kicked back from your uncle."

Lammot gripped his shoulder. "I'm glad you said that, old fellow."

"Then why on earth did you propose it in the first place?"

"You know who signs my pay drafts. Direct orders from Uncle. I'll be pleased to report that you can't be bought."

"You should get away from him yourself, Lammot."

Lammot watched the invisible black edge of the fogbank eating its way through the wharf lights below. "All in due course, Michael. It is not quite as easy as it seems. As for you, my friend, glance over your shoulder now and again. Do not be swallowed up unawares."

CHAPTER FORTY-ONE

1873

Michael Farrell had not drunk to excess in the ten years of their marriage. When Megan saw him stagger in the hallway at two o'clock of a workday afternoon, she knew something had to be seriously wrong. When she got closer she realized he hadn't been drinking at all.

"Mother of God! Are you ill? Here, sit down." She led him to the entry settee, but he waved it off and headed for the kitchen, pulled a decanter from the cupboard and took a long pull straight from the bottle. Then he very carefully replaced the stopper and tapped it home gently with his palm. The color had returned to his face, and now he looked plain angry and a little frightened.

"I was fired today."

"Fired?" She had to laugh. The idea was ridiculous. Only the week before the company president had been a guest at dinner and made himself tiresome praising her husband's work.

"Fired with a demand on my note."

Panic stabbed at her. He was serious.

"But that's foolishness," she protested. "Don't they realize you could drive them out of business in a minute?"

"That's a joke, my dear. It's the other way around."

"Michael, this is spinning my mind. What happened?"

"Last week the company sold a block of shares to raise capital for the new plant in Cleveland. It was a normal transaction in every way but one—the buyer had secretly acquired stock for the past two years in another name. They now own controlling interest in California Powder. Their first order was to quit making high explosives and concentrate on the black powder operation in Santa Cruz. The second was to quit using my patent for Hercules."

"That's insane. You could take the patent somewhere else."

"Not in California. I gave California Powder exclusive rights."

"But if they don't use it—"

"That's not in the contract. It was such a simple agreement. The two of us drew it up in friendship."

"Well, they'll just have to pay if they use it or not."

He saw how distraught she was, but he could not keep it from her, the good or the bad; he had learned that the hard way long ago. "Not so, my love. I wish it were. The royalties are based on pounds of explosive produced. If they don't make it, we do not get paid."

"My house . . ."

He could not look at her, could not say the words.

"Who could be so vindictive, so cruel?"

He did not have to answer that question either. She answered for him.

"That bastard," she hissed.

By 1874 Henry du Pont not only controlled the Powder Trust, with Lammot as president, but his company owned nearly every small powdermaking firm in the country. Even as he applied pressure to his major competitors through the Trust, he was secretly acquiring heavy blocks of their stock. The Panic of '73 continued into following years as banks collapsed and industry with them. One by one the larger powdermakers fell into his pocket. As always, he kept up the facade of their independence— separate companies under his remote control.

When Lammot's sister-in-law Charlotte died while confined in an asylum, Irénée collapsed. He died of a massive hemorrhage six weeks later. There were the usual funerals at Sand Hole Woods and a meeting to reform the company partnership. As things stood after Irénée's death, there were only two executives —Henry as senior partner and Lammot.

Before the meeting, Harry Belin took Lammot aside.

"I'm speaking as head bookkeeper, not as father-in-law, Lammot. There are some things in the company books that deserve your attention."

"You make it sound rather ominous, Harry. I'm hoping I may be able to look at them more leisurely in the near future."

"Then I'll speak to you as Mary's father. You owe it to my grandchildren to examine the ledgers."

"Very well. First chance I get."

"Before the meeting."

"That's hardly possible. It's called for three o'clock. I have to get up to the house now."

Lammot's greatest regret was that he had not chosen to be late for the meeting. He might have had enough ammunition to sway his aging aunts' proxies away from Henry's control. But it was too late to do anything about that now. He listened with building rage as his uncle proposed and then voted in the new panel of senior partners. They were Henry and his two sons, Henry Algernon and William. Neither had ever worked a day in the mills.

Lammot was retained as sole junior partner of the firm.

CHAPTER FORTY-TWO

I thought I'd never see you again."

"I doubt that you cared to, old fellow. Under the circumstances, I'm surprised you didn't come after me with a gun."

"The thought crossed my mind."

"Is Megan out? I was hoping to see her. And I have a message from Mary."

"She chose not to see you."

"Blunt as usual."

"It takes considerable effort just to be civil."

"Look here, Michael. I had no idea of what he had done to you. You should have written. My God, I could have saved your house, placed you in a higher position."

"I imagine so. You people control the whole industry now."

"Henry does. I'm rather small potatoes these days."

"What about the Trust? You head that."

"I've resigned."

"Got your fingers burned good, eh, Lammot?"

"Worse than what I've told. It wasn't just losing the directorship. The company books had a bigger surprise."

"Your shares just melted away."

Lammot was stunned. "How did you know that?"

"It was predictable. You told me a long time ago he had absolute control."

"But he violated our own agreement of '58. He gradually reduced my shares as I drew advances on my salary. My God, most of the money was for company business. And when my brother died, he bought those shares without notice to anyone."

"I feel the inclination to yawn."

Lammot snatched off his glasses and glared. "You're not making this very easy."

"Should I? Why should I listen to you at all? Take a good look around this room. Is this just payment for everything I have done for your damnable family enterprise? What have you been reduced to, Lammot? Four or five thousand a year, a mansion for your wife and kids, and thirty or forty thousand in your shrunken company stock? I bleed for you. Try living on a dollar a day when neither the rent nor the food is free."

Lammot looked away as he polished his spectacles and carefully hooked them on again. He laced his fingers together, took a great breath, and smiled.

"All right. I deserved that, and you don't deserve . . . all this. When I arrived yesterday and found out you were not with the company any longer, I wanted to do what I could. The first thing is some back pay, and the next is getting your job back. A hot wire to Uncle will take care of the job, and I can take care of part of the back pay right now." He reached into his coat and pulled out a wallet.

"Put that Goddamned thing away and forget sending the wire. I'll not ever be beholden to a du Pont again."

"Back pay," Lammot pleaded. "It's no loan, no gift."

"As God is my witness, if you don't put it back I'll cram it down your miserable throat."

Abruptly Lammot rose and began to pace the room. The rough flooring creaked under his weight, and he hunched as though he might brush the grimy ceiling with his head. He frowned at Michael.

"How are the children?"

"Fine. Healthy and happy, I guess. They adapt to things."

"Do you still own the patent?"

"The only thing that is ours, legal and clear."

"Why don't you sell it?"

"I've been tempted. If the right price came along I might do it. I'm not sure that Megan would ever forgive me that."

"She'd surely appreciate the comfort it would bring."

"It would take more than that. She calls it our dream ticket. She wouldn't want to part with it." Michael paused, thinking. "I imagine the Ginger Bastard wants that, too. Is he converted to high explosives?"

"Never. He won't allow us to touch it. Some of the other companies would like to get into dynamite, but the old man keeps freezing them out."

"How much influence do you have with them?"

"They pretty much do what I say as long as Uncle approves."

"How about if he doesn't?"

"Oh, Laflin and Rand are strong enough. Hazard might go along."

"Why not test them? Start your own high explosives factory."

"Would you license us to exercise your patent?"

"For a fee and a percentage of three cents on the dollar."

"What's the fee?"

"Get Megan's house back free and clear, and all my back pay with interest."

Lammot began working on his glasses again, his handkerchief flying over the lenses.

"Give me some time to put things together, old friend. I'll get back to you on this." Then he grinned broadly, a little like the Lammot Michael remembered. "This may be grander than Sebastopol and London combined."

After he left, Michael allowed himself a little smile too. It was good Lammot had not included Gettysburg. He was holding back on dreaming, not daring to hope. But, oh, how he wanted to tell Megan.

Lammot thrust a sheet into Henry's hands and pointed at a cluster of figures. "Last year dynamite sales amounted to one third of all blasting explosives. That was an increase of fifty percent over the year before. Next year the projections are even higher."

"The compound is too dangerous. Mark my words, black powder will survive. Nitroglycerine and guncotton are passing freaks."

"A preponderance of opinion to the contrary."

"The answer is no."

"Is that final?"

"I do not waste words with a mind to contradict them later."

"Then I will have to compete on my own terms."

"You would start a rival company?"

"I do not waste words either, General."

"Then you would forfeit all office and benefits of this company."

"I presumed that."

"Relinquish shareholdings for fair value."

"That's preposterous!"

"Read the ruling on competing industries."

"What a joke! How many 'competitors' do you own?"

"*We* own. At least while you hold shares in this enterprise."

"I couldn't afford that. I wouldn't be able to come up with a third interest. We'd fail before we got started."

"Who are the other two?"

"That's confidential."

"My guess is that Solomon Turck of Laflin is one, and Hazard Powder is the other. Am I right?"

"You have able informants."

"All right, Lammot, I don't want to lose your skill, and I don't want a sulking partner either. You have me over a barrel. I'll allow du Pont to invest one-third if the others agree to put their money where their mouths are. Until you can prove complete safety of product, I want no connection made with du Pont. If this gets out after all I've said about that Goddamned blasting oil, I'll look like a horse's ass. I would dislike that very much."

"But you will allow our agents to sell it?"

"As a separate line, and not from our storage magazines."

"Agreed. I must get your assurance that I can buy into the new company out of my share of profits."

"If you can make any money off that infernal stuff."

"No question of that, sir. I'd want a third ownership."

Henry du Pont nodded. "What about a license to manufacture? Nobel's?"

"Not dynamite. This will be Hercules, and we already have the rights."

"Just remember our deal, Lammot. You still have your obligations to us."

Lammot had his own ideas about obligations. He would scrape together every cent he had to buy out his uncle. That part of the agreement would be on paper in clear terms. He did not fear the other two investors. Solomon Turck was trustworthy, and Hazard would be putty. Now all he had to do was draw up a new agreement with Michael Farrell. It was a pleasure to know that the General would be buying back Megan's home with du Pont money. Since Henry owned over eighty percent of the company, that meant he was personally paying eight cents out of every dollar for the California house. He could hardly wait to tell them!

General du Pont rested easier that night than he had for some time. He had finally brought Lammot back into line. He could not afford to lose him at this point. Henry Algernon was proving to be an embarrassment to the business, and young William just didn't have the salt. Oh, well, he could hang on for another ten years. Lammot was sewn in securely. His new company would never leave du Pont control. It would be du Pont's by two-thirds from the start.

The one thing Lammot did not know was that Henry du Pont owned Hazard Powder lock, stock, and barrel.

"You *told* him?" Michael stared at Lammot incredulously. "Tell me it was a joke! Are you bent on self-destruction?"

Megan groaned and left the table to stand at the rain-streaked window. In the narrow street below she could see the children idling under the tattered awning of a produce store. They looked gray-faced in the moody fog-rain.

"It's the only way I could swing it. He'd have cut off my arms and legs otherwise. I'd have had a company with no capital, no location, and no factory. Besides, this way we'll be able to market the explosives through du Pont agents. Do you know what that means?"

"Greater exposure, but I don't trust him."

"Good choice of a word, Michael. The Trust will ultimately be our avenue to sales. You have no idea how far the organization reaches."

"I've had direct experience, remember?"

"And I have his guarantee of my buying up at least a third of the shares. That ensures control."

"Believe it when you get it, Lammot."

"Speaking of that, I have something in writing for you." He opened a leather case and produced a long document. "Read it over and see if it covers everything."

Skimming the text did not take long. Michael had rewritten such an agreement hundreds of times in his mind since the oversight in his first.

"It looks fine to me, with one exception. If the patent is not exercised or another substituted, I want continued royalties on any and all explosives produced."

"At the same percentage?"

"For fifteen years."

"You drive a hard bargain."

"I don't want to be burned again."

"What do I get in return?"

"The same as me. Exclusive rights to the patent."

"Fair enough, let's write it in and get it signed."

Megan turned from the window. "Don't sign it, Michael. You're forgetting something."

"You must be referring to this, Megan." Lammot smiled, drawing a folded parchment from the case. It was tied with a broad ribbon. "Go ahead and open it up. Michael insisted that it was yours, so it's made out to you alone."

The new parchment crinkled softly as she spread the deed open and they read it together. Then she crossed over to Lammot and kissed him on the cheek.

"Tell Mary that the teapot is always waiting," she said and went to the window. The children saw her immediately, ghostly upturned faces in the swirling fog, and when she beckoned they scampered in a knot for the door and thundered up the stairs.

"All *you* get, old fellow," Lammot said as he thumped a wad of bills on the table, "is the money."

Then he made a show of looking at his watch. "I'll be late for my train east. Can we sign these now, Megan? I have some high explosives to make."

CHAPTER FORTY-THREE

Michael braced himself against the sawing February wind high above the scattered cluster of new buildings. Wrapped to a towering smokestack, the scaffolding trembled under their feet as he and Lammot climbed to the top level, gripped the rickety framework, and gazed out over the vast isolation of western New Jersey. Chunks of tide-thrown ice cluttered the Delaware River shoreline behind them and to the east and north, the property of Repauno Chemical Company stretched deep into the frozen marshland. Lammot pointed with his mitten toward a small delta.

"That stream is Repaupo Creek. Repaupo. I hope the Indian who named it doesn't mind my changing a letter. Repauno seemed more euphonious."

"I'm sure he's not around to lodge a complaint." Michael blinked his eyes free of wind tears and smiled. His friend was nearly bursting with excited pride.

"You've done a remarkable job in such a short time."

"The first delivery was made months ago, Michael. What you see now is the full-scale operation. This is my make-or-break production run."

"Make or break?"

"Yes. Say, old fellow, do you mind if we get down out of this wind?"

After they clattered down the ladders and were warming themselves at a potbellied stove in the construction shed, Michael asked again.

"What did you mean up there?"

Lammot chafed his hands vigorously, took off his steamed spectacles, and chuckled. "I suppose you'll think I'm living dangerously again. Well, that's true to a degree, I suppose, but it simply had to be done."

"You're not cutting corners with this stuff, I hope," Michael frowned. "Nitroglycerine is not as forgiving as potash and brimstone."

"You sound a bit like the General. But, no, I would never be that foolish. Mary would skin me alive."

It was no joke. Michael shot him a piercing glance. "She wouldn't have much left to skin, my friend."

Lammot replaced his glasses and smiled warily. "Nothing like that at all, Michael. What I am referring to is the financing of this infant enterprise. You might say I have all my eggs in one basket."

"Meaning?"

"The deal I struck with Uncle has the proviso that I can buy out the du Pont interest, which is to say the General's interest, with my shares in du Pont and the note I owe him."

"Note?"

"A short-term loan we negotiated personally to get me started."

"I don't like the sound of it, Lammot. That man would not lend money unless he was certain of getting more than simple interest on his risk."

"He has no risk to speak of. My du Pont shares are collateral. And, of course, the one-third of Repauno I would forfeit in the event of default."

"One-third."

"Repauno was capitalized by three separate firms in the Association. I have the option to buy out du Pont's third."

"When does the note come due?"

"June of this year."

"Not much time. How close are you?"

"If we keep up the current rate of production, I'll make the delivery with a month to spare."

"*One* delivery? You mean a single contract?"

"It is a bit unusual but not unexpected considering skeptics in the business. The customer is Northwest Mining, and some of the older members of their board stipulated that we warehouse all of the explosive here and ship as needed. The reputation earned by nitroglycerine still worries our dynamite customers. But I gave them a good price, and they'll accept delivery in our magazine."

"So *you* take the risk."

"Ah, but you and I know how safe it is. It's a bonanza for me. The profit will enable me to pay off the General and secure my third-interest in Repauno."

"Suppose you don't make the deadline."

"I prefer not to entertain that kind of pessimism."

"You'd lose everything."

"Just about."

Megan Farrell smiled as each of the five children withdrew from the table and took turns excusing themselves to their parents' guests. She reached for Michael's hand and gave it a squeeze as the youngest bowed awkwardly and scampered after the others.

"Oh, they're darlings, Mary, all of them."

"That Louisa is going to be a charmer," Michael said warmly. "Thank God she favors her mother."

Lammot laughed. "Loulie is pure gold. Notice how she marshals the others around?"

"Pierre looks like the leader to me—so quiet yet forceful."

Mary leaned forward. "Motty thinks so, too, but he won't admit it. He favors the boy shamelessly."

"Grooming the heir apparent, Lammot?" Michael winked at Mary.

"Nonsense. The boy is quietly assertive, as Megan observed. We'll see what the others have to say about splitting up whatever pie I can serve them."

"From the looks of it, my prolific mate, it will have to be a gigantic pie." Mary eased sideways out of her chair and stood with one hand pressing at the small of her back. "And speaking of that, would you all mind if we had dessert in the drawing room? I need a more comfortable seat. Heir number six is already asserting itself."

Megan stood at the front window of the Gallagher cottage and fingered the lace curtain. The frost pattern on the glass mimicked the lace, and she wondered if her Aunt Noreen had designed it so. She traced the delicate fabric with her eye, seeking remembered flaws, little aberrations in the ordered flow of the design, remembering the agitations that had triggered them.

"Here," she murmured barely loud enough for Michael to hear. "Here is when we found out about Daddy's being sent to Pea Patch Island. And here, near the hem, that must have been when Uncle Brendan died."

"Can you see the kids on the ice?"

"Yes." Her eyes focused through a clear pool in the glass to the frozen sweep of the Brandywine across the road. Three lumpy dots skittered on the green suface of the Crick.

"I'm sorry Noreen could not have lived to see our young ones and Tim, too, of course."

Megan nodded and caressed the lace. "I want these. I'll speak to Aunt Blanche tonight."

"After she's gone, you mean?"

"No, I won't risk it. I'd rather be blunt and take the curtains when I can. Aunt Blanche doesn't care, not as much as I do, anyway. They have no memories for her."

"I remember them, too. Why not buy some fine ones in town? She'd like that."

Megan spread the delicate fabric between her hands and nodded. "Anything, Michael. They are the web of her life here, and mine, too. I'll steal them if I must."

She left the window and slowly paced the small living room measuring everything as though to lock it forever in her mind. Then she shrugged and smiled. "I want to go back now."

"To California?"

"Yes. You don't mind too much, do you? To leave you here alone for a few weeks? I want to get my babies back home."

"Are you sure you can manage by yourself? It's a long ride with three children."

"That won't be as hard as waiting for you."

"Why not wait, then? It will only be a month longer."

She went to him and slipped her arms under his cardigan, pulling him close. "I just want to make sure it's all still there as we left it. I've seen enough here, visited the graves and visited Denny. Aunt Noreen was my only tie, and that's broken. The lace curtains, my babies, and you. That's my life now, love. Hurry and finish with Lammot so we can be together again."

He rumpled her hair gently. "I'll bring the lace," he whispered. "That way you'll be twice as glad to see me."

CHAPTER FORTY-FOUR

From the excited bustling of the downstairs maid as she answered the door chime, Lammot knew before he was announced that the Sunday morning visitor to Nemours was his Uncle Henry. He resented not only the unannounced intrusion on his day with the family but also the distasteful company of the man himself. They had not spoken for months, and Lammot was not yearning for a reconciliation.

"I'll meet him and then quietly withdraw." Mary grimaced. "I imagine this call is more business than social?"

"Why don't you just turn him away?"

"Tsk! Respect for your elder kin, Motty dear."

She left and shortly he could hear their banter as Mary led the General down the hall toward the dining room. Lammot sighed, pushed his coffee away, and rose to meet them. He did not smile.

"Can I get you something, Uncle Henry? It's quite cold out. Have you had breakfast? Hot coffee, certainly. And griddle cakes?"

Henry nodded curtly to Lammot. "Coffee, thank you, but nothing else."

"Come now, Uncle," Lammot heard himself saying. "You must share with us anything from our table. Some crust perhaps to mark the occasion."

"Motty!"

Henry weathered the remark easily. He smiled again at Mary. "Your husband is up to his mettle, I see. Ever the droll du Pont humorist."

She shot Lammot a look that was genuinely cross. "I think I'd better see to your coffee and leave you two alone."

Lammot grimaced. "Send in the man's coffee."

As soon as Mary left, Henry spoke. "I'm not going to go into the reasons for our estrangement, Lammot, though I must confess that your reasons for being irascible are a mystery to me."

Lammot started to speak, thought better of the idea, and removed his glasses instead. Picking up a napkin, he began polishing the lenses deliberately.

"Yes, well, water over the dam. The reason I'm here is to make you an offer of reconciliation, a rather generous offer, if I might say so."

"I have always been in awe of your past generosities, General."

Henry glared, caught himself, and continued. "As you know I have the highest respect for you as an asset to the family enterprise. What I propose is that you be given a guarantee of future participation in the good fortunes of our company."

"I am all ears."

"You have been distressed in the past by losing a portion of your stock through cash draws against it. What I am offering is a chance to restore those shares."

"I see. Just restitution? I am taken with your change of heart, Uncle. But given your feeling, you probably consider the just return of my property an outright gift."

Lammot could see the old man bridling. His proposal obviously was of more value than mere reconciliation—or Lammot's continued services to du Pont. After some effort, Henry's half-smile warmed the frosty glare of his eyes.

"Neither, Lammot. This is a business proposition—one that can be profitable for both of us."

Lammot sipped at his coffee and waited.

"Our agreement that you can buy out du Pont's third of Repauno bothers me. Frankly I do not like the idea of having a family member in competition with the firm."

Lammot's cup crashed into the saucer. "You will not renege on *that* agreement, sir! I have it in writing."

"Hear me out. I have no intention of quarreling with you on that. What I propose is that you exchange half of your interest for the shares in du Pont you drew on in the past and"—he tapped the table for emphasis—"I will tear up the note for the cash you owe me."

"You want to buy Repauno for thirty-thousand? Some bargain!"

"Your du Pont shares, which I'll assign from my own holdings, are worth nearly double that. You'll own ten percent of du Pont and one-sixth of Repauno."

"What would be my role with du Pont?"

"Run the high explosives business, and do essentially what you were doing before this misunderstanding reared up."

Lammot laughed. "You amaze me. In exchange for returning shares which were mine to begin with, you expect me to hand over a thriving company that I built from scratch."

"One-sixth, Lammot. And as a du Pont partner, you'd own part of that."

"I know how much influence my ten percent would carry."

Henry leaned forward, his voice lowered and insinuating. "As it is, Lammot, you only stand to gain a third if you manage to pay me off. Laflin and Hazard control a third each."

"I trust Laflin, and Hazard is a boiled noodle."

"Don't be too sure. Solomon Turck might leave Lafflin-Rand. Who knows where loyalties will lie?"

Lammot slowly rose and walked away from the table. "You're past sixty-five, Henry. When do you plan to retire?"

It was the first time his nephew had ever spoken to him as an equal, and the first time he had mentioned his age. Henry did not like the sound of either.

"When I draw my last breath."

Lammot smiled. "I appreciate the honesty. As to loyalties, who will replace you as director?"

"That will be up to the shareholders."

"Henry Algernon and Billy will inherit your bundle, I imagine. Hardly a fair contest for me or my other cousins."

"I've fought against greater odds," Henry drawled, "and won."

"I am aware of how you won."

"What's that supposed to mean?"

Lammot ignored the question. "Would you draw up an agreement recommending me as interim director for two years following your resignation, incapacity, or death?"

"You drive a hard bargain."

"Harder still. I want control of the Repauno split."

"To what degree?"

"Sixty percent."

He was silent for such a long time that Lammot thought the proposal had been rejected out of hand. But when Henry took his hat and walked toward the door, he left Lammot gaping.

"I'll have the papers ready by the end of the week."

At the New Jersey plant the following day, Michael Farrell was not as enthusiastic about the proposal.

"He has something up his sleeve."

"Not this time, old fellow. I think the truth of his son's inability to manage has finally dawned on him. That and his own mortality. He considers the company more important than his own life—an extension of his life, I suppose. If du Pont continues to grow, he will forever live as part of its history."

"That tyrant will outlive us all, Lammot. Don't agree to it."

"I'm afraid I must. The opportunity is too great to miss. With the extra funds I'll begin to buy out Hazard."

"What makes you think they'll want to sell?"

"They didn't have the capital to buy their third when the partnership was formed. It's a note due in two years. A cash profit will be very tempting."

Michael's face was furrowed with doubt. Lammot slapped him on the back and chuckled," Come on, old fellow, there is such a thing as a happy ending. The Ginger Bastard may be a soft cookie after all."

"Do you mind if I make a trip to Connecticut? Just a few days. The lab can run without me from now on anyway."

"I thought you would want to leave early for San Francisco, but *Connecticut?*"

"Someone I want to see—about insurance."

"Certainly. When will you be back?"

"When will you sign the deal with Henry?"

"This Friday."

"I'll be back before then."

"Well I would hope so. Mary and I want at least one representative of Farrell Laboratories to celebrate with us."

Michael was on the northbound train that evening. It meant a sleepless night, but he needed the time saved to do his research. Lammot du Pont might not have been aware of it, but he had sent his friend on yet another mission of espionage.

The kitchen help at Nemours had caught the fever of Mary Belin du Pont's dinner party for the boss early in the week. By Wednesday, there was not a servant in any of the dozen or so du Pont mansions who did not whisper about the General and his wife coming to Mr. Motty's for supper.

The dinner went off smoothly enough, but Mary felt the edge of apprehension hanging over their conversation. The reason for their get-together never came up, but Lammot was certainly agitated about what lay in the papers Henry du Pont placed on the sideboard as he and Louisa entered. They were in plain view throughout the meal, a distraction she felt was deliberate on Henry's part. It was a cheap trick, but at least Lammot had the restraint to ignore them. When they had finished dessert, Lammot offered Henry a cigar.

"We'll smoke in the library, General. Mary doesn't like me to smudge the walls in the dining room." On the way out he made a point of ignoring the paperwork, and Henry had to circle back and retrieve it unasked.

"Score one goal for Motty," Mary thought. She turned brightly to Louisa. "The children have a piano entertainment for us while those two befoul the air. I'm not certain which will be more endurable, but at least a sour chord will not injure our health."

In the library Henry handed his contract to Lammot without ceremony. "Read it over. I'll pour my own brandy."

Lammot sat at a simple escritoire, adjusted the flame of a

small lamp, and took his time in the reading. The entire document had been handwritten, a trademark of his uncle's lifelong use of the quill. Typewriting machines were proliferating everywhere but on the Brandywine. Henry would not have one within earshot. The script was bold and clear, the terms specific, and everything was exactly as stated the preceding Sunday.

Lammot knew that the directive stipulating his interim leadership of the company was nothing more than a recommendation. Henry would have no appointive power beyond the grave. The shareholders would have to vote his successor. But it had a persuasive weight of its own, a potential weapon for challenging claims of primogeniture by Henry's sons.

The real meat of the agreement was sound. Sixty percent of the du Pont interest in Repauno would be transferred to Lammot, giving him full control of the du Pont third. In addition, all of his pilfered shares in du Pont were restored. That and the effective gain of thirty thousand dollars he would not have to repay Henry meant he could pursue Hazard's third of Repauno as soon as the current shipment of explosives was complete.

"I'll get you a fresh pen, Uncle Henry," he said casually, and arranged the contract neatly as he rose.

"Don't bother. I'll use that damned steel thing. Go ahead and sign it."

Lammot stood at the chair. "After you, General. You're making the offer."

Henry shrugged, moved to the desk, dipped the pen, and scratched his signature on both copies as chimes rang in the hall.

Lammot's face brightened. "Ah, he made it after all. A bit late for supper, but in time for the celebration."

"Who's that?"

"The brilliant Mr. Farrell. I'd better let him in."

Henry's face darkened. "He can wait ten seconds until we finish our business. Here's your pen."

But Lammot was already walking toward the door. In the hallway he crashed into a breathless, wild-haired Michael Farrell.

"I let myself in, rode hard all the way from the station. You didn't sign the contract?"

"You're about to witness that act, old fellow. And not a moment too soon."

Lammot pushed him into the library and the cold stare of Henry du Pont.

"Before you sign, Lammot, there is something you should know."

"And what is that, my friend?"

"Who owns one-third of Repauno."

Lammot laughed, but his gray eyes were already clouding with concern. "Well, du Pont and I own one third, Laflin owns a third, and Hazard owns the other."

"I found an interesting detail about Hazard Powder during my visit to Connecticut. It seems they have a confidential ally, one who has been quietly buying shares in the company, easing them out of their financial difficulties."

Lammot spoke slowly, quietly. "And this ally now holds controlling interest in Hazard?"

"Lock, stock, and barrel."

"You wouldn't know who that party might be?" Lammot gently lifted the contract from the desk and jabbed the pen unused back into its holder.

"Ask the Ginger Bastard standing behind me."

Michael felt the carpet twitch under his feet, and he spun around as Henry du Pont swung a meaty fist at his head. Dodging the blow, Michael caught the man off balance, seizing him by the wrist and bending the arm double behind his back. Henry grunted in pain and bent over helpless.

Lammot acted as if nothing had happened. He strolled the length of the library holding the contract as though studying it again.

"I suppose we will have to stop meeting altogether, Henry. Every social contact seems to end in disaster. Will you behave if I let you go?"

The old man said nothing, but at a sign from Lammot, Michael released him and stepped back. Henry straightened with a face purpled with rage and pain.

"I think I'll keep these for a few days if you don't mind, Uncle. You can understand my reservations? I doubt that I'll ever sign them, but I'll certainly keep my copy as a memento. You'll find Aunt Louisa with Mary and the children in the music room. A pity that you must leave so early."

"You'll regret taking counsel from this traitorous scum, Lammot. You'll end up with nothing."

The sudden departure of the elder du Ponts was awkward, even though Lammot took pains to be pleasant to his aunt. Mary was more concerned about her than she was about Henry's trickery.

"The poor thing has no idea," she said miserably. "Why is it that charlatans marry good women? She's more understanding than all the rest put together."

"In her circumstances," Lammot muttered. "She has had to practice it more than the rest."

"I feel badly about making a shambles of your evening, Mary. If I could have gotten word to Lammot earlier, all this to do might have been avoided."

"No, Michael. Thank God you found him out in time." She shook her head, bewildered, "I keep hoping for the best in people. Now I think I should apologize to you for being so insensitive in my invitations. I mean about the way you must still feel toward him."

Michael suddenly wished he had gone back with Megan. The old angers, the old fears, were edging in. He forced them back and managed a smile. "The important thing now is to meet your husband's deadline. Once that note is repaid Henry will be forced to surrender his third of Repauno."

"One thing that worries me," Mary said, "is that he will still control Hazard's share. If he somehow got control of Laflin-Rand, he could take it from you again."

Lammot shook his head. "That can't happen. One of the agreements Laflin signed with me was that neither would attempt to increase our holdings without consent of the other. If I let Turck know what Henry tried to pull, he would spill the story to the Trade Association."

"There's not much they would do, Lammot. Henry has the Association in his pocket."

"Oh there's quite a bit they could do. Would be forced to do,

Michael, suit for breach of contract and forced divestiture of his Hazard stock."

"But would they?" Mary asked. "The General plays the march they step to."

"He would probably direct them to do so himself if the news got out. After all, the Gunpowder Trade Association is supposed to be a cooperative. That's what makes it work so well for du Pont. It is supposed to represent all the member companies unequivocally. No, Repauno is not worth that to Henry, even as a spiteful gesture."

Michael nodded. "Lammot's right, Mary. As important as the dynamite works is to you two, it is small potatoes to that tyrant. No, all we have to worry about is getting that shipment consigned by the due date."

Lammot smiled broadly and pulled Mary close. "And with Michael ramrodding the lab crew, we'll be ready in ten days."

"Well, that relieves my mind," Mary said and pulled at her husband's tie. He bent down and she kissed him firmly on the cheek.

The following morning Lammot picked up Michael at five o'clock in front of the Gallagher cottage. They had a chilly thirty-minute buggy dash to the Delaware River and a colder ride in the steam launch to the Jersey side. Neither minded the uncomfortable trip or the long job facing them. They would work without letup from now on. As Lammot had said before, all of his eggs were in one basket. Michael Farrell knew that for all practical purposes, his and Megan's fortunes were there, too.

Henry du Pont was up even earlier. He had a call to make at a comfortable little cottage on one of his more remote properties. It was several miles up the Brandywine Gorge, a place he planned to convert into a private gun lodge. The caretaker was still in bed when he thumped his whip handle on the door.

A man opened the door a crack, then wide to let Henry in. His face did not register surprise, annoyance, pleasure, or any other emotion that Henry might have expected. But Henry had long since forgotten to look. As far as he was concerned, the man had no emotions to hide; he was cold. That was his prime asset, that and thorough attention to his work. These were the qualities for which Henry du Pont hired Loughlin Sneed and paid him regularly—and from his own pocket—during the long periods between his special jobs.

It was payday again, a week early by Loughlin's figuring, and as he accepted the cash without comment or expression, he waited for the instructions that were sure to follow.

"It's New Jersey," Henry said without preamble. "The Repauno plant. Get a job there this week."

Sneed nodded. He knew it was a du Pont property but the fact did not matter. He waited.

"There's a bunker nearly filled with stuff for Northwest Mining. It's a new magazine off by itself."

"When?"

"Give it a few days. Wait until the shipment is nearly complete."

"Just the one magazine?"

"Nothing else."

Henry left without another word. He was home well before breakfast, and when his wife came down to join him she was pleased to note how much his mood had improved since the evening before.

CHAPTER FORTY-FIVE

It took nine more days to complete the shipment. During the last week neither Lammot nor Michael left the plant. They slept in the construction bunkhouse and ate on the run. The long hours took their toll, but Michael insisted on everybody getting at least half of each twenty-four hours off, with a stern warning that eight hours' sleep was mandatory. Carelessness induced by fatigue could be a sudden killer in this business.

Toward the end of the production run there was another problem.

"They're all coming down with headache, Michael. I've had one for days."

"It's the nitro. We'll have to work on a way to pull the fumes out and get clean air into the plant."

"Could I induce you to stay a bit longer to solve that problem?"

"Don't even try. As soon as you get Henry paid off, I'll be on the train."

Lammot grinned, took off his glasses, blew on the lenses, and began to polish them with his handkercrief. "I have a plan to expand into a second plant in Cleveland."

"I know what to expect when you start working on those spectacles, and the answer is no. I want to pursue my own challenges, build my own fortune."

"If I offered shares in the new plant?"

"Still no, Lammot. I know there would be more money in it than with my little laboratory operation on the Coast, but my dream, like yours, involves more than wealth."

Lammot hooked the spectacles back in place and smiled. "I won't tempt you further, old fellow, but it's going to be hard explaining to Mary that you and Megan can't be persuaded to set roots closer to us."

"No more tempting? Even that trick won't sway me."

Lammot swung his legs off the littered workbench and stood. "All right. I respect any man's lust for entrepreneurship. God knows it burns deep enough in me. But the fact is I need you desperately, Michael. Look at this shambles of an office! In the old days all we had to worry about were a few grades of black powder and that was it. Now I have to fiddle with a host of other products essential to high explosive—blasting caps, detonating wire, magneto and friction-electric blasting machines, acid recovery, the ventilating problem you just mentioned and," he pointed to a pile of wire and apparatus in the corner of the lab, "now that."

"What is it?"

"The telephone system. I honestly do not have the time to supervise its installation."

"And you thought since I recommended it—"

"Would you?"

"No."

Lammot shrugged off the rejection with a wry smile, "It was worth a try, you'll grant me that. Oh, well, would you trot out and inventory the shipment? The magazine is nearly stacked to the rafters. I'll get the analysis done on this next batch and move it into the mixing stage."

Michael nodded and reached for his jacket. "I want to inspect the loading anyway. Those five new swampers will probably need direction."

The new storage bunker was a squat mound isolated from the main plant by several hundred yards. The March wind whipping across the Jersey marsh cut into him as he jogged along the muddy path, but Michael was glad for the fresh air. His own headache was mild, probably because he was becoming immune to the nitroglycerine poisoning as was the case with long exposure. He drew in deep lungfuls of the salt-laced air, his eyes stinging with the cold, and thought again of Megan on the deck of their honeymoon ship. When he got home again he would take her and the children on a short sail across the bay. Maybe a small boat of their own was not out of the question.

As he drew closer to the magazine, he had a sudden memory of Indian hogans seen from the swaying coach of his transcontinental train. They were much the same, but the dynamite bunker was huge in comparison, thirty feet square on the inside and sunk halfway into the ground with earthen walls twenty feet thick rising sullenly on all sides. From the factory side he could not even see the door which faced away from all the other buildings at Repauno. He wondered how much power filled the place. The shipment would eventually total two thousand fifty-pound boxes of dynamite, fifty tons of seventy percent nitroglycerine. The thought was staggering. At triple the power, the bunker held the equivalent of three hundred thousand pounds of black powder!

As he swung around the hill of compacted earth, he noticed a wagon backed into the low doorway and a crew of laborers strung out into the dim interior as they off-loaded the wooden cases of explosive. He waved to the foreman and a few of the older hands working at a brisk pace for his benefit. He knew that once he was gone they would ease up to a more reasonable level. A time-honored observance, and a smile flickered as he remembered. He waved the foreman over.

"I know the stuff is safe, but don't rush it, Casey. Make the stacks nice and neat with no chance for mashed fingers."

The foreman touched his hat and grinned. In seconds the line slowed its rhythm. The boxes flowed easily into the gaping magazine pungent with the smell of pine and stencil paint and the cloying sweetness of tamed nitroglycerine.

Michael completed his inventory and walked back to the crew. He jotted down the number of cases still to be unloaded, and was adding the total when the foreman spoke up.

"Gettin' close, are we, Mr. Farrell?"

"Close."

"I'll be glad for it to be over. I know it don't make much difference. I mean a couple of sticks is as bad as a wagonload, but this mountain of stuff gives me the willies."

Michael looked at his figures. "Three more days, Casey, maybe two, and you can seal the door."

"I can last that long, I guess."

One of the new men had done something to cause a slight break in the rhythm of the moving boxes, and Michael's eye was drawn to him. The man looked away easily, and the line went on as before. Probably interested in what they were saying, a natural curiosity. Before Michael was gone two minutes, Casey would pass the word anyway. Better set their minds at ease.

"I think there will be other jobs when this one is done," he said casually. "The customers are lining up."

"Thank you for that, Mr. Farrell. The men will be glad not to be laid off."

On the way back to the lab, Michael wondered about the one who had been listening, an older fellow with muttonchops and a mustache. He looked familiar somehow, but the beard looked out of place, and he idly tried to visualize the man without it. So many hairy faces these days! Since the war it seemed that every male beyond puberty was bent on raising whiskers. Even Lammot carried a Lincolnesque growth. Michael stroked his own clean-shaven face, wondering why he had not given up the razor, too? Was it a perverse vanity, he wondered, or simple obstinacy?

The swamper's face popped into mind again, and he had to force himself to dismiss it. "Old muttonchop," he muttered irritably. "I've more important things to occupy my brain."

When Michael reported for work the next morning, only the foreman was in the lab, warming his heels at the stove and sipping coffee. Michael's mood was soured by a throbbing headache. His nitroglycerine hangover had returned with a vengeance.

"What's going on, Casey? The plant shut down?"

"Mr. Lammot's orders, Mr. Farrell. Told me to wait here for that thing to buzz." He pointed his cup at a conical device screwed to the wall.

Michael looked back at the pile of equipment in the corner. It was considerably smaller than it had been the day before.

"Has he been working on that thing all night?" It was an accusation more than a question. Casey got up nervously.

"The Mister calls it a telephone, said it would speed things up nicely. Save time runnin' to and fro. I guess he didn't get much sleep—got *no* sleep, I imagine. Him and two others stringin' wire and such."

"The man's a fool!" The remark burst hot and reckless, but Michael did not care if Casey did hear. The fate of Repauno rested on completing the Northwest order and Lammot was burning up energy playing with Alexander Bell's newest toy.

"Can I get ye a cuppa?" The foreman nervously reached for the pot rumbling on the stove.

Michael shook his head and they both jumped as a loud jangling filled the room. Then there was a tinny squeaking coming from the wall. "Hello, hello, hello. Casey, are you there?"

"How do I work this Goddamned thing?" Michael growled.

"Just, just talk in this, he said," Casey pointed with the pot.

Gripping the mouthpiece, Michael shouted back. "He's here and so am I, Lammot. Why aren't you? We've got dynamite to deliver!"

"Not so loud. Normal voice is fine. That you, old fellow? What do you think? Jimhickey, eh?"

Michael had to smile despite himself. The man was like a child sometimes. He spoke deliberately, "The agent from Northwest is on his way to the lab—*now*. I think you should be here to reassure him."

"I suppose I should, eh? Almost finished here. Exciting device, don't you think?"

"I think you should come over. Where the hell are you?"

"In the new bunker. Put a telephone in five of the buildings. Have to test the connections, now. Goodbye, old fellow."

"Yes. Good-bye."

When Michael replaced the speaking cone, he saw that the visitor had already arrived. Just as Lammot might have predicted, the man was dazzled by the telephone performance. Lammot did not show up for another hour, and the Northwest agent, who turned out to be their senior vice-president, was Michael's total responsibility. He was gone before Lammot returned.

"He'll be back on Friday to deliver your check."

Lammot ignored Michael's sour tone. "Wonderful! I felt you could handle him, old fellow. Now we'll just have to form and wrap the last batch and wait for the money."

"Do you think you can let your electrical project wait that long?"

"Oh, that's about finished, too. Isn't it clever? Now we can call anywhere in the plant from the lab. Saves lots of running to and fro. Would you like to try it? Here, it's quite simple really."

"No thanks. I have work to do. *Your* work, I might add."

"What do you have to do this minute?"

"The first thing is to get over to the packing room for a sample of the putty. I want to do an analysis before they start wrapping the cartridges."

"A demonstration, Mr. Farrell."

Lammot went to his telephone, connected one of a series of blade switches on a panel, and cranked the handle of a small machine consisting of several horseshoe magnets mounted over a rotating coil of wire. He waited a moment, eyes sparkling behind grimy spectacles, and suddenly a voice scratched from the cone.

"Packing house."

Lammot handed the speaking cone to Michael. "Go ahead, tell him."

"Send a putty sample over to the lab."

"Right away, Mr. Farrell."

Lammot took the mouthpiece, disconnected the circuit, made an elaborate bow, and snapped, "Voila! You have just saved yourself a ten-minute walk."

"All right, I see the potential. It's the timing of your excursions that baffles me. I sometimes wonder where you get these impulsive urges."

"Actually you gave me the idea, old fellow. Remember the speaking tube aboard your ship? An old technique applied horizontally with electricity."

"As long as we are wasting time," Michael quipped, "What is the idea of using our blasting machine for the telephone?"

"Oh, that's not one of ours. Looks the same, though, doesn't it. Same principle—a magneto to send enough current to ring the bell at the other end."

"What about the voice current?"

"Dry cells do the trick for that. A much lower power is needed."

They spent the rest of the morning placing calls to each building in the plant and even called Casey at the magazine. Michael finally admitted that the telephone would eliminate most trips from the lab. It was much more than a curiosity, and he wondered how long it would be before it replaced the telegraph lines spanning the country. There was someone in San Francisco he wanted to talk to very much.

For Loughlin Sneed the telephone lines offered a different kind of opportunity. When the foreman had asked for two volunteers the night before, he stepped forward mainly for an opportunity to prowl the grounds without inviting challenges from the watchman. He had no idea that he would be paid by Lammot du Pont to lay the groundwork for his real purpose at Repauno. It was almost too simple to believe. By daylight he had everything in place, and had he been a more sensitive man, he might have felt squeamish about taking the five dollar tip Lammot pressed into his palm after the work was done.

But Sneed was not one to suffer qualms about anything. He took the bonus of a day off to sleep peacefully until it was time to complete his mission. This one would be the cleanest trick of his long career, and he smiled to think of the little "bonus" he would arrange for his boss. Henry du Pont would recognize its value—with compensation discreetly appropriate—for the General knew the value of such things. Especially the value of Loughlin Sneed's sealed lips.

They had a ceremony in stacking the last box of explosives. While the laborers stood by smiling, Lammot carried the fifty-pound crate himself, and Michael made an elaborate business of checking if off the inventory. Then they closed the doors, sent the crew back to the plant, and made their own way to the laboratory office.

"Are you staying the weekend?"

"You know better than that."

"You *will* be here for the delivery ceremony tomorrow?"

"Of course. I want to see that check in your hands."

"My freedom from the du Pont dynasty?"

"Your freedom from Henry the Red is more accurate."

Lammot nodded soberly and then glanced sharply at Michael, "And your patent royalty. You haven't forgotten that, I suppose?"

"Correct."

"Remember the old days, Michael? How we trusted the fellow with all our ideas? Live and learn."

"I don't recall much trust, Lammot. I believe he simply took what he wanted."

"Grasping sort of chap, my uncle. Well, this time he missed out. Should have taken my advice and switched into high explosives."

"He had the chance that day he raided our lab and took all my papers on nitroglycerine. It was there to develop, he just let it slide. Together we might have beaten Nobel to the punch."

"I'm glad you were able to reconstruct your notes." Lammot swept his arm across the expanse of factory buildings before them, "None of this would be possible without your Hercules patent, my friend."

In the distance Michael saw the laboring crew file toward the gatekeeper. The flat angle of the setting sun bathed their laughing faces red. Muttonchops was trailing in the rear.

"That fellow, Lammot, the last man, did he work for us before? On the Brandywine, I mean?"

"Which one? Oh, *that* one. No, he's new to me. Nice chap though, don't know how I could have strung all those wires without him the other night. Hard worker and quick-witted, but as taciturn as they come. I'll have to get his name from Casey. He'd be a good man to keep around."

It was midnight when Michael awoke in the bunkhouse, sat bolt upright in the darkness, and remembered. He saw the face clearly now without the beard, a younger face on a man systematically ransacking his files as Henry du Pont watched. It had been eighteen years before, but Michael could see him as clearly as if he had a daguerreotype. Muttonchops was the Ginger Bastard's spy!

In minutes he dressed and was running with a lantern toward the new bunker. It was dawn before he came out again, red-eyed and exhausted, and headed directly for the lab.

When he entered the office, Lammot raised an eyebrow and stared at Michael's day-old beard and soiled clothing. "My stars, old fellow, did I miss the bacchanal? I thought our celebration was set for this afternoon."

Michael seemed not to have heard. "Is this the only place where you can call up the other telephones?"

"Yes. They can call here but not each other. This is the central switching board. I plan to improve on that . . ."

"Ringing the other stations, this is the only place?"

"Yes. Look here, Michael, I think you might clean up before our guest arrives with his money."

Loughlin Sneed had made his first call on the packing house telephone and stood on the loading dock looking east toward the laboratory building and the distant hump of the loaded magazine beyond. Except for a driverless horse and wagon, he was alone. It was a good vantage point to observe movement between the two places and have a margin of safety besides. After he was sure his target had started for the bunker, he would stroll to the exit gatehouse and send the final message. It was neat and clean. He would be long gone before the smoke cleared.

"Ah, there you are! Hop aboard, lad. We've a quick job for Mr. Motty."

The foreman's voice jolted him, and he turned on his heel as Casey and Farrell sauntered up and prodded him to the rig.

"You drive, lad." Casey said cheerfully as they mounted the seat, one on each side.

"Where to?" Loughlin asked, his mind instantly blocking any reaction to the complication of his plan. There was plenty of time.

"To the bunker."

Michael was watching the man with the reins closely, but there was not a glimmer of reaction. It was disappointing. "Either I have the wrong man," he thought, "or this fellow is the coldest fish I have ever seen."

They drove in silence to the magazine, and when he opened the doors and waved the wagon inside, Casey looked up at Sneed. "Load up ten cases, lad, and we'll be off."

"I think he said twenty," Michael said. "I'm sure it was twenty."

"Ten is what it was, Mr. Farrell."

"Well, I'll make sure. Is this telephone thing working?"

He walked to the machine, gave the handle a vigorous crank, and waited with his back to the others.

"Lammot, was that shipment for ten or twenty?"

There was a chatter from the tinny speaker and Michael turned with a look of exasperation. "Well, look it up please, and call me back."

"I'll be starting then," Sneed said to the foreman and sauntered into the tall stacks of explosive. When he was out of sight of the others, he ran quietly over the packed earth floor to the dim interior of the building and clawed under the corner of one of the cases. His fingers hooked a pair of twisted wires and he carefully followed them up to where they disappeared into the side of a broken carton. Tugging quickly but gently, he freed the wire and nervously felt for the end. There was nothing there but the clipped ends of the wire.

"Looking for this?"

Sneed did not bother to look at the copper vial Michael Farrell held in his hand. He knew it was the electric blasting cap he planted the day before.

"A demented lunatic, a madman! Thank God you caught him in time." The General's voice rumbled with oily concern. He looked from Lammot to Michael and smiled expansively. "And you,

Farrell, again you have done well for the family. If there is ever—"

"Here is my draft for full payment," Lammot cut in. "I would like a receipt."

"Certainly. I'll have Harry draw up the papers first thing in the morn—"

"Write it out now, please."

Henry reached for a sheet of paper, inspected the check Lammot had dropped on his desk, and shook his head sadly. "To have you leave the family business on a sour note grieves me, young man. Think of your children's fortune if not your own."

Lammot's face was stone, the eyes black as anthracite, his lips a white line. The only sound in the General's office was the scratching of his quill. Henry scrawled his signature under the neat line of script and handed over the check without raising his eyes. Lammot glanced at the receipt and turned on his heel.

"There's a foul smell in this place, Michael. I need some air."

Michael did not follow him out, but stood staring at Henry du Pont until the aging tyrant was forced to acknowledge him.

"I imagine your business is concluded as well, Farrell." There was no facade now to mask the cold rage in his graveled voice as Henry spit out the words. "It was you who drove a wedge between us, split the loyalties and strength of this fine family. I'll not forget it, you traitorous mick!"

Michael assayed his old enemy with contempt. The fury he thought beyond control had ebbed to mere disgust, and he finally spoke with a detached precision that gave his words a deadly chill.

"I am a man burdened with certain undesirable skills, Mr. du Pont, some of them so selectively destructive I shudder to think of their perverse ingenuity. I have you to thank for that. The health of your nephew is ever my concern. Lay a finger on him again, and as God is my witness, I will be your executioner."

It was a bone-chilling day, windy with sleet and snow when Lammot and Mary saw him off at their front door.

"We'll miss you terribly, Michael. Give our love to Megan and the children."

"Next winter come visit us, Mary. Make your husband take a month off. I'll guarantee better weather."

"Did you remember Megan's lace, the curtains?"

He nodded and swept his eyes over the misty estate. "This is the last time, I suppose. Good-bye to the Brandywine for all of us."

"Don't you start, Michael. My household staff is up in arms about moving to Philadelphia."

"I can just make out the old lab down there through the trees, Lammot."

"My chapel? First meeting, eh, old fellow."

"There you two go again! I won't listen. Too many memories."

"Good and bad memories," Lammot murmured. Then he smiled brightly. "We'll take the good ones with us and leave the rest to molder here."

"Good-bye, Michael," Mary said abruptly, planting a kiss on his cheek and dashing into the house.

The two men ambled off the portico steps into the freezing drizzle.

"She's more upset about not seeing you and Megan than she is about leaving here."

Michael stopped by his waiting trap and looked out over the snow crusted lawn and chuckled. "Remember Charlotte at the Christmas party?"

"How could I forget."

"Lammot, you said something about leaving the bad memories here. That's a good idea, but don't cut yourself off completely. Your roots are here, ties that can build strength, and love, too. Don't burn all your bridges."

Lammot glanced back at his house and the barren trees beyond. He could just make out his uncle's place. The yellow stucco of the Eleutherian Mills residence gleamed dully through a black interlace of leafless limbs and branches.

"The roots were cut long ago, old fellow. I simply took too long a time to leave."

"One root only, Lammot. It may be out of line, but I have to say it anyway. Patch things up with your mother while you can."

"I think we had better not discuss my mother."

Michael brushed off Lammot's black look. "Whatever mistake she might have made is just memory. Let it fade. Meta du Pont was as much a victim of Henry's scheming as the rest of us."

"Victim? I should think eager accomplice better describes her role."

"All right, accomplice. But from what I have seen she was trying to save something of the company for her children."

"You have not seen some things that I . . . Thank God my father never knew!"

"Let the tired old sin die, Lammot. This business you have put together at Repauno would have made your father proud."

"Small compensation."

Michael gripped Lammot's shoulders and grinned. "Not so small. I think the score is evened up. You've beaten the Ginger Bastard for good."

Lammot said nothing and the silence was filled with a quiet hiss of ice pellets slanting into the crusted grass. It was getting colder. The sleet mixed with flakes that were already coating the frozen ground with a soft blanket. Lammot suddenly tugged Michael into an embrace. His bony frame shuddered as he spoke.

"Thank you, Michael, my good friend."

They parted without another word, and as the buggy pulled away Michael realized that it was the first time he had ever seen Lammot du Pont crack. Real tears. It was about time.